Praise for The Turner House

Awards

National Book Award Finalist • NAACP Image Awards
Nominee • One of the National Book Foundation's "5 Under 35"
• Short-listed for the 2015 Center for Fiction First Novel Prize
• Long-listed for the NBCC John Leonard Prize for a Debut Novel
• Long-listed for the PEN/Robert W. Bingham Prize for Debut
Fiction • Short-listed for the Ernest Gaines Award • Short-listed
for the Winter 2015 Lariat List • A Michigan Notable Book

Named Best Book of the Year by

O, The Oprah Magazine • *Entertainment Weekly* • NPR • *Essence*
Men's Journal • *Buzzfeed* • *Bustle* • *Time Out* • *Denver Post* • *Publishers*
Weekly • *Kirkus Reviews* • *BookPage* • *Literary Hub* • Kobo • *The Week*

A *New York Times* Notable Book of 2015
An Amazon Top 100 Editors' Pick of the Year
A *New York Times Book Review* Editors' Choice
A *Detroit Free Press* "Must-read Novel of 2015"
An Indie Next Pick

"Flournoy's knockout debut is one of those books that should, by rights, be
described as the Great American Novel, as it hits all the points of American
life: family, real estate, money, ghosts and loss."

—NPR, "Our Guide to 2015's Great Reads"

"In this assured and memorable novel, [Flournoy] provides the feeling of
knowing a family from the inside out, as we would wish to know our own."

—*New York Times Book Review*

"When a made-up family feels as warmly real as the Turners . . . your heart
takes note . . . By the time you reach the book's end, you'll almost feel like a
Turner yourself." —*Entertainment Weekly*, "10 Best Books of 2015"

"An epic that feels deeply personal . . . Flournoy's finely tuned empathy in-
fuses her characters with a radiant humanity." —*O, The Oprah Magazine*

"An elegant and assured debut." —*Washington Post*

"Poignant and timely." —*San Francisco Chronicle*

"[Flournoy's] debut does an incredible job of bringing both a family and a city to vibrant, poignant life." —*Buzzfeed*, "24 Best Fiction Books of 2015"

"The start of a brilliant career." —*Bustle*, "2015's 25 Best Books, Fiction Edition"

"Epic, ambitious and strikingly executed . . . A deeply satisfying portrayal of relationships among those to whom we, for better or worse, are related by blood." —*The Root*

"Whip[s] from laugh-out-loud to heart-crushing . . . [Flournoy] proves even bonds that have stretched a mile long have the ability to snap back." —*Essence*

"An utterly unsentimental love story that, rather like the house on Yarrow Street, manages to make room for everyone." —*Christian Science Monitor*

"Beautifully moving . . . This book is deeply personal but also clearly representative of one American city's hope in the face of tragedy." —*Bust*

"Dynamite . . . *The Turner House* belongs on the shelf with the very finest books about one of America's most dynamic, tortured, and resilient cities . . . There are cracklingly alive scenes inside pawn shops and factories, casinos and living rooms . . . Flournoy is an exciting new talent whose debut has enriched Detroit's flowering literature. Read *The Turner House*, and I'm sure you'll join me in waiting, eagerly, to see what its gifted author comes up with next." —*The Millions*

"This is essential reading." —*Detroit Free Press*

"A lamentation for and a paean to Detroit. A funny yet heart-wrenching book, both beautiful and revealing of all the ways close human beings relate to one another (and to places and things) over time." —*Buffalo News*

"A thoroughly engrossing saga. Flournoy is adept at conveying the sense that it is with our families where we can most be ourselves." —*Rain Taxi*

"A gripping, nuanced [read], heralding the arrival of a major talent . . . Reminiscent of other family/city sagas: Jonathan Franzen's *The Corrections*, Jane Smiley's *Some Luck*, [Jeffrey Eugenides's] *Middlesex*, all stories of places and their inhabitants. Do yourself a favor and read *The Turner House*. Once you open its pages, you won't be able to put it down."

—*PopMatters*

"A lively, thoroughly engaging family saga with a cast of fully realized characters . . . [Flournoy] puts her own distinctive stamp on this absorbing narrative." —*Publishers Weekly*, starred and boxed review

"A compelling read that is funny and moving in equal measure."

—*Booklist*, starred review

"Flournoy's writing is precise and sharp . . . The novel draws readers to the Turner family almost magnetically. A talent to watch." —*Kirkus Reviews*

"Profound . . . We rarely find such an honest portrait of what it means to be a sibling — defined by your differences as much as your similarities — as the one Flournoy gives us." —*BookPage*

"*The Turner House* artfully sketches no less than thirteen [siblings] — plus matriarch, patriarch, grandchildren *and* a handful of supporting characters. Beyond this character balancing act, Angela Flournoy's novel is also an impressive work of place, illuminating not only the eponymous house, but also the larger city of Detroit, from the Great Migration through white flight and early gentrification." —*Literary Hub*

"Detroit is a city often portrayed as past rescue, irrevocably blighted. But Flournoy's debut novel retrieves it from this through vivid details and equally vivid characters." —*Time Out New York*

"Moving, beautifully written." —*Men's Journal*

"One of the many strengths of this book — entertaining, well-written and keenly insightful without calling attention to itself — is its clear-eyed, unsentimental vision. Flournoy never ignores the problems afflicting family and place — a thirteen-child clan and Detroit — even as she pays homage to both." —*Milwaukee Journal Sentinel*

"As compelling, unforgettable, and beautifully told a story as I've read in ages. While each of the thirteen siblings (and their parents) could carry a book on his or her own, here they remain indelibly linked by the complicated bonds of history and belonging—and by the promises of their heartbreak city, Detroit."　　　　　—Cristina García, author of *King of Cuba*

"*The Turner House* is masterful: a novel full of history and lies and the myths that can bring a family together, or tear it apart. This is a beautiful, elegant, and living novel, one that you will savor until the last, moving paragraph."
　　　　　—Daniel Alarcón, author of *At Night We Walk in Circles*

"Flournoy is a magician—here is a story that is charming and funny while being whip-smart and profound. Laced through are the hard facts of history and the mysterious workings of the human heart. This is a thrilling debut from a writer to watch."—Tayari Jones, author of *Silver Sparrow*

"An expansive and ambitious novel that descends through the generations of one family's history to achieve real poignancy and power."
　　　　　—T. C. Boyle, best-selling author of *The Women*

"This book is so beautifully written, so perfectly observed and heard—it's about aging and parenthood and above all that misunderstood lifelong union, siblinghood—but it's also pure pleasure to read: funny, heartbreaking, with the sort of characters you'll miss like family when you finish."
　　　　　—Elizabeth McCracken, author of *Thunderstruck*

"Utterly moving and tough as nails, *The Turner House* is a love story as immense as the family it describes, and as complicated as the city that made them. A clear-sighted ode to the bonds that make and break us, to resilience across generations, to shared joys and solitary struggles, Flournoy's debut is as fresh and bold as they come. Commanding and unputdownable!"
　　　　　—Ayana Mathis, best-selling author of *The Twelve Tribes of Hattie*

· THE ·
Turner House

ANGELA FLOURNOY

MARINER BOOKS
HOUGHTON MIFFLIN HARCOURT
BOSTON   NEW YORK

First Mariner Books edition 2016
Copyright © 2015 by Angela Flournoy

For information about permission to reproduce selections from this book, write to
trade.permissions@hmhco.com or to Permissions, Houghton Mifflin Harcourt
Publishing Company, 3 Park Avenue, 19th Floor, New York, New York 10016.

www.hmhco.com

Library of Congress Cataloging-in-Publication Data
Flournoy, Angela.
The Turner house / Angela Flournoy.
p. cm
ISBN 978-0-544-30316-4 (hardback) — ISBN 978-0-544-30320-1 (ebook) —
ISBN 978-0-544-70516-6 (pbk.)
1. African American families — Fiction. 2. Domestic fiction. 3. Historical fiction. I. Title.
PS3606.L6813T87 2015
813'.6 — dc23
2014034423

Printed in the United States of America
DOC 10 9 8 7 6 5 4 3 2

A portion of this novel appeared, in different form, in *The Paris Review*.

"They Feed They Lion," copyright © 1968, 1969, 1970, 1971, 1972 by Philip Levine;
from *They Feed They Lion and the Names of the Lost: Poems* by Philip Levine. Used by permission of Alfred A. Knopf, an imprint of the Knopf Doubleday Publishing Group, a
division of Random House LLC. All rights reserved.

For my parents,
Francine Dunbar Harper
and Marvin Bernard Flournoy,
for being real

In loving memory of Ella Mae Flournoy,
who saw more than I can make up
and loved more than I can imagine

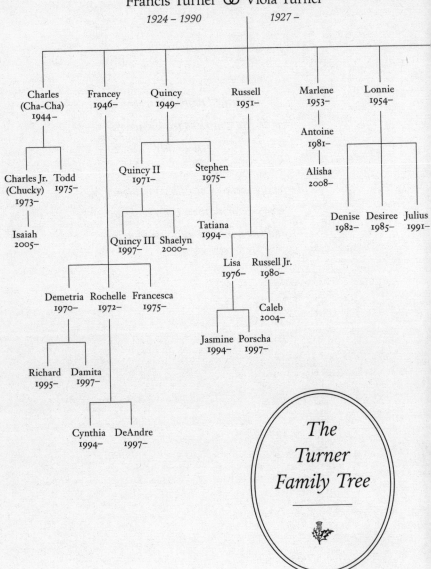

The
Turner
Family Tree

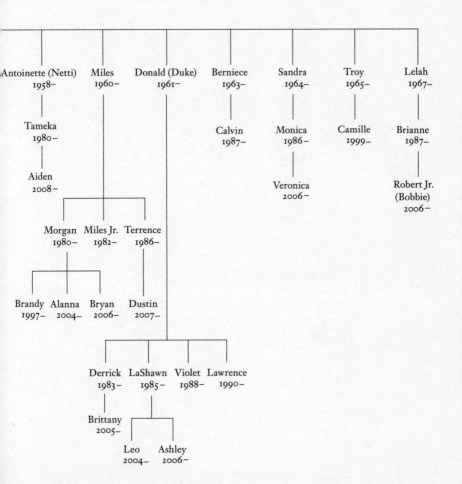

The Negro offers a feather-bed resistance. That is, we let the probe enter, but it never comes out. It gets smothered under a lot of laughter and pleasantries.

—Zora Neale Hurston, *Mules and Men*

    Out of the gray hills
Of industrial barns, out of rain, out of bus ride,
West Virginia to Kiss My Ass, out of buried aunties,
Mothers hardening like pounded stumps, out of stumps,
Out of the bones' need to sharpen and the muscles' to stretch,
They Lion grow.

—Philip Levine, "They Feed They Lion"

Trouble in the Big Room

The eldest six of Francis and Viola Turner's thirteen children claimed that the big room of the house on Yarrow Street was haunted for at least one night. A ghost—a haint, if you will—tried to pull Cha-Cha out of the big room's second-story window.

The big room was not, in actuality, very big. Could hardly be considered a room. For some other family it might have made a decent storage closet, or a mother's cramped sewing room. For the Turners it became the only single-occupancy bedroom in their overcrowded house. A rare and coveted space.

In the summer of 1958, Cha-Cha, the eldest child at fourteen years, was in the throes of a gangly-legged, croaky-voiced adolescence. Smelling himself, Viola called it. Tired of sharing a bed with younger brothers who peed and kicked and drooled and blanket-hogged, Cha-Cha woke up one evening, untangled himself from his brothers' errant limbs, and stumbled into the whatnot closet across the hall. He slept on the floor, curled up with his back against dusty boxes, and started a tradition. From then on, when one Turner child got grown and gone, as Francis described it, the next eldest child crossed the threshold into the big room.

The haunting, according to the older children, occurred during the very same summer that the big room became a bedroom. Lonnie, the youngest child then, was the first to witness the haint's attack. He'd just begun visiting the bathroom alone and was headed there when he had the opportunity to save his brother's life.

Three-year-olds are of a tenuous reliability, but to this day Lonnie recalls the form of a pale-hued young man lifting Cha-Cha by his pajama collar out of the bed and toward the narrow window. Back then a majority of the homeowners in that part of Detroit's east side were still white, and the street had no empty lots.

"Cha-Cha's sneakin out! Cha-Cha's sneakin out with a white boy!" Lonnie sang. He stamped his little feet on the floorboards.

Soon Quincy and Russell spilled into the hallway. They saw Cha-Cha, all elbows and fists, swinging at the haint. It had let go of Cha-Cha's collar and was now on the defensive. Quincy would later insist that the haint emitted a blue, electric-looking light, and each time Cha-Cha's fists connected with its body the entire thing flickered like a faulty lamp.

Seven-year-old Russell fainted. Little Lonnie stood transfixed, a pool of urine at his feet, his eyes open wide. Quincy banged on his parents' locked bedroom door. Viola and Francis Turner were not in the habit of waking up to tend to ordinary child nightmares or bedwetting kerfuffles.

Francey, the eldest girl at twelve, burst into the crowded hallway just as Cha-Cha was giving the haint his worst. She would later say the haint's skin had a jellyfish-like translucency, and the pupils of its eyes were huge, dark disks.

"Let him go, and run, Cha-Cha!" Francey said.

"He ain't runnin me outta here," Cha-Cha yelled back.

With the exception of Lonnie, who had been crying, the four Turner children in the hallway fell silent. They'd heard plenty of tales of mischievous haints from their cousins Down South — they pushed people into wells, made hanged men dance in midair — so it did not follow that a spirit from the other side would have to spend several minutes fighting off a territorial fourteen-year-old.

Francey possessed an aptitude for levelheadedness in the face of crisis. She decided she'd seen enough of this paranormal beat-down. She marched into Cha-Cha's room, grabbed her brother by his stretched-out collar, and dragged him into the hall. She slammed the big-room door behind them and pulled Cha-Cha to the floor. They landed in Lonnie's piss.

"That haint tried to run me outta the room," Cha-Cha said. He wore the indignant look—eyebrows raised, lips parted—of someone who has suffered an unbearable affront.

"There ain't no haints in Detroit," Francis Turner said. His children jerked at the sound of his voice. That was how he existed in their lives: suddenly there, on his own time, his quiet authority augmenting the air in a room. He stepped over their skinny brown legs and opened the big room's door.

Francis Turner called Cha-Cha into the room.

The window was open, and the beige sheets from Cha-Cha's bed hung over the sill.

"Look under the bed."

Cha-Cha looked.

"Behind the dresser."

Nothing there.

"Put them sheets back where they belong."

Cha-Cha obliged. He felt his father's eyes on him as he worked. When he finished, he sat down on the bed, unprompted, and rubbed his neck. Francis Turner sat next to him.

"Ain't no haints in Detroit, son." He did not look at Cha-Cha.

"It tried to run me outta the room."

"I don't know what all happened, but it wasn't that."

Cha-Cha opened his mouth, then closed it.

"If you ain't grown enough to sleep by yourself, I suggest you move on back across the hall."

Francis Turner stood up to go, faced his son. He reached for Cha-Cha's collar, pulled it open, and put his index finger to the line of irritated skin below the Adam's apple. For a moment Cha-Cha saw the specter of true panic in his father's eyes, then Francis's face settled into an ambivalent frown.

"That'll be gone in a day or two," he said.

In the hallway the other children stood lined up against the wall. Marlene, child number five and a bit sickly, had finally come out of the girls' room.

"Francey and Quincy, clean up Lonnie's mess, and all y'all best go to sleep. I don't wanna hear nobody talkin bout they tired come morning."

Francis Turner closed his bedroom door.

The mess was cleaned up, but no one, not even little Lonnie, slept in the right bed that night. How could they, with the window curtains puffing out and sucking in like gauzy lungs in the breeze? The children crowded into Cha-Cha's room—a privileged first visit for most of them—and retold versions of the night's events. There were many disagreements about the haint's appearance, and whether it had said anything during the tussle with Cha-Cha. Quincy claimed the thing had winked at him as he stood in the hallway, which meant that the big room should be his. Francey said that haints didn't have eyelids, so it couldn't have winked at all. Marlene insisted that she'd been in the hall with the rest of them throughout the ordeal, but everyone teased her for showing up late for the show.

In the end the only thing agreed upon was that the haint was real, and that living with it was the price one had to pay for having the big room. Everyone, Cha-Cha included, thought the worry was worth it.

Like hand-me-down clothes, the legacy of the haint faded as the years went by. For a few years the haint's appearance and Cha-Cha's triumph over it remained an indisputable, evergreen truth. It didn't matter that no subsequent resident of the big room had a night to rival Cha-Cha's. None of them ever admitted to hearing so much as a tap on the window during their times there. The original event was so remarkable that it did not require repetition. Cha-Cha took on an elevated status among the first six children; he had landed a punch on a haint and was somehow still breathing. But with each additional child who came along the story lost some of its luster. By the time it reached Lelah, the thirteenth and final Turner child, Francis Turner's five-word rebuttal, "Ain't no haints in Detroit," was more famous within the family than the story behind it. It first gained a place in the Turner lexicon as a way to refute a claim, especially one that very well might be true—a signal of the speaker's refusal to discuss the matter further. The first six, confident that Francis Turner secretly believed in the haint's existence, popularized this usage. By Lelah's youth, the phrase had mutated into an accusation of leg pulling:

"*Daddy said if I get an A in Mrs. Paulson's, he'd let me come on his truckin trip to Oregon.*"

"*Or-e-gone? Come on, man. Ain't no haints in Detroit.*"

Cha-Cha transported Chryslers throughout the Rust Belt on an eighteen-wheeler. The job was the closest thing to an inheritance that he received from his father. After his twenty-fifth birthday the old man took him to his truck yard, introduced him to the union boss, and ushered him into the world of eighteen-wheelers, all-nighters to Saint Louis, and the constant, cloying smell of diesel fuel. Cha-Cha joked with his brothers who'd joined the service that he was more decorated at Chrysler than all of them combined. This wasn't a warmly received joke, but it was true. He held records in the company for fewest accidents, best turnaround times, cleanest cab, leadership, and dependability. He did this for over three decades, until, if what he saw was really what he thought he saw, the haint tried to kill him.

Cha-Cha was driving a full load of SUVs to Chicago during a storm. His rig at full capacity was a sight to behold—five-ton gas-guzzlers stacked like toys in two rows behind him. One, supported by a metal overhang, perched right above the roof of Cha-Cha's cab. He had reached the M-14, just past Ann Arbor, when, according to the police report, a deer darted onto the highway, causing a sedan to swerve into Cha-Cha's lane. Cha-Cha, in turn, veered off the highway and into a ditch.

"He ran me off the road" was the first thing Cha-Cha said when he woke up in the hospital.

"Who ran you off the road, baby?" his wife, Tina, asked. She put a plaintive hand on his arm cast.

"I knew he'd come back."

"Who? Come back from where?" Lelah asked.

Cha-Cha put his free hand on the bed, made to sit up and see who else was in the room.

"Just sit still, Cha," Tina said. "I got the remote right here."

In the awkward seconds it took for the mechanical bed to raise him, Cha-Cha remembered the night before. He saw the car to the left of him swerve into his lane. And he'd swerved, true enough, but only onto the shoulder. Then blue light, that familiar, flickering, and fear-inducing blue from the big room, filled his cab. He couldn't see the road to pull back onto it. He remembered clamping onto the wheel then, and hunching his shoulders forward as he tried to make out the road. He couldn't do it, and just as he conceded this point, he heard a fluttering, similar to the fluttering of the curtains that had roused him from his sleep so many years before. A sound like a multitude of moths, then silence. His old haint had found him and almost destroyed him in a matter of seconds.

His truck dragged along the brush for several hundred feet before slamming against a tree that was big enough to hold its ground. His seat belt did not catch the way it was supposed to in such an accident, and Cha-Cha's body bounced around the cab—up to the roof first, then hard against the driver's side door. He broke six ribs, his left arm, his collarbone, and, as if someone somewhere saw fit to initiate him into old age, his left hip.

Once propped up in the hospital bed, Cha-Cha gained a better sense of the owners of the voices in the room. His mother, Viola, stared at him from her wheelchair. Her neck muscles looked tense, as if the strain of supporting her head was getting the best of her, like a newborn baby. He wondered how long she'd waited for him to wake up. It annoyed him that someone, likely his sister Lelah, considering her proximity to Yarrow Street, had put Viola through the trouble of an unnecessary hospital visit. His boys, Chucky and Todd, leaned against the bathroom door. Francey was there, as was Troy, still in his police uniform. And someone else, too. Someone male, and white, and professional-looking, presumably the doctor, by the door.

"You said somebody found you, Cha?" Viola asked. Her voice sounded weak, weaker than the last time he'd heard it.

"The haint, Mama, remember?" Cha-Cha asked. "There was that same blue light from the big room."

"Cha-Cha, you've got a lot of painkillers in you right now," Francey said. She put her hand on Viola's shoulder, looked around the room in a way that made Cha-Cha nervous.

"Francey, don't look at me like I'm crazy. It was that same haint in my cab, I—"

"Dad," Chucky cut in. "Not. Now." He and his brother wore the same nervous expression. A half smile usually reserved for police of-ficers—and, Cha-Cha recalled, schoolteachers.

The man in the doorway cleared his throat.

Perhaps it was his over-starched dress shirt, or maybe that he'd displayed patience few doctors could have mustered during the previ-ous exchange, but Cha-Cha realized this man could only be one per-son. *The INSURANCE MAN is here*, he thought, and then, *Oh, hell*.

Milton Crawford was not an unpleasant man, but Cha-Cha quickly decided he had no sense of humor. He was fond of peppering sen-tences with *actually*, even if he wasn't clarifying anything.

"Actually, GM Life and Trust takes its employees' state of minds before accidents quite seriously," he said.

"I'm sure they do," Cha-Cha said, "but what you heard wasn't me before the accident, it was me after surgery, and sitting here getting this"—he reached unsuccessfully for his drip bag—"put into my bloodstream for a few hours."

"I do understand that, Mr. Turner, but actually what you just described, a vision of a ghost, has to be included in the report. It may actually amount to nothing, but I'm obligated to transcribe our entire conversation here."

"But he wasn't talking to you," Lelah said. Her hands moved to her hips. "He's lucky to be alive right now. Can't you come back tomorrow?"

"Lelah, let Cha-Cha handle this," Francey said.

"Lelah's right," Troy said. "He didn't even notice you were here. He thought he was speaking in confidence to *us*. You can't go holding him accountable for that." Ever since joining the police force, Troy was quick to become litigious.

Cha-Cha cleared his throat.

"Look, Milton, truth is, I'm tired. If you have to include it in your report, feel free to do so. I'm sure it'll amount to nothing, like you say."

Actually, it did amount to something. Three weeks into his Family and Medical Leave Act insurance, a letter arrived from a Mr. Tindale, who claimed to be Milton Crawford's boss. He said Chrysler would offer Cha-Cha his normal wages for the duration of his recovery, on the condition that he see a company psychologist, who would determine whether he was "personally culpable" for any aspect of the crash. All drivers had to submit to drug testing after an accident, and often a trace amount of alcohol or cocaine (used by the younger guys to help them stay awake) would be the reason they didn't get the money they thought they deserved. Cha-Cha had never heard of a driver being required to have a psychological evaluation.

"They wanna make sure you're not crazy," Tina said. She knelt on her knees in their master bathroom, running water for his bath. Cha-Cha sat on an ottoman near the door, one of Tina's old bathrobes pulled tight around his frame. It was purple and his favorite since the accident.

"Ain't nothing crazy about seeing a haint."

Tina turned to look at him.

"Says you and your family. Sooner or later you're gonna realize that just cause a Turner thinks a thing is normal doesn't mean it is. Not at all."

· WEEK ONE ·

Spring 2008

Swelling Bellies and Wedding Tulle

Lelah stuffed fistfuls of her underwear into trash bags. She was too busy thinking about what to pack next to be embarrassed in front of the stranger who watched her. The city bailiff seemed disinterested anyway; he leaned against her front-room wall and fiddled with his phone. The other bailiff waited outside. Lelah saw him through the front window. He did calf raises on the curb near the dumpster, his pudgy hands on his hips.

She'd always imagined the men who handled evictions to be more menacing—big muscles, loud mouths. These two were young and large, but soft-looking, baby-faced. Like giant chocolate cherubs. It had never come to this before, the actual day of eviction. Lelah had received a few thirty-day notices but always cleared out before the Demand for Possession—a seven-day notice—slid under her door. Seven days might as well have been none this time around; before Lelah knew it the bailiffs were knocking, telling her she had two hours to grab what she could, that they would toss whatever she left behind into that dumpster outside.

Humidity made her wrecked living room oppressive. It was the end of April, but it felt like June. The bailiff leaning on the wall carried a gray washcloth in his back pocket, and he swiped it across his brow from time to time. He pretended not to be watching her. Lelah knew better. He had a plan ready for if she snapped and started throwing dishes at him, if she called for backup—a brother or cousin to come beat him up—or if she tried to barricade herself in the bathroom. He probably had a gun. Mostly, all Lelah did was put her hands on the things she owned, think about them for a second, and decide against carrying them to her Pontiac. Furniture was too bulky, food from the fridge would expire in her car, and the smaller things—a blender, boxes full of costume jewelry, a toaster—felt ridiculous to take along. She didn't know where she'd end up. Where do the homeless make toast? Outside of essential clothing, hygiene items, and a few pots and pans, she focused on the sorts of things people on TV cried about after a fire: a few photos of herself throughout her forty-one years, her birth certificate and social security card, photos of her twenty-one-year-old daughter and her eighteen-month-old grandson, Francis Turner's obituary.

The second bailiff stopped his calf raises when Lelah walked outside with another box. She imagined that the neighbors peeked at her through their blinds, but she refused to turn around and confirm it.

"I'd give you a hand, but we can't touch none of your stuff," he said.

Lelah used her shoulder to cram the box into the backseat.

"I know you're thinkin, like, if we're not allowed to touch your stuff, then how are we gonna dump everything at the end."

Lelah did not acknowledge that she'd heard him. She took a step back from her car, checked to see if anything valuable was visible from the windows.

"We hire some guys to come and do that part," he said. "Me personally, I'm not touchin none of your stuff. I don't do cleanup."

The bailiff smiled. A few of his teeth were brown. Maybe he was older than he looked.

Back inside her apartment, the other bailiff, the sweaty one, sat legs splayed on her sofa. At the sight of Lelah he stood up, leaned against the wall once more. Her daughter, Brianne, called her cell phone, and Lelah ignored it for the third time that morning. She surveyed the room. What to take, what to take, what to take? It all looked like junk now. Cheap things she'd bought just to keep her apartment from looking barren. She snatched her leather jacket from its hook on the hallway closet door. That's it, she thought. The only way to hold on to some dignity, to maintain the tiniest sense of control, was to leave now, with an hour and a half to spare.

Later that night, at her mother's vacant house, she claimed the big room for sleeping.

As the youngest Turner child, Lelah had no siblings to escape from growing up, no reason to seek the cramped comfort of the big room's walls. Still, when her older brother Troy went off to the navy, she'd expected to take his place across the hall, spend her final years at home on that narrow twin bed for tradition's sake. Before she could gather her things to move, her mother had claimed the big room for sewing. Viola Turner claimed so little for herself, who could deny her this luxury? Not Lelah, the child who had the privilege of seeing her parents at a slower cadence. Fewer mouths to feed at the table, long-awaited fair wages keeping the bill collectors at bay. Francis and Viola were older, a bit slower getting around, but she was the Better Times Baby, something she'd known since plaits and barrettes. She'd stayed in the too-large, run-down, Pepto-pink girls' room until she too got grown, and found a way to get gone.

That night, nearly a year after Cha-Cha's accident, and six months since Viola went to live with him in the suburbs, Lelah claimed that long-denied right of passage. One small triumph on a day marked by defeat. She climbed the narrow stairs and creaked down the hall, using her cell phone as a flashlight, and imagined her younger self, sleepy-eyed and ashy-kneed, peeking out of the girls' room door to watch an older sibling take quarter in the big room.

The porch light had been on when she drove up, which meant Cha-Cha still paid the electricity bill. A relief. A house with electricity couldn't be classified as abandoned, and an individual with a key to that house didn't fit the definition of a trespasser. She considered conducting a thorough search. It was warm enough for someone—a niece or a nephew, or, God forbid, a drug-addled interloper—to set up camp in the basement. But she was too tired. After leaving her old apartment, Lelah had driven around the city, no idea of where to go. She refused to beg Cha-Cha or one of her nearby sisters for a place to stay this time. She'd wracked her brain for an alternative solution, some cheap, temporary lodging or genius scheme to hustle up money for a new place. Nothing surfaced, so she'd waited until the sun set and driven to the east side.

The big room had its disadvantages. It was right next to the bathroom, and water knocked on the wall as it traveled through old pipes to the toilet, which continuously ran. The lone window faced the street, which in this part of the city—ever changed, further decayed between each visit—put Lelah at risk of being struck by a stray bullet, or kept awake by intermittent car horns, hoots, hollers, and alley cat screeches. But on this, the first real, spring-feeling night of the season, she thought people had better things to do than shoot up the old Turner house, and having lived here in the eighties when the final, fatal arrival of crack cowed the neighborhood, Lelah felt Yarrow Street had already given her its worst. She hunkered down on the old twin bed, shoes on and jacket draped over her torso, and fell asleep.

She overslept. She'd planned to leave at five, before the block's working residents got up and about their business. She didn't bother to change clothes. She hurried down the empty house's narrow stairs.

Daylight flooding the front room halted her on the first-floor landing. Lelah knew that nearly all of the furniture in the house had been divvied up, save for the old bed and dresser in the big room, which no one had wanted. It hadn't occurred to her that the walls would be bare too. Dozens of brown outlines on the yellow wallpaper—ovals and rectangles—highlighted where picture frames once hung. Not long ago, every descendant of Francis and Viola Turner smiled from the front room's walls. Four generations, nearly one hundred faces. Some afro'd, some Jheri curled, some bald, more balding. Mortarboards, nurses' scrubs, swelling bellies, and wedding tulle. A depression in the floorboards opposite the front door marked the spot where Viola's armchair had stood. Lelah had spent whole afternoons on the floor in front of that chair, watching the comings and goings of Yarrow Street as her mother or an older sister greased her scalp and combed her hair. The memory made her feel safe for a moment, like maybe she'd made the right choice coming back here.

A knock at the door.

"Little Lee-Lee, is that you?" A muffled voice from outside.

A bald, spotted head and a pair of bifocals crowded the front door's high window. Mr. McNair. Too late for Lelah to duck out of sight. She rubbed the sleep out of her eyes, undid the lock.

The door creaked open, and Lelah's eyes focused on a pair of withered kneecaps. They looked like baked potatoes. The old man's face loomed above her. He balanced on an upturned plastic crate, one veined arm pressed against the porch's ceiling.

"Mr. McNair, come on down before you hurt yourself."

Lelah gave him her hand, put her free one on his elbow.

"I only fell the first time," he said. "Sure did hurt though."

"See, that's one time too many. What were you doing, casing this place for a robbery?"

"Hell, don't look like there's much left to take."

They chuckled. He straightened his baggy shorts, carried the crate to a far corner of the porch.

"Your brother Cha-Cha asked me to come by here and look after the porch and yard," Mr. McNair said. He ran a hand along the porch's rail to steady himself. "So I come every once in a while, sweep up, make sure it looks all right."

Norman McNair and Lelah's father had worked in the same trucking unit at Chrysler for thirty-two years. When Francis Turner died in '90, McNair took up the handiwork for his best friend's widow. McNair pretended to be a serious old man, but his fondness for going around with his gnarled, reedy legs showing as soon as the weather warmed up suggested a secret whimsy to Lelah. Francis Turner had never worn shorts.

"Few weeks ago somebody was sittin in Mrs. Bowlden's living room when she came back from New Orleans," Mr. McNair said. "A junkie. Up in there like he paid rent, just livin the life of Riley. Eatin her food *and* makin long-distance calls. He come up through the basement window."

He whistled through his teeth and shook his head.

"So I got the idea to start lookin in at your house through that top window in the door, seeing as how the curtains is always closed."

"Looks like we had the same idea," Lelah said. "I just came by to do a quick walk-through on my way to work. Everything looks all right."

Mr. McNair considered this, nodded. Lelah's phone rang—no doubt it was Brianne. She pushed Ignore.

"Well make sure you lock up real tight, cause these junkies are about ready to thaw out from the winter. Lord knows what they'll be lookin to steal."

The old man peered down the block, brows gathered. Lelah's car was parked across the street from where they stood, and she could see the odds and ends of her life cramming up the windows. If Mr. Mc-Nair noticed the things on the walk over, he was too polite, or bewildered, to bring it up.

"Alright, I'd best be gettin on my way," he said. "Tell your mama McNair says hello."

A rash of dandelions pocked the east side with yellow. The newly arrived spring—the spots of color, the surprise of birdsong—gave the neighborhood a tumbledown, romantic quality. It reassured Lelah that the ghetto could still hold beauty, and that streets with this much new life could still have good in them. On both sides of the Turner house, vacant lots were stippled with new grass. Soon ragweed, wood sorrel and violets would surround the crumbling foundations, the houses long burned and rained away. The Turner house, originally three lots into the block, had become a corner house in recent years, its slight mint and brick frame the most reliable landmark on the street.

Lelah took Van Dyke out of the east side to 8 Mile Road, 8 Mile to Woodward Avenue and into the city of Ferndale. She considered Ferndale, with its coffee shops and pet stores, a decent place for her daughter to live alone with a baby. It was home to a sizable gay community, and the trim, muscled white boys who jogged through the nearby park posed a stark contrast to the folks she'd seen on the street on her drive over. She pulled into Brianne's apartment parking lot at 8:45.

"Gigi!" Lelah's grandson, Bobbie, reached his chubby arms out to her.

Brianne passed Bobbie to Lelah. "What happened to you yesterday? I called a bunch of times."

"Sorry," Lelah said.

"I had to ask Olga across the hall to watch him again. She's too old to have him all day like that."

"I got my days mixed up. I thought you were off yesterday, and then working today."

Brianne shook her head. "I can get a real babysitter, you know."

Lelah said nothing to this. She made to bite Bobbie's cheek, chomping down on the air next to his face. The baby grinned, showing off two bottom teeth.

Brianne was darker than Lelah, shorter too, but with the same heavy chest. She'd inherited her slim hips from her father, not Lelah, who possessed what folks liked to call "hips for days." Brianne reached up and smoothed her mother's hair back. The gesture was motherly, their roles reversed. Lelah flinched before she could stop herself.

"You musta woke up late. Didn't even do your hair. There's some gel under the sink in the bathroom if you want."

Brianne handed Lelah a diaper bag and turned to put her key in the car door. Her nurse's scrubs were a deep red with small black triangles printed in a haphazard pattern throughout.

"I can't believe you go to work in that," Lelah said. "You look like a ninja."

"My scrubs? What's wrong with my scrubs?" Brianne turned back around, searched her shirt and pants for a tear or a stain.

"Nothing, they're just tacky. Nobody wants their nurse to look like they're headed to the club."

"Says the woman with the winter leather on." Brianne pulled at Lelah's coat collar. "You know it's supposed to be seventy-five today? I'm hot just looking at you."

"Wasn't hot yesterday," Lelah said. She shifted Bobbie's weight on her hip while Brianne put on lipstick, the same deep red as her uniform. Lelah could picture old men at the nursing home where Brianne worked planning their days around her daughter. Watching daytime TV in desperation, waiting for the moment she'd come and put her small hands on their frail bodies and make their senses jolt awake.

"Anyway," Lelah said. "When you get your RN, I'ma buy some new scrubs for you. LPNs might be able to dress like that, but *real* nurses wear bright colors. Care Bears and seashells. Or maybe just a nice mint green like they used to wear back in the day."

Brianne scrunched up her lips.

"Real nurses? So now I'm a fake nurse?" Brianne said. She sucked air through her teeth. "Why are you going in on me, Mommy? You're the one who didn't show up yesterday."

"Nobody's trying to go in on you. It was just an observation. It's like nobody can never tell you anything."

"I need to wash clothes, okay? These were the only clean scrubs left."

Brianne scrutinized Lelah once more, ran her eyes up and down her mother's body.

"We're both tired," she said. "But I'm serious about the babysitter thing. If you don't wanna do it, I can figure something else out. I can't be dropping him off with random neighbors when you don't pick up the phone."

Lelah forced a chuckle.

"I'm his *grandmother*, Brianne. You can't threaten to fire me."

Brianne raised an eyebrow, climbed into her car, and drove off.

Lelah walked with Bobbie to the park near Brianne's apartment. She sat him down on a shady bench near the cement pavilion, took off her jacket. She had felt like this before, anxious, cornered, but never had it produced such an uncomfortable physical sensation. Her body ached from yesterday's move, her skin tingled, and her head pounded. She stood up, jogged in place a bit, and stretched. With her hands reaching upward, Lelah knew the skateboarders in the pavilion were getting an eyeful of her softening midsection, of her heavy chest straining against the awkward fit of her teal polo shirt. She bent down toward her toes, displaying her backside to the skaters as she stretched her hamstrings, and tested the limits of her tight jeans. Her cell phone vibrated in her back pocket. This surprise, coupled with gravity's predictable pull on her bosom, threatened to topple her forward. She took a step for balance, straightened up, and pulled out her phone.

A text message from Brianne: "Was 10 minutes late to work."

Then another: "AND I AM A REAL NURSE."

"Huh," Lelah said out loud. She knew all-caps was the equivalent of yelling; she'd once accidentally set her own phone to all-caps and was accused of aggression by a tech-savvy coworker. Bringing up the RN thing had been stupid, but what else did she have to talk about? Usually Lelah fell back on a report of her mother's well-being over at Cha-Cha's house. She'd been avoiding Viola since she got her first eviction notice, so her go-to topic was stale. She couldn't tell Brianne that she was homeless because Brianne would feel pressure to offer her a place to stay, and Brianne needed to focus on working and going back to school.

Licensed practical nurse. That's what Brianne was. It wasn't so much that her daughter's job wasn't good enough, just that Brianne was too young to stop striving. LPNs were easily hired and fired; Lelah wanted Brianne to push for the more secure job. "A woman without no options is waitin for a man to come by and ruin her," Viola used to say, and she was right. Lelah had witnessed too many smart, talented Yarrow Street girls sit around on their porches, looking for excitement, meet the wrong man, and end up in trouble. Not pregnant trouble, but black-eye, bad-credit, women's shelter trouble, or worse. Lelah had married Vernon Greene, Brianne's father, because he was enlisting after graduation and odds were good they would see new things together. Three years after marrying Vernon and less than twenty-four hours after receiving the first and only black eye he'd ever have a chance to give her, she was back on Yarrow Street with little Brianne in tow. She hadn't even left the Midwest. The last time Lelah saw Vernon, some eight years earlier, he'd been nodding off in the freezing rain on a curb in front of a twenty-four-hour Coney Island on Harper. Maybe if she'd pushed herself harder back then, she wouldn't be where she was now.

Brianne acted as if she had no one, as if being a single mom meant she was some solitary mule humping an unbearable burden. It was only true because Brianne was stubborn, Lelah thought. It hadn't been that way for Lelah. Even before moving home for good, she'd seen that staying in the Midwest had its rewards, the most significant being that Brianne received Francis Turner's blessing. A blessing from Francis did not have a spiritual connotation in any formal sense. It meant that Francis would get to know your child in a way that wasn't possible for everyone in his ever-expanding line. In the final years of his life, Francis spent most days on the back porch, eyeing his tomato patch with good-natured suspicion, listening to his teams lose on the radio, and smoking his pipe. He did these things, and he held Brianne. Right against his chest. Francis had nothing cute or remotely entertaining to offer babies; he didn't say anything to them at all. Instead he gave them his heartbeat. Put their little heads on his chest and went about his day. Even the fussiest babies seemed to know better than to cut short their time with Francis via undue crying or excessive pooping. Lelah would stand in the back doorway and watch Brianne sleeping against Francis, his large hand holding her up by the butt, and think she could stand a few more years of being close by. How many babies had he held just like that since Cha-Cha was born, using only his heartbeat as conversation?

But it was also true that things wouldn't be the same for Brianne as they had been for Lelah. Francis Turner was dead, and Viola Turner now lived in the suburbs with Cha-Cha, for her own good, Lelah had herself once agreed. The Yarrow Street matriarchs who had helped raise Lelah, who had helped Lelah raise Brianne, were dead, dying, or tucked away in some suburb with their own families. And Lelah herself had no house to offer, no extra income to share.

She decided a conciliatory response was best for Brianne's text message.

She wrote: "Didn't mean it that way. Sorry."

A moment passed.

Brianne responded: "I know. Just annoyed. Sorry for caps."

Clouds slid into the sky, and Lelah felt a tiny raindrop land on her forehead. She decided to take Bobbie over to the Ferndale library, just a few blocks north of the park. Usually when she babysat she took him to her apartment, where she'd sectioned off a portion of front-room carpet for his toys. Those were all in the landlord's dumpster now. She'd feared they'd look like something worth stealing out of her car, so she'd left them behind.

Almost a Quorum

Cha-Cha was sure he was the first Turner to visit a shrink. His initial visit had been obligatory. The letter from Mr. Tindale, Milton Crawford's boss, sat on the kitchen counter for three weeks, demanding him to go talk about haints with a complete stranger. Cha-Cha tried to picture telling everything to this Dr. Alice Rothman—someone he imagined just as humorless as Milton Crawford, likely too thin and too pale, the type to be uncomfortable with Cha-Cha's wide, tall, brown presence in her office. Her discomfort might be obvious, or worse, she would fancy herself a liberal and make a show of trying to relate to Cha-Cha, a sixty-four-year-old black truck driver who saw ghosts. So desperate to appear politically correct that she would condescend to him, pretend to understand what he felt. He'd met enough of these types at Teamster meetings during those post-riot years in the seventies; he knew they often thought less of him than the blatantly racist types.

Alice Rothman was black, and not even biracial as far as he could tell—skin darker than his, hair kinkier than his, worn natural. Just a black woman with a misleading last name. She looked to be mid-forties, about the same age as Berniece, the tenth Turner child, who lived in Toledo and had just married the same man for the second time—a quiet, balding bus driver who refused to visit Detroit. Odd for Chrysler to hire a young, black female psychoanalyst, Cha-Cha thought. Maybe Alice was married to a white man, a higher-up somewhere in the company who hooked her up with this side gig, helping Chrysler avoid insurance payouts by declaring folks crazy.

"Call me Alice," she said. She did not ask if she should call him Charles, his full name, and Cha-Cha didn't tell her otherwise.

"Your report says you're the oldest of thirteen. Tell me about that."

Cha-Cha pegged her question as some sort of shrink trick, a roundabout way to establish him as a person with too much at-home stress, then she'd be able to move on to his hallucinations with the pressures of his big, rambling family already lined up as an explanation. He started off carefully.

"That's right, there's thirteen of us," he said. "But there's only about six or so here in the city. The rest are scattered around the country and getting along fine by themselves."

Alice Rothman leaned back in her turquoise armchair—hotel furniture, Cha-Cha thought—and tapped her pen on her notepad.

"What are their names?"

"Francey, Quincy, Russell, Marlene, Lonnie, Antoinette, Miles, Donald, Berniece, Sandra, Troy, and Lelah," Cha-Cha said, his cadence more like a song than a list. An image of his younger self, twelve maybe, came back to him. There'd only been the first six then, and he had made up a song for when he was "it" during Dark, a hide-and-seek game they played in the basement with its only light off. He sang in a whisper as he walked through the musty room, the low ceiling already becoming a problem for him, and when he thought he'd found someone's hiding place (behind the water heater, in an old box), he'd stand in front of it repeating the person's name ("Come on out, Quincy, Quincy, Quincy—hey!—Come on out, Quincy, Quincy, Quincy") until someone came out willingly or their laughter revealed them. He'd added to the song for a few more births, but then the novelty of another body in the house wore off on him and he was too old to play Dark anyhow. He didn't share this memory with Alice Rothman.

After names she wanted to know nicknames and the explanations for the nicknames if possible. Cha-Cha explained that his younger sister Francey was named after his father because his parents had named him, their first child, after the preacher who had married them back in Arkansas, a man Cha-Cha never met. It seemed she'd planned a series of questions that had more to do with the Turner family than with Cha-Cha as an individual, maybe to ease him into talking about himself. She wanted to know who had children, whose children had children, who was in school, who came to visit often, who was deployed and where, and who was incarcerated ("Excuse me, miss, *no one* is in jail," Cha-Cha shot back). Alice Rothman glided past this last misstep and switched the subject to memories of Viola and Francis, then to Viola being by herself on Yarrow, then on to Chucky and Todd, Cha-Cha's sons. Finally, when the hour ended, she mentioned Chrysler.

"They want me to send a decision about you sooner than later," Alice had said, "but what do you say we push it to later? You could come again next week. Talk some more. I could move this earlier thing, and you could come at ten."

"Alright," Cha-Cha had said. It was just nice to sit and talk, he supposed, and not lead the conversation if he didn't feel like it, and hold back what he wanted without the other person being any the wiser. Talking to someone who didn't already think she knew his life story was new for him, and interesting.

Three weeks later Alice Rothman declared that Cha-Cha was not "personally culpable" for the accident, at least not from a psychological standpoint. They'd never talked about his haint in any of the meetings. Cha-Cha figured she must have been able to glean whatever it was she was looking for better by not approaching the issue head-on. If that was the case, Cha-Cha had no interest in upsetting his leave payments by bringing the haint up himself. She invited Cha-

Cha to continue to come and talk to her, and he agreed. After his hip healed and he returned to work (no more driving; Cha-Cha would train new drivers now), he started using his own money to pay for visits.

Four months into the meetings, he sat in her waiting room and tried not to sweat. This was the day they'd scheduled to finally discuss his haint. Alice had said that with the "Chrysler business" behind them, Cha-Cha shouldn't feel pressure to hold back.

Her office door opened, and Cha-Cha, not trusting a porcelain hip to hold up his 230-pound frame, used his new cane to help him stand up.

"Good morning, Charles. Come in."

There wasn't a typical leather couch in Alice Rothman's office. In its place stood a mauve suede chaise, a fainting couch was what Alice called it during that first visit. Vintage, she'd said, custom reupholstered. Something a grown man, especially one with a bad hip and a beer gut, had no business lying upon, Cha-Cha thought. He'd dragged a regular old armchair from the waiting room into the office during his first visit. Alice didn't say a word as he did this, and she hadn't said anything about it each time he did it again. Cha-Cha wondered when she'd stop removing his chair after every visit; there was enough room for the chair and the fainting couch both.

"How's your mother doing?" Alice asked.

"She's doing fine, just drugged up a lot from her shoulder surgery, but she's talking more than she's been doing since she came out the hospital."

A pinched nerve in Viola's shoulder had begun giving her trouble recently. Before that, a series of strokes put her in a wheelchair and precipitated her move off of Yarrow. Before the stroke it was gallstones. Cha-Cha told Alice he feared his mother wouldn't make it through next winter.

"You never know, Charles. Your mother sounds like a fighter."

"I hope so. I guess all we can do is pray," Cha-Cha said, although he suspected praying for an old woman with a lifetime behind her to have a few more days on earth was futile, possibly sinful. He knew his wife, Tina, would call it sinful.

"So. Today is haint day, isn't it?"

"It looks that way." He no longer wanted to discuss his haint with her. Back when the meetings were obligatory, before he'd come to know Alice, her thoughts about him and his superstitions—apparitions, whatever they were—hadn't mattered. Now things were different. Cha-Cha feared that after they had finally gotten comfortable talking to each other, Alice might still declare him crazy, and since he knew he wasn't crazy, he'd have no choice but to stop therapy altogether.

"We can start with the first time," she said. She pulled out a new pad of paper from her desk drawer.

He told her about that night in the big room—the curtains hanging out the window, Francey coming to his rescue, his father's dismissal of it all.

Alice nodded but said nothing.

"What? You don't believe me? See, this is why we should've talked about this in the very beginning,"

"I didn't say anything, Charles. But have you ever considered that you might have imagined it?"

"Six people? I've never heard of six people imagining the same thing at the same time."

"Sure you have," Alice said. "A group of kids sit up late at night telling ghost stories, then they all think they've seen a ghost. Happens all the time. Isn't that what happened with the Salem witch trials?"

"I don't know anything about witches, Alice. But I do know a little about haints. And it wasn't just the one time when we were little. It came back."

"Oh, I remember the insurance report. So let me play devil's advocate for a minute. You're driving in the rain on an all-nighter, and you think you've seen a ghost. A lot of people might attribute that to sleep deprivation, lightning, too much caffeine."

Cha-Cha usually enjoyed the sparring nature of his and Alice's talks. She volleyed his answers right back at him like one of his own sisters would. But she took things too literally—a major character flaw, he thought.

"Charles? Were there more times than just those two?"

He didn't like how frequently Alice used his name. It was a way to keep their talks formal, which was fine, but he also thought it was a way to condescend.

"I don't see the point of waiting this long to talk about the haint if you were never going to believe me."

"It's not important whether I believe or don't believe, Charles. I'm curious if there were more times than just those two."

How many times did a body have to collide with the paranormal for it to count for the science-minded? Three? Twelve?

"Fourteen years old to sixty-four years old," Alice said. "That's a pretty long gap, don't you think?"

It didn't seem like a long time to Cha-Cha. Fifty years, a wife, two children, one grandchild; they were not here one day, then all here the next.

"Do you believe in God, Alice?"

"Well, I don't usually discuss my beliefs, but"—Alice put her pen down on the pad—"I'm an atheist, Charles. Why do you ask?"

"An atheist?" Cha-Cha had never known an atheist. When his son Chucky was thirteen he'd declared himself an atheist, but Tina had prayed and whupped it out of him. "Did you *ever* believe in God?"

"I guess I thought I believed at one point," Alice said. "But now I don't think I ever truly did."

"Oh."

"Why do you ask?" She leaned back in the chair but kept her arms on the desk, as if leaving her body open for attack.

Alice wasn't exactly Cha-Cha's friend, but she wasn't like anyone he'd ever met before, and he didn't want to throw their rapport out of sync.

"I don't know," Cha-Cha said. "There are ghosts all through the Bible, and angels, and even demons, not to mention the Holy Ghost himself."

"I'm not sure how that answers my question," Alice said.

"I'm trying to explain."

"Okay, explain then," Alice said.

"Thing is, after that first time on Yarrow, maybe I saw that blue fill my bedroom, and maybe sometimes I felt a certain way, like someone was watching me, but what I would do is hop out the bed, get on my knees, and pray. And after fifteen minutes or so of that, I wouldn't feel or see anything in my room."

Alice scribbled a quick note, possibly a single word, in her notebook.

"So you've been doing this off and on for fifty years?"

Cha-Cha certainly hadn't prayed on his knees, outside of his bed, in ages. Tina prayed like that most nights, and other nights she sequestered herself in their walk-in closet for a half hour, the door closed, the light switched off, trying to get that much closer to God. But just because he didn't hit the floor in prayer didn't mean the haint never paid him a visit. When Cha-Cha was seven he'd had the job of cleaning up the kitchen at the end of the night. He washed whatever dishes remained after dinner, swept the floor, and wiped down the counters. If he waited too late to take care of it, he'd flip on the kitchen light and find cockroaches scampering across the counter, some as long as his thumb, claiming their territory for the dark hours. In the beginning it had made him sick, but he learned to tolerate fighting the insects in silence as his siblings and parents slept. The haint might be similar, something that had always been around but no longer an out-of-the-ordinary nuisance. Except, of course, when it tried to kill him.

"I don't know. Maybe," Cha-Cha said. "Maybe I've seen it, or hints of it a few times over the years."

"And you've never told anybody about it again? Not even your father?"

Cha-Cha laughed.

"No, especially not my father. He said there weren't any haints in this city. I wasn't gonna change his mind."

Alice sat with this last statement a minute and munched on her bottom lip, a habit Cha-Cha noticed she indulged in when devising some sort of plan for him. Lip munch: you need to hold your siblings accountable when they say they're going to pitch in with your mother and don't; it's only fair. Or, lip munch: I think you could use a hobby, Charles, maybe something active, like swimming. Otherwise she kept her face very still.

"This is what I think," she said. "I think you need to pay more attention these next few weeks, find out if this thing is still appearing for you, in any kind of form. Think about patterns. Do you feel a certain way when it shows up? What did you eat that day? Take a note of those things. Then we'll have a better sense of what to do next."

"Okay," Cha-Cha said.

"Good, and maybe later, when you're ready, you can take a visit to your mother's house and spend some time in that room. Could be that you have some loose ends there that need tying up."

"Maybe," Cha-Cha said, but he had no desire to do anything to get closer to the haint. It seemed foolhardy, like thrusting your hand in a faulty garbage disposal, or parking a brand-new Cadillac on the street on the east side overnight.

Whereas the house on Yarrow Street sat high and narrow, full of straight lines, steep inclines, and sharp corners, Cha-Cha and Tina's house on the edge of Franklin Village sat low, round, and wide. The kitchen—which bled into the dining room, which connected to the den—was at the very center of the building. From the den a hallway led to the house's five bedrooms, 3.5 baths, garage, and finished basement. If you kept going, the kitchen inevitably reappeared. Francis Turner suggested such a layout, arguing that in his old age Cha-Cha would want a house that went out and around instead of up and down. It was optimistic advice from a man who in the end never lived to see seventy. In the wake of his accident and bringing Viola here to stay, Cha-Cha appreciated his father's wisdom. He'd bought the land at a considerable discount; the old house was destroyed in a fire, and the owners opted not to rebuild. He took his time planning the layout, aware that with only one above-ground story his neighbors' estates would dwarf his own. He made sure to add touches elsewhere to help his house fit in—a generous back deck, large bay windows, a wide, curving driveway. Now, a few of his neighbors' places featured foreclosure and For Sale signs on the lawns. Cha-Cha's house still stood, deep in the heart of a cul-de-sac and on its way to free and clear.

"Russell's been holed up in Mama's room since he got here," Cha-Cha said. "I tried to listen through the door, but damnit if they weren't in there *whispering*."

He leaned into the kitchen from the front entryway.

"Please, Cha-Cha. You know your brother couldn't whisper at a funeral," Tina said. Every surface in the kitchen supported a tray of pepper-speckled raw chicken parts. She moved from tray to tray, shaking seasoning salt from one hand and garlic powder from the other.

"All I know is that he better be in here in time for this meeting." Cha-Cha hovered in the kitchen entryway lest Tina put him to work. "If he's gonna show up for the weekend unannounced, he can at least help tend to some business."

"I keep telling you he sent us an email saying he was coming," Tina said.

"That man sends an email every hour," Cha-Cha said. "How am I supposed to wade through all them chain letters for the real ones?" He hurried as best he could manage through the kitchen and into the dining room, where he tried to look busy with a stack of receipts.

"The subject line was 'coming to Detroit this weekend.' You had to have seen it."

"That coulda meant that God's coming to Detroit for all I know. Half those emails are always tryna force me to do something or face hellfire. They'll have some scripture, then talkin about 'click this if you love God,' or 'if you don't forward this, you'll be damned.'"

"So do you forward em?" Tina asked.

She looked up at him, her gloved hands out in front of her like a doctor pre-operation.

"Of course not! It's probably some people tryna steal folks' metadata, or spyware, or whatever you call it."

Tina's face did that thing it liked to do when she prepared to say something righteous. Her eyebrows rose, her chin dropped a bit, and her freckles seemed to multiply. Cha-Cha knew the scripture she'd reach for.

"Whoever denies me before men, him I will also deny before my father who is in heaven," she said, with more seriousness than Cha-Cha thought necessary. He opened his mouth to say something clever—he wasn't sure what—and perhaps a bit combative in return, but Russell came into the dining room from the den.

A career military man like his older brother Quincy but not nearly as zealous, Russell was most similar to Francey in that he'd strike up a conversation with anyone, anywhere. He also had a penchant for creating nicknames, including for people he'd just met. The gift of gab resided within every Turner child—fights for parental attention required it—but to Cha-Cha, Russell's level of gregariousness seemed less a product of genetics and more the result of a dogged, often annoying resolution to remain optimistic. His brother, the fourth child, had survived Vietnam, three decades in the marines, throat cancer, and, perhaps most harrowing, the shame of his firstborn son growing up to be a pro-prison, anti-"big government," libertarian-leaning Republican. Russell would hold court on any subject except politics. Unbeknownst to all but Cha-Cha and Viola, he contributed the most money to Viola's care, and his mother harbored a soft spot for him because of it.

"I take it all this chicken ain't for me, the weekend guest of honor?" Russell said.

"Not this time," Tina said. "The women's ministry is hosting a picnic tomorrow."

"Mmm-mmm, now you know I love a women's ministry!" Russell said. He rubbed his hands together.

Tina swatted her spatula in his direction from the other side of the counter.

"You're just as bad as Cha-Cha. Y'all both need more church."

Cha-Cha heard cars pull into his driveway and went to open the front door.

Marlene, Francey, and Netti arrived in one car, Troy in another. Cha-Cha worked his way from one sister to the next, doling out squishy hugs and airy pecks on the cheek. He clapped Troy on the back, suppressed the undying urge to give his youngest brother a nougie.

"Where's Mama? In her room?" Marlene asked. "I wanna say hi before we get started."

She moved toward the hallway, and Russell cleared his throat.

"She just took her pills and *finally* went to sleep," Russell said. "Don't go in there waking her up. Maybe by the time we're done meeting."

Marlene turned back to the living room and rolled her eyes at Russell.

"Fine, but I'm not leavin without seeing her, Russ, you'd better believe. She's not no little baby. She can go back to sleep."

Russell might have garnered favor with Viola through monetary contribution, but Marlene's sense of entitlement to her mother's attention stemmed from time spent and sheer will.

"Anyway," Netti said. "Anyone heard from Lelah? I called her earlier, but her house phone kept ringing. I think she's got a new prepaid cause the cell number I tried didn't go through."

"I tried that prepaid number, and she didn't answer either," Cha-Cha said. He chose a barstool over a dining chair to give his left knee some relief, as did Russell. Turner knees, the left one in particular, became untrustworthy as one aged.

"I don't know why that girl won't go ahead and get a regular contract," Netti said. "She's like one of them drug dealers on TV, doesn't want the government to track her down."

"You've gotta have good credit to get a contract, don't you?" Troy said. "Y'all know Lelah ain't had good credit since high school."

"Oooh," Marlene and Netti said in unison.

"What happened today, Officer Troy? You in a bad mood?" Netti said.

"Alright!" Francey said. "It looks like it's just gonna be us. Three boys and three girls. That's good enough. It's almost like a quorum."

"Yes indeed, Francey-pants," Troy said. "If you wanna make it real official, you can go ahead and take the minutes." He stepped past her to the refrigerator and pulled out a beer.

"I just *might* take minutes, thank you very much. And I'll be sure to note your intoxication levels in the official report."

"Never mind Officer Troy. Can we kindly get this show on the road?" Marlene asked. "I'm tryna catch a rummage sale in Windsor early in the morning, so I need my beauty rest."

"*Roomage* sale?" Russell said, imitating their mother's pronunciation. "Thought it was called a flea market nowadays. You turning into an old lady on me, Marly Marl?"

"Mama pronounces it *roomage*, I'm gonna at least say rummage, out of respect. You know what I mean."

Viola no longer had the energy for the requisite bargain hunting and haggling, but Marlene still ran the clothing booth that they had manned together at a local flea market for years. She handed half of the proceeds over to Cha-Cha to help in Viola's care.

"Alright," Cha-Cha said, trying to sound formal. "Let's get to business."

"Yes, let's," Marlene said.

"After being on hold for forever, I finally talked to the bank about Mama's house. Apparently, under the advice of I don't know *who*, Mama refinanced in '94 after Daddy died. A couple years before I got in charge of her affairs."

"That was my advice," Netti said. "And it was good at the time. All of y'all were broke or busy feeding your kids, and those social security checks weren't enough for Mama to survive on." Netti, the seventh child, worked for an accounting firm. She was a lead administrator, not a CPA, but she had a general handle on money, always put more aside than most.

"Nobody's blaming you, Netti," Francey said. "Cha-Cha is just laying out the facts."

"Thank you, Francey," Cha-Cha said. "So anyway, Mama owes about forty thousand, but that house, even though it's the nicest one on Yarrow, is only worth four thousand dollars."

Gasps and epithets filled the dining room, even a "What in the *hell?*" from Tina, the born-again non-curser, in the kitchen.

"That's the same thing I said," Cha-Cha said, referring to one of the curses, or maybe all of them. "But let's not act like Yarrow ain't been doin bad for a while now."

"Doin bad, sure, but four thousand dollars?" Netti said, "You can't even buy a car with that."

"The appliances me and Richard just put in there cost almost half that amount," Francey said.

"I *know.* But four thousand is just a number we're all gonna have to accept. This meeting isn't about that number. It's to decide what we're gonna *do* about the Yarrow Street house."

"What do you mean, *do?*" Marlene asked.

"Well, it's pretty obvious," Cha-Cha said. But here he paused a beat too long, which made everyone fearful of what he'd say. "We'll have to short-sell it, unless we can come up with some other option."

There was no uproar here, no additional curse words flung into the air. Instead all the siblings got familiar with the carpet on the dining room floor, ran through assets and expenses in their heads. Everyone knew what short-selling meant; the depressed housing market had made the term commonplace. You stopped making payments on your house, then the bank agreed to sell it for what it was currently worth. You didn't see a penny of the sale money, but at least you didn't owe the difference. Each sibling also took a quick assessment of the level of personal guilt in the situation. When was the last time they'd lived on Yarrow? The last time they'd visited, or added equity to the house in some way or other? There was an email sent out by Marlene, right around the time of Cha-Cha's accident, asking who might be able to come live on Yarrow, to help Mama manage, so she wouldn't be alone. Everyone had been too busy with mortgages, or their own grandkids, or spouses. Well, everyone except for Lonnie, who was out in California and living God knows how, but no one wanted him back on Yarrow, getting into God knows what kind of trouble with his old friends. Silently, to themselves, the six siblings in the dining room all concluded that they were culpable in some way or other, even if it was just for not having enough money saved up to hand over the $40,000 right now.

"Well, we're not selling the house, especially not for no four thousand dollars," Marlene said.

"Yeah," Netti added. "We sell it today and in ten years Donald Trump or somebody will buy it, build a townhouse, and sell it to some white folks for two hundred grand."

Everyone, faces stricken, acknowledged the truth in this.

"That's the way the east side is gonna go eventually," Russell said. He balanced precariously on the barstool; it was a bit too narrow for his behind. "People are just walking away from their houses, and the city's makin it too hard for other folks to buy them. Talkin about you have to pay the back taxes and what all else. Even on empty lots! They should be happy somebody wants to mow the grass."

"But let some millionaire offer to buy a whole bunch of lots at once," Troy said, "and all of a sudden the city will start cutting deals for them. Pennies on the dollar, I bet you anything."

"Well y'all don't have any other ideas, do you?" Cha-Cha asked.

A moment passed in silence. Cha-Cha wondered why he'd even called this meeting in the first place. A Turner family meeting rarely ended in agreement.

"What does Mama say?" Marlene asked. She looked from Cha-

Cha to Tina, who was leaning on the kitchen counter, and back to Cha-Cha again. "What's she wanna do?"

Tina coughed and turned away to check on her chicken in the oven.

"Cha-Cha? Please tell me you clued Mama in to all this." Marlene's eyebrows folded into a frown, causing her high forehead to break into a series of ripples. "I keep telling y'all she's not a baby. It's *her* house, she shoulda been the first one to have a say."

Cha-Cha would have liked to remind Marlene that he was Viola's legal guardian—a role he took on after her last stroke—and that he would be the executor of her estate when she passed, pitiable as that estate might be. He would have liked to tell her that as far as the law went, Viola might as well be a baby because his decision was the only one that would matter in the end. But Marlene's wrath was infamous, first exhibited at age nine when she plotted for an entire week to get even with her younger brother Lonnie for breaking her Easy-Bake Oven, and finally found vengeance by dropping him on his head in front of the entire family during an impromptu performance of Ice Capades (wherein the children "skated" on socks across the waxed living room floor). Lonnie had needed ten stitches. Cha-Cha had no desire to call forth such rancor now.

"Fine," he said. "Let's go ask her."

Viola's room shouldered a burden designed for a much larger space. The pictures that once crammed the common rooms on Yarrow Street had been shoehorned into this one, producing an effect not unlike the famous-patron photos that smothered the walls of pizzerias and Greek diners throughout the city. Every relative pictured looked a little more important than they were in real life. The room, chosen for its abundance of natural light, had belonged to Todd, Cha-Cha's younger son, before it was Viola's, and despite new furniture and professional carpet shampooing, a faint smell of adolescent armpit and athletic socks lingered. Marlene entered first, with Russell on her heels and Francey and Cha-Cha behind them. Troy and Netti stood in the doorway. Tina opted to stay in the kitchen.

A matriarch, even one who demurred at that title and its pressures as often as Viola did, is a hard thing to lose. The Turners had to reckon with the loss of their matriarch every day they laid eyes on her. Viola had been a thickset woman, the origin of the Turner hourglass shape that had set east side men to drooling for five decades. Time had finally claimed those curves in Viola's seventies, and the stroke the year before had withered her still-shapely legs. The right leg was all but immobile now. She'd held together for ages, then every part of her seemed to collapse within six months. Marlene, Russell, and Francey appeared unbothered by the tight confines of the room, but Troy and Netti, more sparing with their visits, were shaken. Cha-Cha lived two bedrooms down from Viola, and still he felt a shock every time he came through her door. His mind held a crystallized image of his mother from a specific epoch in his own life, and it was hard for him to reconcile it with current reality. Cha-Cha would always imagine her in her late fifties, all thirteen children born, wide-hipped and heavy-chested, carrying both of his young sons with more ease than even Tina, thirty-something at the time, could muster. The woman lying on the bed now, not at all asleep, using the remote control on her lap to flip through TV channels, was a stranger. More than Francis Turner, Viola had always seemed the type to just drop dead one day, not wither slowly. She lowered the remote and regarded this incomplete amalgamation of her brood.

"Now I know it can't be my birthday already, can it?" She said. "Russie, why ain't you tell me we were celebratin my birthday today?"

They moved toward her, kissed her cheeks and gripped her papery hand.

"Mama, you know it ain't your birthday," Marlene said. "You're more than a month out. We're having a family meeting tonight."

"Oh Lord," Viola said. "About what? Y'all votin on something? You know Cha-Cha's gone do what he wanna do. Ain't no democracy in this family."

Cha-Cha felt his face burn and heard his siblings snicker. Troy snorted.

"No I'm not, Mama," Cha-Cha said. "If we vote, I'ma listen. One man or woman, one vote."

Russell sat on the edge of the mechanical hospital bed and put his hand on Viola's good leg.

"It's about your house," he said. "We owe the bank more than it's worth now. To be exact, we owe forty—"

"Bottom line, Mama," Francey interrupted. "Do you think we should sell the house? Or do you want us to figure out a way to keep it?"

"Well, it's not that simple," Russell said. "That's why I was tryna break it down for her."

"She *understands*, Russell, god-lee," Marlene said.

"Just let Russell finish," Netti said. "Before Mama gets confused."

"Who's confused?" Viola asked. "Y'all ain't even said nothin yet. I know how much we owe the bank, Netti. You forget I was there when we did it?"

Netti, chastened, said she remembered.

"And I don't wanna lose it," Viola continued. "I plan on movin back just as soon as I get strong again. Just a couple more months."

Viola continued to flip through channels. She paused briefly on a megachurch telethon.

"Why everybody lookin at me crazy? I'm serious. A few more months is all I need, so just sit tight. Shoot, I ain't fixin to be up in this room forever."

She flipped through channels some more and finally settled on an old western, replete with covered wagons and *pew-pew* gunshot sound effects. She leaned back on her pillows and yawned, signaling she no longer wanted to be bothered.

Back in the kitchen, Tina was dicing a mound of boiled potatoes for salad. The Turner siblings returned to their seats in the dining room. Each felt a coward for not pointing out the obvious to Viola. She would never live on Yarrow again.

"You short-sell that house, it won't even be worth four thousand," Troy said. He'd found a toothpick and talked while jabbing the thing at his gums. "Mrs. Gardenhire's son, not the one strung out on herr-on but the younger one, Dave? He bought that house next door to them for only fifteen hundred. And that was back in '03. What we should do is short-sell to somebody in the family, but someone that you can't prove is family on paper. That way we still own it, and only have to pay what it's worth now."

Cha-Cha suspected that Troy was referring to his girlfriend, Jil-lian, and he didn't like it. She and Troy's relationship was so volatile that Jillian just might burn the house down out of spite.

"If anyone without a Turner name should buy it, it should be Ra-hul," Netti said. She and Rahul, an Indian man who worked in ac-counting at her office, had lived together for fifteen years. He held more clout among the Turners than Jillian, but he still wasn't blood.

"Rahul owns all those properties in Dearborn—"

Here an argument broke out, because Troy didn't see what was wrong with Jillian being the buyer, and Netti came too close to telling him what the rest of them thought. Then Tina said the whole plan felt dishonest, which set everyone's eyes to rolling and forced Cha-Cha to side with his wife, despite wanting to roll his eyes too. Russell and Francey were both willing to see the Yarrow house go, and Mar-lene burst into tears when they admitted this. In true Turner fashion, the only thing they all could agree to (after Russell agreed to treat) was tabling the matter in favor of finding somewhere to eat dinner. Troy said he already had dinner plans. Marlene volunteered to stay back with Viola and keep an eye on Tina's wings.

Motor City, Friday Night

Francis Turner's garden had turned to weeds shortly after his death. The house's surviving residents had their reasons for not picking up trowel and hoe in his memory: Lelah was working two jobs, not to mention taking care of Brianne, and Viola said simply, "Francis never liked me pokin around with his plants when he was alive, so why would I start pokin now?" No one had a good answer to that. The state of the garden, coupled with a string of car thefts on Yarrow, prompted Miles, the eighth Turner child, to invest in a garage. He said a garage accessible through the back kitchen door would not only protect a vehicle or two but also provide a way for passengers to get into and out of the house during the winter months without slogging through the snow on the street. So the backyard was paved, and an aluminum-and-wood two-car garage fitted to the back of the house like a caboose.

Lelah, not wanting to risk another night with her car in plain sight, planned to park in the garage. She turned in to the alley behind the house, a poorly paved strip that separated the Turner property from a boarded-up house that faced Fischer Street, and climbed out of her car to unlock the back gate. She tried to ignore the blackness of the

alley behind her as she fumbled with her key. The trees from neighboring lots hung low, and she felt the hard bodies of unripe mulber-
ries crush beneath her feet. They should have sprung for an automated gate like Mr. McNair's, she thought, because once she drove
through the gate she had to get back out of her car to lock it behind
her. After this she manually unlocked and raised the garage door.

She couldn't bring herself to go into the house. Inside the garage
she smelled mildew and damp earth through her rolled-up windows.
Various medical supplies stacked haphazardly in the small space and
hanging from the rafters created a geriatric phalanx around her Pontiac. An old walker and its dirty, impaled tennis balls, a disassembled
hospital bed, boxes and boxes of gauze, huge boxes of adult diapers—
male ones Francis hadn't lived long enough to wear and newer boxes
of female ones that Viola could probably use. Too much. She wasn't
sleepy at all, so getting out of the car meant how many hours alone in
the big room, in the dark, with nothing but her thoughts? Too many.
She backed the car out, closed the garage, and exited the backyard.

The chips looked like candy. Pastel, melt-away things that didn't
make sense to save. The feel of them, the click and dry slide of them
in her palm, was gratifying. Some people in Gamblers Anonymous, a
place she hadn't been in months, claimed the tiny ball, spinning and
spinning around on its wheel, was the reason they loved the game.
"It's like you get a bonus, a little bit of a show from that ball," Zach, a
white man who always wore a suit and tie, once said. Other people in
the group had nodded knowingly.

Lelah stood at the foot of the roulette table. Just having a look, she
told herself. If she were playing, she would never stand here, so far
away from the wheel and the top half of the board, a position where
she'd end up asking strangers to put her chips where she wanted them
to go. If she were playing, she'd request the orange chips, depending
on the dealer. But she couldn't play right now. She'd spent the last of
her cash on lunch for herself and Bobbie, and she didn't know whether

she'd be approved for unemployment, so she couldn't spend the $183 in the bank.

"No more bets," the dealer said. He waved a pudgy, upturned palm over the table. People settled back into their chairs.

The ball landed on double zero. There were a few cheers but mostly groans. It was a crowded night in Motor City Casino.

"The one time I take my money off those zeros, they come up," the light-skinned woman next to Lelah said. "I been splittin the zeros all night."

She looked at Lelah, waited for a response.

"I know, I saw you," Lelah said. "That's how it always goes though, right? That means you'll hit soon."

"Shit, I hope so," the woman said. Her fake eyelashes made her look drowsy, like a middle-aged blinking baby doll. She wore a rhinestone-trimmed dark denim jacket and matching jeans. Brown cowboy boots with a low heel. "All I know is that I'll be back to splittin these zeros from now on."

Lelah grinned at her. She enjoyed this false camaraderie almost as much as she did the chips.

She told herself she'd come to Motor City to eat. Her twenty-five complimentary tickets for the buffet were the only tangible benefit of thousands of games of roulette. She also had a Motor City VIP card. The irony of being a homeless, "very important" anything was not lost on Lelah as she had presented the black and purple card to the valet out front. She had anticipated a strange stare or at least a smirk as he helped her out of her overflowing car, but he hadn't seemed to notice. It had occurred to her, slightly depressed her, that she wasn't the only homeless gambler in Motor City tonight.

It was a low-stakes table, $5 to get on the board. The woman in the cowboy boots split the zeros again with $25 worth of lavender chips — an amount Lelah considered risky, seeing as how double zero had just come up. She said nothing though. Faux camaraderie was appreciated, but outright advice was not.

Lelah knew she was an addict. She'd come to terms with this truth long before her eviction, which marked a new low. The first indicator had been almost four years earlier when she'd been desperate enough to ask Brenda, her cubicle mate at the phone company, to loan her $200, just until payday. She asked Brenda instead of one of her siblings because she didn't want to have to lie about where she would spend the money. That $200 had bloomed to $1,000 in about a year's time, and after she had paid Brenda back, she found other coworkers to befriend and borrow from. A few hundred from Jamaal, a sweet, chubby twenty-year-old with dreadlocks who worked on the third floor and maybe had a crush on her; $60 from Yang, an older Chinese woman who used to sell pork buns from her cube before management forbade all sales except for the Girl Scout variety; $1,200 from Dwayne, a fifty-year-old widower with a potbelly and a gold-plated left incisor who absolutely had a crush on her but insisted he wanted nothing in return for the loan. "Now that my Sheila's gone, I got nothing and nobody to spend on," he'd said.

Dwayne proved to be a problem. He waited by her Pontiac in the parking deck after her shift a few weeks after he'd loaned her the money, and as Lelah approached the car she realized his pants were undone, and that little brown bump Dwayne was rubbing his thumb over so quickly was not the knuckle of his other thumb but in fact the head of his lonely widower penis. They fired Dwayne, but at the grievance meeting HR brought up the money she'd borrowed going all the way back to Brenda. They claimed she'd borrowed more than five thousand dollars over the four years, but that didn't sound right to Lelah. She could only account for about three thousand, and she'd paid back everybody but Dwayne. "Jesus, you could've told us you were pumping little old ladies for cash before we got in here," her union rep had said. She had been suspended without pay for over a month now and was still waiting to see if she would be terminated.

She followed her own code when it came to playing roulette. She never bet all inside, or all out; she spread her chips around the table, she never begged the dealer to let her play out her last chip, and she didn't make loud proclamations, speak directly to the little white ball as if it gave a damn about her, or pray for those inanimate, albeit beautiful chips to behave any particular way. She tried not to act like a strung-out, desperate addict, even if that was how she felt.

"No more bets."

The pit boss, a busty redheaded woman in a pants suit, whispered something into the dealer's ear, looked hard at the people gathered around the table, then walked a few paces away. Even this moment of choreographed intimidation was a familiar comfort to Lelah.

The ball landed on 27.

"Aw hell," the woman splitting the zeros said.

Lelah always played 27. Brianne was born on the twenty-seventh of February, as was Troy, the closest sibling to Lelah in age. Lelah's chest tightened, and somewhere near her sternum she felt a bit of warmth. She wanted to play. Badly. Now was a smart time to move on to the buffet, she knew, but she couldn't take her eyes off the dealer. He swept up all of the chips, a jumble of sherbet-colored winnings for the casino, because no one had bet on her number.

She stood up. Took off her jacket. She should have walked away, but she couldn't. It was awkward, being at a table but not playing at the table. You had to smile, look indifferent and simultaneously interested enough to justify taking up space. Her armpits started sweating.

Several chips covered number 27 this turn. Too late for them, Lelah thought. The woman put the rest of her lavender chips, Lelah estimated twenty, between 0 and 00 again. She looked up at Lelah and winked.

"No more bets," the dealer said.

"I knew it! I knew it! I knew it!" The woman next to her jumped up from her stool. The ball was on 00. Lelah congratulated her as the dealer slid her a small fort of chips, more than five hundred dollars.

If she were a seasoned gambler, this woman would stay put and ride this upswing out, likely eating away at her winnings in the process. This was what Lelah would have done. But the woman asked the dealer to give her the chips in twenties and stood up to go.

"For you," she said to Lelah. She handed her a blue and yellow $20 chip.

"For me, for what?"

"You said I'd hit and I did."

"You would've anyway. I can't," Lelah said, even though she knew she could.

"Like hell you can't," the woman said. Then she leaned in closer, whispered, "Roulette ain't a spectator sport."

Lelah closed her fingers around the chip but did not sit down at the table.

"Well, thank you. Here." Lelah looked past the woman toward a cocktail waitress, put up a hand to get her attention. "At least let me buy you a free drink. I can afford a free drink."

They both laughed.

"No, I need to run out of here with my money before I get pulled back in." She dropped her remaining chips into her purse, a sturdy, designer-looking purse, Lelah noticed, and headed toward the cashier.

This happened to Lelah sometimes in the casino, a stranger high off of a big win gave her money just for bearing witness, and each time she felt like crying. Because she wanted the money so much. Because a stranger could be so generous, when she'd never once thought to do that after a win. Because she perhaps looked as desperate as she felt. Because, truthfully, it didn't take much to make Lelah feel like crying. But feeling like crying was not the same as actually crying, and Lelah was up $20.

She'd been down to less than twenty bucks and pulled ahead before. Her mind ran to wild possibilities of success. There was a red convertible sitting on top of the Wheel of Fortune slots, and though she detested slots as an amateur, vulgar game, she imagined winning so much at a table that they gave the damn thing to her; just put a ramp over the front slots so she could climb up, drive her new Corvette down, and pick up the rest of her winnings at the cashier. Or maybe she'd only get a few hundred, but it would be quick and enough to buy her some time, so she'd resist the urge to try to flip the money and run out of there, hundreds in her pocket, and check in to a nice hotel. Yes, a nice hotel would be a good start, and then she'd take a day or two to figure out what to do next. This was a lot more feasible than the car scenario, she knew; she just had to strategize.

She figured she should eat first, before they ran out of the good stuff at the buffet, then she'd come back and try to make the chip last. Split it into ones at the $5 minimum table, spread it around.

As she piled limp green beans onto her plate, she thought she saw half a dozen people she recognized. The woman near the pop fountain with the red sequin hat was definitely someone Lelah had seen before; she always wore that hat, and she kept rolls of quarters for the slots in her fanny pack. Lelah made a conscious effort to keep her eyes on the food, lest she run into someone from her GA meetings. The defeated did not like to acknowledge one another mid-backslide.

It would follow that Lelah returned to the table where the woman won the chip for her, but every open seat there made it so you could see the craps table behind it. On a Friday night the craps crowd was too lively, and Lelah couldn't risk being distracted. She chose a five-dollar-minimum roulette table near the bar where an older black man named Jim was dealing. Lelah couldn't recall anything spectacular happening to her at Jim's table before, but she didn't have any negative recollections either, so she gave him a try. It was considered bad form to take up a seat when you had so little money to play, but Lelah was determined to make this money grow. She planned to act like she had more cash until it became a reality.

She put ten outside on black, two on 27, and three in the corner between 7, 8, 10, and 11. Jim spun the ball and it landed on 8. That meant she'd get ten from her outside bet and twenty-four from the corner. This brought her to $54, a much more reasonable amount to work with. She took off her jacket.

Lelah never kept a strict count of her money after every play. The exact amount wasn't as important to her while in the thick of the game as much as the feel of her stack of chips. Could she cover them with her entire palm, or did she have tall enough stacks that her hand sat on top of them, and the colors—the orange ones she preferred, persimmon, in fact—still peeked from between her fingers? Yes, this was the thing to measure by. Let the dollar amount be a pleasant surprise after several rounds. She kept playing inside and out, sometimes black, sometimes red, a few corners, a few splits, but always straight up on 27.

Her tablemates came and went. She registered their movements—new faces and body shapes—but not the particulars anymore. The camaraderie seduced her in the beginning, it was a way to warm up to the task at hand, but after a while if she didn't go broke she'd slip into a space of just her and her hands and the chips that she tried to keep under them. A stillness like sleep, but better than sleep because it didn't bring dreams. She was just a mind and a pair of hands calculating, pushing chips out, pulling some back in and running her thumb along the length of stacks to feel how much she'd gained or lost. She never once tried to explain this feeling in her GA meetings. She couldn't even share with them the simplest reasons of why she played. They were always talking about feeling alive, or feeling numb. How the little white ball made them feel a jolt in their heart, or maybe how the moment of pulling on an old-fashioned slot handle for the first time in a night was better than an orgasm. Lelah did not feel alive when she played roulette. That wasn't the point, she'd wanted to say. It wasn't to feel alive, but it also wasn't to feel numb. It was about knowing what to do intuitively, and thinking about one thing only, the possibility of winning, the possibility of walking away the victor, finally.

"You want to change some of those for twenties?" the dealer asked.

He's talking to me, Lelah realized, and she looked down for the first time in at least ten plays. Her hand rested on a cluster of persimmon stacks about six inches tall. Three hundred dollars, give or take, she could feel it. Jim, the dealer, stared at her.

"Sure," she said. "How about one hundred in twenties, one eighty in fives, and whatever's left in ones again."

Jim obliged, and Lelah slid a cobalt $5 chip back to him for his assistance.

She had enough for a hotel room now. She knew she should leave. Slide her chips into her purse like that generous woman did earlier and make a beeline for the cashier. But her watch said 11 P.M. Just another half hour and she could be up $600. With $600 she could find a place to stay for a week, maybe two weeks if she settled for a shitty motel. She could flip the money into something worth leaving with. Not could, she *would*. She just had to try. She put $60 on black, $10 on oo because it hadn't hit yet, $40 on the third 12 of the board, and $20 on 27.

No matter how still Lelah's mind became as she played, she was never careless; her purse stayed in her lap, her cell phone tucked in her front pocket. Vernon was the one to tell her that over two decades ago, back when they'd taken trips off base in Missouri to the riverboat casinos. "The same guy sitting next to you shooting the shit all night will steal your wallet in a heartbeat," he'd said, and she'd nodded. This was toward the end of their marriage, and the riverboats, newly opened, were one of the few places where the two of them still had fun. Neither of them was interested in winning money, but Vernon had an engineer's knack for figuring things out, breaking systems down into their parts. They conceived Brianne after one of these trips, and although they weren't exactly in love anymore, Lelah believed they had created their daughter in hope.

"No more bets."

The ball landed on 14. She had no chips on 14, which meant $120 was gone. The remaining $180 was still more than she had in the bank, but what could you get with that? Not much. If you walked out with $180 when you could have had $600, you didn't walk away the victor. She put money on the same spots again, just half as much.

It wasn't Vernon's fault she'd ended up a gambler; she would never say it was. A few years after the divorce and her return home Lelah started going to Caesars in Windsor on her own, and that's when the feeling found her. The stillness she hadn't even realized she'd needed up until then. When she felt like she was flailing, back on Yarrow not doing anything worth anything with her life and tired of being alone, she could sit right here, put her hand on the chalky surface of the chips, and be still for a moment in the middle of all the commotion of the casino floor.

"No more bets."

Lelah looked down. Her twenties were gone, gone before she even thought to admire the shiny redness of them. Cobalt and persimmon were left—it felt like forty dollars. Her watch said 11:27. Forty dollars was like no money at all, so she might as well let it play. Straight up on 27 twice and it was gone, and with it, the stillness. She heard the slot bells first, then noticed the stink of cigarette smoke in the air. Lelah found herself part of a loud and bright Friday night in Motor City once again.

One North

A city had its own time and cruelty. There was cruelty in the country too, but it was plain. Not veiled beneath promises of progress, nor subtle when it manifested itself. Francis took in the high-domed roof, the glittering marble floors, and the multitude of corridors as he walked. One stepped into a place like this—a palace like the kinds that Abraham and his wife, Sarah, turned up in, he thought—and felt impossibly small. Just a dim light, easily blown out. Francis arrived at Michigan Central Station with a small bag, his only pair of shoes on his feet, $15 in one pocket, and a letter for a pastor in the other.

He'd hoped for a different letter from the one he carried. It did not introduce him as a clever young man worthy of apprenticeship in the Lord's work. That letter and any chances of a preacher's life were gone.

Reverend Matthews,

I trust that you will be able to assist Francis Turner, of my flock, with securing housing and a good word at one of the fabled places of industry in your city. He is open to any work available. He and I will both be much obliged.

> With Faith in Our Lord,
>> Reverend Charles Williams Tufts
>> Spring of Faith Missionary Baptist Church, Arkansas

Francis had opened the letter as the train thundered through Kansas. It was early morning, and the sky out the window stretched wide and black and endless. That phrase, "of my flock," was impersonal, as if he and Reverend Tufts had not lived under the same roof, as if they were casual acquaintances. He deserved more warmth than that, a few words to lift him from the ranks of ordinary congregation member to favored almost-son. The reverend could have called his friend ahead of time; he had a phone line in his house, and Francis was sure the other man had one too. Putting the letter in Francis's hand ensured that he would have to look the man up, humble himself before a stranger, and beg his case. He couldn't bring himself to use such a letter, especially not one so impersonal. He kept it in his pocket for the duration of the train ride. This was how it had been done since Henry Ford first took a paternal interest in Negro employment and the cheap labor it provided: manufacturers depended on Up North ministers to supply them with reliable workers, and those ministers reached out to their southern colleagues for help filling the positions. But that was before the war. Who needed a note of introduction in a city on the forefront of the war effort? Francis had read that there were more jobs available in Detroit than in the entire state of Arkansas.

Pride had always played a prominent role in the Turner psyche. Its source went back further than Cha-Cha and Lelah's generation, past Francis's too. Officially, Francis Turner Sr. died in 1930 from a rusty-nail puncture to the bottom of his left foot, but it was pride that did him in. He stepped on the nail walking back from the fields he sharecropped, and the soles of his shoes were so worn that nothing pre-

vented the corroded metal from piercing him nearly to bone. He
hobbled home to his wife and six-year-old son and let his wife dress
the wound. Francis Sr. ignored Cynthia Turner's pleas to go see a
doctor for monetary reasons but also out of pride. There were no
doctors in their town, and Francis Sr. could not imagine sending for
a white Pine Bluff doctor over a cut on his foot. He doubted the doctor would be willing to even step inside his house, and he would not
let any doctor tend to him in the yard as if he were an animal. His was
not an arbitrary, selfish sort of pride; for Francis Sr., losing the little
dignity he'd held on to as a black man in the South seemed a more
concrete defeat than death. Two weeks later Cynthia was a widow,
and the debt Francis Sr. left her led to eviction. She and her son
moved into a one-room shack that was one bad storm away from being no more than a lean-to. After two years of scraping by, Cynthia
found a live-in maid job in Little Rock. She entrusted young Francis
to Reverend Tufts, a widower himself, and sent money when she
could.

If Francis hadn't inherited enough pride from his father, Reverend
Tufts supplemented what he lacked. The man had a congregation of
fewer than three hundred poor people, but he indulged in frequent
haircuts, a two-story house, and a new car every five or so years, even
while paying tuition for his only daughter at Tougaloo College. His
brand of pride—heavier on self-regard than Francis Turner's, but
still rooted in the same desire to feel a man when the world told you
otherwise—extended to his pulpit. The reverend had three deacons
and he would have preferred none, but these three were so old and
respected, there before he even moved to town, that he couldn't rid
himself of them.

During his sixteenth summer, Francis stopped receiving Cynthia
Turner's small packages of neatly folded money and sweets. She had
maintained one-Sunday-a-month visits with him up until then. She
would take a bus out or hitch a ride, and the two of them would sit on
the reverend's porch and talk. A stranger driving past might have mistaken the two for teenagers embarking on a courtship via sanctioned

Sunday visits. If they were lucky, the reverend would join them and fill up their awkward silences with self-congratulatory chatter. On her final Sunday, Cynthia said her white folks were moving to Dallas, where the husband had some sort of work lined up, and they had asked her to join them. Francis was not surprised that his mother had said yes; the white folks had seven children, and he'd long suspected that the line between blood and water — questionable water at that — had gone blurry for his mother. His sixteen-year-old pride prevented him from showing his disappointment. He took a long look at her smooth, wide face, the high eyebrows he'd inherited, and said a variation of something he'd heard the reverend tell many a congregation member when they moved away: "I'll be prayin for you, Mama. You call or write me if you ever need a thing."

Pride worked in mysterious ways on Francis, much like the God he worshipped. Pride prevented him from using Reverend Tufts's letter of introduction to get a good job and maybe even free rent for a while. But he was not too proud to ask strangers for help. At the train station in Detroit he chatted up a porter who directed him to a janitor who told him to head to a house off Hastings and see about renting a room. He had a gift for conversation, for making people feel at ease. It wasn't his words, exactly; Reverend Tufts always said that Francis was eloquent in his head but still too much a country nigger out his mouth. It was his looks, he supposed. He was tall and slender without lapsing into frail, and his skin was the color of baked-right cornbread. He'd learned early on that folks assigned all sorts of qualities to skin like his, and that a certain type of middle-aged woman would always consider a yellow boy somehow trustworthy. The sort of young man who would help carry a load of groceries and not run off with them. He asked colored person after colored person for advice until he climbed aboard a streetcar headed for Paradise Valley.

The best way to avoid feeling too small for a place was to pretend you'd been there before. It was Francis's first time on a streetcar, but after the lurching claustrophobia of the train ride (another first), the wide-open windows were welcome. On Hastings, among so many citified Negroes, Francis tried to feel like one of them. He dawdled in front of a chicken shack he didn't dare spend his money in. He stood in front of a vegetable cart and lamented the pallor of Up North to-matoes. He broke down and bought a plum, found it sour but ate it anyway. Poor folks and the better-off were out, couples shopping and mothers with children in tow. It was Saturday. He'd only had liquor a couple of times in his twenty years—a neighbor's moonshine made his throat swell when he was thirteen—but he thought that after see-ing about a room he'd find himself a nice place to sit and have a drink. There would be workingmen at a bar, and maybe he'd find his way into a job.

A room. The boardinghouse was crumbling. Ash-gray rotting wood showed through the black paint, and greasy sheets hung in the windows. The porch sagged as if it were sometimes tasked with sup-porting more than a dozen Negroes at once. The house sat on a street narrower than Hastings, and poorly paved. The smell of garbage and sewage made Francis's mouth tingle with nausea. He knocked, and a sharply dressed young woman with a wide, pouty mouth opened the door. Too good-looking for such a place. Francis thought she might be a whore, and this place some type of cathouse. Still, he took off his cap.

"You a soldier?"

"No ma'am. I just come up from Arkansas," he said. "You only ren-tin to soldiers?"

"I didn't say that," she said. She looked him over again. "You just look like a soldier, the way you stand. Not much the way you dress, though."

Francis made a conscious effort not to adjust his posture. He re-peated that he'd just come from Arkansas, added that he didn't have much money, but if she had space for him, he'd never miss rent. The woman's eyes dropped to his mouth as he talked, and Francis won-dered if this was because he sounded so country or because she saw something there she liked, or didn't like. He had a gap between his two front teeth, and people were often of two minds about it.

The woman suggested he split a room to save his money. He'd get the room to sleep at night, and during the day a Mr. Jenkins, who worked nights, would have it. She would hold his belongings downstairs.

"You're lookin at me strange, but this here's the best setup for a fellow like you." She swept one arm in front of her like a circus ringleader presenting to a crowd. "You all keep coming up on every train and bus, and y'all find work, sure enough. But it'll be *a lot* harder to find yourself a decent place to live. You wait and see."

Francis didn't believe her. He'd read about the race riots up here the year before. He'd read that on top of rumors of a black baby thrown into the river or some other specific injustice, the fighting had been over housing, and that the government had finally broken down and guaranteed space for Negroes in the city. Housing projects, they were called. He kept these thoughts to himself. Part of the job of being the mistress of a crumbling boardinghouse was to present housing as scarce, he supposed. He had no doubt he'd find a better place to live once he found work, so he left his bag with her. She introduced herself as Miss Odella Withers after he'd paid his rent for the week. He wandered over to Beaubien Street, back toward the heart of the Negro commerce stretch that he did not yet know doubled as the center of Negro nightlife. He passed over a place that two conked-haired men in suits entered and followed a man with rolled-up shirtsleeves and well-worn trousers into another. He sat at the bar and ordered a scotch, the only liquor he'd ever seen Reverend Tufts drink.

Viola was expecting a call. Francis imagined her sitting in Jean Manroy's ramshackle house far down the road from her own, trying to be polite so that Jean didn't change her mind about lending the phone. He'd said he would call when he was settled, but who could consider half a room and no job settled? Francis looked around the Up North bar and drank his scotch like the other patrons—slowly, carefully, as if it had been on his mind all day.

Two South

· SUMMER 1944 ·

The Reverend Charles Tufts left a message for Viola with her neighbor Jean Manroy. He said that his pastor friend Up North had not heard from Francis, and furthermore that it was not advisable for Viola to contact him about it again, seeing as how her husband was now in the business of turning his nose up at favors. Jean relayed this message with a nasally, phony-white accent meant to mimic the reverend's intonations. It was a known secret that the reverend who claimed New York was originally from North Carolina and had trussed up his diction upon setting foot in town. Viola did not laugh. She left Jean standing barefoot in her raggedy front yard and walked back to her parents' house to check on Cha-Cha.

Six weeks had passed since Francis left town on a bus bound for the train station in Little Rock, and local tongues wagged. Eventually the ones in Viola's own house joined in. Her overworked father was too tired to care about gossip, but her mother, two older sisters, and four younger brothers took to aggressive whispering. *Ain't he have a job lined up? They got phones Up North, don't they? Well, at least he married the girl, fore he run off. I heard they roundin up colored men at the train station and sendin em to the war if they don't have no proof of work.*

He supposed to be preachin with Tufts, why'd he run outta here in the first place? He liked to do right, but with a mama like his maybe he just ain't got it in him. When Viola entered a room in their two-bedroom shotgun house, voices retreated abruptly, like water from the shore.

Francis could have stayed in their tiny town, devolved into a drunk and a whoremonger, and Viola's family would have supported them with fewer complaints. Aspirations to leave set her and her new husband apart. Ever since the Budlongs of Brunswick County, Virginia, had found their way west to Arkansas, no woman in her family had left for anyplace farther than Pine Bluff, which was less than twenty miles east. She had two brothers in Cleveland and a third in Omaha, but they were men and their lives their own. And Francis *was* supposed to be preaching. Viola had met him in church when she was thirteen years old, shortly after she stopped going to school. He was already tall at fifteen, golden and thoughtful. He usually read the opening scripture for Reverend Tufts on Sundays, and Viola noticed that he knew most of the Old Testament by heart. A more impressive feat than memorizing the new one. The Reverend Tufts was not a tall man, but he was handsome and imposing in his Sunday robes. Viola imagined that Francis would one day look even better in those robes because he would be more humble, and not clutter his sermons with flourishes like Tufts did. When you got the call like that, so early in life, what was there to do but preach? You didn't necessarily need a college degree like Tufts had, you just had to know the scripture and feel the pull of the pulpit for admirable reasons.

When Francis said they were moving to Detroit, that Tufts had given him a letter of introduction and a little money to send him on his way, Viola had insisted she wouldn't go. "Just cause somebody tells you to up and move don't mean you move," she'd said. "This time it do," Francis had muttered back. They were in his room in Tufts's house, on the first floor behind the kitchen, their makeshift honeymoon suite, and they could hear the reverend creaking around upstairs. It was the first time she'd sensed that she ought to hold her tongue with Francis, that she should tamp down the flurry of questions in her throat to spare some part of her new husband's pride. A difficult feat, but she managed it. Francis left two days later.

On her way back from another fruitless visit to Jean Manroy's telephone, Viola saw her sisters, Lucille and Olivia, standing on the porch of her mother's house. Lucille carried Cha-Cha, just four months old, in her arms. When she came closer she saw that Olivia held a white envelope in her fist, so tight it looked like she meant to crush it. Viola ran up the walk and snatched it out of her hand. Its seal was intact, and it had an incomplete return address.

> Dear Viola,
>   I am in Detroit. Grateful enough I have a job and somewhere to sleep. I am saving my money and will find a way. I do miss you.
>   F. Turner

Francis had enclosed $7. Seven dollars! Not enough, not at all. Viola had left school to work in the fields with her older brothers and sisters on their father's sharecropping plot. The boys picked cotton and the girls held out the stiff burlap sacks for collection. The longer Francis stayed away and kept sending such little money, the more the fields called her. It was either that or housework for white folks, which is what Olivia and Lucille had opted to do a few years back. She tried to think of which job would spare the most of her dignity and afford her time with the baby. A preacher's wife shouldn't be forced to choose between field work and white folks, she thought.

"So he ain't dead," Olivia said.

"No, he ain't *dead*," Viola said. "Who thought he was? I thought the goin rumor was he run off."

"Well he ain't said he's leavin you for good, or you'd be cryin," Lucille said. She handed Cha-Cha to Viola and put her arm around them both. "You oughta be smiling, girl. Plenty girls sittin around waitin for a letter like that, and it ain't never comin."

Viola tried to see it that way.

Spring 2008

It Sure Ain't Free

With the exception of his graduation from navy basic training—all those white uniforms, the green lawn, the crisp rows—any time an event reminded Troy, the twelfth Turner child, of a scene from a movie, things turned out poorly. Occasionally on his beat when he pulled someone over or responded to a call he'd have this cinematic déjà vu, and trouble always followed, be it an irate arrestee or a senior officer with brass on his shoulder who barked in Troy's face. This evening had all the makings of a scene from a white-collar crime thriller, and Troy's nerves responded accordingly.

"Pull over right here," David Gardenhire said.

Troy parked his SUV at the curb in front of a little park with a gazebo abutting the river.

"Here? We're only a couple blocks from your apartment," Troy said.

"So? We don't need to drive into the woods. This phone just doesn't get good signal inside."

David pulled out a phone Troy had never seen before. A cheap flip-up one, not nearly as nice as David's new smartphone.

"You got a prepaid just for this one call?" Troy's voice cracked at the end of his question.

"Yeah," David said. "Last time I dealt with this dude I used a pay phone. Shows you how long ago that was."

The need for an untraceable phone line increased Troy's suspicion that he was acting out a Hollywood scene. He wasn't a detective, but beat work and crime shows had proven that if a prepaid phone was necessary, the perpetrator was into something extra dirty.

Over the previous few days his original idea about the Yarrow Street house had crystallized into a plan. He and his girlfriend Jillian might not have the $40,000 needed to absolve Viola of her debt, but they had enough to buy the house for the price any interested stranger would be expected to pay. Less than four thousand, Troy estimated. Of course, short-selling at the current market rate to relatives of the debtor wasn't legal, or else everyone would shimmy out of bad loans as quickly as thin women out of dresses. As Troy had pointed out during the meeting at Cha-Cha's, on paper Jillian Farmer had no connection to the Turners at all. The larger issue, Troy knew, was his siblings' lack of confidence in his and Jillian's relationship. Troy himself had a middling amount of confidence in them as a couple, but not having the approval of his siblings had become one of the most appealing incentives for short-selling the house. He used to crave their approval with a desperation that dictated his life. Since coming back to Detroit and becoming "Officer Troy," a name his siblings used to mock him, he'd discovered that it felt good to do what he damn well pleased.

"So you ain't worked with this guy since forever ago, and you trust him to just up and help us now?"

Twilight was turning into evening on the RiverWalk, but Troy could still see the whites of David's eyes as he rolled them. Both David's dark skin and his lankiness had been fodder for teasing growing up. Now Troy thought these features made his friend look ageless; he could have been twenty-five or fifty-five.

"This ain't a big money deal, Troy. It's four grand at most, which means this guy's cut is only a couple hundred. Not worth snitching over, trust me."

David turned the prepaid on, and the car filled with green light.

"This is more of a precaution for you than me," he continued. "I had a buddy who did real estate in San Diego, and he had this guy who would help him out with people's credit sometimes. The feds brought the guy up on fraud charges, and my friend had to testify in front of the grand jury. They subpoenaed him for all his emails, phone records, receipts, checks, everything from ten years back. But he'd only ever dealt with the dude in cash and spoke to him on one of these, so they couldn't stick anything."

As ambivalent as he felt about being a cop, Troy didn't want to end up disgraced. Three years before, he would have said that he hated the police, especially in Detroit, where they could take over an hour to respond to 911 calls yet expected residents to respect them. Now that he was one of "them," he knew that limited resources *did* play a role in delayed response times, but he'd also seen his colleagues, both black and white, shrug off calls to protect and serve folks in the worst parts of the city in favor of others. Francis Turner had never liked Detroit police. He'd told Troy that the only difference between a southern cop and a northern one was that if the northern one killed you, he would try harder to make it look like an accident.

"Alright," Troy said. "Just call him."

He took off his seat belt, reclined his chair. If he were patrolling this area, he'd shine a light into a suspicious car like this, or at least drive by at a crawl to encourage the driver to move on. He considered himself fortunate that his district, the Central District, didn't include much of the waterfront. He'd heard of cops stumbling upon major drug drop-offs from Canada, catching idiots attempting to dump bodies or guns into the river, violent confrontations. The water attracted a higher-skilled breed of lowlife.

David made the call on speaker. The line rang once, then he hung up. Troy began to say something, but David cut him off.

"This is how we do this," he said. "I let it ring once, then he calls back."

David pulled out his smartphone and played a game. Solitaire. Out of all of the new interactive, drag-and-drop and bubble-pop games available on a phone like that, David picked solitaire. Above all, Troy Turner valued potential, and he had begun to suspect that David's potential for success was outpacing his own. Maybe it was because David had simple desires. He didn't want everything, like Troy did, so it was easier for him to work slow and steady toward his modest goals. Small business installing cable and Internet; a loft on the newly revitalized RiverWalk; a couple cheap properties throughout the city. It was more than Troy possessed but far less than what he desired.

A few nights before, Troy had sat on his sofa, Jillian's head in his lap, his hand on her angular shoulder, and tried to conjure up a segue into the topic of his illegal short sale. They watched one of the many food and travel shows that Jillian liked. This one featured a white man in a rumpled dress shirt and slacks in what looked to Troy like Bangkok, peering into pots of local fish stew. The show broke for a commercial, a perfect amount of time for Troy to say what he needed to say and get an answer from her with minimal follow-up questions.

He'd pitched his plan matter-of-factly, as if being concise would make it feel less illegal. He never mentioned forging signatures or falsifying deeds. He'd kept his hand on her shoulder, kneaded it a little.

"Basically, cause you know how these banks are, running through your whole family tree trying to get their money, I was thinking we could short-sell to *you*. I'd pay the money."

Jillian jumped up from where she was lying. Troy's hand flew from her shoulder and smacked him on his own chin.

"What the fuck, Troy?"

"What the fuck what?"

"We just talked about both of us putting more into the savings, and now you're tryna get me caught up in some money scheme with *our* money?"

"It's not some money scheme, Jillian," Troy had said. "It's my mama's house. Damn."

He had dabbled in less-than-sure things in the past. Once he'd bought in to a classic pyramid scheme, ostensibly selling poorly crafted cell phone accessories, but the real money was made by getting other people to sign on underneath him. That lasted a month. He'd been seduced at mansion parties out in the suburbs, where self-appointed tech gurus, health and fitness gurus, and experts in the emerging Michigan wine market had convinced him to "buy in" to this or that product or service, then foist it onto his loved ones and coworkers for meager profits. He'd never recouped his seed money from any of these "investments." But he was done with that sort of thing, had sworn it off after the winery venture didn't pan out.

"I'm really disappointed right now . . . you haven't put any money . . . in the savings account since February . . . I checked."

Jillian took a deep breath every few words. Around the holidays they'd had a shouting match that caused her to have an asthma attack so bad she'd ended up hospitalized. Afterward she and Troy agreed not to yell anymore. Deep breaths were how Jillian diffused her anger. Avoiding eye contact and feigning indifference were how Troy attempted to control his.

"It's not that much money, compared to what we actually owe. It's the best way to get my mom out that loan—we short-sell it, and the bank just writes off what she owed them as a loss. I'll start putting more in the savings each month, starting on the first."

"That's what you said in February . . . but it never happened . . . How bout you just let me know . . . if you want out of the savings . . . altogether?"

They'd opened a joint account right after Jillian earned her cosmetology license. At thirty-two she'd quit her job as a flight attendant and begun pursuing a dream to own her own salon. The savings was for a down payment on some sort of split-level property in a decent neighborhood where she could have a salon on the first floor and they could live on the second. They'd met at a job fair at Cobo Center three years before, back when Troy was living with Viola on Yarrow. He'd been out of the service for six months, still smarting from the way his ex-wife, Cara, had left him and taken their daughter to Germany. He and Cara had not been doing well, true. He'd cheated three times, yes. Still, Troy thought he was owed one more chance, one more opportunity to straighten up. He never got it. His sister Netti, always thinking dollars and cents, had harangued him into going to the job fair, reminding him that his pension for twenty years of service wouldn't be enough to live on after paying child support. Jillian was there, a volunteer rep for the airline she worked for at the time. Once she'd sussed out that he was a pensioned vet, not your average deadbeat, she introduced him to the guy at the Detroit Police Department table, talked Troy up to the man as if she'd known both of them for years. There was a big sign at the table saying INFORMATION ONLY. DEPARTMENT NOT HIRING, but Troy still received a call for an interview. Back then, Jillian oozed potential from her pores. When they moved in together, Troy made a vow to himself to do better this time, to simply leave before cheating again. He was getting old for the lies required, all of the ducking and dodging. He'd kept that promise so far. But he now wondered if there wasn't a better way for Jillian to harness her potential. She had been doing hair for nearly two years and had yet to secure a decent roster of clients to justify her booth rent.

"Do you know how many weaves I'd have to put in to get that money back?" she had continued. "A lot of fucking weaves, trust me. And it's not like your family needs more reasons to hope we break up. Do you want em to hate me?"

"It's not even that much money. Like two thousand—"

"The money's not the point." Jillian had turned off the TV and searched Troy's face. "Why do you wanna do this? Why you and me? You act like you're the only one of the thirteen that could buy the place. Rahul could do it, and I'm sure he's got better credit than me."

Troy couldn't say, and because he offered no convincing reason, Jillian had refused.

Now the prepaid phone tinkled and bleeped on the dashboard. David accepted the call and put it back on speaker. Wheezing, followed by nothing for several seconds. Throat clearing with considerable push-back from what sounded like bronchitis-grade phlegm.

"Dave-O, that you?"

David sat up straighter in his chair, as if the man on the other end of the phone could see him.

"Hey, uh, what's up, man? Yeah, it's me. Dave-O," he said.

Troy would have made a joke about this nickname, but David had warned him not to speak unless prompted.

"Long, long, *long-ass* time, huh?" The man chuckled, then caught something in the back of his throat. Hacking ensued.

"Yeah, man," David said. "Working for myself these days. You know how it is."

"I do, I definitely do. No days off, and if you take one, ain't *nobody* payin you for it!"

More laughing, more hacking.

"So what I need help with is a little thing," David said. "A minor paperwork thing."

A muffled thud on the other end of the line, as if the phone had dropped on carpet.

"Hold on right quick, Dave-O," the man said.

He yelled to someone near him, "I said lemon pepper, nigga! You know the buffalo ones is nasty. Hurry up and go back fore they close."

"Alright, I'm back," he said. "So a little thing, huh?"

"Yeah, my boy's worried about his mom's house. She's not doing too well health-wise, and she's behind on her mortgage. He wants to go ahead and get a short sale done in his girlfriend's name before anything happens."

An impressive, selective truth, Troy observed.

"Smart man," the voice said. He made a glugging noise and gasped for air. "Thing is, you know with this housing crisis blowing up, banks are looking twice at everybody's papers."

"Which is why we're seeking your expertise," David said.

"It ain't free, though. It *sure* ain't free."

Troy blew out air through his nose and slumped down in his seat.

"Of course," David said. "Don't worry about that. We'll take care of you. Right now we just need to know what paperwork he has to get in order."

The man outlined the extensive dossier required to work his fraudulent magic. Viola's social security card, Jillian's employment history, and so on. Troy knew all of Viola's important paperwork stayed in a plastic freezer bag in her top dresser drawer at Cha-Cha's in case of an emergency. He could get those easily. The voice said Cha-Cha's signature was required if he was currently on the deed. Well, that signature would have to be forged. Luckily Cha-Cha had the signature of a teenage girl, all loops and legibility. He'd written Troy enough checks over the years for Troy to imitate it.

"I'ma need all those plus the mother's signature and thumbprint for my notary guy to make it all official," the man concluded.

"Thumbprint!" Troy yelled. "What for?"

Silence on the other end.

"Dave-O? Everything good over there?"

David sighed.

"Yeah, it's fine," he said. He put his hand up to silence Troy, who shook his head violently. "We'll get it together, then I'll hit you back. Thanks for this, man. 'Preciate it. Eat some carne asada fries for me out there. I miss them things."

David hung up without waiting for a response. He switched on the overhead light.

"If you want to do this, you're gonna have to get her thumbprint."

"Apparently," Troy said. But how? He couldn't imagine doing it himself. Picking up his mother's gnarled hand, dropping her finger onto a pad of ink, pressing it on paper, and baby-wiping away the evidence. Not even if she was in one of her pain-pill hazes.

"That's gonna be a problem?" David asked. He drummed his fingers on his knees, and his nails looked especially shiny. Troy wondered if he buffed them. Could he remain friends with a man who buffed his nails?

"I mean, I can figure out a way to do it," Troy said.

"I know it's weird. I'd have to think about it before I did something like that to my own mom."

"You already own her house though, and damn near half of the east side."

"Shut up, man. I don't own anything close to that."

Troy was again reminded of David's success, of how different their lives had turned out. Their first tour was on the USS *Carl Vinson*, a ship that would later gain fame for delivering Osama Bin Laden's body to the bottom of the Arabian Sea, but was just a run-of-the-mill super-carrier in 1990. They'd gone to different high schools and were not as close as they'd been as kids, so each man sailed for three months without knowing the other was on board. One day Troy was eating on the mess deck, trying to remember the last time he'd seen the sky, when he heard someone with an accent like the long-lost twin of his own telling a story about a house full of sisters he once knew.

"I'm tellin you, you could get blue balls just walkin to the corner store. There was six of them, and the oldest one was like forty, but she was *still* bad. I'm talkin Pam Grier bad, you know, just getting older and finer? They all had these thick thighs and small waists."

The surrounding men had whistled in admiration. Troy stood up from his table and located the speaker. He recognized David's face — skin like ink, high-contrast white teeth, and a Roman nose — but out of context and so far away from the east side, he couldn't recall his name.

"You ever get with any of them?" someone asked.

"Nah, not really, but I'ma try again when I get back. Even if they put on some weight, none of them had the type of bodies to get sloppy, you know? The youngest one was around my age, and I fingered her once in high school, but then she got married and moved away."

Troy knew from the beginning of the talk that his six sisters could fit the seaman's description — he wasn't blind, after all — but the last bit about Lelah doused him in a proprietary rage he'd never experienced before. It wasn't a fight as much as a quick pummeling of David's face, but both men were assigned thirty days of on-boat restriction and thirty days of labor. The latter half of their 30/30s, when Troy and David spent four hours a day suspended from cables to paint the starboard side of the ship, bonded the two sailors, their differences overshadowed by a shared longing for home.

David looked at the time on his phone.

"I bet Jillian is waiting for you. Go head and drop me off."

Troy had planned to buy him a few rounds of drinks for setting the call up, but it felt like David was in a rush to get away. He dropped him off and headed home.

Hamtramck, a small city surrounded by the larger city of Detroit, had experienced several lives over the past century—German farming community, Polish immigrant enclave, even one of the most rock 'n' roll cities in America, according to one magazine. None of these lives had ever included enough black people for Troy's liking. He sometimes liked to sit in his patrol car on the street in front of his rented duplex to remind his Eastern European, Chaldean, and plain old white neighbors that he (A) was gainfully employed, and (B) had the law on his side. Tonight he parked his SUV, walked up to his door, stopped with his key in the lock, and sniffed the air. He could smell Jillian's dinner from outside, something with Worcestershire sauce. Lamb chops. He heard her singing along to one of her quiet storm mixes. It was a female vocalist with a voice too deep for Jillian to mimic. Anita Baker. He rolled his shoulders back and stepped inside.

His ex-wife, Cara, had been all curves and softness. Big ass, fleshy thighs. Jillian was the first woman Troy had dated who was linear and firm. Nearly as tall as Troy at five feet ten. Like a model, is what he'd thought back at Cobo Center when they met. He watched her shoulder blades work up and down as she grated parmesan cheese onto a salad in the kitchen. Quitting the flight attendant job had stripped her of some glamour—she rarely wore makeup outside of lip gloss now, and kept her hair in ponytails more often than not. But the hours on her feet sewing in weaves, washing and flat-ironing hair hadn't affected her posture. She was statuesque. She had the sort of even complexion—medium brown with orange undertones—that, coupled with her athletic frame, suggested continuity, an unwillingness to mottle or sag.

"Camille tried to chat with you earlier," she said. "I was checking my email on your laptop when she called. I told her to try again tomorrow."

"I'll catch her in the morning," Troy said. He sat on the ottoman in the living room and took off his sneakers. His nine-year-old daughter, Camille, and his ex-wife lived in Kaiserslautern, an American military community outside of Frankfurt. He'd bought her a new laptop with a webcam so they could talk for free online.

He and Jillian ate on TV trays set up in front of the couch. Jillian associated sitting around the table every night with the strained family dinners of her childhood in Lansing, when she and her younger two sisters had to report on the highs and lows of their school days before they could eat dessert. Table or no table, Jillian had never broken the habit of recounting her day in detail. He listened to her talk about a man who came into the salon with a shopping bag full of bootleg DVDs. A customer gave him a $100 bill, expecting change, and he ran out with the money.

"I promise you, you never seen a old-ass man move that fast," she said. "And we tried to play the DVD he gave her. It was blank!"

Troy laughed. They were skilled at this, being good when things were good between them.

"We need to go ahead and start looking into flights for Camille this summer," Jillian said. "It's almost that time."

He walked into the kitchen with their dirty plates. This was their agreement: she cooked and he cleaned up afterward. He'd never made such agreements with Cara, or the women he'd dated before. He had cleaned up plenty of times with other women, but it always felt like a favor he was doing them, rather than an expected contribution. Now he felt mature enough to where it didn't hurt his ego to clean the kitchen or fold the laundry without being asked.

"Babe? Did you hear me?" she called from the couch. "I said it's time to start looking for flights before they start going up."

"Mmm-hmm," Troy mumbled. He sponged Worcestershire sauce and cold lamb fat from the skillet. Every summer Troy sent for Camille for a month. For three years it had been the only time he'd seen her in person. Jillian had come to look forward to the visits too. Troy knew she wanted a child of her own, a child that he was not poised to give her. Viola had always called him the Lucky Boy because he was the last son born, and Francis had tried harder to be present in his life than he had the six boys before him. They'd gone fishing on Lake Saint Clair, to countless Lions games out in Pontiac. One summer when Troy was twelve, Francis, inspired by an announcement on the morning news, had tracked down the SwimMobile for Troy and two of his friends. He dropped them off on the west side. He must have noticed their apprehension at swimming with kids from unfamiliar blocks because he'd told them, "This whole city belongs to you. Specially at this age. Don't let nobody stop you from enjoyin it." He'd sat in his truck as they splashed around in the mobile pool—an eighteen-wheeler with an open cargo container in the back filled with hydrant water—listening to the radio and smoking his pipe. Francis even attended Troy's graduation from basic, something he'd never done for Quincy, Russell, Lonnie, Miles, or Duke when they finished boot camp. This extra time spent was not enough for Troy, because Francis still existed behind a wall of formality. You could not go to Francis for advice about girls, or bullies, or even siblings. He would shrug off responsibility with something like, "Your mama got a better head for that sorta thing," or "Might as well ask Cha-Cha, what's an old man know?" It was if his father had finally figured out the value of sharing his time with his children but not his heart. Troy tried to give more than this to Camille, via video chats, spontaneous gifts in the mail, and support of her extracurricular interests, which ranged from German and French classes to ballet. It took a lot of energy, and Troy did not think he had enough reserved for another child, nor enough money.

"We should put her in a little summer program," Jillian said. "She's old enough now to do a day camp, or maybe a short sleep-away one. There's this one in the Upper Peninsula that's a week long about ecosystems and stuff. Maybe Cara would help pay."

He dried his hands and came over to the couch.

"I met with Dave earlier tonight."

"Oh yeah? What's he talking about?"

"Um." Troy hopped back up and went to the fridge for a beer. "Ha. It's funny. We was talkin about my mama's house, actually."

He could feel her eyes on him, even as he faced the fridge in mock deliberation (they only had Heinekens to choose from). He knew her head was cocked, that she was incredulous that he'd brought the issue up again. Soon her neck, that beautiful, elongated, near limb that had drawn him to her in the first place, would be tensing up, shrinking into her shoulders.

"Dave knows a guy who can help with the house paperwork, but it'll cost extra. And, um, I was thinkin maybe we could wait to bring Camille out here till the second half of the summer, like late July?"

He turned around to find her posed just as he'd imagined.

"What the fuck, Troy? What's there to even . . . help with? Huh? We had this . . . conversation not three fucking days ago."

"Yeah, but the more I think about it, we gotta do this, Jill."

He sat on the couch, ignored her hostile posture, and moved in close. If they were willing to be close to each other, it could not be considered a fight yet. He put his hand on her thigh.

"Why?" she asked. "You need to . . . to really *think* about why. You're gonna piss folks off . . . damn near *everybody*. And the house is basically worthless. Why?"

"Cause people like Cha-Cha and them always get taken advantage of," he said. "So scared of breaking the rules, like somebody is even thinking about them. Wasn't nobody thinking about us when they *made* these rules. But they wanna sit around and follow them."

There was a difference between violent, destructive crimes and bending rules that were prejudiced or predatory to start. Over the last few months, as the housing bubble burst, he'd read article after article about banks pressuring black and Latino homebuyers, even those whose income and credit scores could have warranted a better deal, into subprime mortgages. It was illegal and deplorable to steal from your neighbor, yes. Manipulating a housing system that had manipulated people who looked like you for decades? He saw no harm in that. But for as long as he could remember, Cha-Cha and Tina had acted like the integrity police. They had been above getting illegal cable installed in the nineties when everyone had "black boxes." They wouldn't let anyone drive their cars if they weren't on the insurance, not even around the corner. A couple years back they had overextended themselves financially to prevent their son Chucky from filing for the unemployment compensation he was entitled to. It was a particular sort of Turner weakness: self-sabotaging self-righteousness masked as self-reliance. It made Troy sick.

"You know, Cha-Cha's not the only one who put some money and time into that house," he said. "When I first got out the service, I lived on Yarrow with Mama, and Cha-Cha *never* came over to see how I was doing, let alone how Mama was doing. He came over to 'handle business,' like check on the water heater or whatever, but that's it. And doesn't spending time count more than his stupid money, especially cause his money comes with strings attached? Like, when I was in high school I had to take the bus out to Cha-Cha's house early every morning, and Tina would take me and Chucky and Todd to school. It's cause they had a better basketball program over there, and by that time Kettering was a shithole. I'd wake up around six just to get there, and wait for Tina to wake up around seven-thirty and take us. I had made it on this traveling team, and I needed new team shoes and a special jersey. Daddy and Mama didn't have the money, so they told me to ask Cha-Cha, which is what they *always* said when they didn't have the money, but that's not my fault, right? Remember I'm only fourteen, fifteen years old. The shoes and jersey were like a hundred dollars.

"Do you know that before he would give me the money he made

me get to his house at *five in the morning* for a month? He didn't want me to shovel snow, or do any chores or nothing. I just had to get there at five, and he'd come down the stairs in his pajamas when he felt like it, let me into the house, then go back to sleep. And his own sons were upstairs sleep the whole time! Fuck was the point of that, huh? Even in the navy, if they made us wake up at the crack of dawn, there was a point, we did some drills or whatever. Me standing outside, I couldn't even do my homework, I stood there on the front step looking like a fucking burglar. I know he just did it cause he *could*. And every day that I had to go to practice without the gear I felt like shit cause you know the white boys on the team came back with their money the *very next day.* You know how cold it is at three-thirty in the morning in the winter? I'd be standin at the bus stop on the east side hopin I didn't get jumped, freezin my ass off."

Troy breathed quickly. The veins in Jillian's neck relaxed.

"I'm sorry, babe. He probably thought he was building your character or something."

"It's true," she added after a while. "The banks *are* being extra predatory right now. I saw it on the news. They know people can't pay their mortgages, they knew it when they gave them the loans or let them refinance, but they refuse to renegotiate."

Troy nodded. He hadn't intended to tell her about Cha-Cha and the basketball gear. It was a stupid, old, humiliating story, but it had done the job.

Outta the Fields

Had his childhood been a happy one? The question felt irrelevant. Cha-Cha had made it through. He couldn't recall being extraordinarily unhappy—he was clothed, fed, never molested, and never *beaten* beaten. Alice had posed the question to him earlier that morning, and now he posed it to his sister Francey in her Oak Park kitchen. He lay on his stomach underneath the kitchen sink, breathing in mildew and straining to snake the plug for her new alkaline water-filtration system to a power outlet in the adjacent cabinet. Francey's husband, Richard, had electrocuted himself as a boy by jamming a fork into a socket, and now he avoided even minor electrical work. Every once in a while Francey would call Cha-Cha over to hook up a sound system, install a new light fixture, or fix the sprinklers, and during these visits Richard was nowhere to be found.

"What a weird thing to ask," Francey said. "You say this woman's black, huh?"

"Darker than you and me."

Plug finally secured, Cha-Cha rolled onto his back on the tile. Francey hovered over him. The track lighting on the ceiling made her close-cropped silver afro glow. With her cat-eye glasses and sparkly green earrings, she looked extraterrestrial.

"That's really what goes on in therapy? They ask you to drag up a whole bunch of stuff from childhood? I thought that was just on TV. We're so old! At some point that stuff doesn't matter no more."

"I said ... the same thing," Cha-Cha said. He tried to catch his breath. Sweat trickled down the back of his neck. "Unless something crazy had happened."

"And nothing crazy did," Francey said.

Cha-Cha sat up, reached his hand out, and Francey yanked him to his feet. At sixty-two years old she was surprisingly strong. Stronger than he was, Cha-Cha suspected.

"Uh-huh. But Alice kept going on about deep-seeded trauma, and how something old like that could be a reason I see this haint."

"Weird," Francey said again. "We weren't traumatized. Just poor."

"Right. Which means you've got holey socks, maybe, hand-me-downs."

"And you eat starchier food," Francey said. "Lord, we ate so much greasy, nasty food growing up! I can't hardly stand to think about it now. Just pork, pork, pork, *pork*. Mama cooked damn near *every*thing with pork."

"Oh hell," Cha-Cha said under his breath. Unhealthy food was Francey's favorite hobbyhorse. There was nothing to do now but wait her out.

"That's why when folks say they can't understand how I'm a vegetarian I always say I got enough meat in my system to last me the rest of my life."

"Mmm-hmm," Cha-Cha mumbled. He opened Francey's refrigerator and scanned the jugs of prune juice, carrot juice, and some sort of green juice that had separated into three distinct and disconcerting layers. If this is what it took to be as strong as she was at her age, Cha-Cha could live with being a little feeble. He settled on water.

It had been warmer out this morning than the previous week's visit. Alice took off her purple cardigan halfway through the session. Her arms looked soft but not flabby. She had some of the smoothest-looking skin Cha-Cha had seen on an adult—supple, with a sheen he attributed to some sort of body oil. She had a light splotch of skin about the size of a dime on the inside of her right biceps. Cha-Cha couldn't stop staring at it as they talked. Either a birthmark or a burn scar, he figured. He'd wanted to rub his thumb across it to feel if it was smooth or textured.

"Alice asked me if I think life would've been better without so many siblings," he said.

Francey spun around from the far counter where she'd been bent over writing something, all the while still listing the perils of pork. She hissed through her teeth.

"What a stupid question. I mean, yeah, it *coulda* been better. But what do we know? What you say to her?"

Cha-Cha saw Francey's question for the setup it was. Outside of joking about hand-me-downs handed down for far too long, or waking up at the crack of dawn to be first in the shower, the Turner children rarely discussed the disadvantages of being one of thirteen. Scrutinizing too closely why Viola and Francis had not stopped at two, or seven, or even ten children felt like wishing a sibling never born. And yet, each child thought about it, Cha-Cha was sure.

"I said what I always say. I don't have time for what-ifs. Don't see no point in it."

In truth, since he'd started seeing Alice, his stance on what-ifs had softened. Now he caught himself analyzing many aspects of the way he was raised, when before he would have been content to remember the highlights and skim past the rest. It seemed a self-indulgent, pointless endeavor, but he couldn't stop. Vignettes from this time or that time kept bubbling up in his memory. The logical next step was to think about how these experiences had helped make him the person he was. What if there had only been two Turner children, or five? Who might Cha-Cha have become?

"Remember when you and me and Mama and Daddy lived in that rented house off Lemay and Mack?" he asked.

"Oh, the not-so-ghetto ghetto." Francey chuckled. "We thought we had it made cause the water stayed hot, and we had our own stove."

"We did have it made, compared to that place in Black Bottom," he said.

There had been three whole years between Francey's birth and Quincy's, then another two before Russell was born. By five years old Francey was already the boss, never mind that Cha-Cha was older. She'd gone on to teach third-graders at various Detroit public schools for twenty-five years until she was forced to retire, her obesity having led to a string of health issues. She'd devoted a good chunk of her life to wrangling children, and now all of her grandchildren lived out of the state.

"Plus," he added, "Daddy stopped workin at the salt mine so he could work for Chrysler, which made him less depressed."

Francey frowned and picked up the magnetic dry-erase board she'd been writing on and stuck it onto the fridge.

"I don't know if I'd say he was *depressed*. Since when did you decide he was depressed? Alice help you with that?"

The dry-erase board held a to-do list, which Cha-Cha watched Francey check off and strike through.

Juice leftover apples   ✓
Soak and clean juicer   ✓
Kyle bday present
~~Look into Head Start for Bobbie?~~
Breathe!   ✓✓✓
Smile!!   ✓✓

Who needed a reminder to breathe? Cha-Cha was certain the last two entries were for his benefit, Francey's way of communicating that she had larger and more important concerns than he did, or that life was too short to not smile, or to take it "one breath at a time," or some other Francey-approved feel-good slogan. She wore black stretch pants hiked up to the middle of her loose, smallish belly, a teal tank top tucked into the stretch pants, and white aerobic shoes. Somebody's athletic, health-obsessed granny, Cha-Cha thought. She probably weighed 150 pounds now, but just as Cha-Cha had to reconcile Viola's current physical condition with his own memories, he often had to do the same with this thin woman before him. Francey had been large for most of their adult life, 350 pounds at her heaviest. Nearly ten years had passed since she lost more than half of herself, thanks to bariatric surgery and a lot of juice.

"I *know* depression exists," Francey said. "I'm not one of those old black ladies who doesn't believe in mental health, but the threshold has gotta be different for different eras. Lots of folks had a bunch of kids back then; it's just what they *did*. Mama was one of ten herself. And remember, Mama and Daddy's parents and grandparents were sharecroppers. Shoot, sharecropping killed Daddy's father. And their great-grandparents were probably born slaves. *Slaves*, Cha. What's a big family and a crummy job in Detroit when you're only two generations or so outta the fields?"

Slavery. Did there ever exist a more annoying way to try to make a modern-day black man feel like his troubles were insignificant, that he should be satisfied with the sorry hand society dealt him? Cha-Cha thought not. The line of reasoning was faulty; it was precisely because his grandfather's father was born a slave that he should expect more from life, and more from this country, to make up for lost time at the very least.

"I'm not comparing anything to slavery, Francey, come on," Cha-Cha said. "And I don't know nothin about thresholds. Let's keep it simple: Daddy was sad a lot. And he drank too much. Can you admit that?"

Francey threw up her hands.

"I don't know, Cha-Cha, *sure*. But he wasn't no raging drunk. He wasn't in the house raising hell, hitting his wife and children. You make it sound like he was abusive."

"I never said that."

Cha-Cha's plan had been to come to Francey's, hook up her filtration system, and ask her about his haint. He'd even brought a book, Zora Neale Hurston's *Mules and Men*, which the Internet told him mentioned both black folks and ghosts. He hadn't come here to talk about depression, or Francis Turner. Now Cha-Cha was irritated. It was frustrating, the way his siblings worshipped their parents. What part of their worlds would crumble if they took a good look at their parents' flaws? If there was no trauma, why not talk about the everyday, human elements of their upbringing? Call a spade a spade.

Cha-Cha drank down the rest of his water.

"Alice says my role in the family is kinda like the prime minister of England."

Francey chuckled.

"Cha-Cha, if this woman is helping you, then great. But I don't know if I can stand to hear any more of her ideas."

"You gotta let me explain before you laugh at me. Now, she says I'm like the prime minister cause I handle the everyday business of the family, but when people think of who *runs* the family, who is the symbol, they think of Mama."

"As they should," Francey said.

"Okay, but the thing is, being the prime minister means you handle all the ugly stuff that the royal family doesn't really get into. Like, me and Daddy worked together, remember? So you would think that back when I still lived on the east side we would carpool when we both were doing short runs, but we never did. He said he liked to drive alone. But Mama stayed on me to make sure he came straight home after work. Daddy knew I tailed him home in my truck. What he'd do is park across from the basketball courts on Lambert and throw back a couple of those small bottles of Miller Lite, remember he used to call them short dogs? Then he'd drive home, and I'd follow him into the house like nothin happened."

"But what does that have to do with anything?"

"Why do you think Mama made me do that?"

"You know why. So that everybody didn't have to see him drinking."

"Exactly. But what about *me*, Francey? Wasn't I his child too?"

Francey made a sound somewhere between a chuckle and a snort.

"You know, I took a psych class or two in school, and I can tell you this much: if this Alice person is encouraging you to do anything other than *get over it*, she's wasting your money. You were already *grown*, Cha. And what does it matter to you now, old as you are, that your daddy drank too much and your mama delegated too much onto you *and* onto me? Don't act like you were just the prime minister and I was off in the countryside not helping out. Lord, I don't even *like* this metaphor, and here you got me using it! I helped out until I couldn't anymore. You know that. Don't act like you don't."

Up until her bariatric surgery Francey had been just as involved as Cha-Cha in settling familial squabbles, remembering birthdays, looking after Viola, opening up her home to down-on-their-luck nieces and nephews, and providing leadership in countless other ways. Cha-Cha was still not sure why the rest of his siblings didn't do more for Francey following her operation. Maybe opting to have the surgery was too decisive a step among a family of people who talked about improving their health but generally left the things that ailed their bodies and minds unattended. Francey contracted an infection after the operation and was hospitalized for nearly a month. None of her siblings visited more than once, save for Cha-Cha, who, in part due to Tina's insistence, had visited almost daily. After she got well and got skinny, she distanced herself from all familial obligations. She remained cordial, and social, and it was clear she still loved them all, but there was no more hand wringing over other people's problems, no more open-door policy to relatives in need of money or beds. She wouldn't even offer a ride to the airport.

"Oh, come on, Francey. I'm talkin about myself right now," Cha-Cha said. "I never said you weren't there. You helped out too when we were comin up, and I was there for you when you needed it, so don't try to make me feel guilty."

"You know what," Francey said. "Richard's gonna be back soon. Seeing you up in here with your tools and stuff makes him embarrassed about his electricity phobia thing."

Cha-Cha made no move to leave. This morning he and Alice had talked about how he thought Turners were prone to addiction. There was Francis, who Alice had called an alcoholic, but Cha-Cha thought the word was too clinical to truly convey the sort of secret, sad drinker Francis was. He took no joy in his drinking; it was as if he drank to punish himself for some past misdeed. There was Lonnie, no longer little and peeing in the hallway, but he had dabbled in heroin as young as thirteen and was clearly still on something, Cha-Cha didn't want to know what, at the age of fifty-three. Troy, bless his heart, was obsessed with success, but he hadn't figured out how hard work begot it. There was Marlene, and with her Viola Turner herself, not really hurting anyone with their obsession, Cha-Cha supposed, but there had been a decade or so when they were downright absorbed with that flea market stall, even through Marlene's chemotherapy, and despite never having turned a profit. The duo had scoured the Midwest for *things*. Cha-Cha never understood their need for things to sell just to say they had them to sell—fur coats, vintage pocketbooks, lamps. There was Cha-Cha's own wife, not a Turner by blood, but thirty-odd years rubbed off on people. He felt a pinprick of guilt calling Tina's church involvement an addiction, but that's how he thought of it. Now here was Francey standing before him, obsessed with nutrition and vegetarianism and kitchen gadgets. Turners seemed incapable of doing anything in moderation. Maybe Cha-Cha himself was addicted to being in charge of the family, or to going to therapy with Alice, or even this revived idea of a haint. Well, he wouldn't let his obsessions get the best of him; he would take them apart and figure out where they came from. He pulled his book from underneath his bag of tools.

"Can we switch gears right quick? I said I'd come over here and put your water filter in cause I'm tryna learn more about this haint. I been lookin around on the Internet, and I found this book."

Francey eyed the book, allowed Cha-Cha to put it into her hands.

She walked to the couch in her living room and sat down. She was one of two Turner siblings who'd finished college, the other being Lonnie, who had a bachelor's but had been too busy chasing pop music stardom to put it to good use. Francey had taken correspondence courses while raising her three daughters and earned her BA after seven years. She was the only Turner sibling with genuine bookish inclinations.

"If you haven't read it, then never mind," Cha-Cha said. "I just thought maybe."

"I read this a *long* time ago," Francey said. "Good book. A lot of the stories and jokes reminded me of going down to see Auntie Lucille and Olivia when we were little. You know how, when Mama says something that makes people mad, she'll say, 'Don't like it, don't take it, here's my collar come and shake it'?"

"Yeah."

"That's in the book. You start reading it?"

"Not yet, I just got it."

"You said 'this haint,' like it's yours. You still seeing it?"

Cha-Cha explained what he'd realized with the help of Alice, that he had felt the haint's presence on and off throughout his life, although he hadn't actually seen it save for that time in the big room and the night of his accident. He was glad Francey seemed to be relaxing. He never took for granted her ability to bounce back from potential discord. Too many of his siblings were incapable of doing the same.

"You think you're too smart for this kinda thing to be happening to you?"

Yes, Cha-Cha thought. "No," he said. "Being smart's got nothing to do with it."

"Please. You're not a touchy-feely person, Cha. You're a logic person. So even though you know you seen something, had an experience, you either need to find some logic in it or get rid of it."

"What's wrong with logic?"

Francey smiled. She had small, straight teeth and a slim gap between the front two, like Francis Turner.

"What's wrong with it is that you end up acting like the white folks in scary movies, who either provoke the ghost or try to get rid of it, when really they don't have to do anything. That's a Western thing, being afraid of ghosts. And really, it's a *new* Western thing. They used to have all kinds of spirits they believed in before they decided they knew better. Look at *Hamlet*. Matter of fact, a lot of them still believe in stuff like that, but they like to make black folks feel stupid and superstitious for doing the same thing."

Ever since becoming a healthier person Francey had taken an interest in non-Western everything, preferably anything with African or Middle Eastern roots. It might have had something to do with the dreadlocked brothers and Yemeni immigrants who ran the juice bars she frequented. It had never really bothered Cha-Cha one way or the other, not like it bothered Quincy, who was too conservative—too interested in appearing upright and unsentimental—to sit around without eye rolling and listen to Francey talk about architecture in ancient Kemet, or Asanti funeral traditions. Cha-Cha was just happy Francey backed up all her talk of the Motherland and libation rituals with book knowledge and specificity.

"I never said I'm afraid."

"You are, Cha." She smiled again. "You checked out a book from the library? You're doing *research?* You're afraid. You need to work toward acceptance. Science can't explain why you and I are alive when so many folks we grew up with are dead, but you're able to accept that."

"I think that's statistics, or probability," he said. "We had two parents, and then you and me were the third and fourth parents for the ones under us. It was harder for folks to get into trouble, and there was more support around."

"Don't buy in to that, Cha. Folks got into plenty of trouble. Lonnie especially. Don't give me that two-parent-household junk. Other folks had two parents, and a bunch of siblings, and they're not around anymore. It was chance, or fate or God, but it wasn't science. You know, the Yoruba in Nigeria, they believe in what they call Orishas for all sorts of things. So do black Cubans and Brazilians in their own ways; they kept believing right through slavery. Then you have Vodou in Haiti, which, you know, made its way to New Orleans. And plenty people around the world believe that ancestors can intercede on our behalf, which I'm not saying this is, but you never know. I used to have a book about it, someplace. If I can find it, I'ma bring it to you."

The storm door slammed shut, and Richard walked in with a white butcher-paper bundle cradled in his arms. Meat, which Cha-Cha guessed he would grill out back since it was now warm enough to do so. Francey didn't allow it to be cooked in her kitchen. He clasped hands with his brother-in-law and hugged him. The same height as Cha-Cha but thinner, the same bald head and skin tone as Harry Belafonte.

Richard picked up *Mules and Men*, pulled the book to arm's length to read the title better.

"What's this about?"

"I gotta run," Cha-Cha said. "Good to see you though, Rich." He didn't want to have to sit there while Francey told Richard about his haint; he'd feel ridiculous. He gathered up his tools, pecked his sister on the cheek, and let himself out.

"Hey, Cha?"

Francey had followed him out to the driveway.

"One thing you gotta remember is he stopped," she said.

"Huh?"

"Your daddy stopped drinking. He found the willpower to quit. You can't go around tellin his story to your therapist or whoever without mentioning that."

Cha-Cha said nothing in return. He drove home. A memory kept bothering him, one that seemed to fly in the face of the narrative of his father that his siblings cherished. He wasn't sure if he'd made things larger as an adult, whether time had inflated the importance, but since seeing Alice this morning it had played in his mind on a loop. He hadn't even told her about it, because he did not know what it meant.

IN THE SUMMER of 1967, when Cha-Cha was twenty-three, he worked at the Lynch Road Assembly Plant putting together Dodge Chargers. In June of that year Viola announced she was pregnant again, at forty years old. This thirteenth and final pregnancy might have been the most memorable event of the summer if only Detroit, the country, and maybe even the entire world had seen a different July.

On the morning that Detroiters began to realize the skirmish on Twelfth and Clairmount had morphed into something larger, Cha-Cha and his fellow line workers went to the plant as usual. Anxiety crackled off of people like static. Nervous behavior led to carelessness, and by lunchtime Cha-Cha's coveralls were splattered with the blood of another man, a man who let himself get distracted. He left the plant determined to find a new job.

Before that July a burning building felt like a particular and tragic occurrence to Cha-Cha. The smell of brick and clothes and small pets smoldering urged a person to stand tall like a prairie dog and crane his neck in search of the emergency. Afterward, a burning house became an olfactory norm akin to skunk spray; as long as the source of the odor wasn't too close, you eventually ignored it. Cha-Cha's shared apartment on Forrest and McDougall had no kitchen, so when he felt particularly lonely, he used the excuse of needing a home-cooked meal to come back and check on things at the Yarrow house. If he'd had no younger siblings to worry about, he might have joined his own friends from the neighborhood in search of new shoes, lightweight appliances, anything with resale potential. He wasn't above recreational looting. But as the eldest, he kept in mind that the fires, the looting, and any police beatings all qualified as reasons a Turner boy might get into serious trouble, or maybe even die. He felt responsible for making sure nothing happened. Quincy was in army boot camp in South Carolina. Miles, Duke, and Troy were all under the age of eight and therefore still under Viola's thumb. This left Lonnie and Russell. The two of them were standing on the porch when Cha-Cha pulled up.

"Everybody in the house?" Cha-Cha asked.

"Yeah," Lonnie said. "Except Daddy's not home yet. They're sayin on TV there's a curfew tonight. They got snipers on the roofs shootin at the police."

Lonnie stood with his chest puffed out, his bony shoulders thrust back. He was thirteen but already as tall as Russell, with tight knots of pubescent muscle on his arms, and his father's strong chin. Neither him nor Russell asked Cha-Cha about the blood on his collar.

"Where y'all goin?" Cha-Cha asked.

"To get bricks," Russell said.

Cha-Cha stared at his brother as if he didn't comprehend. He knew Viola was kneeling on the couch on the other side of the front window, listening. He walked toward the door.

Russell stepped in front of him.

"I said we're gonna go get bricks, Cha, and we want you to come with us."

"I heard what you said. You see all that smoke? They probably shooting niggas on the west side by now," he said.

"Well, we on the east side," Lonnie said.

"I heard they looting on Harper too," Cha-Cha said.

"So? I'm not finna sit up in that house like a girl, watching everything on the news," Lonnie said. His new, deeper voice cracked as he spoke.

"Kowski pays a *nickel* a brick," Russell said. "All this shit goin on, you think anybody cares about the bricks we take from tore-up buildings? We could be doing a lot better money-wise, but ain't nobody gonna shoot us over bricks."

When he was sixteen, Cha-Cha had also felt and looked as much of a man as Russell did. He knew that no matter what Russell felt like inside, living in the Yarrow house meant he was still considered a child. Still reduced to bickering with younger siblings and begging Viola for pocket money. To wait patiently while Viola, eyes closed, mouth scrunched, rooted around in her purse and extracted a few crumpled dollars was the ultimate humiliation. Russell sometimes worked for a Polish man he called Kowski, short for a longer name Cha-Cha never knew. He swept up trash and debris on construction sites in East Detroit. A nickel per brick could add up quickly.

Cha-Cha agreed to go with them. He wasn't old enough to forbid Russell and Lonnie from doing what they wanted, or strong enough to drag them both into the house. And if he stayed home and something happened to them out in the streets, what then? He turned his back on the window where his mother was likely spying on them, and offered his truck for the transport of bricks.

Every block seemed devoid of women. Most porches were empty. A half dozen were occupied by young men and older boys, their postures communicating a readiness to protect whatever resided on the other side of their thresholds. Cha-Cha knew most of them had guns within easy reach. Old hunting rifles brought up from Down South, and newer, lighter weapons acquired here. But who would they shoot, the police? They surely wouldn't shoot their neighbors.

Russell guided them to a house several streets west of Yarrow. It sat on a block abutting Harper, and its overgrown yard suggested it had been vacant even before flames from the neighboring dry cleaner burned through its roof and much of its second floor. By 1967 whites had already started their retreat to the suburbs, leaving vacant houses in their wake if black folks couldn't afford to buy or rent them quickly enough.

Cha-Cha stayed on the sidewalk while his brothers went to the side of the house. Judging from the way Lonnie walked ahead and Russell kept looking back, it was clear that the younger of the two had set this plan in motion. Although he was underage, Lonnie had talked himself into a job with Ron Vollick's Universal Teen Sales Club. Vollick organized carloads of colored teens to go door-to-door in white neighborhoods selling overpriced goods (dish soap, thermometers, measuring cups) to fearful housewives. Lonnie was a top salesman that summer, an expert at convincing ostensibly smart people to do stupid things.

Alone out front, Cha-Cha heard the *whup-whup-whup* of helicopters and the frenzied bleat of fire truck sirens. The sounds seemed to be moving away from him, toward the northwest of the city. He realized they should have had a better plan, one including a wheelbarrow. They wouldn't be able to make very many trips without attracting suspicion, and they needed twenty bricks just to make a dollar. The ferric scent of blood from his work shirt made him queasy. He should have at least changed clothes.

Cha-Cha's particular duty on the assembly line at work was to wait until a team of three men led by a fellow named Bryson bolted the body of the Charger to the lower frame. A train track-style conveyance then brought the car to Cha-Cha's bench. He had to reach under the body, connect a hose to the gas pump, and use a set of brackets to secure the rear axle. At first the line had moved smoothly despite everyone's nerves, but soon Bryson's team fell behind. Each bench had an approximate minute to complete its job before another car came down. Plenty of time in normal conditions. To prevent any backups, one relief man oversaw a clump of benches, and jumped in to help speed a job along if necessary. Cha-Cha and Bryson's relief man was Michel, a large, curly-haired white boy from Montreal.

Maybe it had been too long since Michel had helped out the line. Maybe Michel's mind was on the fighting and the fires in the streets. A minute should have been long enough to get Bryson's team caught up before the next Charger reached them. In a minute's time Michel managed to lodge his thumb between the lower frame and the upper body of the car, and Bryson's team bolted the two pieces together without noticing. The line stopped moving. Cha-Cha looked down and saw the blood sprayed across his own coveralls.

Now Lonnie and Russell loped toward Cha-Cha with large heaps of bricks in their arms. They dumped them into the back of the truck. Russell's chubby cheeks were smudged with soot, the front of his shirt drenched in sweat.

"Come on back and help us, Cha," he said. "That way we can get outta here quicker."

Cha-Cha agreed.

Lonnie and Russell sorted through the bricks, and Cha-Cha cradled the ones they passed to him. Russell had brought along a tiny hammer to knock off bits of mortar from the edges of the bricks. Lonnie wanted to climb down into the ruined basement where most of the bricks would have fallen, but Russell pointed out that the bad air quality might suffocate them.

What kind of adulthood was this? Cha-Cha wondered. He watched his teenage brothers hastily appraise ruined bricks for their resale value while the streets raged less than a quarter mile away. He had the feeling that he would always be this person, seesawing between adult and child, as long as he stayed in Detroit. Quincy was gone, and in a year's time Russell would enlist and be gone too. Francis and Viola would surely force Lonnie to leave the city when he was of age; a boy as smart and reckless as Lonnie would come to ruin otherwise. Cha-Cha knew he'd stay here through riots and layoffs and whatever else came.

On Cha-Cha's third trip along the side of the house he saw a police car parked behind his truck. The officer was white, wide around the middle, and peering into the brick-filled cab.

You get into trouble. You throw a ball where you shouldn't, you try to brush up against the wrong girl's ass at a party. You take off running. Cha-Cha dropped his bricks, turned around, and ran back to his brothers. Ran past them. There was no time to stop and explain. Russell and Lonnie followed him through the backyard of the house, and the three of them jumped the gate to an alley. They separated as soon as they reached a side street. Cha-Cha should have stopped running. Better to walk as if he'd been walking all along, then make a slow circle back to his truck. But he couldn't stop himself. He wasn't skilled at acting natural. He thought it smarter to get back to Yarrow as quickly as possible. He ran east through alleys parallel to Seneca. He heard sirens up ahead where Seneca intersected Lambert. He panicked. A house to his left had a raccoon-sized hole in the lattice under its porch. He crouched down, kicked the hole a bit wider, and scooted feet first until he was inside. He lay on his back with his arms folded on his chest. Under the porch smelled like dead leaves and wet fur. Cha-Cha listened for the rustlings of rodents but heard none. He heard sirens instead, still as close as before, as if the police had parked on the block. He heard himself wheezing long after he believed his heart rate had slowed. He blamed the smoke in the air.

Taking refuge under the porch was not the smartest decision. He would be covered in dirt when he came out of the hole, and coupled with the blood he already had on his shirt, that would make him look more suspicious than ever. He still heard sirens.

Cha-Cha's mind might have wandered for less than five minutes or a dangerous fifteen minutes. He heard footsteps crunching through the dry summer grass toward him. The sirens had stopped. Slowly, Cha-Cha turned onto his side. He recognized those boots. That slue-footed, toes-outward walk. It was his father. Francis was a hummer and a smacker. He hummed the same song mostly, about a train headed to Glory, and he smacked as if something sticky was lodged in between his molars.

Why didn't he crawl out then, and walk with his father home? Cha-Cha didn't know. His heart told him to keep still. Francis stopped very near to Cha-Cha's hole in the porch. He stood there and hummed. Francis burped and Cha-Cha realized he was drunk; he could smell the beer from where he hid. Only Francis Turner could find time to sneak away and drink during an uprising. Cha-Cha heard him unzip his pants.

Earlier that day, when the body of the Charger crushed his thumb, Michel had said, "You can't." Just "You can't" once, quickly, and then a low-register wail when the bolts were removed and the rest of his hand freed. As Bryson's team carried him away, Michel mumbled a string of words in French that no one understood. Cha-Cha wanted to yell "You can't" from under the porch, but he didn't. He merely closed his eyes.

Most of the urine did not reach him, but an unforgivable amount splashed onto his forehead. It took nearly two minutes for Francis to relieve himself, and Cha-Cha was convinced that Francis had done it to him on purpose. A few years later, when Cha-Cha started tailing Francis on Viola's orders, he would learn that this corner on Seneca and Lambert was Francis's preferred one for clandestine drinking and occasional public urination. The knowledge did nothing to change his initial beliefs. His memories of the event were not swayed by reason. They were the culmination of the wrong kind of day, and too many realizations about the kind of life Cha-Cha felt destined to live. His father had pissed on his forehead when he should have been at home protecting his family, and this seemed a special, premeditated disrespect.

Francis shook himself, zipped up, and walked away, still humming about his train to Glory. Cha-Cha waited until he heard Francis slam his car door and drive off before he crawled out and walked back toward his truck, no longer worried about how suspicious he looked.

Memories

What folks said about idle hands and the devil was true for Lelah; busyness was her best defense against the urge to fondle those chips. She manufactured things to do in earnest. Weekdays proved easiest. She left Yarrow Street around dawn to pick up Bobbie and spent the day with him, either in the park or the library or, when the weather was too wet or cold, in Brianne's apartment. Strange to feel the need to tiptoe around your own daughter's home, but Lelah did feel that way, careful to put things back, never eating enough cereal or whatever leftovers were in the fridge to offend Brianne. A week passed and Lelah had spent less than thirty dollars.

The real danger lay in the weekends. Saturday arrived and Lelah drove to Brianne's early in the morning. She hoped to pick up Bobbie again, maybe give Brianne some time to herself, but Brianne was already dressed and getting Bobbie ready for the car when she arrived. She said she was driving to Rob's in Chicago.

"Two weeks in a row?" Lelah asked.

"Two weeks in a row. Is there something wrong with that?"

The same sass from that all-caps text message, Lelah thought. But how to address it?

"Nothing," she said. "It's just, how come he never comes up here?"

Brianne didn't reply. She looked over Lelah's shoulder into the parking lot as if her car might have taken off without her.

"Are you two seeing each other again? You can tell me if you are."

"Mommy, *no*," Brianne said. Her shoulders squirmed and for a moment she reminded Lelah of a younger, more secretive version of herself. "It's just nice out and he said he wants to take Bobbie to see the Bean."

"Okay, I'm just asking. We've got nice parks up here, too." Lelah crossed her arms for lack of something better to do with them.

"I have to go now, Mommy," Brianne said. "But you need to call Uncle Cha-Cha. He said he's been trying to reach you all week."

Brianne carried Bobbie down the stairs before Lelah could ask whether she planned to spend the night out there, and if so, with whom. She tried to convince herself that it was none of her business.

Alone on Yarrow, Lelah knew desperate measures were necessary to keep her from herself. She decided to clean the entire house.

She started in the big room, armed with a wad of old T-shirts she found in one of her duffel bags and a bottle of all-purpose cleaner. This room was the most intact. Her two duffel bags and three trash bags full of clothes were tucked under the big room's bed and pushed up against the wall so that someone would have to be looking hard to find them there.

The girls' room, still a dismal shade of Pepto, had an old headboard leaning against the wall, but no frame or mattress anymore. The boys' room was empty save for pink insulation heaped in the middle of the floor. In the far corner of Francis and Viola's old room, still painted sea-foam green, the ceiling door to the attic hung open, and more insulation frothed out from up above. It was as if the house, once vacated, decided to come undone, letting loose its innards in places they didn't belong. Lelah gave the insulation a wide berth.

In the kitchen most of the cupboards were bare save for cat food above the sink. Two stacked columns of generic aluminum cans for the strays Viola used to feed behind the garage. For a brief, self-pity-ing moment Lelah envisioned resorting to these cans of kitty chow for dinner, eating straight out of them like the old, eccentric mother-daughter duo she'd once seen in a documentary. She needed more money.

Francis Turner's AM/FM radio was still bolted to the side of the cabinet near the kitchen's back door. It switched on when Lelah tried it. She swept the floor while an oldies station played a Keith Sweat song. His nasally voice wasn't nearly as seductive to Lelah as it once had been. When Francis was alive, the radio stayed on sports stations, and if he wasn't listening to the Lions on the radio, he was at the Pontiac Silverdome watching them live. He took Troy with him often, or Cha-Cha, or whichever boy happened to be on leave and in town. Only once did he invite Lelah to come along.

"That's how you know he's getting old," Berniece had said. She watched Lelah curl her bangs in the bathroom. It was the early eighties, and Lelah's hair, died light brown and feathered to mimic Sheila E.'s and Tina Turner's (she'd brought both pictures to the salon), featured more bang in the front than ponytail in the rear. She was sixteen. Three years away from marrying Brianne's father and moving to Missouri, yet already desperate to leave Detroit. She'd begun savoring each bit of quality time with her parents in anticipation of the near future, when she hoped to live far away from any Turner for as long as she could stand it.

"Daddy *never* takes girls to the games," Berniece had added. "And maybe he shouldn't. Who curls their hair for a football game?"

"I do," Lelah had said. Berniece was the only sibling to truly tease Lelah. It might have been because as the tenth child, Berniece had been born right after Miles and Duke, the self-appointed family comedians, who were inseparable and insufferable in their teasing of her. She made fun of Lelah for remaining flat-chested through freshman year of high school, then when Lelah sprouted triple Ds a year later, Berniece took to calling her Jug-a-lug and joking about how Lelah would never make it on the track team because she might knock herself out with a breast during the hurdles.

"Anyway, I don't wanna go to the game," Berniece had said then. "I heard he still gets drunk at games. You better get ready to be embarrassed."

Francis bought tickets for what Troy called the Loitering Section: for less than $15 you could purchase a seat with views so bad patrons used the tickets as an excuse to stand around inside the Silverdome, buying all the hot dogs and beer their stomachs could bear and watching the game on the big screens. Francis had indeed smuggled a silver flask in under his Lions hat—Lelah saw him position it as they walked from the car—but once they were inside the stadium Lelah didn't see it again. He definitely didn't get drunk. He was chatty and relaxed. He drank his pop, crunched on his Better Made chips, and insisted that this would be the season Billy Sims took the team past the first round of the playoffs. "We got some talent now," he'd said. "Them jokers just gotta play smart. Play smart and stay healthy." It seemed the flask under his hat was more a lucky charm than anything else, as if he'd always brought it to games and was therefore hesitant to go to one without it. Later Lelah would be thankful neither she nor Francis had been at the game a month later that ended Sims's career. She wouldn't have known how to console her father, a man who rarely expressed hopes for anything, had she been there to see Sims's knee destroyed.

Back then Francis's sobriety was something of a disappointment to Lelah; her older siblings were always talking about the old days when Francis would do or say ridiculous things after a case of beer, but she never even saw him tipsy. She imagined it would have made him smile more, make his hybrid Arkansas-Detroit accent harder to decipher. Now, considering her own gambling issues, she wondered where and how her father found the strength to kick his habit, and whether or not that strength might lie dormant somewhere in her DNA.

Now in the basement, Lelah found what looked like mouse droppings in the corner by the sink, next to the skeleton of a rusted Schwinn. Her brother Lonnie used to rehearse with his band down here. He'd drape green tarps over the high windows, string up Christ-

mas lights, and burden the house's electrical system with his old am-
plifier. She couldn't have been older than seven, sitting on the steps
watching Lonnie and his friends practice. They'd fancied themselves
a Delfonic, pre-funk, pseudo-gospel outfit, and Lonnie's spastic dancing would serve as Lelah's blueprint for cool for several years before
she learned better.

A stack of boxes underneath the far window bore the label Memories. Lelah had been here on the first few packing days, helping everyone decide which things would go where, and trying to convince Viola to throw a bunch of knickknacks no one wanted into the garbage.
Being the flea market connoisseur that she was, Viola could not be
convinced. "These here is all my memories," she'd said. "You don't
put your memories on the side of the road like that. Might as well put
yourself out there."

So Lelah and Marlene had packed up the countless Precious Moments statuettes—those big-eyed, egg-headed celebrators of the
Lord's Word—along with an assortment of ceramic, glass, and crystal
candy dishes; a crumbling stack of certificates ranging in importance
from Perfect Attendance to Participant: Ypsilanti 1996 March of
Dimes 5K; copies of ultrasounds for which no one could remember
whose baby was pictured; a tangle of tarnished high school track and
field medals likely to be claimed someday by Russell but in actuality
won by Quincy; and even a few of the chintzy airline wing pins given
to children who were able to visit the cockpit and say hello to the pi-
lots pre–September 11. The boxes were labeled Memories so that
everyone understood that they held (a debatable amount of) senti-
mental value and no monetary potential at all.

That is, *most* boxes had no monetary potential. One box, smaller
and sturdier than the rest, had been on Lelah's mind during the past
week. She pushed a stack of larger boxes to the side and found it. This
was the box of things that she hadn't trusted herself to take home
back then.

Inside was a black case the length of Lelah's femur and five inches wide. Engraved in a silver rectangular panel on the front of the case were the words LELAH MARIE TURNER, 6257 YARROW STREET. The case held a twenty-nine-year-old Gemeinhardt flute in admirable condition. Triple silver-plated with a solid silver head joint, according to a yellowing card tucked into the velvet interior. Cha-Cha and Tina had purchased the instrument, but it was Francis and Viola who thought to get it engraved.

The local YMCA had a ragtag youth orchestra in which Lelah earned first chair at fourteen years old. She went on to hold prominent positions in her high school marching band, but what she remembered most fondly from those musical years was teaching herself all of the flute sections from the *Super Fly* soundtrack. She'd hated the movie, what with its half-naked women and everyone looking sweaty all the time, but Troy wouldn't let her use his boom box to play her cassette, so she was forced to watch the VHS more than two dozen times one winter break to get the notes down. Before putting down the flute junior year in favor of other pursuits (she couldn't remember what those pursuits were anymore, likely boys), she'd also memorized a good amount of Schubert, Haydn, and Bach. With her fingers in place now (not her mouth, for fear of mouse germs) she could make out only "Pomp and Circumstance" by memory. Disappointing.

The remaining items in the box weren't hers. Since no one else claimed the things and they didn't quite fall under the benchmark of worthlessness required to be lumped into Viola's boxes, she'd saved them. She'd first found the wide Japanese-looking dagger with the ivory handle wrapped in canvas in a drawer under Viola's china cabinet. It probably belonged to Troy, or Miles or perhaps Duke, as those three were the only ones who Lelah recalled having Asian tours while in the service. There was also a pair of door-knocker earrings, presumably gold, presumably belonging to Sandra, the eleventh Turner child, who'd worn so many heavy, dangly earrings in the seventies and eighties that the holes in her lobes were now long slits. Rounding out the collection of possibly valuable forgotten things was an old-fash-

ioned pipe made out of dark wood—perhaps cherry or mahogany—
that undoubtedly belonged to Francis Turner.

CHAINS-R-US was on Gratiot, less than a mile from the house. She
hadn't been there before, but she'd been to the White Castle just
south of it and the check-cashing place a little farther up. She didn't
admit to herself as she cleaned that morning that she'd end up doing
this, but part of her knew it would happen soon. The box had been
somewhere in her consciousness since the first night back on Yarrow.
On the periphery like a repressed memory. A low, persistent sound,
like feedback from a television.

The space that housed CHAINS-R-US had been a banquet hall
first. Brotherly Banquet was the site of Viola's sixtieth birthday cele-
bration as well as Francis's retirement party and a host of baby/wed-
ding/welcome-back-from-deployment gatherings. Its wood-paneled
walls had witnessed many a Turner *Soul Train* line. The owner, Mr.
Clive Brothers, had pink fluorescent lights installed in the women's
restroom and blue fluorescent lights in the men's.

According to a scrolling LED banner out front, CHAINS-R-US
specialized in cash-for-gold exchanges but provided traditional pawn
services as well. The woman behind the bulletproof window was what
Lelah, for lack of a better reference point, would call ghetto-Asian.
The charm on her necklace said THANH in tiny gold cursive, so Lelah
assumed her to be Vietnamese, maybe Hmong, but Thanh's hair was
slicked back into a ponytail with the baby hairs gelled down like teenage girls around the way had been doing since time immemorial, and
held in place with a plastic balls hair tie. Lelah fought the urge to tell
Thanh the same thing she wanted to tell every around-the-way girl:
you're beautiful, now go wash that gunk out of your hair. Thanh's
nails were long, electric blue, and acrylic, and she popped her gum
like her life depended on it.

"You're going to have to give me stuff one by one on the carousel,"
she said.

Her voice sounded high and sweet, maternal even, not how Lelah had imagined. The dissonance unnerved her. She looked down into her box, at the flute case that was hers and all of the rest that wasn't. The pipe couldn't go. No, you could not pawn a dead man's things, especially if that dead man was your father. She put the pipe in her back pocket. The rest she would come back for, she promised herself. Starting with the door knockers, she placed the items on the plastic carousel for Thanh to spin around and retrieve on her side of the window.

Thanh rubbed the earrings between her palms, held them up to the light.

"These are only gold *plated*. I'll give you twenty."

Lelah opened her mouth to speak, perhaps to point out how heavy the earrings were, but truth was, she'd only pawned things one other time and didn't know the weight of gold from that of brass. She nodded.

Next was the dagger. Thanh unfolded it from its canvas envelope, ran one neon nail along the blade, then carried it into the back, presumably for a second opinion.

"I'll give you two hundred for this," Thanh said upon her return.

"Wha?" Lelah said, not to Thanh as much as to herself. The dagger was likely worth a lot more than she'd expected, and maybe she could haggle Thanh up a bit, but it could also be that Thanh and Co. didn't know a good fake when they saw one. She decided to not rock the boat.

"Two hundred sounds about right."

"Okay, good," Thanh said. She opened the flute case, read the old information card, checked the pads, removed the head joint, and weighed it in her palm.

"Fifty for this."

"Fifty? That's like thirty years old, and the head joint is solid silver."

"I know. I felt it." Thanh's eyes trailed to a small television in the corner. A cooking show was on, and the host molded ground meat into patties.

"It's in almost new condition! Won't people pay extra for an antique like this?" Lelah's inflection went up a little too high for her liking at the end of this question. She was begging.

Thanh's eyes returned to her.

"Most dealers count something to be an antique after one hundred years, so no, this *isn't* an antique. What it *could* be is vintage, but flutes don't automatically go up in value with age. Maybe if it was *solid* silver, or gold, or platinum, somebody might call it vintage, but it isn't, okay? Besides, do you see any kids running in here to buy some *flutes?*"

Lelah turned around and saw one boy, maybe thirteen, in an oversized T-shirt that had seen better days, eyeing a silver chain on display behind more plastic. No use in pushing her point further. It appeared that Thanh knew her stuff.

Back inside the Yarrow Street kitchen, a feeling like nausea forced Lelah to sit on the floor. She hadn't asked Thanh how long she had to buy the items back. *You won't go back for them, and you'll piss away this money at a table.* This thought was the true thought, never mind the promises she'd made to herself beforehand. She'd just sold things that weren't hers, maybe for a lot less than they were worth, and the crushing, life-changing regret she hoped to feel hadn't arrived. An act like this should've spurred so much shame that she would have no choice but to make a vow to herself to change. The people in GA often talked about hitting rock bottom. One woman, heavyset with a vaguely West Indian accent, said turning tricks out of her back shed while her kids slept in the house had done it. She'd gone too low and knew she was in danger of permanently becoming someone else if she didn't stop. Lelah was waiting for that moment, an act that put her so close to the precipice of losing herself that she'd have no choice but to shake the image of those chips from her brain, the feel of them from her sensory memory. She knew it wasn't this, wasn't now, because she'd already partitioned sixty dollars off in her mind for a gambling "emergency." If it wasn't this, then what and when would it be?

At some point the notion had entered her mind that she was special, that she deserved more than a healthy baby girl, a roof over her head, and whatever job she could find. A dangerous, selfish notion to leave unattended, Lelah thought now. And one so hard to get rid of once it was there. She might have been in this very kitchen, tucking ant baits into corners on the butter-colored linoleum when it happened.

Far from Any Pulpit

· FALL 1944 ·

Jobs Francis Turner held in his first 6 months in Detroit : 4
Jobs willfully abandoned: 1½
Rooms rented: ½
Money sent to Viola: $7
Alcohol consumed: Many paychecks' worth
Women slept with: 1
Number of times he slept with her: He stopped counting.

Here is the truth about self-discovery: it is never without cost. Not now, in the age of create-your-own college majors, the Peace Corps, and yoga retreats, and definitely not during World War II for a young black father newly migrated to a strange city. That very first night in Detroit, after nursing two scotches for three hours, Francis talked his way into a dishwashing job at the bar on Beaubien. The owner and cook, a redbone man named Clydell, had family down in Little Rock and hired Francis based on shared Arkansan roots. For a month Francis washed congealed plates of leftover corned beef hash, smothered turkey, and oxtails from two in the afternoon until one in the morning. An unfortunate schedule because it cut into time on his rented half room. Once off work, after getting something to eat and cleaning himself up, he usually had three or four hours to sleep before the sun came charging across the low midwestern horizon and Mr. Jenkins came knocking for his space. Mr. Jenkins, a short, husky fellow from Kentucky, either worked in some sort of brewery or was a beer-loving drunk, Francis gathered. The smell of sour, yeasty sweat lingered in their shared room throughout the night. Francis took to gulping down coffee throughout his shift to fight drowsiness. The coffee made him jittery by the time work was over, and to help him relax he frequented a blind pig on Saint Antoine and Gratiot where for a nickel a day he rented a little locker to store his own hooch. He discovered he was a bourbon man, not a scotch man like Reverend Tufts. He'd sit in that upstairs illegal establishment and think about how his mother had washed dirty dishes and drawers so that he'd be a preacher, not a dishwasher himself. He'd also think of his father, with gapped teeth like his own, and other facial features he couldn't quite remember. He thought he remembered his father sitting on their porch in the afternoons, chewing snuff and spitting into a pail, but often this memory would bleed into one of Reverend Tufts sitting on his porch and reading the Bible. Reverend Tufts would go to Pine Bluff once or twice a month and come home very late at night or early the next morning, leaving Francis alone in the two-story house. These one or two nights alone were when Francis would think about his father the most. It hadn't occurred to him until the last summer he was in Arkansas that Tufts might have had a woman he saw in Pine Bluff, some romance that a widower pastor had reason to keep in the dark.

If nothing else, he had learned from Reverend Tufts the dangers of making one's dreams and desires too public. Someone could take them from you, exile you to a cold, flat, and distant place. Francis was not naïve about the dangers Down South, but it was home. His father's grave in an old colored cemetery. His mother gone, but Texas more feasible to travel to from Arkansas than Detroit. Had he left of his own accord, this hankering for home would not have been so strong.

On the first freezing day in October, Francis discovered that the back of the bar on Beaubien had poor insulation. The patrons basked in warmth, but even Clydell's sizzling griddle could not prevent the kitchen from slipping into the thirties. On Clydell's advice, Francis spent the small amount of money he'd saved on a heavier coat to wear throughout his shift. No use. Whenever he pulled his hands out of the dishwater, his knuckles ached like he had a bad case of early-onset arthritis. He started spiking his coffee with bourbon to stay warm. Soon enough he called Clydell a stingy, pock-faced, crooked nigger under his breath (too loud, alas) and got the boot. It was a milestone. He'd never given words like that a go out of his own mouth, not directed at someone in particular. Never mind that Clydell's face wasn't marred by pocks as much as heavily freckled, or that Francis hadn't quite cussed the man to his face; he felt one step closer to holding his own up here where men were crooked but pretended to be magnanimous.

That feeling lasted until rent on his half room was due. To say that Francis slept with Odella Withers, the mistress of his boardinghouse, to secure free housing would not be accurate. He might have slept with her sooner had he seen her for longer than the moment when she handed over his bedding each night. Lonely as he was, Francis might have slept with one of the prostitutes he often saw smoking cigarettes and laughing alongside men in Paradise Valley bars, had he thought he could afford one. Odella Withers had a wide mouth, very straight, square teeth, and bright pink gums. A mouth that made her look happier than Francis thought she was. Brown skin, not as dark as Viola's but close. Francis Turner had a predilection for darker women. Perhaps it was a subconscious effort to prevent potential offspring from defecting to white, or maybe it was because his own mother had been darker than his ill-fated beige father. Francis would sit in the armchair across from Odella in the boardinghouse's miserable little parlor and tell her about his long day of looking for work. How he'd hitched a ride down to River Rouge to see about work, only to have the slots for black men snapped up before he arrived. How he was in line to see about work at a foundry when an ambulance pulled up and word spread that a man had been nearly cooked alive. He told her about his week and a half working as a runner at the salt mine, how it reminded him of the time he'd traveled down to the Gulf with Reverend Tufts for a revival and felt his lungs fill with salty sea air miles before they got close enough to see the coast. He didn't tell her that he'd quit the salt mines because, sea air notwithstanding, he could not bear to be so far underground, the white walls dwarfing him, his own shadow a stranger as he hunched over and shuttled carts of supplies to white men similar to how he imagined Hebrew slaves carting stone at Egyptian quarries. Few people think about the individual lives lost to make something huge, but Francis thought about it often, had thought about it since the first time he read Exodus as a child. He feared he'd die in that dried-up ocean cave, either from a blast gone wrong or plain old sun-starved misery.

He found Odella reasonably versed in the Bible, and she knew about the goings-on both overseas and in Detroit thanks to her fondness for the radio.

The *Fibber McGee and Molly* show had just come on the evening Francis decided to sit directly next to Odella and see what that wide mouth felt like pressed against his own. They were in her little apartment downstairs with its banging radiator by the time the show's ham-fisted Johnson's Wax opening commercial ended. Odella was the second woman Francis had ever slept with, and he was very grateful for the experience, adultery be damned. So grateful he repeated the act as often as she let him.

Sleeping with her was not enough to absolve him of rental obligations.

"*Every*body's got to pay rent, soldier," she said one morning. "Even a body like yours."

They'd drunk a half pint of cheap bourbon the night before, and Odella stood in an ivory slip in front of her kitchenette making a water and baking soda concoction for their hangovers. The thermostat outside read in the twenties, but Odella's basement apartment was always steamy, which she claimed was good for the lungs and bad for her hair. She liked to call Francis a soldier, and Francis never could decide whether she meant to make him feel brave or like a coward. She did not ask him about back home, and he did not ask how she came to rent out a big old house by herself. He guessed her to be in her late thirties, but this guess was predicated only upon the way the skin between her breasts folded like a tiny accordion when she put them in a brassiere.

The first job Odella found Francis involved painting houses with an outfit run by the same man who had painted the boardinghouse years before. This job Francis enjoyed. He had some skill in painting, thanks to summers spent touching up the church back home, and he got an opportunity to see more of the city than bus and streetcar fare could afford him. He tracked the pockets in neighborhoods where Negroes were living, and those where they seemed to have the best chance of encroaching. Out near Eight Mile and Wyoming, country life claimed its last foothold, but as much as a small farm and a modest house appealed to him, Francis knew Detroit was not the place for it. While outhouses and water pumps were ubiquitous back home, up here they heralded dire straits. He rode in the back of the truck and watched junk collectors traverse Black Bottom, their rickety carts overloaded with treasure scavenged from the many garbage piles that lined the back streets. Forty years later, he would think of these men when scrappers descended on his neighborhood. He would imagine them running around the east side at night, placing the bits of metal they pried off of houses into the same rudimentary carts. From the men who worked with him he discovered that a fellow could pay to get his name moved up on the wait list for the new housing projects, and that the only real way a colored man could get past the racist real estate pacts in white neighborhoods was with a whole bunch of cash, connections, and luck. It was useful information, if not encouraging. By the middle of November snow wrapped its obstinate fingers around the city's neck and the painting work dried up.

The second job Odella found for him was the most Jim Crow job in all of Detroit, or so Francis thought. Odella knew a few members of the Urban League who knew a member of the Nacirema Club, a social club for Negroes with status (*American* spelled backward, she told him; Francis found this foreboding). The Nacirema man hired all of the caretakers for the cars that executives at a certain major manufacturer drove to work each day. They'd switched to defense building for the war, yet their own cars still received special attention. The company preferred Negroes with genteel mannerisms to serve the executives, but they settled for those with light skin in a pinch. Francis greeted the bosses when they came to work, washed and serviced the cars as needed, and drove them back out front when summoned. A stable boy for twentieth-century horses. The type of job Francis was born to lose.

Two sorts of men worked with him: those who took immense pride in the measure of intimacy they were granted with the executives, and Francis's type, who would just as soon crash the boatlike vessels into a wall. Of the latter group Francis found a friend in Norman McNair, a young man near his own age up from Alabama, with a receding hairline and a habit of chewing tobacco in lieu of lunch. "Rather eat breakfast and dinner," McNair would say. "Do those two right and lunch ain't on your mind." He and his wife rented a room not far from Francis's half room, over in the poorest section of Black Bottom, but they had no access to the kitchen, so meals were expensive. His wife worked as a housekeeper for a black undertaker's family in the Conant Gardens neighborhood. The McNairs were an example of what Francis should have been doing—working hard, saving for a house—but he could not manage it. Even if he somehow made the money, he thought it would take twice as long to make the right connections. His country conversation skills did not do the long-term charming up here that they had done back home. During his third week, one of the "other" sort of colored men working as a valet accused Francis of stealing a pair of driving gloves out of an executive's car. Francis was fired without deliberation.

He would come to think of these first months in Detroit as his heathen period, the beginning of his walk from God. Not completely away, but farther than he'd ever been before. Since stepping off the train, Francis had felt the call to preach receding within him, like a sonar ping growing fainter with each knot traveled. Nothing replaced it. He went to church once, to Bethel AME, and felt insignificant, sitting in a back pew in his faded trousers and sweater. More than a purpose, being part of Reverend Tufts's church had given Francis identity. He was no one in Detroit. One more migrant in a city where so many stepped off of trains and buses each day. No one knew him up here to judge him, because no one knew him up here at all. So he drank and screwed and lost his jobs. He did not call or write his wife.

Better Than a Burlap Sack

Viola had to work for white folks after all. She needed the money, and in the end she couldn't bear to be in those fields. As far as the fraught dynamic of interracial housekeeping went, Viola believed she fared well. Ethel Joggets, newly married into the Pine Bluff Joggetses, did not condescend more than Viola expected, nor did she degrade. Ethel had a son named Harold around the same age as Cha-Cha. The two women had origin in common; their people came from roughly the same spot in southern Virginia. When they figured out the connection, Ethel had said, "Small as that county is, we might be *distant* cousins!" She laughed long enough to highlight how absurd she found the prospect. Viola had an older, more complicated relationship in mind, but she kept it to herself.

The Joggetses lived thirteen miles from Viola's shotgun house (she would always call it the shotgun house), and it took two buses to get there. On the first one she rode with her sisters, Olivia and Lucille; they set out an hour before sunrise and parted ways at first light for their respective second buses. Gas rationing meant the second buses were overcrowded; sometimes Viola and a handful of other colored maids waited for several to pass before a driver deigned to give his last few inches of standing space to them. On the ride home she'd listen to the geese honking or the humpback crickets singing and imagine Francis on a bus or a trolley of some sort as exhausted as she was, only he was going off to spend his money on what? Viola couldn't imagine. People talked about how a good war-effort job paid at least six dollars a day. Almost six times as much as Ethel Joggets paid her.

Viola had no intention of playing the disgruntled, abandoned wife for long. In 1944 it already felt cliché. And no, she wouldn't resign herself to the work of her sisters and half the women in town. She had no inherent gift for organization, no real skill for cooking or cleaning, which was something her sisters knew when they found her the job. "I oughta get into the pictures, way I was lyin to that woman," Olivia had said. "Lord knows you don't know *nothin* bout puttin things back where you found em." Being the third girl and child number six out of ten had buffered Viola from certain singularly female duties. She was better at delegating, and managing the expectations of her father when she and her siblings worked in the field, or of her mother when it came to the status of housework. She might have operated a successful housekeeper-dispatching business—a sort of precursor to Molly Maid—but back then housekeepers were hired by word-of-mouth reference only, and the salaries were so small, no housekeeper would pay a fee for a go-between. Ethel Joggets assumed Viola knew how to make dishes that she'd never learned to cook and that Ethel herself couldn't prepare. (How to make hot-water cornbread? What *was* tuna casserole?) She also expected Viola to have a facility with children that Viola did not yet possess. Cha-Cha did not cry like Harold did, for what felt like hours at a time. Each day Viola arrived anxious that she would be outed as unfit for this job that she now needed to keep.

On the way home from work three months after Francis's departure, Viola walked past Jean Manroy's scraggly front yard. She realized she had no urge to stop in and see if there was a message for her. In fact, the last time she'd stopped by, the front of Jean Manroy's property had been a mess of gardening tools and dry, overgrown summer grass. Now red and gold leaves covered the lawn.

Spring 2008

Downtown Sunlight

The line for the unemployment department's Problem Resolution Office in New Center stretched out of the building's tinted-glass doors, past the neighboring FedEx, and several hundred yards to the corner. At least sixty people waited outside, not to mention the snaking line within, and the office had only been open for forty-five minutes. Lelah joined at the very back, behind an obese white woman who sat on a red combination walker/chair contraption. All sorts of people populated the line: teenagers, the elderly, the shabbily dressed, the suit-and-tie types, the shabby-suit-and-tie types. To Lelah's surprise there were near-equal numbers of whites and blacks waiting. Lelah had been laid off from her job at the airport in 2002, and when she had visited the unemployment office then, the overwhelming blackness of her fellow unemployed seemed to be clear evidence of injustice. But the proliferation of these new white jobless was more disturbing. If this many white folks couldn't find a job, times were certainly tough.

In fifteen minutes Lelah moved up a few feet, and the line behind her grew by nine people. She overheard people discussing extensions, training programs, and appeals, but she had no desire to join a conversation. Experience had taught her that this sort of talk was pure speculation, and getting excited about one's case based on the shaky advice of the fellow jobless a waste of time. Instead she played a maze game on her phone over and over, beating her previous high score each time.

After another twenty minutes someone tapped her on the shoulder. A short, skinny, balding man in slacks and a T-shirt.

"Hi," he said. "How long you been in line?"

"About half an hour," Lelah said. She brought her phone up to her face again.

"You mind if I ask what you're waiting to find out?"

Lelah looked the man in the eyes. He had shaved recently, and this seemed like an indication of sanity to her, never mind the incongruity of crisp slacks and dingy T-shirt.

"What do you mean?"

"I'm trying to figure out what kinds of problems they solve before I stand in this line for the rest of the morning," he said.

Lelah opened her mouth to respond, but the woman in the walker butted in.

"Anything and *everything*, sweetie," she said. "If you couldn't get your answer through the phone or on the computer, you have to come here and hope they figure it out. No exceptions."

The man didn't appear satisfied with this answer, but he said thank you and moved to the back. The woman in the walker looked up at Lelah conspiratorially. The flaky makeup on her jowls reminded Lelah of powdered doughnuts.

"There's always that type here who thinks they can cut," the woman said. "Like if they just ask someone closer to the front, they'll find a way to bypass the line. But we all gotta stand here and suffer until it's our turn, right?"

Lelah smiled with her mouth closed. She didn't enjoy talking to strangers outside of the casino. Without the clanging of jackpot bells and the headiness of free booze to bolster them, people generally only had inane or rude things to say. The woman chuckled to herself and scooted her walker up as the line edged forward. Lelah turned to see the line stretching back to the Fisher Building, an art deco behemoth she had been inside of only a handful of times.

The interior of the PRO office smelled of stale breath and popcorn. Signs hanging above the representative windows instructed those in line to have their ID cards, social security numbers, and a copy of their initial correspondence ready. Lelah dug around in her purse for several minutes before acknowledging that she had no idea where her official unemployment rejection letter was. Likely balled up in a corner of her old apartment, next to the stack of unopened delinquent account notices. Francis's pipe still lay in her purse. She decided to carry it around as a reminder of the things she needed to retrieve from CHAINS-R-US. She couldn't stop thinking about her flute. She had decided that she needed discipline; maybe she could trick her brain into finding stillness while making music instead of gambling, and abandon its other preoccupations.

At the window, a woman behind the counter took Lelah's ID and entered her social security number into the computer. There should have been an easier system than this, Lelah thought, a computer kiosk where people could input their own information and get basic answers. She'd waited two and a half hours to watch someone push buttons on a keyboard.

"It says you're not eligible," the woman said.

"I know it says that," Lelah said. "That's why I'm here. I got suspended from my job without pay, so I *should* be eligible, right?"

"Your employer hasn't put anything in here," the woman said. She was fair-skinned but not quite white. Lebanese, maybe, or Egyptian. She had green eyes, a long, slender nose, and a small, pretty diamond stud in her nostril. She did not look Lelah in the eye.

"What happened when you called Martha?" she asked Lelah.

"Martha? Who is Martha?"

"M-A-R-T-H-A," the woman said loudly. "Michigan Automated Response Telephone Hotline for Assistance."

She slid Lelah a pamphlet titled "Meet MARTHA: Your Guide to Filing for and Receiving Unemployment Benefits." Lelah folded it up and shoved it into her purse.

"I couldn't get through to anybody when I called the numbers online," she said. "That's why I came down here."

"Was it MARTHA you called, or some other number?"

"It was MARTHA," Lelah said, but she wasn't sure.

"Well, what's the status of your suspension? When will they tell you if you've been terminated for good?"

"I have no idea," Lelah said. "But I assume I'm pretty much fired at this point."

The woman scrunched her brow and pulled her lips back into a kind of closed-mouth grimace, a look intended to communicate empathy.

"You need to find out for sure and get something in writing," she said. "It might be better to go ahead and get them to officially cut you loose if you think they're going to anyway. That way you'll have something solid to input into MARTHA's system when you call. Most of the time, MARTHA can help you more than we can."

Lelah relinquished the window to the next person in line. She almost laughed to herself as she walked back to her car. This was her new life, she thought, begging various people for money through windows, as if the whole world had morphed into one big, stingy casino cashier counter.

She realized the mail might be to blame. She always remembered to check her email at the library, and aside from the usual spam sales offers and chain letters from Russell, she never had anything new. But she'd been without physical mail for nearly two weeks. Off the grid, unreachable. All sorts of money could have been tied up in postal purgatory—a little bit of refunded 401(k) cash, a severance offering, an important message from MARTHA. She'd forgotten about real, hold-in-your-hand mail, and the things that could only come to you through it. She drove to the post office near Jefferson and Lemay, the closest one to her old apartment. No mail for her there. She bought a six-month PO box for $21 and filled out a change of address form just in case.

There was a choice to be made now. She could go about her day and wait to see what arrived in the PO box. Go to the library, maybe, or straighten up the Yarrow house some more. Or she could be proactive. Find out once and for all whether she would ever work at the phone company again. There were risks associated with finding out, the potential for added humiliation high. She'd felt awash in relief when she learned that Dwayne the lonely widower was fired for his actions on the parking deck, both because the act itself was so unsettling and because the chances of him being able to ask for his money back decreased if they didn't work together. She even wanted to thank her manager for expediting the grievance process to get Dwayne out. Then her own scandal surfaced and she had nothing to say. She sat silent as that same manager enumerated all of the money she'd borrowed, and Misty, her union representative, shook her head in disappointment. She'd never felt so exposed in her life.

But money was money. She decided to go downtown and try to speak with her union representative instead of her manager. She'd paid her dues out of each paycheck like everyone else, so even if Misty didn't like her, it was her job to provide assistance, wasn't it?

She recognized the security guard on duty at the desk in the lobby. Sheldon had always struck her as a decent, reasonable person.

"Shelly! Long time no see," she said.

Sheldon put his hands on the desk and leaned forward to peer at her in mock suspicion. His eyes traveled up and down her body. He leered in an absent-minded way; Lelah thought he was not even conscious of what he was doing. She'd always had the sort of figure that certain men stared at out of habit. While Turner men were blessed with beautiful faces—long eyelashes, smooth skin, square jaws—a Turner woman's beauty originated below the neck. This wasn't to say that Lelah thought she and her sisters were homely; they all had large, doe eyes, full lips, and the capacity to grow an impressive head of hair.

But the Turner hourglass figure was their greatest gift, as well as a potential curse. A Turner woman's lifelong challenge was to keep the proportions in check, to prevent her ample top from ballooning and drooping, to keep her waist discernible, to prevent her bottom from spreading and sagging. The fact that Sheldon always gave Lelah this extended once-over confirmed that she hadn't lost the proportion war yet.

"Lelah Turner? I thought you'd won the lotto or something. Where you been?"

"I been around. Definitely didn't win no lotto, though."

"That's too bad," Sheldon said. "You going up to your floor? I don't know if you know, but they just put this new card scanner system in. It's a pain in the ass cause I have to swipe everybody in and out now. They give you the new badge yet?"

Lelah leaned an elbow on the tall desk, tried to appear casual. Two women in jeans and phone company polo shirts came up behind her, and Sheldon swiped them through. Lelah waited for them to get on the elevator before answering. The phone company was strict about who entered any of its buildings, but this building, full of non-salaried call center employees, had the most rigid visitation requirements of the entire downtown complex.

"No, no new badge yet," she said. "I'm just here to see if Misty Crespi is in today? I would've called her office, but my cell phone up and died on me this morning."

"Sounds like it's time for an upgrade," Sheldon said. He picked up the desk phone and scrolled through the directory. "Hi, it's Sheldon from downstairs. Lelah Turner is here looking for Misty Crespi. Can I send her up?"

Sheldon's thick lips disappeared into his mouth.

"Alright," he said. "I understand." He hung up and gave Lelah a look a person might give an energetic dog when leading it to a kennel.

"Lelah." His voice was too soft. "They say upstairs that you're suspended, and because of that you can't be on the property. I'm sorry, love, I have a list of suspended and terminated folks right here, but I didn't even think to check when you came in."

"What, they think I'm gonna shoot up the place?" She attempted a laugh.

"It's my fault for even calling up," Sheldon said. "It should have said something about you not being able to come here in whatever paperwork they gave you. You have to wait until they invite you back. Safety precaution."

"Yeah," Lelah said. It came out like a whisper. "That makes sense."

Sheldon, still wearing his apologetic face, held out his chubby hand. Just then a chatty group of employees with colorful lunch bags exited the elevator and Lelah seized the opportunity to leave. She walked through the lobby with her head down. She needed to get to her car before the tears came.

She'd made it to the door when she heard her name. It was another man calling, not Sheldon. Lelah ignored it and stepped outside. The large shadows cast by the high-rises had shifted, and she walked through a triangle of bright sunshine.

"Lelah Turner! Hold on a second, please."

There was a limit to Lelah's capacity for rudeness, even when she'd been humiliated. The nice part of her, that same agreeable part that wouldn't allow her to say what she really wanted to say to Brianne or anyone else, for that matter, prevented her from walking away from someone calling her name. Especially in broad downtown daylight. She stopped at the corner and turned around. A tall, dark-skinned man in khaki chinos and a light blue button-down shirt took long strides toward her. He looked like a lanky teenager from far away, but as he moved nearer she saw that he was closer to her own age. A boy she used to know from Yarrow Street, morphed into a full-grown man. He panted.

"I thought that was you," he said. "It's me, David Gardenhire, Troy's friend? Hi."

"What do you want?" This was ruder than Lelah imagined she could get.

David wiped sweat from his forehead with the back of his hand. He rolled up his sleeves, smiled nervously. His square, white teeth seemed a special torment to Lelah, too insistent.

"I'm sorry, I wasn't tryna chase you down," he said. "I was just up there meeting about a contract. You work here?"

"Yeah."

"I saw you when I got off the elevator, and man, it's been like twenty years."

They stood there for a few seconds. David looked at his watch and Lelah hoped this meant the conversation was over.

"It's lunchtime," he said. "You have time to eat? There's this barbecue place near here, and I know the owner, so we could get food pretty quick."

It hadn't been twenty years. Lelah remembered seeing him a few years back, when family gatherings were still held on Yarrow. She'd stepped out onto the porch to help Sandra with a couple boxes of pop, and he had been among the men in the empty lot next to the house. He leaned against a truck with Troy and a guy from the neighborhood that people called Trigger. Troy said something and David bent over laughing. He had not come into the house to say hello to Viola as many of the neighborhood men had, so Lelah never saw him up close that day.

She followed David's van in her car. A moment ago, out in the sunlight, it seemed easier to agree to lunch than come up with an excuse, but now Lelah felt trapped. Troy's friends were uniformly sleazy. Too loud, aggressive, flirtatious, always looking for an angle. Why would David be any different? She followed him onto the I-94 and ten minutes north, to the Eastland mall, eating away precious gas in the process. Before she pulled into the parking lot, she screamed once, loud and long with her windows rolled up.

David waited for her on the sidewalk.

"I called ahead to my friend, and he said they had a big convention crowd right now, so I figured other places downtown might too. Then

I remembered this place was close. I didn't have your number, or else I would have called you in the car."

It was a regular old Applebee's.

"It's fine," she said.

On his side of the booth David looked cramped, and when he tried to casually put his long arms out on the table in front of him, they nearly crossed the distance of varnished fiberboard over to Lelah's side. He draped one arm across the back of his seat instead.

"So," David said. "Last I heard about you, you were moving to Missouri with your husband."

Lelah shook her head.

"That was a long time ago."

"What you been up to since then?"

"You really wanna know?"

"Yeah, why not? That's why I invited you to lunch, right? To catch up."

"I don't know," Lelah said. "Let's see. I was married in '86, divorced by 1990. I got a daughter named Brianne who's twenty-one, and a grandson who's almost two. That's it."

David whistled.

"Makes me feel old. What's your grandson's name?"

"Bobbie," Lelah said. "Short for Robert like his father."

"Congratulations," David said. He sounded like he meant it.

The waiter arrived to take their drink orders, and Lelah asked for a Diet Coke. David ordered a Heineken, so Lelah changed her order to the special margarita advertised on the front of the menu. She hoped tequila and sugar could carry her through the awkwardness.

"Margarita, huh? You must not be going back to work."

"I'm off this whole week," Lelah said. The lies had a life of their own.

"Cheers," David said when the drinks came. He reached over to touch the tip of his bottle to Lela's glass. Her margarita bowl was too large to lift without spilling.

After a few sips Lelah felt pleasantly woozy. The cheap blue Curaçao in the drink tasted like melted gummy bears. With the exception of Marlene, who could hold her own with her brothers, Turner women had no capacity for drinking. Their predilections ran cheap and sweet. While Turner men pounded their way through cases of beer and fifths of cognac, the women usually split a couple wine coolers and a few bottles of dessert wine, then called it a night, their heads aching from the sugar and their stomachs craving grease.

In the time it took the food to arrive Lelah had told two stories about Bobbie making a scene at the library, and David laughed at each one as if they were as funny to him as they were to her. His burger looked slider-sized in his hands. Lelah had canceled out any health benefits her salad might have offered by opting for crispy chicken and bleu cheese dressing. It tasted wonderful.

"So," she said. "Why were you at my job this morning?"

"I install cable and Internet." He flung his hand over his shoulder in the direction of his van outside. "And I got a friend who told me the phone company was looking for independent contractors, so I set up a meeting with the field manager."

David finished his beer and took a long drink of his water.

"They told me to check back in a few weeks," he added. "Today was me checking back."

"Sounds impressive," Lelah said. She looked down into her drink, surprised that so much of it remained. "How do you go from being in the navy to installing cable and Internet?"

"You're gonna laugh," David said. He drenched his remaining french fries in ketchup.

"Why would I laugh?"

"I went to an Internet college. You know them commercials that make you feel guilty when you're sitting up in the house watching TV in the middle of the day?"

"Shit yes," Lelah said. "I hate them. They're designed to make people feel triflin. They don't even focus on what courses they offer."

"I know, but they wore me down. I had just moved back to Detroit after my divorce, and since I had only been in the service for ten years, you know, I didn't get a pension like Troy. I was just back on the east side with my mom, tryna figure out what to do next. I called the number on the screen, just like they say to. A year later I had an electrical engineering certificate, and I used that to get work installing for Comcast. It was kinda like the network engineering stuff I'd done in the navy. Then I got a hookup on a van, got my permits together, and started getting contracts."

"Damn," she said. "They should put you in the brochure."

David stopped eating and looked at her.

"They did. I was on the front page of their website for a long time, too."

Lelah laughed to the point of choking, and didn't regain her composure until after she drank some water.

"I told you. See, you laughed," he said. "I've got good business from being up on that website though, so I'm not mad about it."

The server cleared their plates, and David ordered another beer. Minor brain freezes had further slowed Lelah's progress on her margarita.

She and David talked about the state of the old neighborhood, both of their mothers' health, and the ongoing scandal with the mayor. It surprised Lelah how easily she could do this after falling out of practice; talk to a person about grown-up things, laugh at jokes, be a little funny herself. David never questioned Lelah about her job, and since he'd unwittingly done her this favor, she decided not to mention his brother Greg. Even from the vantage of the big-room window she could tell he was still strung out; he shuffled up and down the street in an old oversized pea coat that was too warm for the weather. He wasn't like the few crackheads she spotted on the block— skinny, jittery, and paranoid—he had the drowsy, old-man gait of a heroin addict. He often stopped and squinted up at the sun.

"I have this one tenant over by City Airport," David said. "A man in his early fifties, and his great-aunt. The man pays me three hundred a month to rent the house, and he works for the city, so I know he can afford more than that, even with the furloughs. Few months ago the *Free Press* put out a report saying his zip code was one of the deadliest in Wayne County, but he won't move. Says he thinks moving will kill the aunt. It's crazy, right? A stray bullet might kill her too."

"I don't know," Lelah said. "It's his prerogative. It might be nice to know you can do better than a place but stay there anyway. It's better than the other way around, when you're just being delusional and living somewhere you don't belong."

David squinted at her, as if trying to gauge her level of seriousness.

"I think I'd rather scrimp and save to afford something better," he said. "Somewhere safe at least."

Lelah laughed.

"That's that Heineken in you talking," she said. "You just said the man was doing it for his *aunt*, not cause he didn't have the money to move. Why did you buy all these properties in the first place?"

"Somebody's gotta do it," he said. "I get them so cheap, I don't even need tenants. If I just hold on to them, they'll go up in value eventually."

Lelah thought they'd both be dead before that happened, but she didn't say so. In some ways, she had begun to feel less like a squatter in the Yarrow house and more like a rightful tenant. After Saturday's trip to CHAINS-R-US she did not leave the house for nearly forty-eight hours. She ate a few Cup o' Noodles, the water from the tap in the kitchen just hot enough that she didn't have to boil it. She'd sat on the bed in the big room and surveyed the street below. The boarded-up house directly across the way had orange numbers spray-painted on its door. They looked more municipal than gang-related, and Lelah spent a considerable amount of time trying to guess what they meant. Sunday saw more traffic on the street as younger relatives in sedans and SUVs picked up their parents and grandparents for church service. Twice Lelah thought she saw someone she remembered from growing up, but the only person she was sure about had been Greg Gardenhire. Odds were the others were relatives, younger facsimiles who mirrored the gait of a person she used to know, drove in the same leaned-back, one-handed fashion. Mr. McNair never stopped by. She felt possessive about the property, imagined her presence might be beneficial. She'd even put a few of her pots in the hard-to-reach cabinet above the stove.

"I have a place on the river, too, a loft, right up Jefferson," David said. "All the buildings around there used to be industrial. You should come see it sometime."

Lelah nodded, and hoped she came off as slightly interested but not too eager. He was Troy's friend, after all, not hers. The waiter brought the check to David, and he quickly paid in cash.

In the parking lot they exchanged numbers, and Lelah warned David that she wasn't the best at returning missed calls. They hugged quickly. David climbed into his van and pulled out of the lot.

She sat in her Pontiac and regretted not getting one last glass of water. She felt overstimulated. The lunch, pleasant as it ended up being, was more small-talking, face-to-face lying, and semi-serious flirting than she'd done in months. She did all of these things at the casino, but there her behavior operated on autopilot, a mindless warm-up to a serious game during which she spoke to no one. Even when the casino flirtations led to a few ill-fated dates, or clandestine meetings in hotel rooms upstairs, she was not presenting her true self, only her casino self, a bolder personality that could not be conjured up in the outside world. Her true self wondered if her lies were convincing this afternoon, her conversation engaging, and whether this was a charity lunch not to be repeated in the future. She closed her eyes and rested her forehead on the steering wheel.

She was at the precipice of a parking lot nap when her phone rang. It was David.

"Lelah? Hi. My three o' clock job just canceled. How'd you like to come see my loft right now?"

She said yes.

He waited for her in the lobby. He'd changed into a pair of jeans and a black T-shirt. He looked even younger, and a little nervous.

"So you just seen the garage," he said. "Let me show you the rec room and the roof deck."

He held the elevator open for her and followed her out to the roof.

"The condo association has deck chairs that they bring out when it's warm," David said. "No one hardly comes up here, but it's nice in the summer."

They were eleven stories up, and the air was chilly. Lelah had been to rooftop bars in Chicago. She couldn't recall being on a roof this tall in Detroit. Facing south she saw the GM logo at the Renaissance Center, the central cylindrical steel and glass structure standing upright like a bullet among the cluster of skyscrapers downtown. To the east was Canada, and Lelah recognized the white, red, and gold of Caesars, her old home casino before the ones on this side of the river had been built. A squat lighthouse to the immediate northeast of David's building looked like a set piece from a theme park or miniature golf course. To the west was the city, the real city, a dull mosaic of green trees and brown rooftops, and a smattering of feeble gray columns of smoke.

"There used to be beavers in the river, like a hundred years ago," David said. "But then they all left or died from the pollution. Now they're coming back."

"Must be some brave beavers," Lelah said.

They took the stairs two floors down to David's apartment. This was her first time in a loft, and with nothing but movie depictions of New York–style, high-ceilinged, granite tombs as her reference, it surprised Lelah to see how much this loft looked like a regular apartment, just with more open space and cement floors. She'd imagined a place with no walls.

David left her in the living room as he used the bathroom. Lelah heard keys jangling in his pockets, and since the walls were thin enough for this sound to escape, she anticipated hearing the sound of his urine hitting the water in the toilet, or at least the sound of flushing, but she didn't. He was opening drawers, rummaging, it sounded like. He's looking for a condom, she realized, and her heartbeat accelerated. How strange to be listening to the unemployment woman talk about MARTHA one moment, then listening to this sound, and knowing what it meant so soon after. She stood in front of the sofa and looked at a framed blueprint of a 1960s US Navy aircraft carrier on the wall. On either side of the blueprint were smaller prints of Japanese woodcuts. Ink-rendered oceans flanking the plans for a ship.

"I got those two small ones in Japan," David said. He stood behind her. "And I found the blueprint at a stall at Eastern Market last summer."

"They look good together," Lelah said. She turned around and faced him. He smiled at her, a big, toothy grin that Lelah might have described as stupid on another person.

"What?" she asked.

"You look the same," he said. "I'm still tripping off of it. *Exactly* the same, maybe even better."

This, of course, struck Lelah as a bold-faced lie, but it was the impetus she needed to act on an urge she'd had since the parking lot of the restaurant. She stood on her toes and kissed him.

Twenty-five years ago they had gone on one real date, a trip to Belle Isle in David's father's menthol-clouded Regal. David had parked the car and they'd begun kissing. Lelah remembered his knuckle grazing her clitoris through her underwear. Just a few up-and-down strokes and Lelah had made him stop because the backseat of a Regal on a less-than-concealed part of Belle Isle would not do for the first time. He'd stopped without protest, bit his bottom lip, and grinned at her. Grabbed her hand and put it on top of his. His fingers were slick. "You feel that?" he'd asked. "Your mind's just about the only part of you not ready." Well, that was all too much too soon for Lelah, even though he'd been right, so a few days later she said she wasn't interested in him "like that," said he wasn't "worldly enough" for her. This explanation came to her on the spot, and it worked fine enough.

Now there was no such thing as too much or too soon.

David pulled her shirt over her head, pressed her against him, and undid her bra. He kissed her neck, her breasts, her stomach, her breasts again. They fell onto the couch, and for a moment Lelah was pinned under David's surprisingly substantial weight, his hips kneading hers. He pulled off her jeans and panties and knelt over her, one hand cupping her breast and the other on her waist. Soon enough he was naked and still kissing her. She felt his dick, warm and solid against her thigh, then his fingers inside of her, and as much as she preferred to say nothing at all, she said "condom" and he said "uh-huh" and he pulled it from his back pocket and it was on and he was inside of her. He breathed into her neck and she could see over his shoulder down the gentle slope of his back to his muscular ass. She wrapped her legs — Prickly? Ashy? Who cares! — around his back so his chest was flush against hers. *You look the same*, he'd said. Good lord, Lelah thought. No one should have to go so long without feeling this feeling.

When it was over, and David shuffled to the restroom, Lelah lay on her side and breathed. What would happen when he returned? There are few moments more telling, more ripe with the possibility of humiliation, of implied derision or unwanted sympathy, than when a lover returns from the bathroom after sex. In the hotel rooms at Motor City, when Lelah had occasionally been in this position, her expectations were nil. She'd be dressed, her ponytail smoothed back and her purse on her shoulder by the time the man returned. Running out wouldn't do much good right now. It had been a long time, but she still knew David. And she wasn't remorseful. She took her time putting her bra and shirt back on, renegotiated her panties, and considered beginning the dance required to get into her jeans. David opened the bathroom door. She waited, jeans in hand.

His jeans were back on, but not his shirt. This opposing yet similar ratio of undress seemed a good omen to Lelah. He held a pair of navy blue basketball shorts out to her.

"You wanna put these on?" He looked her in the eye, and she knew it wouldn't end badly. At least not yet.

"Sure," she said.

"Want some water? All I got is water and beer, and I guess coffee if you want."

David walked into the kitchen and took a Heineken out of the fridge for himself. Lelah asked for water.

"You can turn on the TV if you want," he said. He sounded so relaxed. As if she'd been here before, in this living room, wearing his shorts.

"So when's the last time you seen your brother?" David asked.

"Troy? Maybe last month. My sisters Sandra and Berniece were in town."

David took a swig of his beer.

"I seen him a couple days ago. He and Jillian got into a little fight, I guess, and we went out for drinks."

He shrugged and chuckled a little, as if he were talking about two crazy kids he and Lelah knew and often talked about. She didn't laugh though; she couldn't. Troy and Jillian's dish-breaking shouting matches worried her too much. The two of them reminded her of being stranded on that base in Missouri with Vernon and the night that made her leave him. After Jillian's bad asthma attack last winter Lelah had tried to convince Troy that all of that fighting—all that aggression and volatility—wasn't healthy, but who was she to tell him anything? Troy told her it was none of her business, and that it was not as crazy as it looked from the outside, so she'd left the matter alone.

David lowered his arm onto her shoulders, pulled her closer. His deodorant smelled freshly applied.

"I'm not gonna tell Troy what just happened," he said. "You don't have to worry about that."

Lelah had never been worried. Once she was in David's apartment she hadn't thought past kissing him and feeling his weight on her and putting her hands on his back. But she said okay because he seemed to need it.

David kissed her on the forehead, then the neck. His hand moved to her thigh. Lelah stood up, took off the basketball shorts and straddled him. She did not think of Troy or Jillian, or Brianne or Viola. Only herself.

This Was the Surprise

Speak something into existence. Give it a name and give it life. Had Cha-Cha done this? Did he believe this could be done? Certainly not after so many years of relative peace, and not as quickly as it was happening.

There was someone, something, sitting on the windowsill in Cha-Cha's bedroom.

This is how it begins. A moth-like sound, and a light too blue in a corner of your bedroom. If you ignore it, it does not exist. But speak its name and you've invited it into your mind. Like hearing voices, or seeing the face of Christ in a freshly laundered shirt. What happens cannot be manipulated, refuses to be controlled. But what we *acknowledge* as having occurred, what we tell others, can metastasize, grow ubiquitous overnight. He'd acknowledged it there in Alice's office, and now the control he had over what happened was gone. Cha-Cha hadn't started recording his feelings as Alice suggested, or thought about patterns, or visited the big room, but he had started remembering.

He couldn't show Tina because Tina was on a Women's Ministry retreat; somewhere along Lake Huron she slept on a cabin bunk with proverbs swirling through her dreams. He couldn't carry or wheel

Viola in to see his haint because the old woman's sleep was precious. He couldn't even get out of his bed and down on his knees to pray like he had prayed so long ago because the truth was that he couldn't move. Fear didn't paralyze him as much as surprise. And disappointment with himself. He awoke because he felt the air in the room shift, as subtle as a single hair falling on his skin, and tried to keep his eyes closed. A futile attempt because the noise was there, too. Like the beating of wings so papery and thin a drop of water could have dissolved them. He'd recognized the sound.

Two hours and the light on the windowsill hadn't moved. Just an orb of brightness like the spots of light one saw after blinking too fast. It hadn't condensed into the glowing, wispy-haired man-child marauder of the big room. Hadn't grabbed him by his ashy foot and dragged him into the dewy April night. This was the surprise. No confrontation at all.

I am here, was all it seemed to want to say. I have always been here.

Enter Doubt

When faced with the fantastic, those unfamiliar with that world often regard the phenomenon through the safe lens of logic. Logic was how Cha-Cha made it through the night. When the sun came up the haint slipped away, or perhaps it dissolved during those hours of exhausted delirium when Cha-Cha was neither fully asleep nor awake. In either case, before dawn an uncontrollable curiosity gnawed at the kernel of fear tucked deep within his body. This haint had always been a presence. He was willing to accept that as fact. A blue thing on the edge of his life. But was it a menace, or merely a benign constant that he'd misinterpreted as threatening? Perhaps it existed somewhere between the two. He needed to figure out how it worked.

He edged out of the bedroom, careful not to get too close to the window. Would that spot be hot or cold from the haint's visit? He didn't dare find out. Wrapped in the protective terry cloth of Tina's purple bathrobe, he made his way to his office nook—a desk and a swivel chair—in the living room. A few days before he had stacked the pages he'd printed from websites about haints into two piles: "likely" and "unlikely." Those tales that felt too tall, the ones that seemed ripped out of a B-movie thriller, he stacked in "unlikely." The "likely" pile was smaller, as feasible information on haints proved hard to come by online. He'd learned that in the Carolinas people painted their porches, doorjambs, and even their tombstones haint blue. Blue to mimic the ocean, because haints were thought incapable of traveling across bodies of water. They tended to stay in the house or the town where they lived when they were alive. In the New Orleans hoodoo section of *Mules and Men*, Hurston also mentioned that water was a barrier. Sedentary ghosts. Perhaps his haint glowed blue because it was proud to go where it pleased.

He wanted to send Alice some of the likelier links, but he didn't have her email, so he looked her up online. The "images" tab popped up. He clicked it. There on the first page of results, underneath all of the Alice Rothman, PsyD's who were not black, was a captioned image of Alice and her elderly white parents at a gala downtown. He didn't know what to make of the picture, besides that she was obviously adopted, but he printed it out nevertheless. He broadened his haint search by inputting "blue light ghosts." He scrolled through the results. These websites, old and shoddily put together, offended Cha-Cha's limited web-presentation sensibilities. Ancient Angelfire, GeoCities, and LiveJournal pages featured everything from Blue Light Ghosts: A Rockabilly Band to poorly spelled firsthand accounts of UFO probes. Haints, Cha-Cha decided, must be relegated to oral accounts. But they were the only type of ghosts he knew. Even Francis never denied their existence; he just did not believe them capable of traveling so far north. And Viola's sisters, his aunts Olivia and Lucille, had been full of haint tales when Cha-Cha visited them in Arkansas as a child. Olivia and Lucille were dead now, but Viola was not. He went to her bedroom.

"Mama?" Cha-Cha knocked twice, softly.

No noise from within. He edged the door open.

"Mama? Are you awake?"

Cha-Cha moved closer to Viola in her adjustable hospital bed. She slept on her back, her eyes scrunched closed. Under any other circumstance, waking Viola would have been heinous. Not this morning.

"Mama," louder this time. "Are you up?"

Viola's eyelids fluttered, her lips parted.

"Get me some water," she said.

"I will. But I have a question."

"Lord, water first, please," Viola croaked. "Then questions."

Was she always this cranky in the morning? Cha-Cha couldn't recall. In fact, Cha-Cha could not remember the last time he'd been alone with her for more than a few minutes.

Water in hand, straw positioned to Viola's lips, he tried again.

"Mama, last night I think I saw something, like a light or something in my room? I think it was the haint."

"Where's Tina?" Viola asked.

"Tina? Mama, I'm tryna talk to you about something. To tell you about the haint."

Viola looked up at Cha-Cha, scrutinized him anew, as if she'd just now realized her firstborn, and not some other person, was in the room.

"What haint?"

"You know, the haint from the big room and the accident," Cha-Cha said.

"I don't know nothin about no haint, Cha-Cha."

She looked past him to the doorway. Cha-Cha smelled the Pond's face cream that Tina helped Viola apply every night.

"Mama, how are you gonna sit up here and say that? The haint? The ghost that me and Francey and everybody saw and then I saw again when I had that accident?"

Viola took the cup from Cha-Cha's hand and drank the water down. The veins in her neck pumped as she swallowed.

"Mama—"

"You remember what your daddy said?" Viola's voice was low, deliberately cold. She waited for Cha-Cha to nod, or respond at all, but he didn't move.

"You remember. 'Ain't *no* haints in Detroit.' And he was right. You know what else he said to me?"

Cha-Cha did not respond.

"He said maybe somethin's off up in Cha-Cha's head." She took a finger, the nail painted a thick, dull pink, and tapped her temple.

"Come on now, Mama," Cha-Cha said. "He never said that."

"Yes he did. So you be careful who you go runnin around tellin stories to."

There never seemed to be a point in being angry at Viola. Even when old age wasn't her excuse, she was overworked, underappreciated. This morning felt different. Cha-Cha was angry, but underneath that anger lay something more terrifying. Viola had planted doubt.

"Mama, you don't mean that."

"My legs are startin to hurt, Cha-Cha. I need my morning pills. Where is Tina anyway? You don't never take care of me like Tina does."

He imagined shaking her, denying her the pills, turning her out onto the street, but he knew he would not. He counted out the pills and left them in a pile on the nightstand.

THERE WERE DUES to be counted at church, Women's Ministry members to track down and shake down for money, but Tina headed home the morning after the Lake Huron retreat. Cha-Cha should have been at work, and she didn't like to leave Viola alone for long.

When she walked into the living room, Cha-Cha was asleep on the sofa. His mouth hung open, as did the purple bathrobe, exposing his bare sagging belly and his blue and yellow checkered boxers. Printer paper fanned out on the floor around his feet. At first Tina feared the worst: heart attack, hours ago when he was getting ready for work, and no one around to help him. She stood frozen in the entryway, her own mouth open, no single thought caught in her head. But then, praise God, he snored. Tina shoved him awake. Cha-Cha jerked up and yanked his bathrobe close.

"What are you doing home, Cha?"

"I called out from work."

"You called out from work. You sick? What's wrong?"

Cha-Cha was a strategic hoarder of sick days. Nothing short of a harrowing case of food poisoning could make him waste a day. He sat up straight and made room for Tina on the sofa, but Tina remained standing.

"I saw the haint," he said. His eyes were wide, and for what couldn't be but felt like the first time, Tina noticed a cluster of tiny moles on both of his temples, like three-dimensional liver spots.

"You saw the haint. When? Where?" Tina knew Cha-Cha hated it when she repeated him like this, but she couldn't stop.

As he told her about the night before, about a light both natural and unnatural, about the air shifting, Tina was conscious of her purse sliding to the floor, her arms folding, her brow knotting up. But did she realize these gestures screamed I DON'T BELIEVE YOU to her husband? Not really.

Tina was both a believer and a skeptic. She understood the value of practicality as well as the power of miracles. There were events that could only be processed and accepted through faith: raising the dead, angelic visitations, praying cancer out of a body. But she did not believe a haint had been in her bedroom the night before. In the room she'd decorated in earth tones and cherry wood. Where the pillow shams matched the curtain tiebacks. Near the remote-controlled bed she'd picked out less than a year ago. Her bedroom was too ordinary, too familiar to be the site of an event as fantastic as what Cha-Cha described. On a mountaintop, in the middle of a blustery summer storm—these were settings where she could imagine something amazing happening.

"Are you sure?"

"Yes, Tina, I'm sure. Now you're soundin like Mama."

"What Mama say?"

"She didn't say anything helpful, that's for sure. She damn near called me crazy."

Cha-Cha gave Tina a searching look, and Tina quickly shook her head to let him know that she didn't think he was crazy.

"You know what," Cha-Cha said. "I'm gonna go try and see Alice."

"You're gonna go see Alice? Why?" Tina hoped her panic didn't show on her face.

"Alice is the reason it came back. She got me to thinking about it, and how I grew up."

"She *got* you, is right. You paying that lady an arm and a leg to talk about your feelings, and now you think she can help you with spirits? You gotta go see Pastor Mike, if anybody."

She wiggled her cell phone out of the front pocket of her jeans, feeling glad that she'd gone ahead and put the pastor's personal number on speed dial.

"I just saw Pastor Mike an hour ago, matter of fact. I'm sure he'd love to talk to you today."

Cha-Cha hoisted himself up from the sofa and snatched the phone out of Tina's hand.

"I don't *know* Pastor Mike, Tina. I know Alice."

Tina blinked away the tears she felt welling up in her eyes.

"But does Alice know God? She doesn't even *believe* in him, Cha."

This should have been the end of the argument, Tina thought. Why would anyone want to go to someone who didn't believe in the spiritual for help with spirits?

Cha-Cha bent down to gather up the paper at his feet and stacked them into a messy pile on the sofa.

"Alice is my friend," he said. "I can trust her to help me sort this out."

"Alice is your *friend?* You *pay* her, Charles. Don't you forget that. You pay her a whole heap of money for this so-called friendship. If anybody is your friend, it's *me*, isn't it?"

Cha-Cha sighed heavily. He might as well have rolled his eyes. He walked past her toward the guest bedroom, where he kept his casual clothes. Was he afraid of their bedroom? Tina wondered. He would probably have the nerve to try to sleep on the couch tonight.

"How can you know she won't just tell you what you wanna hear, huh? Are you that afraid of this thing that you want somebody to *lie* to you?" She said this to his back.

Cha-Cha turned around in the doorway. The look he gave was one she'd seen before but never directed at her. Chucky's first wife, Yvette, cheated on Chucky when he was deployed during Desert Storm, and she'd come around to the house begging Cha-Cha and Tina to convince their son to take her back. Cha-Cha gave her a look Tina had never seen him make before, devoid of the intimacy and flicker of empathy that he afforded everyone in his family. His eyes were cold, and something in the way his lips sat suggested disgust. It was a look that at the time Tina thought appropriate, but now, on the receiving end of it, she thought poor Yvette didn't deserve a look like that. Who was this Alice Rothman? Tina was suddenly afraid to find out.

"This is *my* thing, Tina, and you just need to respect that," Cha-Cha said. He was dressed and gone within five minutes.

Tina and Cha-Cha met the summer of 1971 in Kansas City, where Tina grew up. A short woman, she just made five feet two with the best posture she could muster, and here was Cha-Cha, a six-foot-two trucker from Detroit, hanging around the pharmacy where she cashiered, looming over her, making up excuses to talk to her. The first time he came in was legitimate; he had a toothache and was determined to make his run to Nashville on time, so he needed painkillers.

"This says you shouldn't operate heavy machinery," Tina warned. His eighteen-wheeler parked on the curb in front of the pharmacy cast a shadow on the entire storefront. The cars on the top deck shone like beetles in the sun.

"I'm from Detroit, miss," Cha-Cha said. "We learn to operate heavy machinery in grade school."

Tina laughed, more to encourage Cha-Cha to keep smiling than because she cared for the joke. He was thin back then, unhealthily thin, Tina thought, and she had a desire to feed him. An alien, maternal desire she'd never felt for another person before. It made her afraid. She had looked after her three younger brothers her whole life. She took the job at the pharmacy in hopes of saving up enough money to move out with a girlfriend and take care of no one but herself for a change. Cha-Cha left that afternoon without asking her on a date.

He came back two Saturdays later, then again in another two weeks. Tina thought that Detroit to Nashville was his regular route; she would not know until after they were married and she'd moved up to Detroit that he had begged and bartered with his own father to have the route that summer.

They moved into a two-family flat off of Van Dyke, not far from Yarrow, during the fall of 1972. Cha-Cha was saving furiously for a house, and it took Tina time to find work as a medical transcriber. The neighborhood was just as poor as the one she'd left in Kansas City, but the riots had left it uglier. Charred husks of buildings lined Harper Street, and those businesses that still operated did so halfheartedly, with decreased hours and pitiable attempts to repair their façades.

"It'll be better in the spring," Cha-Cha reassured her. "The green will help make things look nice."

Tina didn't have to wait for spring. After the wedding Cha-Cha's sisters pulled her into their ranks, and Tina felt what it was like to be a part of a web of familial love and connections. Weekends were full of birthday celebrations and looking after one another's children. Lelah and Troy were only four and seven when Tina met them.

After Chucky and Todd were born, Cha-Cha became more determined than ever to move out of the neighborhood. The move to the suburbs changed everything for Tina. Just her and her three men, out there in a neighborhood she'd never even had a reason to drive through before, where she'd never felt welcome. Francey and Marlene and Netti and Sandra and Berniece still came by, and she still went to see them, but she was not as "in" as she'd once been, she could feel it. It wasn't even that they felt she looked down on them; *they* looked down on *her* for some reason. As if a big new house in that white neighborhood made her less connected to their children trouble, their man trouble. As if she'd morphed into some type of Stepford wife overnight. She became "my sister-in-law" in introductions, when she'd always just been called a sister, and while her boys and Cha-Cha were still barraged with calls, cakes, and visits on their birthdays, Tina's own birthday mysteriously vanished from folks' calendars. The exception was Lelah, who Tina felt she had helped raise just as much as Viola had, if not more. It was Lelah who told her about any girls' night out lest she not be included. But Lelah, first as a teen, then as a new mother, also depended on Tina for sporadic loans and frequent childcare. She needed Tina more than the others did, had a reason to keep her close.

Just when it felt like the old, suffocating loneliness from Kansas City threatened to smother her, Tina's hairdresser invited her to New Dawn, a church in Southfield with a young pastor and a bevy of ways to get involved. When she talked to prospective members now, Tina liked to say that the Word drew her in, but the people closed the door behind her. She'd found a place. A decade had passed and Cha-Cha still called her involvement a phase. But how else would she have been able to give all that she continuously gave? Organizing quarterly birthday parties for the legion of Turner grandchildren and great-grandchildren, pretending to be just as "in" with the family as always. Her crown would be in heaven.

Tina went to Viola's room with a bowl of oatmeal. She didn't knock. Viola slept on her side facing the far wall. Tina set the oatmeal down on the nightstand and put a hand on the pillow next to Viola's head. The pillowcase was damp, perhaps from sweating, or could it have been from tears? She leaned over and looked at her mother-in-law's face. Without wakefulness to animate it, it was easy to see how this face had made its way into the features of her thirteen children. There were Russell's long eyelashes, Lelah's high forehead, everyone's small nose with its delicately flared nostrils and shallow arch. Cha-Cha's thin lips, the top one just a touch more brown and the bottom more pink. Tina was not blood, she knew, but Lord, how she loved these people! So much sometimes it made her ashamed. They were hers. She didn't let the move to Franklin Village push her out of the family, and she decided she wouldn't let Alice Rothman do it either.

She cracked Viola's window on the way out of the room. Whether she had been crying or sweating, fresh air would do her some good.

CHA-CHA HUSTLED THROUGH the lobby of Alice's private counseling consortium, into the elevator and out to Alice's floor, past the young female receptionist who never asked him whom he was there to see. He had never shown up unannounced, but it didn't occur to him to wait for Alice to come out of her office. He had forgotten his printouts, and he cursed himself for this mistake. He knocked on her door.

Alice opened it. Her mouth was full of food, her office empty.

"Charles," she said. "It's lunchtime. What's going on?"

Her standing there, surprised, worried, her hair pulled up into a type of high, fluffy halo that he'd never seen before, made Cha-Cha both regret coming there and desperate to touch her. Just some physical contact to confirm that they were indeed friends. That she would see him through this thing. He hugged her before he could stop himself. A chaste church hug, his pelvis as far away from hers as possible. Alice patted him once on the back but was otherwise still.

"It's alright," she said. "Please come inside."

Cha-Cha forgot to drag his customary armchair into the room, and once inside he couldn't bear to walk back outside to get it; he might have lost his nerve and run out of the building. He collapsed onto the fainting couch, let his cane fall to the carpet, and told his story for the third time that day. Unlike with Tina and Viola, he was precise as possible with Alice, preempting questions by including what he had done beforehand (a little haint research, babysat his grandson); what was on his mind right before he went to sleep (the Yarrow house, his grandson's preoccupation with the word *stupid*, an email from Russell announcing another visit); and even what he'd eaten for dinner (hot wings, not as spicy as he would have liked). These details came out in a torrent, and for most of the telling he kept his eyes closed. When he reached the end he looked over at Alice.

"Well," she said.

"Well?"

Alice spread her fingers out on her desk. She looked exhausted.

"I'm concerned, Charles, if you want to know the honest truth." She did not blink as she looked at Cha-Cha. Was that fear he saw in her eyes? Or was it just an intense effort to remain detached?

"I feel responsible because I encouraged you to explore this haint situation further."

"Oh, I don't blame you," Cha-Cha said. "I know maybe having to remember certain things helped me see it again, but now I'm pretty sure it's always been around."

"That's the problem, Charles. It was unprofessional of me to allow you to indulge in these hallucinations, but now I think we need to start a more constructive dialogue."

"Hallucinations? What are you talking about?"

The look he'd seen a minute ago was indeed detachment; that mask of professional indifference that Cha-Cha feared Alice would wear before he even met her. Here it was. It had been underneath the surface of her all along.

"Again, I apologize for not calling them that sooner. You're holding on to these visions, which *are* essentially hallucinations, for a specific reason, and unless we speak about them in the correct terms, I don't think things will improve. There are techniques we can utilize, more direct approaches that I now feel I should have implemented sooner."

Cha-Cha sat up as straight as possible on the chaise.

"I'm not hallucinating a damn thing!" he said, then, "I'm sorry for raising my voice."

"It's fine," Alice said.

"Listen, I had things to show you. I printed out some research I been doing, stuff I found about haints online. A lot are individual testimonies, but they prove that what's happening to me isn't so crazy."

"Charles, I really am sorry," Alice said, and she did look pained as she spoke. "But I think it's dangerous to keep discussing this haint as if it's real. It is clearly real to *you*, but the goal has to be to get you to a point where you don't need to believe in it anymore."

At sixty-four years old, Cha-Cha could count on one hand the number of times he had ever cried. When he was nine and Marlene was a newborn, she'd contracted a kidney infection and Francis sat the children down to tell them she would likely die. Cha-Cha had held the baby girl three, maybe four times, and the only remarkable thing he recalled was her skin; she was the darkest of his siblings yet. The thought of a casket small enough for a baby had made him weep. Quincy, Francey, and Russell had wept as well, but Francis shot Cha-Cha a look across the kitchen table, a look that told him to pull it together and be strong for the younger ones. Cha-Cha cried again in 1973 when Edgar Bullock, his best friend and first roommate, was killed in Vietnam, just days before he was scheduled to come home. The last time Cha-Cha cried was more than thirty years earlier, when Chucky was born. It was the only time out of the three when he hadn't been at all ashamed. If he were younger, perhaps, or the son of another man, Cha-Cha would cry now. At the very least he should leave this woman's office, he thought. Alice suddenly seemed ignorant, and much, much younger than she was. But who to tell next? Where to go with a story this incredible? Cha-Cha searched his mind for the right face and drew a blank.

"Charles?"

He'd been sitting quietly for nearly a minute.

"I understand if you're upset with me," Alice said.

"Who are you, Alice?"

"Excuse me?"

"Who *are* you? I've been telling you all about myself, my family, hell, even *personal* things about my marriage. I figure I should at least know some basic facts about you before I listen to anything else you have to say."

Alice straightened up in her seat.

"Me as a person? That's not how this works, Charles."

"You know what?" Cha-Cha said. "I find it funny that all of a sudden you're all about rules. Few months ago you were *lying* to Chrysler, encouraging my 'hallucinations.'"

"I've got nothing to explain to you, Charles."

"No, you don't, because I've got Google like everybody else. I've seen your parents."

Alice's eyes widened for a moment, then she began straightening the pens on her desk.

"So you've seen my parents. My parents are white. What does that have to do with you and the things you need to work through?"

Cha-Cha stood up to go. Why had he trusted this woman so quickly? Because he was lonely, and because she was beautiful. He could see her beauty even now. It was there in her worried eyes and smooth, nervous hands. In the way her plump lips pulled back tight when she was upset. He'd felt so fortunate to have a young, good-looking woman pay attention to him that he'd never fully analyzed what it meant that she charged him a fee for this attention, and that her reasons for seeing him might differ from his own.

"You damn near seduced me," he said.

Alice opened her mouth to object, but Cha-Cha continued. "You had me up in here thinking you cared about all of this shit, this stuff going on in my life. Making it seem like this was more than another check for you."

"Charles, I think you should take a minute to calm down."

"I couldn't figure what you could possibly want me in here for," he said. "Not my brilliant conversation, I know that much. I guess you just wanted to know what it was like, huh? To grow up around your own kind. Or maybe just what it was like to grow up black *and* poor."

"Charles," Alice said.

"Stop saying my gotdamn name. I'm the only person in here."

Her nose crinkled up as if she might cry, but the moment quickly passed and her face glazed over with detachment again. Cha-Cha walked toward the door.

"I'm not a lab rat, or some stupid monkey in a cage."

He shut the door behind him, but he could still hear her say, "I never thought you were," as he exited the waiting room.

Corned Beef and Cabbage

The story of black Detroiters and corned beef is nearly as fraught with racial tension as the story of the Pilgrims and corn. Long before European immigrants gave up fighting to keep the newly arrived black masses from becoming their neighbors, they were working next to them at the plants, distilleries, mines, and government agencies that made the city hum. It was easier to sustain hate for a monolith than to keep hating Earl from two spots down the line (even if you called him Nigger Earl, *Mavro* Earl, *Mulignan* Earl, or some other epithet when he wasn't around), so tenuous friendships were forged and eventually recipes shared. Add to that the scores of blacks working in all manner of domestic and food service in the city, and an unintended result was that the Negro transplant had occasion to pick up new cuts of meat at the butcher. If black folks in the Southwest lay special claim to their own offshoot of Mexican food (and they do; think tamale pies, enchilada casseroles, and the like, all sprinkled with Lawry's, pork added where it wasn't before), then their midwestern cousins maintain a similar toehold in the world of brats, beer, and brisket.

Lelah felt she did not deserve nor could she feasibly manage a real relationship, but that didn't stop her from trying to make what she'd started with David closer to her ideal. To this end, she offered to cook, to show up at David's house during a respectable hour and make the two of them a proper meal. Corned beef and cabbage.

For the past week, their relationship had centered on simple, hungry lust. Sex for the sake of it. She'd slept over David's three times. It was as if she'd suffered from scurvy and that chance meeting with him was a booster shot of vitamin C. She dissected their meetings after she left him, ran their touches and jokes through her mind too many times. She tried to ration this reminiscing but could not. It had been too long. His mustache on the ridge of her top lip when they kissed. The way he pulled his mouth away from time to time and breathed into her neck, as if the kissing itself was too much and required breaks. His elbows and knees the same color as the rest of him because he was dark enough for that, for very little wear or discoloration to show. She hoarded these details. She was here and already in the future looking back at here. Editing, perfecting, reliving it. She feared what lay around the corner, what two weeks, a month of their coupling might mean. Lelah and David were what Brianne would have called hanging *out*, messing *around*, hooking *up*. Two adults over forty couldn't do that for long without one of them asking what's what. At the very least David would want to see her apartment, catch her in a lie or two. And that would be terrible. Lelah preferred to leave David's apartment while he showered—a self-preservation tactic, so that she would never be asked to leave—and she took meandering routes back to Yarrow. She had no reason to suspect he would follow her, but there were only so many main thoroughfares on the east side and not much traffic. How terrible to be caught at the wrong intersection with him.

The beef was in its pot, the cabbage cut and cleaned, the pickles sliced. Lelah joined David on the living room floor in front of the couch. She grunted as she settled next to him.

"I've never met a grown man who liked the floor as much as you do."

"It's my back," he said. "What I get for slouching my whole life."

He sat cross-legged with his back flush against the couch. His knees jutted out and made him look froggish. Lelah couldn't manage to sit cross-legged for long, so she folded her legs under her. The TV was on ESPN, but David had it on mute.

"This how you meditate, down on the floor?" Lelah asked.

He raised an eyebrow at her.

"How'd you know about that?"

"I'm nosey," Lelah said. "And I can read. Those CDs on your nightstand."

"I don't think Troy even knows I meditate."

"Troy wouldn't care. Or he'd just care long enough to make fun of you."

"Ha. Probably."

"I didn't think it was a secret cause the CDs were out in the open. Nobody's supposed to know?"

He put his arm around her. The smell of him was clean and unfussy. She'd found no cologne in his apartment.

"Not everybody gets to come into my bedroom, Lelah."

She rolled her eyes at this. He kept meditation CDs on his nightstand, and the small bookshelf in there was full of motivational books about making money, like *Rich Dad Poor Dad*, *The 7 Habits of Highly Effective People*, and even a few touchy-feely talk show favorites. He seemed to be very interested in fixing himself as well as fattening his wallet, in finding out how to make concrete adjustments for the better.

"So why do you do it?" she asked.

"Do what?"

"Meditate. What do you get out of it?"

"Nothing," David said. "I don't necessarily get nothing out of it."

But the set of his mouth suggested the contrary. Maybe this was none of her business. After all, hooking up required keeping personal revelations to a minimum, didn't it? To hell with that, Lelah decided.

"When'd you start doing it? I'm not trying to make fun of you. I just . . . is it religious? I remember Angela Bassett in *What's Love Got to Do with It?* when she dumped Ike and found Buddha. You remember she had that chant? That's ignorant, I know. Are you even supposed to say 'found' Buddha like folks say they found Jesus? I bet not."

David laughed.

"Nah, it's not religious." He flopped one of his legs on top of hers. Heavier than it looked. "It's just a long story. You really are that nosey, huh?"

"It's like a sickness. Comes from being the youngest."

"Alright, fine. So I met this girl when I was in San Diego and we got married. She was from out there. She had a big Filipino family, and I got along with everybody pretty good. I used to play basketball with her cousins. She was even close with my mom, even though she wasn't black and my mom is old school, you know."

Of course Lelah felt jealous listening to him. Of course she felt ridiculous for feeling this way. She tried to imagine a petite Asian woman with light brown skin next to David. She could and she couldn't.

"Anyway, after like two years we were ready to start having kids, but I didn't wanna be gone on tours and stuff with a baby, so I started thinking about getting out of the service. This was like, '96, '97. Long story short, I volunteered to go back on a ship to try to stack up some money, and I ended up cheating on her when I was away, and I told her about it. Maybe if we had kids she would've stayed, but we didn't. I quit the navy and moved to LA for a little bit, but my money was low, so I moved back home."

"And the meditating?"

"Yeah, I bought a tape at this African marketplace when I first moved to LA, and I been doin it ever since."

"Why?" Lelah asked again. David spoke as if this was the logical next step after his wife leaving him, but it wasn't to her.

"Cause it worked? I don't know. I was tired of feeling like everybody hated me, like because I had fucked up in this one way her whole family was done with me. The tapes helped."

"With what?"

"With being alone, I guess." He shifted his leg on top of her. "If you can get used to being alone, sitting quiet for a long time with just you, then you can do anything."

This sounded like a line out of a self-help book to Lelah, or the type of easy solution they pushed at GA meetings.

"So why do you need to meditate to get that? Isn't it just gonna *happen* regardless? You get older, you get divorced or whatever, and then you're alone. It just happens."

The pot of water for the cabbage boiled over and hissed on the stove. David lifted his leg to let Lelah up. She went into the kitchen and turned the fire down.

"Yeah," he said. "But that's not the same as being alright with it. I bet we both could name a *lot* of people who aren't alright with it."

"Mmm," Lelah said. She wanted to say something about how when you have a child it changes the way you feel when you're alone, how you are never alone in the same way again because there is a live, independently thinking part of you out in the world that you can never fully push out of your awareness, even if you try. She did not say these things to David; he mentioned that he had wanted kids, and he had none.

They ate at the kitchen bar because David had no dining table. The conversation moved on. They talked about how she used to play the flute, his early aspirations to play basketball, and how everyone would be better off when they had a new mayor and a new president. They shared their guarded optimism that Barack Obama might be the next president, like an expectant couple talking about the health of a baby doctors told them they could never conceive. After dinner they had sex in his bedroom. Missionary, slow and close.

"You ever bring any of the dudes you dated around your daughter?" David asked. They lay on their backs on top of his sheets. He moved his arm behind her neck and snaked it around so that his hand rested in the hollow between her breasts, where there was surely sweat, as well as direct access to the accelerated thump of her heartbeat.

"Mmm, not really," Lelah said. "No, actually there was one guy when Brianne was around ten or eleven. Named Damien. Security guard at the airport, back when I used to work at the airport. He never lived with us, but I let him take me and Brianne out. Didn't work out though."

Damien, with the big, adorable, Will Smith–looking ears and an accent that didn't bother with the last consonant of most words. He'd wanted to marry her, Lelah explained, move her and Brianne down to Atlanta where he was from. She pictured him cheering Brianne on as she went down the giant slide on Belle Isle by herself for the first time one summer. Brianne's nervous, eager-to-please grin.

"I didn't wanna take Brianne that far away from her dad," Lelah said now. "I still thought he might get his stuff together and start coming around. Plus, my own dad had passed and I didn't wanna leave my mom up here."

A catalog of past relationships was inevitable if she and David were to do more than hook up, Lelah knew, and she'd likely opened the door for it by quizzing him about his meditating. Still, she was unable to tell the full truth. There were other factors in her refusal of Damien's proposal: fear of being far away and alone with a man again, as she had been in Missouri with Vernon. Her having already ruined her credit gambling at Caesars and not wanting Damien or anyone else to find out. Smaller, seemingly insignificant things, like the way Damien immediately reached to put his boxers back on after they had sex, as if he could only stand to be that vulnerable around her for the shortest time necessary.

"Atlanta's a cool city," David said. "Got a lot more business and stuff goin on since it had the Olympics . . . I mean, it's not no Detroit, though."

"Not even close," Lelah said. She couldn't tell if he was joking or serious, but having never been to Atlanta herself, she still felt confident the cities had little do with each other.

Save for Damien, whom she dated for three years, Lelah had had no relationships more serious than sporadic sex partners and preliminary dates for more than ten years. Either she stopped calling the men or they her, the mutual interest petering out like the last few seconds of a song. What she'd said earlier about the inevitability of ending up alone had transpired in her own life without much fanfare. The time had passed, and one day not being with someone began to feel like the norm.

"What about you?" Lelah said. "You ever start coming around one of your girlfriends' kids?"

No answer. Judging from the slow rise and fall of his chest, David had fallen asleep. Lelah turned over and watched the river outside of the window.

A Life to Get on With

By the fifth month of Francis's absence, the chances of him and Viola reconciling and having one more child, let alone twelve, were quite low. Viola no longer believed he would return for her. She started saving money to leave Arkansas as soon as she could. She might have considered staying Down South, living in the shotgun house for the foreseeable future, had she not worked for the Jogget-ses. The work itself was not the problem; it was the commute. The bus ride began jovial enough, with her, Olivia, and Lucille cracking jokes and gossiping. Once they were on board there was a light, com-munal feeling among the other colored passengers. But as the dis-tance to Pine Bluff shrank, faces closed in on themselves; eyes dulled and jaws tightened. Viola imagined the indignities that others—maids, nannies, cooks, drivers, gardeners, construction workers, wait-ers—faced at their respective destinations. She would not let Cha-Cha grow up and face such indignities himself.

On one ride to work Viola caught Barry Stuttle staring at her. Twenty-five-year-old Barry Stuttle, son of Deacon Stuttle, one of the three old deacons at Reverend Tufts's church, must have had no clerical aspirations himself, because he wore a white chef's coat and cradled a tall paper chef's hat in his lap. He smiled when they finally met eyes. He had an underbite but was not terrible-looking. Viola did not smile back.

Lucille whispered in Viola's ear. "About time you noticed. He been eyein you like you owe him money for at least a week."

Viola shrugged.

"Wish I could pay him to look the other way."

She had attracted suitors since she was fourteen, some more promising than Francis in her parents' eyes. Men who were closer in age to Olivia or Lucille had shamelessly inquired after Viola instead. Olivia had never shown interest in a man. Lucille—the eldest, as quick to laugh as to curse folks out—once had a steady boyfriend, but he'd been drafted early on into the war, and she hadn't heard from him since.

The next morning, as they waited for the bus, Barry Stuttle cautioned a wave. Viola nodded, then turned away from him.

"You know," Olivia said. "Ain't no shame in movin on."

"None whatsoever," Lucille added. "Shoot, you did all what *you* was supposed to do. Ain't your fault the man ain't made good on his part of it. You got a child to feed and a life to get on with."

Viola had stopped going to church because she feared the disapproving eyeballs and the prying questions. She wondered if Reverend Tufts himself would judge her for moving on. The last time she'd gone to service, about a month after Francis's departure, she'd noticed Reverend Tufts moving in her direction through the after-church crowd. On impulse, she hurried out of the sanctuary before he could reach her. She wanted Tufts's approval and also felt angry with herself for caring what he thought. Every time Viola had spoken to him in the past she'd felt cornered, or scrutinized. Despite being short, he had a looming presence; he shrank others down when he spoke. Most women found him handsome, but Viola and her sisters weren't sure his looks made up for his demeanor.

"He so pushy," Lucille had said once. "He look like the type to bring a list with him into the bedroom, and he ain't done makin love till he check off *everything* he got in his mind to do."

Tufts represented a larger truth that troubled Viola: if she stayed in town, she'd always be defined by Francis's abandonment. He would be a shadow over her and Cha-Cha's life. She refused to let her husband's poor decisions define her life; she would save up and leave. Another month passed with Viola working sometimes sixty hours a week and saving three dollars out of every week's pay. She estimated that she'd need at least seventy dollars to feel good about her and Cha-Cha moving, to be able to contribute at whichever brother's household would have her until she found work. She wrote friendly, generic letters to her brothers up in Cleveland and Omaha in an attempt to feel out which location was better, whose wife would be the most welcoming. Clyde, James, and Josiah mailed short responses devoid of any useful information, and Viola suspected their wives had written the letters, given the neat penmanship. No matter, she would just have to take a chance on one of them when she had the money.

All of the planning and saving made her feel older, more confident about starting a life alone. Her love for Francis began to feel like a remnant from her juvenile past. What had there been between them, anyway? He'd seemed a prize, standing in that pulpit, the yearning to make people believe in him so clear on his face. And she'd won that prize. So much for all of that. Next time around she would look for a simple, hardworking man with a good heart, humble aspirations. It was just as Lucille had said: she was eighteen years old and had too much life in front of her to be without love.

Gotham in Detroit

· WINTER 1945 ·

A secondhand brown wool suit, a fur-lined hat, leather wingtips, and a pair of galoshes. Francis used the money he made working at a stamping plant on Jefferson to better equip himself for winter and improve his appearance. It was his fifth job, and it didn't pay as well as the salt mines, but he'd managed to work at the stamping plant a whole month without quitting or getting fired.

Galoshes were most appropriate for a night as icy as this one. Still, Francis wore the wingtips. They pinched his toes. He aimed to take Odella to the Gotham Hotel. He'd passed by the hotel on the bus, heard that Paul Robeson, Joe Louis, and local political figures had dined there. He would take Odella and elevate himself in her eyes, perhaps his own eyes too.

Lately, starting over seemed more feasible than returning to Arkansas, begging for Viola's forgiveness, and bringing his wife and child back up to Detroit. There was a good possibility that Viola would not forgive him. He had no way to explain the long months of silence. Better to make that silence permanent, to look forward, to push the guilt away from him and focus on making something of

himself with the woman he had in front of him. Odella was not exactly his woman, not yet, but he thought he might alleviate her apprehension about his young age and pennilessness by staying on at
the stamping plant and taking her on proper dates. Then, once he'd
saved up, he'd see about enrolling in school for something, maybe
becoming an electrician.

Francis drank a swallow of bourbon from his flask, balled up his
bedding, and headed downstairs. Odella sat in the parlor in a steel-
gray dress that hit below the knee and hugged her hips. She'd
rolled her hair at her neck and pinned a matching gray beret onto
her head at a fetching angle. Not the fanciest outfit Francis had
glimpsed in her basement apartment, but perhaps understated was
best tonight. You could dress so rich that you came off looking
poor.

Amos 'n Andy yammered on the radio. Francis turned the dial
down.

"Well, look who's finally turning into a city fellow," Odella said.

Francis moved to kiss her on the cheek, but she ducked out of
reach, picked up his bedding from where he'd left it on the sofa, and
put it in a closet.

"This who I am now," Francis said. He reached for her again, suc-
ceeded in kissing her on the temple. "I'm livin in the city, may as well
dress like it. Sides, if I aim to keep the attention of the likes a you, I
can't go around in no dusty duds."

Odella patted his shoulder.

"Aw, soldier," she said. "What I tell you when I first met you? You
already had the *posture* of a gentleman. But I guess it doesn't hurt to
have the clothes, too."

Life in Detroit did not slow down for winter, as Francis hoped it
might. Detroiters simply bought more coal or kindling for their heat
and piled fur on their backs. Odella wore such a fur—fox, with tails
shimmying along the shoulders, and one tail missing on the right
side. Francis had seen the fallen tail sitting on Odella's dresser, await-

ing repair. The first time she'd worn the fur Francis must have made a quizzical face because she quickly explained that it was a gift "from another life." He didn't ask for elaboration; he liked that both of them had other lives they'd left behind, secrets they would not force each other to share. Now he told Odella to wait in the parlor while he walked to Hastings to hail a cab.

"Where are we going, soldier? We can't walk?"

"It's downtown, and I don't aim to have you walkin no way. Not even round the corner."

"Downtown? Well, as long as we have reservations, that should be nice."

He kissed her again, this time right on those velvety lips that always encircled his own.

"I'ma dazzle you tonight, girl. Just wait."

He felt silly as he pulled on his coat and hat, his back turned to her. He'd never said such things to Viola. Where had the words even come from? Those damn radio shows, he guessed.

"Be ready when you hear the cab honk," he said.

The cold reached down his throat and snatched at his lungs, as it always did when he first stepped outside. The boardinghouse was a block away from Hastings. Francis had never thought of the distance in terms of actual steps before. Tonight he tiptoed over icy patches in his too tight shoes, the street desolate. It seemed to take ages to pass two houses. He was nervous about showing up at the Gotham. He hadn't made a reservation, hadn't even known to make one. Hell, if they couldn't get dinner, they could at least have a drink or two at the bar.

Up ahead, right before the corner, was an ice slick about three feet long. To his left Francis saw that the street was full of murky, brown, half-frozen sludge. He went gingerly forward on the ice. He chuckled at himself moving so softly, hunched over like a picture-show burglar in the middle of a heist. A whistle blew—a police whistle—and Francis stood up straight on instinct. He slipped. Slid on his right hip across the stretch of ice, the cold so fierce it felt like fire.

"Stop right there," the officer said from across the street, and Francis wanted to laugh. Where could he go without slipping again?

He stood, brushed off his suit as best he could. His wingtips had lost their shine.

"Just tryin to get a taxi," he told the officer. "Slipped on the ice."

The officer crunched across the street in shiny black boots. He had a smooth white face, save for his ruddy cheeks. Outside of work, Francis had experienced minimal contact with white people in Detroit, and no police run-ins at all. He'd heard that they did this, randomly approached colored men on the street and questioned them, tried to make them nervous. He was not yet nervous.

"Have you been drinking tonight?" the officer said. His name badge read WILLIAMS. "How many drinks have you had tonight, friend?"

An off-duty taxi slushed by. Was "friend" the Up North version of "boy"? Francis wondered.

"I ain't had no drinks," he said. "Just wore the wrong shoes."

He lifted up his leg to show the wingtips and nearly slipped again.

"No drinking at all?"

"None, sir."

"Where you headed?"

There were at least a dozen places within walking distance Francis could have named—bars, jazz halls, pool halls, restaurants, even Clydell's place on Beaubien, where he'd washed dishes. Instead he puffed out his chest and said, "Gotham Hotel, downtown. Got a lady friend waitin for me to come round once I get a cab."

The officer widened his eyes, pulled a side of his mouth up into a smirk.

"Alright, I think you'd better show me some identification, friend. Empty out your pockets too."

Francis didn't move. His flask was in his breast pocket, half full of bourbon. An older colored couple walked by, and Francis looked at them with pleading eyes. They did not seem to see him. He thought about Reverend Tufts, and how during the ten years in his care he'd never seen the man humiliated by anyone, colored or otherwise. What was it about himself that people in this city wanted to knock down?

He saw no way out of following the officer's instructions. He reached his hand into his coat pocket for his wallet.

"Oh, hello, Officer Williams."

Francis turned to see foxtails flying and a familiar pair of legs skipping across the ice in high heels.

"Odella Withers," Officer Williams said. "This man is a friend of yours?"

Odella appraised Francis, no doubt noticing his wet trousers and scuffed shoes.

"A tenant of mine," she said. "Which means he pays me money every week. Better than a friend, wouldn't you say?"

Odella's smile made Francis furious. Too wide, too gummy. Desperate. It didn't do that mouth of hers justice at all. In return Officer Williams offered her a quick grin but then tightened his lips once more.

"Your tenant is drunk," he said. "Says he's headed to the Gotham Hotel. Tonight."

Francis opened his mouth. Odella reached out and squeezed his arm.

"He's not drunk," she said. "Just clumsy, and not too familiar with restaurants and such up here. He's from Down South. It's his first Detroit winter."

"One of those newcomers, huh?" Williams looked at Francis with renewed contempt. "They're as likely as anyone else to be intoxicated in public. More likely, in my experience."

"Not this one," Odella persisted. "He's as green as this snow is cold."

"Well, you make sure he learns to be quick about showing identification when an officer of the law requests it." He turned and walked down Hastings without waiting for Odella's response.

Odella put her hand on the small of Francis's back. He shifted away.

"What?" she said. "Let's go on home, soldier. You're soaked, and I can feel you shivering."

It had started to snow shortly after Odella appeared. Now a snowflake landed in Francis's eye. A fire truck's siren wailed a few streets over.

"We still going to that hotel," he said. "I said I was takin you out tonight."

"And here I am, and we are *out*, aren't we?" Odella giggled and put her hands on her hips. "But the Gotham? Even with a reservation we'd have a hard time getting sat, no-named and colored as we are. Without it?" She tsked.

"What's my name matter?" Francis asked. "I got money to spend. And it's a colored hotel, ain't it? You tryin to tell me I ain't welcome there, or you just ashamed to be seen with me?"

Again she put her hand on the small of his back.

"You know what I mean, soldier. It's ran by our folks, sure, but you and I don't have the clout to just stroll through without reservations on a Friday night. Say, let's just get a bite someplace nearby. That'll be nice."

"You go on back to the house," he said. "I'm goin to the Gotham."

Francis walked off in that general direction. The sidewalk on Hastings was salted and shoveled, easier to traverse. He was a grown man, he reminded himself; why should he be afraid of getting a drink in a fancy hotel bar? It wasn't as if the bar was whites only; this was Detroit, not Pine Bluff. The worse that could happen was he'd get the menu, see the prices, and not be able to afford anything special. Still, he could afford a couple fingers of bourbon.

At Saint Antoine Street he lost his nerve, made a right instead of continuing to downtown. He climbed the stairs to his favorite blind pig. He sat in a dark corner and drank. At around 3 A.M. a barback nudged him awake. Francis sat up, then doubled over in his chair and vomited all over his scuffed-up wingtips.

· WEEK FOUR ·

Spring 2008

The Lucky Boy

When Troy and his partner, Higgins, first arrived at the house—
a two-story brick bungalow near the corner of McNichols
and Livernois—it had looked salvageable. Sure, the garage was up in
flames, but since even halfway decent houses usually had a thick fire-
resistant wall separating the garage from the living areas, he thought
it would be a short ordeal, over before noon. He watched the firefighters spray the roof with water, and slate smoke columns lick the
sky. He and Higgins helped keep onlookers at a safe distance. Higgins
was better at this; he was shorter than Troy but older at forty-nine,
and fatter. He used his belly like a flare, directing people away from
the house and fire engine. Troy used a more apologetic approach.
While Higgins said, "Stay back, I'm not gonna tell you again," Troy
offered, "Do me a favor and keep off this side of the street, okay?"
When he'd first joined the police force he realized he was just a little
too light-skinned, too young-looking—too pretty, really—to pull
off being the bad cop, especially next to Higgins. It just made people
giggle. The mother and two little girls who lived in the house were
fine, but a relative drove them to the hospital anyway, much to the
disappointment of the EMT guys in the ambulance. They'd wanted
something to show for having arrived on time.

Troy had stood witness to at least one hundred fires during his two and a half years as an officer. Accidental fires like this one appeared to be, fires in which the arsonist was caught, fires in which no arsonist was sought because the property had already been condemned and there weren't enough investigators to spare. He had never gone out on Devil's Night, the eve of Halloween, when mayhem and flames used to engulf certain parts of the city. Francis Turner was no great disciplinarian, but he prohibited anyone from leaving the Yarrow house on October 30. He'd sit in the armchair facing the door with a seldom used hunting rifle across his lap and a protective scowl on his face that remained even after he dozed off. Troy might have found ways to sneak out if he really wanted to, but the sight of Francis putting forth so much effort had made him feel loved.

The wind suddenly kicked up and the fire spread. All of the house's windows seemed to blow at once. There had been only one truck on the scene, eight firefighters in total. In less than twenty minutes the house was gone.

No sooner had the last hose been shut off than a big black pickup truck, an F150 with DENNING & SON GENERAL CONTRACTORS lettered in yellow on the side, came speeding up the street. A skinny old man driving, with a younger skinny guy — the son, Troy presumed — riding shotgun. They wanted to talk to the owners about rebuilding, give them an estimate. They'd heard about the fire on their police scanner. Troy told them to get lost. Higgins seconded.

"All we wanna do is leave a card with someone," the older one said. Troy couldn't tell if it was the sun or some kind of texturizer that was making the man's hair tint orange. "Or give us a phone number. They gonna need somebody to help em rebuild."

Someone from the small crowd of onlookers lobbed an empty Vernors bottle at the truck. It was plastic, and bounced off the rear bumper, but Denning and son wanted Troy and Higgins to arrest the thrower. Higgins laughed until he nearly choked, his whole body jiggling under his bulletproof vest. The contractors drove off.

The rest of the shift went by slowly. He and Higgins wrote fix-it tickets for broken headlights and too-dark window tint. At lunch Troy showed Higgins a grainy video on his phone of Camille's dance recital in Kaiserslautern, a gaggle of nine-year-old girls pirouetting to a song that sounded both Russian and Disney. Higgins played one of the newest beats that his twenty-one-year-old son had produced. It was very J Dilla–esque, Troy thought, with mellow drums and looped snatches of soulful vocals in the background. If he could somehow just fast-forward to having a son at that age, full-grown and already out the house—someone to hang out with, but without the burden of being a disciplinarian—he wouldn't have minded.

"You heard about these furloughs, right?" Higgins said, his mouth full of gyro. "They tryna get city workers to take one day off a month now for free, maybe more later."

Troy had not heard.

"They better not pull that shit at the department, alls I know." Higgins dabbed yogurt sauce from his mouth with a napkin. "But if they do, I'll give you a heads-up soon as I hear. Give you some time to save up."

All week Troy had wanted to tell Higgins about his plan to buy a house on the east side, mostly because the few people who knew the particulars—that the house was worthless, that it was his mother's house—weren't impressed and he hoped Higgins might be. Higgins was a believer in the city, one of those Detroiters who'd stayed in his neighborhood on principle (although that was easier to do when one lived in Chandler Park, versus on Yarrow Street, where crime was higher and the population smaller). But Troy held back from saying anything because Higgins was a gossip, had been with the department for fourteen years and knew too many people.

"I doubt they do that," Troy said. "It's about to get hot. They know niggas start killin each other when it gets too hot outside."

Higgins nodded.

"True. They probably won't change nothing before summer's over.

Maybe no more overtime though. I know one thing, we gotta stop voting these crooked niggas into office. For the sake of our own paychecks at this point."

Troy couldn't debate the crookedness of their current mayor, but it bothered him when people, particularly black people, bought in to the notion that black politicians were really the ones who'd run the city into the ground. He knew enough history to understand that things had begun to go bad way before that. David Gardenhire and he often talked about resources—both the personal and the public—and how the problem with Detroit was that it had experienced a resource vacuum during white flight. Hundreds of thousands of black people who were never really welcome here, a lot with no access to higher education, were essentially left to run the city. They did a decent job in the beginning, back in the early days of Coleman Young, the first black mayor, but the surrounding suburbs hadn't wanted to do business with them—they essentially boycotted the newer, blacker Detroit—which would devastate any city's economy. During that same time the automakers made poor decisions, which made things worse. But it was the removal of money, the *resources*, he and David agreed, that had put things on a downward trend. Troy knew Higgins would argue him to death over this. Higgins would list off every corrupt mayor, councilperson, and committee chair since the eighties at least. Troy had heard him go through his Who's Who of city crooks before. So Troy ate his gyro and asked to hear Higgins's son's beat again.

"I'm thinking about getting a tattoo," Higgins said. "First ever."

"Ain't you bout to turn fifty? What for? Midlife crisis? Get a bike or something. A new car."

"Nah, I got fifteen years of service comin up. Longer than I'd ever thought I'd make. So it's either a tattoo or a party. I like parties, but not throwin them. Too much hassle."

Higgins said he was deciding between two Latin phrases, which Troy found oddly pretentious for a man who liked his burgers to consist of only meat and bun. It had taken Troy months to convince him to try the gyro with a little yogurt sauce.

"Either 'Speramus Meliora,' which means 'We hope for better things,'" Higgins said, "Or 'Tuebor,' 'from the badge.'" He tapped his finger on the shield pinned to his chest. It was silver, with the word TUEBOR in the middle of a crest, flanked by two stags.

"'I will defend,'" Troy said, proud to have retained something from training. "Not bad."

"Yeah, but a bunch of guys already have Tuebor tats. 'Speramus Meliora' is from the city flag, part of the motto. I never seen that on nobody. But 'Tuebor' relates more to being a cop. I don't know."

If Troy had ever learned the Detroit city motto in school, he must have forgotten it years ago.

"Don't get 'We hope for better things,'" he told Higgins. "It's weak."

"How's it weak? Everybody wants better things. Shit, *you* sure as hell want better things. And you got a million schemes cookin in that little bird brain of yours to get em." Higgins chuckled.

"Fuck you," Troy said. "I don't just sit around hopin for nothing. I *do* shit. It's the 'hope' part that fucks that line all up. You should change it to somethin like, 'We *fight* for better things,' or 'We *work* for better things.' Or 'We *plan* for better things.' That's what's wrong with this city; it ain't about the mayor. Too many people busy *hoping* shit will get better to actually figure out a way to *make* shit better."

"You're thinkin too hard, Turner," Higgins said. He often accused Troy of doing this. "I'm not changin the words. I'll just get 'Tuebor.' 'Speramus Meliora' sound like a disease anyway. Like a rash."

"It sounds like a spell," Troy said. "Like from those Harry Potter movies Camille watches. Some shit you say before you turn somebody into a toad."

After his shift Troy hurried to an office supply store for an ink pad, then drove over to Cha-Cha's house.

A ranch house. Troy still didn't get it. Why would Cha-Cha build this sort of low, wide, wraparound house in a Detroit suburb, where the heating system had to work double time to warm the spread-out rooms? He'd seen these one-story, hallway-centric designs in California. They made sense there; they stayed cool. They made no sense here.

He had a key because everyone had a key to Cha-Cha's house. He saw no cars in the driveway but knocked anyway, just in case someone besides his mother was home. Tina never left Viola alone for more than an hour or two.

Tina yanked the door open. Her short hair stuck up all over her head.

"Cha-Cha ain't here," she said.

"I came to see Mama."

"Really? You know what? That's perfect, actually."

She turned and left him in the entryway. He heard a door slam, water running, keys jingling. The house smelled stale, like they hadn't opened a window all week. Rarely had he come by here and not smelled food in the air from something Tina had cooked earlier that day. He remembered standing in this entryway as a teenager, having been let in from the cold, but still waiting for Chucky and Todd to get ready so Tina could take them all to school. The tile on the floor was different now, and they'd added a fancy little console table that held keys and mail. He used to feel like an interloper, as if he were standing on the outside of a more perfect family.

Tina returned with a baseball cap on her head and her purse on her shoulder.

"I need to step out right quick. Just gonna drive around. Yeah. No more than a hour, hour and a half."

"Alright," Troy said. Tina's small eyes were wide open. She looked haggard, a little wired. Troy remembered that on some of those mornings she would come out of her and Cha-Cha's room in a purple terry cloth bathrobe. Her thighs would peek in and out of view as she rushed around making lunches and ironing clothes. He remembered being thirteen or fourteen, hoping for these quick glimpses of her legs, and feeling a jolt in his crotch when he got them.

She put a hand on his arm, whispered in his ear, "She's sleep right now, and I think she's upset about this uh, I don't even wanna get into it. Something her and Cha-Cha were talking about earlier. She'll probably wake up soon."

"Well if it ain't my Lucky Boy," Viola said. She was not asleep. Troy had never walked into a room and found Viola asleep when others said she was. He'd come to think she was just a great pretender and only slept a few hours at night. She looked him up and down. The dresser drawer with her social security card and identification was to the right of him. Had she been asleep, he could have copied these things before having to finagle the thumbprint. He carried the ink pad in one pocket and a folded-up piece of printer paper in the other. The fat man on the phone hadn't advised on the best method to secure the thumbprint, so Troy would improvise.

"You come to harass me too?" Viola asked. "Cha-Cha done already beat you to it."

Troy walked over to the far side of the bed and kissed Viola's dry cheek.

"Yep, he already got me worked up. That boy's crazy. Got me locked up in this house all day *every* day, then has the nerve to come in here and mess with me."

"Nah, Mama, I just came to say hi." He did not want to hear about Cha-Cha. Viola could complain about Cha-Cha all day if you allowed her, just as she could Francis Turner, never mind that he was dead. The constant complaining suggested that she cared for them most.

"Mama, I'm tryna do an ancestry thing, like a family tree thing? And I need your birth certificate and stuff to look up our history on the Internet." He inched toward the dresser. Viola used her arms to help her sit up straight. Troy wondered at her upper-body strength.

"Come here. You really lookin like the Law today, with them shiny shoes on. One a these days you gotta come by in the *whole* uniform. That'll be nice."

He sat at the foot of the bed and put his hand in her outstretched one. Viola spent a full minute looking at him. His face, his hand in hers, his face again. Troy knew he was spoiled. Not in the way that many people think of being spoiled, with things; he'd been spoiled simply by being noticed. Noticed in a way that all of the boys between him and Cha-Cha weren't, noticed in a way he didn't think any of the girls were noticed by virtue of their womanhood, and the utilitarian, unsentimental that way Viola and Francis had raised their young women. He never felt lucky because of this. The extra attention felt like scrutiny, not doting. He stood back up.

"They got a database of fingerprints . . . kinda like we have at the police department, but it's a lot more."

"I don't have no fingerprints in nobody's database."

"I know, Mama, but they can match family members, they can look for a close match. If I take your fingerprint, the thumb, I can scan it into the computer, send it to them, then they'll match it."

"You shoulda done that for your daddy. I already know *my* people. You know Josiah and James passed, but you met they children before. And Clyde still alive, still old and mean. Olivia and Lucille passed, but—"

"I'm not talking about your siblings, Mama. I mean family from Virginia, and even before Virginia. They can take the fingerprint and match it to tribes in Africa, sometimes. Like I said, they got this uh, technology, that can search and match up people from a long time ago."

Viola laughed.

"What's funny?" He tried to smile.

"You know what I do all day, Lucky Boy? I sit right here and I watch that TV. I got my stories, I got my church shows, my judge shows, the show where they build the houses, all kinda shows up in that TV. And then I got the long commercials, they got a special word for them long commercials, what's that word?"

"Infomercials, Mama." The view from Viola's window was of the cusp of the cul-de-sac, where instead of more houses there was a tiny park. Just a mowed patch of grass and a bench surrounded by trees.

"That's it. *Info*mercials," she said. "Oh, I know all of em by heart. They come on when I can't sleep at night cause, you know, my chest hurts, and up under my arms hurts. Don't get old, Lucky Boy, lemme tell you. Anyhow, I watch them *info*mercials with the sound down low most times, but I already know the words. They got the one for the fancy treadmill where they look like they flyin, you seen that?"

"Mama, I don't know. I was tryna explain to you how the ancestry—"

Viola smiled and went on talking.

"They got another one that I see *all* the time, every day, seem like. It's all about paper, shredding paper, getting rid of the mail with your name on it, all that kinda stuff. You seen it?"

"Nah, Mama. I haven't seen that one."

"Well, it starts out with a couple men in all black, they got masks on so you can't even see if they black or white, but either way they lookin like thugs. They run up in somebody's house at night, but— and this where I *always* get surprised—they not looking for the jewelry, or the china, Lucky Boy. They lookin for papers! They go straight to the office and start rummagin through papers. And then a white man come on the screen in a suit and says, 'Nowadays'"—Viola did a deep-voiced impression—"'your identity could be the most valuable thing in your home.' He's not a bad-lookin white man, either, which is how I remember."

She smiled again. Her glossy eyes twinkled.

"Here," he said. He stood up, opened the drawer, and took out the plastic bag full of documents. "Let me make the copies first, then I'll come back and explain how the fingerprint works, cause it's not like you think."

He was actually impressed. His mother, who had always been sharp, still had her wits about her. This had been the case three years earlier, when he lived on Yarrow for a short time after retiring from the navy, but she'd had two strokes since then. He'd mistaken her physical degeneration for an intellectual one as well. Fucking infomercials, he thought. He couldn't imagine spending so much time watching television that he began to take the infomercials seriously.

He made copies of her social security card and birth certificate on Cha-Cha's printer-scanner-fax-copier. The living room was a mess. A stack of printouts sat on the loveseat, a cold cup of coffee sat on the floor. He did not look at the papers; whatever Cha-Cha and Tina had found interesting enough to print out from the Internet would surely not interest him. He once again thought of his teenage self, standing in the entryway and wanting to belong here. Now Cha-Cha and Tina's lives seemed terribly boring, as did their son Chucky's, as would Todd's once he left the service. He went back into his mother's bedroom.

He put the originals back in her dresser drawer and sat on the bed again, this time closer to Viola. She smelled like strong soap and baby powder. There were various small yellow plastic buckets stacked on the nightstand. Troy couldn't imagine their purpose. He wondered if she used a bedpan or just wore Depends.

"So the fingerprint isn't public unless you want it to be," he said. "You gotta opt in to making it part of the public database, and the way it works is that so many other people have opted in that *that's* how you get a match. But I wouldn't make your fingerprint public cause then, you're right, somebody could steal it and maybe steal your identity."

Viola nodded.

"Mmm-hmm. Now I understand. You say you need the thumb, right?"

She stuck out her hand. She clearly saw his explanation for the bullshit that it was, but she loved him, and it seemed as if his lying had tickled her, provided a bit of entertainment. He pressed her thumb onto the ink pad, onto the piece of folded-up paper, and then used a sheet from the box of baby wipes on her nightstand to wipe the ink away.

They sat there not saying anything for a while, Viola looking Troy up and down again.

"You know, Lucky Boy, I'm in a lotta pain," she said. "Folks think I like to exaggerate, but I'm not. All in my arms and my chest it hurts, like I said. Especially right now cause I ain't had enough pills this morning. And on top of that Cha-Cha got me feelin down. You know what you could do for me?"

"What you need, Mama?"

"Take me for a ride, like how you used to drive me around the east side. You got your truck? You just gotta lift me up into the seat, we don't gotta bring the wheelchair. Just ride me around for a little while."

He felt he could not spend another minute with her today. It was impossible. He stood up, collected his papers, and kissed her on the forehead.

"Next time, Mama. I gotta go."

BACK ON THE east side, Mrs. Gardenhire listened to the TV but did not look at it. Meerkats and large African lizards scampered across the 46-inch screen.

"Mama, why not face the TV instead of the door?" David asked. "It's got a great picture."

"Picture's *too* clear is the problem. Makes me feel like the animals is here in the room."

"Well, I thought you said the old one hurt your eyes."

"That's what I thought was hurting them," Mrs. Gardenhire said. "But now that you brought this new one, I figured out they just plain hurt."

She faced the doorway where David stood, but her focus was on the TV in the far corner. She tilted her head toward it, and when the creatures sounded like they were in peril—a lion stalked onto the scene, say—she shot a peripheral glance at the screen until the danger receded.

David's brother Greg had pawned their mother's old 32-inch flat panel two months earlier. It was a move too stereotypical to be heartbreaking for David—a drug addict stealing his mother's TV—but it did anger him. Mrs. Gardenhire, queen of second and third and thirtieth chances, waited three weeks before telling David the TV was gone. Three whole weeks without her animal shows. David bought her a brand-new 46-inch LED flat screen and vowed to stop by more often.

"Where's Greg at?" he asked.

David leaned against the front door's frame. He planned to stay in the front room the duration of this visit, as he did most visits if he could help it. The house was crammed with pictures he'd rather not see. Of Greg when he still looked related to David, before his long-term relationship with heroin aged him a good twenty years. Of their dead father, Gregory Sr. Of David's ex-wife. His mother wouldn't look at the television head-on, but she cherished frequent glances into the past. David did not.

Mrs. Gardenhire shifted her weight in her armchair.

"What's today? Tuesday? If it's Tuesday, then I ain't seen him since last Thursday."

"It's Tuesday," David said.

"Well, he ain't came around since Thursday, then. I gave him fifteen dollars to weed my annuals, and he took off," she said. "He ain't weeded nothin before he left, either."

Mrs. Gardenhire had a twitch in her shoulder that made it bounce up and down involuntarily. A delicate movement like a bird preening its feathers. David fought a familiar urge to put his hand on the shoulder to calm it down. His mother didn't like attention called to her condition.

"I'll take care of the annuals right now, Mama. You just stop giving Greg your money."

A genuine two-shouldered shrug from Mrs. Gardenhire, followed by a sigh.

Outside, David took off his T-shirt and left it folded on the porch. He knew nothing about weeding but figured anything that wasn't pretty should be yanked up. He'd bought the lot next to his mother's house as a sort of garden annex several years before. Then he purchased several other properties on the east side, places where people had once worked hard, hazardous jobs to pay their mortgages, all for less than five thousand dollars. He owned property in a more desirable neighborhood downriver, but he liked to tell people that one day the east side houses would make him rich. Truth was, landlording his east side properties was more time-consuming than he'd expected, and he planned to purchase empty lots moving forward.

Words like *ghetto*, *dilapidated*, and *run-down* were inadequate to describe this portion of the city, David thought. An apt descriptor eluded him, but Kyle, a geeky kid on his installation team, had come the closest.

"This isn't postindustrial, post-white-flight, or post-automobile-boom," Kyle had said. "It's like, post-zombie-fucking-apocalypse. This is like after the zombies have turned everyone they could find, and then they burn down the buildings to run out the last survivors—right into their clutches and shit."

They'd been sitting on the back bumper of David's van drinking a beer; Kyle had just turned twenty-one.

"Okay, I can see zombie apocalypse," David said, although comic books had been his brother Greg's thing, not his. "But what about the houses still standing?"

"Simple. Just-turned zombies are still sort of human in the brain, you know? They're prone to human sentimentality in the beginning. So the houses they lived in, they naturally don't go as hard on them. Maybe they do a rudimentary prowl of the rooms, but they can't bring themselves to burn them down. So if their families are in the basement hiding in airtight saunas or whatever, they get passed over."

The airtight saunas had thrown David for a loop, but the zombie-apocalypse part stayed with him. He liked how unabashedly nerdy Kyle was, and wondered if he'd had to fight to keep himself that way coming up over in Brightmoor, or if things were different now.

In his basketball shorts and sneakers David could have been anyone. He could have been the David from twenty years before, and he could still have belonged to this block, barren as it was. He was not like Troy, who held on to a notion of still fitting in the neighborhood. David knew that if it weren't for his mother and his few tenants, he'd have no reason to visit the east side. But he was not from anywhere else, either. Not San Diego, where he'd kept an apartment for ten years for the sporadic periods when he wasn't on a ship. He didn't belong to where he lived now, near the river; no one was really *from* that fledgling neighborhood. He'd looked into more established "hip" neighborhoods in Midtown, but they weren't for him. He was too smart to pretend he was alright with being a token in a city with such a large black population, with walking into new restaurants where the all-white patrons looked at him with suspicion, as if his very presence suggested that they weren't as close to "revitalizing" the area as they'd hoped.

Mr. McNair rattled the garden's gate. Short pants, Redwings cap, and polo shirt. David let the old man in.

"Betsy got you out here gardening?" Mr. McNair asked.

"Nothing too skilled, just some weeding," David said.

It bothered him that Mr. McNair always called his mother by her first name. McNair never called Troy's mother by her first name, nor Mrs. Breedlove from up the street. True, David's mother was some fifteen years younger than the other two women, but it still seemed improper.

"Weedin? Boy, looks like you just yanked up some good stuff," McNair said. "Let me see."

Mr. McNair took the bunch of curling leaves from David's hand and sniffed them. Then he laughed and slid them into his shirt pocket.

"These is basil, David. Good basil. I'll just take em and you can blame me if Betsy comes lookin."

Embarrassed, David stood up and went to the porch for his shirt. When he returned to the garden Mr. McNair was patting his shirt pocket and looking at David oddly, as if trying to decide whether David had committed some crime he'd heard about. The ropy veins in McNair's neck bulged.

"What's going on, Mr. McNair? Something bothering you?"

This could be more bad news about Greg, David thought. In the winter McNair had caught Greg stealing aluminum siding off of Mrs. Breedlove's house. Ever since Viola Turner moved away, Mrs. Breedlove had been his mother's only remaining friend. The news about Greg's theft humiliated her so much that for weeks she'd begged off of Mrs. Breedlove's invitations to come play pinochle. Or maybe it was not about Greg. Maybe it was finally time for McNair to confess that he was more than a friend to David's mother. Maybe he would make an honest woman out of her, old as they both were.

"You talk to Troy Turner lately?" McNair asked.

David chuckled out of relief.

"I seen Troy Turner a couple weeks ago. Why?"

"Somethin's goin on over there on Yarrow," McNair said. He looked over his shoulder in the direction of the street.

"What do you mean? Something like what?"

"Well, somethin like *somebody*. Somebody's been in and out of there for a few weeks." Mr. McNair lowered himself onto a log in the shade of the house.

"Used to be, right after Mrs. Turner moved out, folks would stop by all the time," he added. "But nowadays Cha-Cha only comes by when I call to have him check something out. So something ain't right."

"They're coming in and out with a key?" David asked.

"Looks like. They got a key to the gate, the back garage, and the house."

So what's the problem? David wondered. The sun shone from high in the sky, and he was ready to get back home and into the shower. An hour or two of silence would do him good right now, he thought.

"What do you want me to do, Mr. McNair? It sounds legal."

"Hell, I don't know about legal or illegal. All I know is it's strange. I wouldn't think so if it was Troy or somebody." Mr. McNair paused, leaned in closer. "But it's little Lelah, David. What business she got sneakin in and out of there like some junkie thief?"

David did not wince. Both of them knew these last few words were too much. The old man opened his mouth to apologize, but David raised a hand to say it was okay.

Lelah could have been scheming on the house too, trying to figure out a way to short-sell or otherwise profit from it. The thought saddened him. That house wasn't worth more than three thousand dollars if it was worth a dollar. Troy might have had his reasons, but a family of adults fighting over a scrap of worthless land was too depressing. Lelah who collected her brothers' postcards in a scrapbook in high school. Lelah who had told David he wasn't "worldly" enough for her, even though neither of them had ever traveled outside Michigan. Lelah who looked the same, her extra weight having settled in all the right places.

"I think it's nothing to be worried about," David said. He wiped his hands on the front of his shirt and ushered McNair to the gate. "If they got a key and there's nothing left to steal inside, then I say leave it alone."

Mr. McNair pulled the basil out of his pocket and sniffed it once more. He nodded.

"I suppose she's got as much a right as any of the other ones to be in there. You tell Betsy I came by."

David watched Mr. McNair cross the street and round the corner. He wondered what he'd really been trying to get at. The conversation had a doublespeak quality to it, like the way two spies in a movie can appear to be discussing holiday travel plans when they're really plotting an assassination.

Addiction Is Real

When Lelah dropped Bobbie off the night before, Brianne had pressed $40 into her palm, and Lelah took it without protest or question because she was eager to get to David's. In the big room she'd added the money to her meager stash in the pocket of a duffel bag under the bed. She should have questioned Brianne about the money, tried to put up a fight for appearance's sake, but also it was about time her daughter compensated her a little. Childcare was expensive. Maybe Rob had finally made good on his promises of child support. At the very least Lelah should have found out if the money would be recurring, or where it came from. Something in Brianne's behavior suggested a secret, and under normal circumstances Lelah would have drawn it out by now. Maybe she was seeing someone new. That could be a good thing, Lelah supposed. Far be it for her to begrudge someone a chance at romance. But taking money from a man was a different story. No time like the present to find out what's going on, she thought. She showered and dressed. She had hang-dried her clothes on the bathroom shower rod, and the wrinkles in her jeans didn't disappear after she squeezed herself into them. She took the $40 back out of the duffel bag. She'd stop by

Eastern Market for some of that pineapple-coconut cake Brianne liked, then pop by her daughter's apartment, clearing-the-air cake in hand.

A man stood on the porch in front of the window. Lelah could tell from where she stood on the staircase that it was David. His body was already that familiar. His pointy elbows were up and out, his long hands over his brow. He was trying to see through the curtains. It's going to be over already, she thought. She opened the door.

"Hey," he said. "I, uh."

"Come in if you want."

David ducked as he walked in, as if the doorframe wasn't tall enough for him. He smelled like fresh dirt, cut grass, and sweat.

Lelah looked him in the eyes, reminded herself that days ago he was any old person she used to know on the street. He looked away, past her to the living room's bare and dingy walls.

"I don't know why I'm here," he said. "I was just over at my mom's, and Mr. McNair told me he saw you."

She could laugh. Of course it was McNair—he'd likely known since the first morning, and told everybody on three blocks each way from Yarrow. She hadn't put enough thought into this. How easy it was to fool oneself when desperate.

"What do you want from me?" she asked. She sat down on the second-to-last stair. David stood above her at first, but he seemed to still be having trouble making eye contact and opted to sit down next to her. Their hips touched. He did not turn to look at her.

"What do you mean? I just heard you were here, and I don't know why he was telling me in the first place, like he was asking me for advice or something. I guess he wanted me to tell Troy, but I couldn't do that, considering."

"Considering what?" Lelah asked. She looked at the side of his face.

David stretched his long fingers away from one another.

"Considering," he said, "that I didn't even know if it was true, or what the situation is."

The skin of David's palms had none of the pinkish undertones of Lelah's own. It was yellow, and his lifelines deep and dark.

"Also considering that we been seeing each other, Lelah. And if *that's* none of Troy's business—"

"It *isn't*," Lelah interrupted.

"Then I figured I'd come over here and see what this is all about. Maybe this ain't any of Troy's business either."

He looked at her now. He had no right to come here, she thought. Asking for an explanation, expecting to get one just for showing up.

"I don't need saving, David. I'm here, you've found me out, that's fine. But I don't need anybody to save me."

"God, nobody's trying to save you," he said. "I don't know. I didn't think everything out before I came over, but here I am, right?"

Lelah felt the situation was plain; she was there because she had nowhere else to go. But maybe it wasn't clear for someone like David, someone who had likely never been evicted and had connections all around the city.

"Your apartment," David began, and Lelah saw that he was going to make her say it all out loud, that he wouldn't just break off whatever they had and leave.

"My apartment does not exist."

"Your job?"

"May or may not exist, it's still up in the air."

"What happened to your stuff, like furniture and clothes?"

He's never been evicted, Lelah thought.

"I'll show you," she said. She jumped up and turned to climb the stairs. David followed.

Lelah stepped into the big room, and David lingered in the doorway. She didn't know what she hoped to accomplish with this. Maybe the meager furnishings—an ancient twin bed, a flimsy chest of drawers—would repulse him into leaving her be. David did not appear repulsed.

"This used to be Troy's room, huh? I remember this upstairs window."

"It was everybody's room at some point," Lelah said. "Except mine."

And then, because waiting for his questions was excruciating, Lelah confessed. Not a true confession, but an abridged, smoothed-over version of what she'd done to end up back on Yarrow. That she had fallen behind on rent because she "used to gamble" and had some "bad debt." That Dwayne the lonely widower sexually harassed her at work. That she'd borrowed a couple hundred dollars from him long before that, and because of this the phone company was investigating.

David didn't say anything after she finished talking, so she felt compelled to repeat, "I'm not looking for you to save me. I'll have it all taken care of soon."

"Why not stay with your daughter?"

Lelah sighed and passed her hand through the air in front of her.

"Have you talked to someone about the gambling?"

"Yes," she said. "I been to Gamblers Anonymous. I haven't gambled in a long time."

"That's good," David said. "Addiction is real."

How was it possible that Troy and this man were friends? Lelah wondered. "Addiction is real" were three words Troy Turner would never say, and words for which Lelah had no response. They were three words that cut to the heart of a certain kind of truth but still failed to capture the seriousness of the problem. Lelah and David sat quietly, and the sounds of the street amplified. The chirrup of squirrels making mischief in the lot next door. A distant tire screech and the bass-induced rattle of a car's cheap sound system.

"Why do you, I mean, why *did* you do it?"

Lelah couldn't say. She could have talked about Missouri, and Vernon chasing her around their little apartment and the fleeting look on his face of genuine hate before he punched her in the stomach, the chest, the mouth, and finally the eye, but wasn't that a long time ago?

Lelah knew she was supposed to be past it. She wanted to say something about the nature of the stillness, but she didn't have the right words to explain that feeling. She thought of comparing it to David's own cherished meditating, his need for silence, but she knew they weren't the same thing. When David meditated, he wanted nothing. When Lelah was still at the roulette table, she wanted everything. The story of her day-to-day stopped and was replaced by possibility for as long as she could maintain the stillness. She could walk out and be anyone, and more than a specific fantasy, the multitude of outcomes captivated her. Just turning the idea over in her head right now made her crave it. She could feel it in her thumbs.

"I can't explain," she said, and David nodded, as if he'd never thought she would. They sat in silence again.

"Really," David said finally. "You're grown, and you don't have no overhead here."

Lelah wasn't sure if he was trying to convince himself or her. It was too soon for her to be so desperate for his approval, but she was. He didn't need her, yet it was clear he still wanted her, and even though she hadn't told him the whole truth, she felt unburdened for finally telling someone a portion of it. He hadn't left yet.

"You ever been up here before?" she asked.

"Me? No, I feel like every time I used to come see Troy your mother was in her chair right by the stairs, ready to pounce on me if I went up."

Lelah smiled.

"Yeah, by the time Troy and me were growing up she'd gotten real paranoid about being robbed, so she didn't let anybody up who wasn't family."

She stood. If she did not act crushed by his presence here, if she could act natural, then he still might respect her.

"Let me give you a tour, then," she said.

She showed him the tiny teal-painted bathroom, thankfully devoid of her drying underwear. She told him about how she and Brianne had lived in the girls' room when they first moved back from Missouri, and her sister Marlene, newly divorced, had lived in the boys' room. When Brianne was four she'd announced that she needed her own dresser, a place where her clothes weren't up against her mother's. Marlene and Viola found her a child's dresser and vanity at a flea market, miraculously painted a terrible shade of pink similar to the girls' room walls. Brianne had insisted on taking the dresser with her when she and Lelah moved off Yarrow, and she continued to drag it from little apartment to little apartment, all the way up until she went away to college. Lelah wished she knew what had happened to it.

Back downstairs she re-created the living and dining rooms for him, where furniture used to be, who used to like to sit where at the table. In the basement Lelah told David about Lonnie's band practices, and did her best to seem uninterested when he pulled a clump of track and field medals out of a memories box to inspect.

In the center of the basement, over a drain in the cement floor, an ancient water hose hung over an exposed beam. The other end of the hose was attached to the sink against the wall.

"You ever use this?" David asked.

"Not since I was twelve," Lelah said. "That was for the boys in the summer. They'd take showers down here so us girls could have more time in the bathroom upstairs."

David walked over to the sink and turned the faucet. In the light coming through the high windows Lelah saw the hose twitch, then the water gush out brown. She took a step back from it. Soon it ran clear. David took off his shorts and shoes and shirt and smiled at her, a look she'd come to recognize. Although it was chilly and she feared spiders or mice, she undressed as well. She joined him under the hose, pressed her breasts against him for warmth. He lifted his arms up, reached behind her head and unwound her hair band. In another life this would have been presumptuous, wetting her hair without asking. But in this life in which she hadn't felt another person touch her scalp in too long, his fingers were welcome. She kissed his collarbone, reached up for his neck.

When David entered her, what Lelah felt was relief. She didn't need him to save her, but she did need this, whatever it was and no matter what it meant, for as long as she could manage to hold on to it.

Sometimes It's Gotta Be You

After being denied three times (the biblical significance was not lost on him), Cha-Cha drove around Detroit for several hours. All the way down Grand River to Warren, up Warren to Van Dyke and past Kettering High School, where Russell had been among the inaugural class. He wound his way through smaller residential streets, surprised by his ability to navigate them intuitively. They were like a system of familiar tributaries leading to a vital body of water. He lacked the nerve to face the house on Yarrow, ostensibly the site of his undoing, so he made his way to East Grand Boulevard instead. The old Packard plant stood in more or less the same state of decay since the last time he'd driven by it—blasted-out windows, cryptic messages graffitied across the walls, the scars of past fires evident here and there. What depressed him more than the ruined factory were the houses farther up the boulevard that he'd coveted growing up, now blighted and abandoned. Those big houses, with their high porches so far off from the street, could have easily housed a family with thirteen children. Now the wide center islands on some blocks were so overgrown with weeds and grass, a child could hide in them.

He took Mack over to Gratiot and drove north for more than a half hour until he reached the cemetery where Francis Turner's remains resided.

In the center of a row of flat gravestones, Francis's own stone was so besieged by untended lawn that only

ANCIS R. TUR
ELOVED FATH
I Corinthians 13:

could be made out in the center. Cha-Cha kicked back the weeds, whacked at them with his cane. He considered stooping over to yank up a few tufts but knew the effort would be futile. Viola was the only one who visited the place, and even she hadn't been by for at least a year. The space of grass next to Francis's stone remained empty in anticipation of the day that Viola would occupy it.

He stood there for a long time, looking to the rest of the cemetery like an estranged son or brother finally paying his respects. The urge to cry rose up again, but Cha-Cha knew better and tamped it down. His father would not have wanted tears at his gravesite or anywhere else. It was likely the reason so few Turners visited this place; they could not imagine their father encouraging them to talk to the ground, to whisper or weep before a granite slab. There was a wrought-iron bench several rows out from Francis's grave, closer to the narrow road. Cha-Cha sat down. His left eyelid twitched, as it used to when he drove long distances overnight. Fatigue. There could be haints here, Cha-Cha thought. The entire cemetery could be populated with ghosts that chose not to show themselves to him. His father could be among them.

The second sighting of something extraordinary is not supposed to live up to the first. Cha-Cha expected to feel less bothered, less fearful in the presence of his haint on subsequent nights. The opposite was true. Still no fanfare, no boogieman theatrics. The light and the sound remained the same. Was it a hallucination? He'd read online that when a person's vision failed—from cataracts, say—the brain could transmit images that mimicked actual seeing. Colorful shapes. People in elaborate costumes. Scenes remembered, and even some never witnessed before. Our brains could be that generous to us. But Cha-Cha thought his eyesight was fine. He'd never even worn reading glasses. For three nights he moved from room to room in his house, hoping each time he would be able to sleep. Insomnia was its own kind of haunting. He became familiar with the clicks and sighs of the house, the soft breathing of his wife, which he hadn't paid attention to since the nights they slept in shifts with newborn babies nearby. Viola seemed to sleep in two-hour intervals. He'd hear her wheezing breath settle into a steady snore, then sometime later her TV clicking through channels, the volume raised a few decibels.

The haint was a large and fathomless unknowing. A challenge. A taunt. On the third night, when Cha-Cha tried to sleep in the basement, he found the nerve to get up and put his hand to it. The blue light felt like nothing, the same temperature as the air around it, and his hand glowed as it might in front of his big screen when he switched the input to DVD. A spotlight from nowhere.

The following afternoon he decided to contact his siblings. He had no friends, and the sleepless nights made him desperate. Plus, Alice had told him several months before that he needed to start "tapping into his resources" for emotional support, seeking help from the people he helped all the time.

Francey, Second Child, Sixty-Two Years Old:
"You wanna know what I remember from the actual incident? Hmm . . . Honestly, I been thinking about this more since you came over and put in my filter. Now that I stopped eating meat, I feel like I can

remember all sorts of things better, you know. Like it's all high-def now. Of *course* I remember *thinking* there was a haint up in your room."

"And?"

"And what, Cha-Cha? We were young, and when I moved into the big room I didn't have any problems, so I don't know. You been reading that Zora book?"

"A little. I been reading up on hallucinations too."

"Jesus, don't read that, Cha. You're not hallucinating."

"According to Alice I might be. I don't think I am, but—"

"You need to let go of that Western mindset, I keep telling you. Had I listened to them after I got sick, I'da ruined my liver and kidneys by now, taking a million pills a day. These white folks don't know everything, trust me."

"Alice isn't white."

"Still. You know what I mean. Anyway, what's going on with the house? Rahul told me that you could maybe get some type of tax write-off if you short-sell it."

"Francey, do you remember what it looked like? It was blue, right?"

"He didn't show it to us yet. He said it's called an MI-X form or an MI-2 maybe, if you want to look it up."

Quincy, Third Child, Fifty-Nine Years Old:
"The problem is all those *women* up there with you. You know I love our sisters, Cha, but they're *hysterical.* I don't doubt they'd drive me crazy too."

"I'm not crazy, Quincy."

"Of *course* you're not crazy. You're my big brother, and a Turner man. Listen to me though: that haint might be real, it might just be in your imagination, I don't know. But your reaction to it is a *choice.* All this hysteria over a ghost? You can *un*choose that, Cha. Turner men don't choose hysteria."

Russell, Fourth Child, Fifty-Seven Years Old:

"Tina said you upset Mama, and every time I call Mama she say she ain't up to talk."

"Mama's confused, Russell, and that's not what I called to talk about."

"Well, what you call for then?"

"I called about that haint from the big room. I want to know what you remember."

"All I remember is what Daddy said."

"I know what Daddy said, Russell. Come on, now. You remember the haint as being real, don't you?"

"Sure it's real. Or *was* real. No one ever saw it again, so that's got to mean something too."

"I saw it on Sunday, and every night since. Plus that time when I had my accident."

"Aw, nobody thinks you really saw it when you had that crash. Tell you the truth, we all thought it was them painkillers."

"So you're telling me it could happen only once on Yarrow, and then never again?"

"Sure. Isn't that how the world works? We were all just at the wrong place at the wrong time back then, or the right place at the right time, depending on how you look at it. You should read the emails I send out, Cha. They're all about miracles and chance encounters. Things like that only happen once."

Marlene, Fifth Child, Fifty-Five Years Old:

Via text message:

(Part 1 of 2): I'm too upset to pick up the phone. I hear you're moving forward with the short sale. If you sell the house I will never forgive you. I don't put down my

(Part 2 of 2): foot on anything in this family, not ever. But you do this, and you break my heart. Not trying to be dramatic, just how I feel.

Lonnie, Sixth Child, Fifty-Three Years Old:
"That was the only time I remember peeing on myself. Ain't that impressive? I was what, three? And I just stopped cold turkey after that night. I could never forget that."

"What would you say if I told you I saw the haint again here in my own house?"

"I believe you. Why wouldn't I?"

"I don't know. Thank you, Lonnie."

"Lonnie?"

"I'm here. I'm looking for the back of my earring. I figured out it's easier to locate things when I take a minute to be quiet."

"Oh . . . well, can you stop looking until after we hang up?"

"Sure, Cha."

"Thank you. You're the first person out of everybody to really say they believe me."

"I am? God. You know, sometimes our siblings disappoint me, Cha."

"I know, but I don't think they mean to. I hope they don't. But anyhow, I'm glad *you* believe me. The problem is now I can't sleep anywhere in the house without seeing it. I'm not really talking to Tina, and I'm sleepin on the couch, so my back and hip is hurting. I even tried the basement and it's there too, no matter where I go. It's still only showin up at night though. I don't know what to do."

"You only got one option. Or two, actually. You could pray really hard, but knowin you and Tina, y'all already tried that. So two: you could try to talk to it."

"And say what?"

"Shit."

"Lonnie?"

"Lonnie, are you all right?"

"Huh? I'm here. I just lost the stud. I wasn't thinkin and I kept the stud in my ear while I was looking for the back and it fell out too. Shit. I bet you this ear's gonna close up. This is my third try this *year*, Cha. First time I got the wrong ear. I had forgot that the right ear's for sissies. So then I took that out and got another one put in the left ear, but then I was visiting some girl in Hawthorne and—"

"Gotdamnit, Lonnie, I'm trying to talk to you about something important!"

"Hello?"

"I'm still here, Cha-Cha. I'm sorry. I haven't eaten all day, and you know how I get when I'm lightheaded."

"It's fine. You were sayin I should talk to the haint. What should I say? I'm not tryna fool around with any séances or them Ouija boards. Francey's acting like I need to take it back to Africa to figure this out, but I don't know how she expects me to do that."

"To tell you the truth, this sounds like some kind of reckoning. And you've got to take heed of it, not be scared of it."

"A reckoning for what? Why haven't you eaten yet? It's already three o' clock in LA. You need some money?"

"Money? No, I mean, I get my check on the first, so that's what? Couple more days. I still got some stuff around here I can eat."

"I'm gonna send you a hundred dollars."

"Thank you, Cha-Cha. I really appreciate it."

"It's nothing."

"I just been a little down lately is all, and I'm tryna figure out why. This girl from Hawthorne, Lily—"

"Lonnie. What's that you said about taking heed?"

"Huh? Truth is, Cha-Cha, I can't call it. Maybe you shouldn't even talk to it. Just listen harder. If you need to go someplace for a while and think, you know you can come here. It's just me in this apartment. And I get paid on the first."

Netti (Antoinette), Seventh Child, Fifty Years Old:

From: TurnerGal7@coolmail.com

To: CTurner1@isecs.net

Subject: RE: I need to talk to you. [Auto-reply: Vacation Away Message]

Namaste,

I am on vacation in India, will return May 29th. If this is work-related, please contact my second-in-command LaShelle Dozier.

Kisses from the Taj Mahal!

—Antoinette Turner

"Be the change you wish to see in the world." —Gandhi

Miles and Duke (Donald), Eighth and Ninth Children, Forty-Eight and Forty-Seven Years Old:

"Cha-Cha! What's goin on?"

"Hey, I uh, what's all that noise?"

"I'm up in Oakland with Duke! It's Padres versus A's. Hold on, let me put him on the phone."

"Never mind, I'll—"

"CHA! Miles is over here talkin about a blowout. He thinks the Padres are finna win by *three* runs. I got fifty says he's talkin out the side of his neck. You wanna put in?"

"Gimme the phone back. That's enough of that. Cha? It's Miles again. Don't listen to Duke, he's drunk. You need to come out here during football season. Me and the girls usually drive up from San Diego the night before. Everybody starts partying at eight in the morning. Y'all try to tailgate like that over around Ford Field, somebody's liable to end up shot!"

"Cha-Cha?"

"Cha-Cha? Hey, Duke, whyn't you tell me he already hung up?"

Berniece, Tenth Child, Forty-Five Years Old:

"Funniest thing, Cha-Cha. I wouldn't have believed you a few years ago, but did I ever tell you about the last time I visited Mama on Yarrow? Last June right before she got real sick and I stayed a whole week?"

"No, what happened?"

"Well, we were driving to church, or I was driving and Mama was riding, and I was gonna go up Seneca to Gratiot, I don't know why, I just felt like it. But Mama said, 'Don't you go up Seneca, Niecie,' and I said, 'Why, Mama? What difference does it make?' I think I sounded kinda smart, but I didn't mean to, you know Mama is the queen of backseat driving, even though she was up front that day, but you know what I mean. Anyway, so I asked her why and she said, 'They killed two boys on Seneca and Medbury and I don't wanna pass that corner by. It's like there's haints over there now. It don't feel right.' And I said, 'What you mean, haints on the corner of Seneca and Medbury?' cause all I know about haints is that joke y'all all used to say about Daddy. Mama didn't answer me, and I didn't push it because I was scared Mama was having a senior moment, you know? Now I guess I should've asked more questions, like did she actually *see* ghosts there or was she just being dramatic, but like I said, I was scared, so I left it alone and went up Maxwell instead. A couple days later I was driving to the store by myself and I took Seneca. Sure enough, right on the corner in front of the light pole somebody had set up one of those shrines with the stuffed animals and the candles like they do when somebody's been shot or hit by a car."

"My God."

"I know, right? It's scary. I mean, it could have also just been a figure of speech. She could've read about the shooting or saw it on the news. I don't know. But let me say this too, Cha. You be careful who you go around asking about this. Everybody ain't so open-minded. Hell, *I* wasn't open to this before last June, and I still have my doubts. No offense."

Sandra, Eleventh Child, Forty-Four Years Old:
"You check your mail today?"

"No, why?"

"I sent you a check for five hundred dollars."

"For what?"

"For the house. Marlene told me you were trying to sell it, and that seems like a mistake to me, so I just sent you what I had. Go ahead and put it in the pot to keep the house."

"I haven't decided anything, but five hundred ain't nearly enough, not even if all thirteen put in five hundred."

"Shit, I *know* Francey and Richard got more money than me, and Netti and Rahul, and Russell and what's-her-name, Julie, Julia? And probably Miles and Duke too—California ain't cheap. I'm just putting in what I have to give. Problem with black folks is that we're too quick to cut our losses and let white folks decide what happens in the cities we live in. Sure the mayor is black, damn near the whole council is black, but we don't have the real money or the *property*. That's how they keep us on the run. Speaking of running, I gotta go. I'm driving and I don't have no headset with me. Don't want a ticket. Keep me posted!"

Troy, Twelfth Child, Forty-Three Years Old:
"You patrolling? I can call back."

"Patrolling? I'm not a slave catcher, Cha. Just ask if I'm at work. You say patrolling and I feel like it's the 1800s."

"You at work or not, Troy? God-lee."

"At home. What's good?"

"Uh . . . you ever catch up with Lelah?"

"That's what you called me for? To talk about Lelah? What's going on with the short sale? That's what I wanna know. I been thinkin about it, and really, at this point I think we need to—"

"Hold on there. Ain't no reason for you to be thinkin about it on your own at all. We're gonna decide as a family, like we said at the meeting. Whatever you wanna propose, wait until everybody hears it out."

"As a family? Come on, Cha. We can't even agree on what kind of food to cook on Christmas, let alone—"

"I'm not *calling* about that anyway. I was calling to ask you about something else... something personal."

"So you wanna ask *me* something personal, but can't even listen to me for two minutes. Some things never change, huh? I guess it's only up to *you* what we talk about. It's always up to you what we talk about, ain't it, Cha?"

"Lord, never mind, Troy. I'll talk to you later."

"No no no! I'm listening, I really am. What's eatin you, Cha? How can I help?"

"Seriously?"

"I'm serious."

"Okay. I don't know if you remember hearing about this, maybe you were too young, but there's this story about how I saw a ghost?"

"Uh-huh."

"Well, I think the ghost, the haint, I guess, has come back, or it never really left, but now it's showing itself again."

"This really is a trip, Cha."

"What?"

"You! You're a trip, calling me to ask for advice on something minor like this—you having bad dreams, basically—and meanwhile important family business is just pushed to the back burner until *you* feel like dealing with it."

"This ain't minor, Troy, this is my life. And I'm not talkin about bad dreams."

"You know what? My line's beeping. I gotta go."

"Hold up, Troy."

"Troy, you there?"

"Gotdamnit."

Lelah, Thirteenth Child, Forty Years Old:

"Where you been hiding? I haven't heard from you in damn near a month."

"It hasn't been a month, Cha. I've been around, just busy with work."

"Too busy to answer a text message?"

"Plus, when I'm not at work I've got my hands full with Bobbie."

"I must have sent twenty texts by now. I sent an all-caps text that said EMERGENCY CALL ME NOW, and you didn't even respond. I had stopped callin this number cause I figured you'd got a new prepaid."

"But you just called it right now. And here I am, right? What's going on?"

"I. Well. You don't even know about the house, do you?"

"I have no idea what you're talkin about, but to tell you the truth, I'm in the middle of something. Can we talk about this at the party next weekend?"

"What party? There's not gonna be no parties around here."

"Tina just left me a voicemail about five minutes ago. Talkin about a party for the spring birthdays next Saturday and does Bobbie eat chocolate."

"I just talked to everybody else and didn't nobody mention a party."

"I don't know, Cha-Cha. All I have is the voicemail. Maybe Tina's workin backwards up the list or something, so I finally get some information before the whole world gets it. I'll see you there though. Tell her Bobbie eats chocolate but he can't have any peanuts. They make his skin act weird."

"Lelah—"

"I really have to go, Cha."

"Alright. But you might wanna go ahead and pay your last visit to Yarrow Street, cause we're not gonna keep that house."

"Lelah, did you hang up?"

"No, I'm here."

"Are you crying? Aw hell, I didn't mean it. I just got too much on my plate, and people aren't being realistic."

"Can we please talk later? I really have to go."

Feeling equal parts frustrated and confrontational, Cha-Cha stomped up from the basement to find Tina on a barstool in the kitchen, the cordless phone tucked in between her ear and raised shoulder, her leather-bound address book open. She looked up at him and lifted one finger—a church-lady gesture that meant "Hold on one minute" but could also mean "Excuse me, I'm trying to get to the bathroom" or "One Kleenex over here, please" or "You'll have to wait until the prayer is over to enter the sanctuary," depending on the circumstances. Cha-Cha rolled his eyes, but he waited.

"Yeah, if you could maybe bring a salad or some fruit, that would be good," she said into the phone. "I'm gonna order some pizzas from Buddy's and then make spaghetti and some chicken too if I have time. If not, I'll buy a few of those whole rotisserie ones from Meijer's and cut em up."

Cha-Cha cleared his throat.

"Anyway, Sandy, I'd best be going if I'm gonna make it all the way up the line tonight. Uh-huh, I *know*, girl. See you soon."

Tina returned the cordless to its cradle and made a mark in her address book.

It had been dark by the time he returned from the cemetery on Monday. Tina was on the loveseat when he came inside the house. She'd stacked his printouts neatly on his desk. She was calm, had the beginnings of a smile on her lips. "I want to be with the man who swept me off my feet in that pharmacy all those years ago," she said, "and I know he's still in you. I'm not givin him up. I'm not givin *you* up, Cha-Cha, so you want to talk about this haint? Fine, let's talk about it." This, of course, was too little too late for Cha-Cha, and what infuriated him was her insinuation that her only motive for helping him now was so that *she* could get the husband *she* wanted back, not because he was quite possibly going out of his mind and needed her to believe him. He'd ignored her proposed truce and started his migration through the guest bedrooms and basement for sleeping, finally settling on the couch. She still cooked his dinner, packed lunches for the workdays he slogged through in a sleep-starved haze.

"Can I help you, Cha-Cha?" she said now.

"Why are you callin people and scheduling a party without asking me about it first?"

"Because it's almost June, and May is usually when we celebrate the spring birthdays, isn't it?"

"I'm not in no kind of state or mood to have a party here, Tina. I think you know that."

"Well, Cha-Cha, the party isn't until Saturday. And I might even push it back until the following Saturday because Troy said he might be sending for Camille, and since neither of us has seen her since she was *yay* big, I think it might be nice if she was here, too, don't you?"

"You talked to Troy?"

"Just a few minutes ago."

"I was talking to him and he hung up on me. He picked up the phone for you?"

"How else could we have talked? So anyway, I figured, or maybe I *hoped* that in a week or two you'd have come around and started having real conversations with me, and we'd sort this business out together."

Tina gave Cha-Cha an innocent smile. He refused to smile back at her.

"What if I don't want a party, Tina?"

"It's not your party, Cha-Cha," she said, the cordiality fading from her voice. "It's for the spring birthdays. If you recall, *I'm* a spring birthday, and more importantly, your *mother* is a late-spring birthday, Cha-Cha. June fifteenth. And she's not gonna be here forever. I know you've been avoiding her room like the plague, but she's lost some weight just in these last few days. She's not eating as much and talking about pain in her arms and chest. They're even running some tests when we go to the doctor tomorrow. People need to see her while she's still *here*."

"Come on, Tina. Don't talk like that. I didn't make her sick."

"Plus, there's been two new babies since Christmas, and people wanna *see* them. Tameka's new boy and Antoine's baby girl. You can choose not to be here that day. Go ahead and *luxuriate* in your misery if that's what you need to do. But there's gonna be a party, with or without you."

She picked up the cordless again and ran her finger down the page of her address book.

"There's meatloaf and green beans in the microwave if you're hungry."

Her plan must have been to obliterate him with condescending kindness. And food. And babies. Cha-Cha was a sucker for a new baby. Not wanting to suffer through another descent down the basement's narrow stairs, he gathered his printouts, his MP3 player, and a saucer of meatloaf and stationed himself outside on the back deck.

It was too early in the year for cicadas, but the crickets did an impressive impersonation as the day grew dark, singing in loud insect harmony. When the sun finally sank behind the Hendersons' stand of pines two houses to the west, the collective cricking dropped a few octaves to a low hum. He sifted through his printouts. Each day he lost a bit of faith in his research, but he still liked to hold the growing stack of papers, a tactile reminder of his efforts to be measured and reasonable. After his first miserable day back at work, Cha-Cha had returned to Hurston's *Mules and Men*. He'd stayed up late Tuesday and Wednesday thumbing through the stories, heartened by the casual mention of ghosts that mingled among the living. The book suggested that many ghosts sought retribution. Cha-Cha couldn't think of anyone he had seriously crossed in his life, much less any former foe who had died. The appendix outlined practical, root-centered remedies for just about every problem—catching a murderer, making someone leave town—except for getting rid of a ghost. Furthermore, these ghost stories happened in the South, and despite Francey's claims of diasporic connectedness, Cha-Cha still felt that what happened down there so many decades ago couldn't be of much insight up here. He considered the South a place mired in the past, never mind the desperate efforts of its larger cities to prove otherwise. A place his father never even bothered returning to, and where on visits to his aunts as a child in the fifties his mother always briefed him on how he should and shouldn't behave in the presence of white folks. It was the twenty-first century now, and Cha-Cha lived in Detroit. He was convinced that he should be able to unthink this haint, mentally shoo it away, just as he had for all of those years after the night in the big room.

The motion-sensor light kept shutting off, so Cha-Cha, too lazy to get up and switch it to the permanent ON, took to rocking back and forth in his deck chair. The rocking also helped fight the evening chill.

He hadn't mentioned Alice to Tina all week. He wouldn't give her the satisfaction of knowing that Alice also doubted him. To her credit, Tina hadn't brought up Pastor Mike during any of her "let's talk about this" entreaties. Cha-Cha missed Alice. He regretted the things he'd said to her, although at the time he believed them. Why else would Alice bother with him, if not to glean some knowledge of living the kind of life that he lived? There was, of course, a more pedestrian answer, one that seemed both increasingly plausible and ludicrous as each day passed. Alice might just *like* Cha-Cha. He resisted this explanation, because if he accepted it, he was tempted to think about the nature of her liking, as well as his own affinity for her. Before the haint's return he had trusted his attraction to her as a friendly one; now it was specious. Why had he felt the need to hug her on Monday? Why had she diverted from protocol and delayed discussing his haint for months? He felt foolish to indulge his imagination in this way, and the fact remained that she hadn't called him since. He could picture her sitting there in her turquoise chair, fiddling with the pens on her desk, absent-mindedly patting her afro. She might have been thinking about him. She might have even considered picking up the phone to check on him, her patient who was on his way to becoming her friend. Or did the image of a sixty-four-year-old, stubborn, former truck-driving, ghost-seeing man make her angry? Did it fill her with pity? It would hurt Cha-Cha too much if the latter were true.

How would a person know if he was going insane? Cha-Cha wondered. There might exist a specific symptom, some indisputable piece of evidence that would prove one unstable. Rocking back and forth on the deck, nibbling a cold disk of ketchupy meatloaf in the chilly evening might be proof enough of a deteriorating mental state for some people.

Growing up, whenever a child went through a habitual lying stage, or blamed his siblings for all of the trouble he got into, Viola would put her index finger to the child's chest and say, "Everybody else cain't be wrong all the time. Sometimes it's gotta be *you*."

What if it was him?

A Typecast She Couldn't Shake

On the walkway to Marlene's Harper Woods bungalow Lelah tried to sort out a game plan. She had just gotten back to Yarrow after meeting up with David when Cha-Cha's call came. She hadn't thought as she put her car in reverse where she might be headed, to whose door she would come knocking. Now that she was here, Marlene felt right. Lelah would need allies to get Cha-Cha to change his mind, and Marlene had spent almost as many years as Lelah had back on Yarrow as an adult.

She knocked. After a few seconds with no answer, she pounded. Marlene opened the door with the chain on.

"It's you. I'da thought you didn't know me, the way you've been ignorin my calls."

"I know you, I know you, okay? Let me in."

Marlene closed the door to remove the chain, opened it again. The small house smelled of furniture polish and incense, flea market aromas wafting off of Marlene's collection of flea market finds.

In the living room Lelah sat across from an ancient floor-model TV that miraculously still broadcast a few channels with the help of a converter box. Marlene hustled past her to the kitchen to turn off the faucet.

"I'd complain about you not calling first, but I know how you are," Marlene said. "You want something? Water? I'm on my diet shakes again, so I don't have a lot of *food* food."

Over the counter Lelah watched Marlene's backside thrust in the air as she bent for something in the back of the fridge. She wore gray cotton shorts, and the fat on her dark brown legs bulged around her knees.

"I've got a bag of oranges Miles mailed me a while ago," Marlene said. She straightened up, held a rumpled paper bag above her head. "I coulda swore it was illegal to send produce across state lines, but people seem to do it all the time now."

"I don't want any oranges," Lelah said. "Sit down."

Marlene was fifteen years older than Lelah, but at some point it had stopped feeling that way. When Lelah came home at twenty-two, heartbroken, Marlene came home to Yarrow shortly thereafter, heartbroken at thirty-seven with a divorce in the works and her only son living with his father. If Lelah were ever to have her life together enough to have a best friend, to maintain such a relationship, Marlene would be that friend. Lelah knew many of their other siblings feared Marlene, particularly the men, who took her fabled dropping of Lonnie on the head as everlasting proof that she was too quick to get angry and too long to forgive, but Lelah knew that Marlene simply loved hard. She was blunt and forceful with her love, but if she cared about you, she would do everything in her power to help you.

Marlene settled in a plastic-covered gold jacquard armchair across from Lelah. The cushions wheezed.

"What's going on with you?" she said. "You look like you lost weight."

Her eyes flitted over Lelah, then back to the orange in her lap. She peeled it slowly, around and around so that the rind made one large, connected spiral.

"Cha-Cha just called me," Lelah said.

"Asking you about a ghost? Girl, isn't he a *mess?* I didn't answer when he called me, but Francey said that's what he's going around asking everybody about. It's just *like* him, I think. Looking for attention, or pity, or both, I bet."

Lelah stared at Marlene, who, oblivious to her confusion, was quickly breaking off sections of orange and popping them into her mouth.

"I don't know what you're talking about," she said. "He told me he was selling Mama's house."

"Oh, that. Yeah, that's why I didn't pick up when he called me. I texted him my thoughts, which are basically he can go to hell if he goes through with it."

"And what did he say?"

"He didn't answer yet," Marlene said. "But you know Cha-Cha, he's gonna do what he wants. Or should I say he's gonna do what he thinks is best for 'all of us,' seein as how he's the de facto patriarch."

"He can't do it though, can he?" Lelah asked. "I mean, can he legally do it? And what does Mama say?"

Marlene extended the last section of orange out to Lelah. Lelah refused it.

"Girl, that's a whole *nother* issue. That night we went over there for that meeting about it, everybody left to get dinner and I stayed back with Mama. She was fine then, or at least fine for Mama, talkin about stuff she wanted me to get her from the rummage sale in Windsor for when she got to move back home. This was barely three weeks ago, remember. She still had plans to move back, talkin about getting new furniture or making everybody give back what they took from the house, what she let them 'borrow,' she said. It was kinda sad. But apparently her and Cha-Cha had some kind of argument since then — what's *wrong* with him, arguing with a sick old lady? I just talked to her the day before yesterday, and now she's sayin she doesn't care about the house, that she knows she'll die at Cha-Cha's."

"*Die* there?" Lelah said. "What are they doing to her?"

"I don't think they're *doing* anything. You know Tina loves her some Mama. I think she just said it to make Cha-Cha look bad, and maybe the pain pills make her more emotional. She wants a higher dosage, Tina said."

A few weeks out of the loop and already drama abounded. This was why the other boys would never move back home, Lelah thought, why Berniece and Sandy kept their distance. To be in Detroit was to be at the epicenter of familial rumblings.

"Marlene, I don't want Cha-Cha to sell that house."

"Me neither," Marlene said. "But he's worried about how much Mama owes. Says Mama's so upside down on her loan that as soon as she dies the bank will just take the house anyway. Unless somebody agrees to keep payin that inflated mortgage."

Marlene continued rattling off reasons, but Lelah had stopped listening. She was mustering the courage to confess, if not to everything, then to one specific transgression. Perhaps her earlier pseudo confession to David had broken some sort of seal, because now it felt like if she didn't tell Marlene, she would suffocate, never be able to get up off of her dusty couch.

"I'm living there," she nearly yelled. "I'm living on Yarrow right now."

Marlene stopped shredding the orange peel. Her eyes narrowed.

"You? You are not."

"Yes I am. I been there for about three weeks. Since right after the first."

Marlene put a hand to her temple, where her baby hairs were curling and gray. Lelah waited for her to ask why, why would anyone hole up there with so many beds and couches to crash on? If she asked, Lelah would say it was because she was tired of needing help. Tired of asking. She was forty, her daughter was grown, she had no one to look after but herself, so she should have the right to hide out in her childhood home for a few weeks until she could figure things out. She would say something about them all being one bad month away from relative poverty, that even Cha-Cha in his fancy house, almost free and clear, could not survive on his pension should he be forced to retire early. That they were all overextended. She would say that truthfully, anyplace she went she'd be a burden.

Marlene did not ask why.

"You feel safe there?"

"I don't know," Lelah said. "Nobody's bothered me, and apparently Mr. McNair knows I'm there. I lock up good when I leave."

"So you got evicted."

That it was a statement and not a question frustrated Lelah. She didn't respond.

"And Brianne doesn't know," Marlene added. "Nobody knows."

To be that person, the one who never pleasantly surprised her siblings, rarely had good news. To be the one with nothing, periodically destitute, was a miserable position. It seemed like ever since she'd come back from Missouri with baby Brianne, this had been her perennial burden to bear. A typecast she couldn't shake, even during her stretches of stability.

"Me and Brianne are overdue for a talk," she said. "I didn't come over here for pity, Marlene. I came over to see if you agreed with Cha-Cha about the house. Even if I wasn't staying there right now, I'd care about that house."

"But since you *are* staying there, it matters a whole lot more," Marlene said. She got up from her chair and sat next to Lelah on the couch, put a hand on Lelah's knee, and breathed deep.

"Oh, Lelah. You know Brianne calls me, or should I say used to call me. Before she quit school and started nursing, me and her used to talk."

"Of course I know that, Marla," Lelah said. "Why *wouldn't* y'all talk?"

Marlene returned her hand to her lap.

"Just say it, Marla. Say whatever you want to say."

Lelah's heart clanged in its cage, but outwardly, she and her sister sat still. Of course Brianne talked to Marlene. And Brianne was no fool. She and Lelah had lived together for too long and were too close for Brianne not to have noticed anything. Lelah used to keep spare chips in a candy dish on her dresser, and the two of them often used her comp tickets for casino buffet feasts when money was tight. But there was no way Brianne or anyone else could know the extent, Lelah believed. She'd been careful to ensure that.

Marlene got up and walked back to the kitchen.

"All I'm sayin is that you know this family, Lelah. We're too prideful, and I think we get that from Mama."

She opened and closed drawers. A Tupperware lid popped open.

"But we're also convinced everybody can do fine all by themselves, that nobody ever needs someone to call them out and set them straight. To *intervene*. That's a Francis Turner trait if there ever was one."

Marlene returned to her spot next to Lelah on the couch. She held a white envelope, the kind the bank gave out for large withdrawals.

"This is nine hundred and fifty dollars, Lelah. But this is also me not doing like my daddy. I'm calling you out."

From the way she clutched the envelope to her breast, Lelah suspected she might not give it at all.

"You always slipped through the cracks cause you're the baby and everybody was so busy doin their own thing. But you're *grown*, Lelah. You've gotta promise me you'll get some help. You can't go back there and throw my money away. This money was supposed to be for my new grandbaby, just in case Antoine ever needed help."

"I don't want it," Lelah croaked. "I don't want that money."

Marlene placed the envelope in Lelah's lap and moved back to her plastic armchair.

"It's yours. You could put a deposit down on a place with it, or at least pay off Brianne's rent so you could feel better about staying over there for a while. I know you won't stay *here*, or you'd be staying here already."

Lelah put the envelope on the couch cushion next to her. She pulled her purse onto her shoulder to go. She wondered how often David Gardenhire had given his brother money, and how far in his estimation Greg dropped each time.

"I really won't take it, Marla," she said. She stood up to leave. "But thank you."

Marlene stared down at her tiny fists as they kneaded her fleshy thighs.

"That's that Viola Turner stubborn pride," she said. "Do you know after Mama's stroke last year the doctor told her that if she stayed alone in that house, she'd end up paralyzed? There's no downstairs bedroom, Lelah, and even if there was, there ain't no bathrooms down there. Doctor told her if she didn't get someone to move in and help her with her mobility being impaired the way it was, she'd have a 'final fall,' is what he called it. And because of the nerve damage she already had, that would be it.

"But of course I don't find all this out until she's at Cha-Cha's, as good as paralyzed cause of all the pain she's in and sad about moving out of her house. More sad about that than not being able to really walk. Why didn't she tell anybody *sooner*, huh? Pride. Too much pride to tell even one of the thirteen children she raised that she needed someone to help her every day. I know you or I would have done it if we knew it was that serious."

Marlene sniffed. Teardrops made splotchy polka dots on her shorts and shirt. Lelah handed her the box of tissues from on top of the television. She perched on the arm of the plastic chair, put her hand on Marlene's shoulder.

"I'm gonna pay you back."

"Girl, I don't care about that. Shit, just don't blow it all on *slots*, Lelah, please. I may not be able to look at you the same if you do."

Lelah had half a mind to tell her sister that slot machines would never get this money, that if anyplace got her money, it would be a proper roulette table. She felt ashamed of herself for the thought.

A Prudent Wife Is from the Lord

A hand on his shoulder and Cha-Cha jumped.

"It's only me," Tina said. "Come on back inside."

She wore his spare house shoes—a pair of moccasins Russell had mailed him from the Grand Canyon—and her feet looked tiny in comparison.

"What time is it?" Cha-Cha asked.

"Past nine already. You've been out here for two hours."

She picked up the saucer that still held a nub of meatloaf and extended her free hand. This small, capable woman, Cha-Cha thought. If only she was as understanding as she was nurturing.

He gave her his hand, accepted her help to stand upright, bundled up his printouts, and followed her inside.

In the living room his comforter and pillow were missing.

"Where's my sleeping stuff?"

"I put them back in the guest bedroom," Tina said. She squeezed his arm just above the elbow. "You're gonna sleep in the bed you belong in tonight."

A younger, naïve Cha-Cha would have pitied Tina for what it appeared she was doing, begging for his companionship. But after more than three decades of marriage Cha-Cha knew better. It was Tina who pitied him, and as much as he snored, she certainly was not eager to have him back in the bed. She thought he needed this, a gradual return to normalcy. She thought he needed her. And maybe he did, but he wished he didn't. They would humor each other for the night.

Cha-Cha had missed their bed. It was a fancy one they bought after his accident, when their old bed had started to feel like a torture mechanism. This new bed had a remote to control the firmness of each side, so that Tina could have hers firm and his could be as soft as he needed. Worried that Tina had been fiddling with his settings in his absence, Cha-Cha tossed off his bathrobe, settled himself on his side of the bed, and started tinkering with his remote.

Tina made a clucking noise and Cha-Cha looked up. She was at the foot of the bed, on her knees, looking at Cha-Cha expectantly.

"You know that hurts my back," he said.

"It's only for a few minutes, and you *know* you need it."

"I've been praying since I knew what praying *was*, Tina. Don't act like I'm some heathen."

At this Tina made the face—her high-eyebrowed face of righteous indignation—and Cha-Cha decided to beat her to the punch.

"But you when you pray, go into your room and when you have shut your door, pray to your Father who *is* in the secret place, and your Father who sees in secret will reward you openly."

Tina's eyebrows dropped down into a scowl, but soon the expression disappeared as she located an appropriate rebuttal in her mental concordance. When had they become these people?

"House and wealth are inherited from parents," she said. "But a *prudent wife* is from the Lord."

She shifted on her knees to make more space on her left.

"Just come *down* here, Cha," she said. His verse had been a better choice than hers, and Tina knew it. "If you want to say your own prayer in your head, that's fine."

Accepting this minor concession, Cha-Cha climbed out of the bed. Being on his knees didn't actually hurt as much as getting down on them; the bracing and muscle control required were the hard parts. Cha-Cha saw Tina's lips moving in the dim light. He closed his eyes, and the first thing he thought of was Alice. The look on her face when he'd left her office. He felt doubly guilty—for thinking of her first when he should have been praying, and for the things he had said to her. He thought he should pray for forgiveness.

Cha-Cha favored short, earnest prayer, and he often wondered what took others so long. It had something to do with excess supplication, he suspected. He never presented a long list of specific requests to God, had always felt uncomfortable with the presumptuousness of "Ask and you shall receive." This might have been a result of pride, or his own middling ambition, but mostly Cha-Cha's prayers were a series of thank-yous and I'm sorrys. *I'm sorry I told Chucky's first wife, Yvette, she was a cheating whore. Thank you for my health insurance coverage.* If God knew what we needed and the right time to bestow it upon us, then why remind Him all the time? This was one of the many differences between Tina's way of worshipping and his own. "Jesus is on the main line, tell Him what you want" had to be one of the most ridiculous songs created since Negroes grabbed a hold of tambourines, but Tina loved that song. He, on the other hand, could see the beauty and benefit of singing a song like "I need Thee, oh, I need Thee, every hour I need Thee," because it was more an acknowledgment of the necessity of the constant favor of God, and less an entreaty to treat the Host of Hosts like a twenty-four-hour fast food drive-thru, or an act ACT NOW! special on the Home Shopping Network. This was the sort of lighthearted theological banter he and Tina used to partake in after leaving their AME church, but then she jumped ship and became a holy roller. The most disconcerting part was that it wasn't for show, Cha-Cha realized. Her fervor was consistent, even when no one witnessed it, and because he couldn't match it she had pushed him into a corner.

He looked over to find her still deep in prayer, lips working, fingers interlocked, so he closed his eyes again and said his usual—the Lord's Prayer with a few special thank-yous tacked on the end. *Thank you for my health, my family, my job, that my mortgage is almost paid up, that my son the soldier has stayed out of harm's way.* Then he added, *Thank you for my sanity,* because speaking as if it were still intact, not showing any doubt, seemed the smartest way to proceed.

Tina finally shifted, so Cha-Cha placed both hands on the mattress and leveraged himself into a stand. Tina patted him twice on the shoulder.

"That wasn't so bad, was it?" she said, and walked into the bathroom.

It was as if he were a toddler and she'd just cajoled him into bucking up for a trip to the doctor. He couldn't sleep here, not with this woman treating him like he wasn't potty-trained.

When Tina emerged from the master bathroom she caught Cha-Cha with his pillow clutched to his chest and his bathrobe back on. She stared at him as if he were truly disappointing, a sad case.

"Please, Cha-Cha," she said. "Get back in the bed."

She held out a glass of water and his blood pressure pills, pills he'd neglected to take all week. The oversight startled him. More evidence of just how much his day-to-day well-being was dependent on Tina's vigilance. He had set it up this way, encouraged her to stop working, practically forbade her from working. He facilitated this metamorphosis into pushy caretaker, clingy nursemaid. It had made him feel like a man, an old-fashioned, all-capable man like his father. Now he felt like a child. Trapped in the cage of condescension and coddling that he'd built for himself.

Cha-Cha took the pills, swallowed the water, and returned to the bed.

Historically, Cha-Cha and Tina's sleeping arrangements were designed to accommodate an all-night spoon. Cha-Cha preferred to sleep on his right side, so he claimed the left side of the bed in order to be the big spoon to Tina's little spoon. Many things had interrupted this arrangement over the years—kids in the bed, sickness or soreness, too hot summer nights, and arguments—but the unspoken agreement between the two of them was that barring the aforementioned, spooning should be afoot come lights out.

Before Cha-Cha could decide how best to get out of spooning while still sleeping on his preferred side, Tina inched her rear end into position, flush against his pelvis. All that was left to complete the formation was for Cha-Cha to drape his arm across her waist. He hesitated, and he was sure Tina interpreted it as resistance, maybe even rejection. He smelled the Avon Haiku perfume that she sprayed onto the crown of her head every day for his benefit. Ever since menopause she'd started using a silk pillowcase so she wouldn't have to wrap her hair at night.

Then something unexpected happened. An erection. Cha-Cha registered the tingly, nervy sensation and figured he had to pee, but no. It was a different sort of urgency he felt. The real thing. Tina, likely more out of habit than out of genuine interest, shifted her rear against it, just a subtle resettling of her hips. The erection persisted.

Not long ago, sex had still been very much a part of Cha-Cha and Tina's life. He used to quietly thank God that all of Tina's extra churching hadn't shamed away the desire in her. Then Cha-Cha had his accident, and his favorite positions became frustrating, even painful, as his hip healed. He'd once complained to Alice about it, and she'd said, "If the problem is mechanical as opposed to having to do with desire, then you two will figure it out. If Christopher Reeve was still getting off after *his* accident, you can too." He now felt embarrassed for sharing his "mechanical" sex issues with Alice. But Tina had been upbeat about it all, and the two of them found a way to make it work. Then Viola moved in, and Cha-Cha felt uncomfortable doing it with his mother only two doors down. There was no way to know whether she was asleep or awake because she kept an erratic schedule. The house on Yarrow had a hallway not half as long as this one, plus the boys' room shared a wall with Francis and Viola's room, but Cha-Cha had never heard his parents' lovemaking, only Francis's fervent baritone during arguments. It had been two months since Cha-Cha and Tina last made love.

Tina moved against him again, and Cha-Cha thought they could really do it. It might help right everything wrong between them, or at least help him sleep better. He brought his arm around her waist, and Tina rested her hand on top of his. After much post-accident trial and error, they discovered that their traditional sleeping arrangement was also the easiest on Cha-Cha's hips for sex. Tina had thought being on top might work, but her compact stature belied her heaviness, and Cha-Cha feared his porcelain might crack if she got too spirited. So the spoon became their go-to. He slid his hand underneath Tina's flannel pajama top and onto her belly, where a smiling scar from a teenage appendectomy ran smooth under his fingers. Tina moved closer still, arched her back just a little, and Cha-Cha knew that she too thought this might be enough to fix it all. Cha-Cha wanted to be strategic, as a hasty grope or shift might ruin everything. He figured his next move should be a reach for either breast or booty, but Tina reached back and grabbed his erection through his boxers. Too soon for that, he knew; he wasn't ready for a full-on grab, and just as quick as the stiffness had arrived, it subsided. Cha-Cha forced the breath he'd been holding out through his nose and backed away, lest Tina try to revive him.

"Well," she started. Her voice sounded hopeful.

"Good night," Cha-Cha said. He nearly barked. He moved a few more inches back and drew up his knees some, effectively breaking the spoon.

Nothing could be solved so easily.

Let Her Say Yes

"G ood morning, Bobbie," Brianne said. She picked him up and
sniffed his diaper, tested for wetness with a finger. Finding everything just as dry as she'd left it, she decided to fix him his breakfast
before commencing the daily struggle of dressing him. Her shifts ran
long and Bobbie's bedtime was early, so Brianne usually woke up at
six to spend quality time with her son. Today she was an hour behind
schedule. She'd stayed up late, past 2 A.M., video chatting with Rob.

As soon as Brianne set Bobbie on the sofa he found the remote and
pushed the red Power button, the easiest to locate and the only button he had learned to make do what he wanted. Brianne took the remote from him and flipped through channels until she found PBS,
where *Donnie* was on. Though imaginative, the pale, bald four-year-
old hero of the show whined too much for Brianne's liking. Bobbie
was obsessed with him. Since he'd discovered the show a few months
earlier, a large part of morning quality time now included Brianne
stomaching Donnie's yelping exploits.

She put a mug full of water in the microwave for coffee and looked
at her shadowy reflection in the glass door. The skin under her eyes
was swollen, and her hair looked smashed on one side because she'd

forgotten to wrap it the night before. That was the downside to video chatting. One had to keep up appearances when one would usually be able to look a mess for bed without the person on the other end of the line being any the wiser. Rob had seen Brianne look disheveled before, but everything between them felt new now.

After she and Rob partook in a bit of awkward, pixelated video sex last night, Rob had asked her to move in with him. She had refused. The boy still didn't have an intuitive bone in his body, so instead of gleaning her feelings and gradually working up to this sort of proposal, he had blurted it out apropos of not much, only a few weeks of being on good terms again. They'd had the same plans in college: get a bachelor's in nursing, then get a master's in public health and become a hospital administrator somewhere. Make more money than all four of their parents combined. It would have still worked with a baby, especially because Rob was going into his senior year, but he'd hesitated. Said he wasn't sure if he was ready to be a father. So she did it all alone. She'd enrolled in night school immediately to get her LPN, just in case she couldn't go to grad school right away. She'd wanted to stay at Eastern Michigan, maybe work in a local nursing home or somewhere part-time until she finished her BS, but it was too much once Bobbie was born. She needed help watching him, and more money than part-time could offer. She came back to Detroit. A few months after Bobbie's birth, Rob had been accepted into an MPH program out in Chicago; he said he wanted to be in his son's life. This was fine with Brianne, but she could not forget those months when she was alone. It had been the darkest, hardest period of her life. She was not was ready to fully forgive him, and had had to move away from the webcam to hide the confusion and annoyance on her face this morning. She told Rob that she didn't think he wanted her, that he was just excited about finally having a relationship with his son.

"*God*, Brianne. I know what I want," he'd said. "I didn't ask you for joint custody, I asked you to be my girlfriend again."

"Girlfriend" seemed too casual a term given that they had a child together, given that he wanted her to uproot herself and move to Chicago, where Rob's rent was double her own and childcare was expensive. He had refused to accept a hard *no* (Brianne blamed the cyber sex for this), so she said she'd think about it.

"Come sit in your chair," Brianne called to her son. She always said it despite his not being able to get into the chair on his own. Bobbie tottered over to her, his *Donnie* pajama pants bunching around his knees, and she lifted him into the highchair. Over his shoulder and through the dining room window Brianne saw her mother emerge from the stairs onto the landing outside. Her mother didn't see her, so Brianne watched her prepare to knock. Her mother smoothed down her ponytail with one flat palm, pulled at her shirt. Brianne felt an urge to pick up her baby and run into the bedroom like she did to avoid a Jehovah's Witness, and like she fantasized doing to her nosey landlord. Then she noticed a McDonald's bag in her mother's other hand. The problem with Witnesses and landlords was that they never came bearing breakfast. Brianne thought they should.

"You're so early," she said.

"Here." Her mother handed her the bag of food. "I left the orange juices on the roof of my car. I'll be right back."

"Mick Donna! Mick Donna!" Bobbie said. He clapped his hands and pushed his rice cereal a few inches away from him. That an eighteen-month-old could already be so enamored with a food he rarely ate scared Brianne.

When her mother returned, Brianne scrutinized the cheerful expression on her face. She could tell Lelah was straining to keep her eyes bright, the set of her mouth resolute.

"You're so early," Brianne said again. "Thanks for the food."

"I woke up a couple hours ago and just felt like McDonald's, you know? Breakfast is the only thing they know how to make there, so I figured I'd bring y'all some."

She wanted something. Brianne could practically smell the question forming in her mother's mouth. *She wants something, but she's gonna see what kind of mood I'm in first,* Brianne thought.

"Gigi, I want the toy," Bobbie said. He leaned in his highchair, gripped the paper bag and turned it over. Ketchup and jelly packets tumbled to the table.

"Aw, there's no toys at breakfast, baby. Only in the Happy Meals."

Brianne watched her mother scoop up the packets and rub Bobbie's head with them. He giggled.

"You heard about the party at Uncle Cha-Cha's, right?" Brianne asked. "Auntie Tina said she was having trouble reaching you."

Her mother spread jelly on half an English muffin and placed the muffin back on its corresponding sausage.

"Yeah I talked to her. She wants us to bring something. I figured I could make macaroni and cheese over here while I watch Bobbie."

She liked to do this, Brianne knew, find excuses to do things here that she could just as easily have done at home.

"Stop playing with your food, Bobbie," Brianne said. Her son ignored her and continued to roll a fistful of hash browns into a greasy ball between his palms.

"When you were his age you used to put oatmeal on your face," her mother said. "Mama caught you doing it and said 'What's that girl doing, somebody told her she got eczema?'"

Brianne's laugh was pained and perfunctory.

"So what's going on with you?" she asked. "How was your weekend?"

"Good," her mother said. "I stopped by your auntie Marlene's last night, hung out with her for a while. Did you stay in town or go to Chicago?"

Brianne finished chewing her sausage biscuit, gulped down her juice.

"I stayed here. We're going back on Thursday, though."

"And where do you stay when you go?"

"Mommy."

"Mommy what? I'm just curious. You're not too old to have some-one know where you are. *Nobody's* ever too old for that. It's common sense."

Brianne rarely knew where her mother was these days, and she doubted anyone else did either.

"Bobbie stays with Rob, and I've been staying with my friend Tawny."

"Who's Tawny? I don't remember any Tawny."

"You'd remember if you saw her," Brianne said. "She went to East-ern Michigan with me. She's tall, light-skinned. Freckles."

Bobbie, bored with his hash-brown ball, grabbed the sides of his highchair and rocked back and forth. He looked like a sailor stuck in a crow's nest during a storm. Lelah picked him up and patted his butt.

"He needs to be changed," Brianne said. "I gave him his bath last night, but he's still wearing the diaper he slept in."

"I'll do all that after you leave," her mother said. "I don't know why you go through the trouble every morning like I'm some hired babysitter."

Brianne did not explain that the "trouble" was part of their morn-ing ritual, a way for her to feel essential to him before so many hours apart. She sat down across from her mother, checked the time on the microwave display. Tawny often talked about her mother in a way that made them seem like girlfriends. Brianne and Lelah were closer in age, but a formality existed between them that Brianne's growth into adulthood hadn't shaken. Lelah rarely got Brianne's jokes, was awkward discussing romance and refused to stop worrying.

"Speaking of babysitters," Lelah said. "I wanna give you this money back."

She reached into her bra and pulled out two $20 bills. Brianne eyed the money on the table, now certain that her mother wanted something larger. She imagined her mother putting the money in her bra in the car, practicing the casual way she'd pull it out. Embar-rassing.

"If I wanted money from you for this, I'd have asked for it," her mother said.

"Well I thought you could use it," Brianne said. "Rob's got a job lined up consulting for KPMG for when he graduates in May. They gave him a signing bonus, so he gave me extra money this month."

The name Rob and the words "signing bonus" sounded strange in one sentence, Brianne thought. The goofy boy who used to play too many video games in college had finally grown up.

"Consulting? I thought he was getting a public health master's."

"He is. They do that kind too."

"Oh," her mother said. "Anyway, I guess I should go ahead and ask what I need to ask you before you run off to the shower."

Brianne raised her eyebrows, tried to look intrigued instead of terrified.

"I've been thinking, I know you want to go back to school for your BA and RN, and you know how I've been working this night shift. Between that and being with Bobbie during the day, I'm hardly ever at my place. What if I moved in here? That way we could save on rent, and you could go back to school."

Brianne had forgotten her mother claimed to be working graveyard. It didn't seem feasible that she had been working all night and then babysitting for nearly twelve hours a day.

"Who said I was going back to school anytime soon?"

Lelah scrunched her eyebrows in confusion.

"You did, didn't you? I thought the plan was always go back for the RN as soon as you could. Brianne, you know you can't be an LPN forever."

One of the many benefits of the girlfriend quality of Tawny and her mother's relationship was that they seemed to speak directly to each other, even when angry.

"It hasn't been *forever*, Mommy. It's not even two years yet."

She wanted to scream at Lelah, remind her that she never went to college, remind her how hard it was with no Yarrow and Granddaddy

Francis or Grandma Viola to prop her up. All she had was a mother who never kept more than a few dollars to her name, who held a rigid ball of secrets close to her breast. Brianne stood up and said she had to pee.

Leaning against her bathroom sink, she saw the situation for what it was. Lelah had likely lost her job, finally frittered away her money to the point of eviction. Lelah needed saving, and who but her daughter could provide the sort of lifeline that could keep her pride intact? Brianne turned and looked at herself in the mirror. More than messy hair and puffy eyes, she saw her mother's high forehead, and skin the color of a father she hardly remembered. From pictures of Vernon in his trim army uniform she knew her slim hips were his, her small, diamond-shaped ears, too. It wasn't enough to know about any relative, let alone one's father.

Lelah hadn't planned on going about it this way; she'd planned to be honest but turned coward as soon as she walked through the door. Better to make Brianne feel as if Lelah was doing her a favor than to admit to being desperate. She wouldn't blame Brianne for rejecting her now. Only please God let her say yes.

When Brianne returned, Lelah could tell the answer would be no, that her daughter would not have her if she could at all help it. She really had been blessed with a child as mild-mannered as Brianne. She seldom had to even make threats of punishment to get her to do right because guilt was enough to keep Brianne in line. She knew if she could formulate the right words now, she could turn Brianne's no into a yes.

Lelah opened her mouth to speak, but Brianne blurted out, "I'm moving to Chicago with Rob."

Lelah said nothing.

"I'm putting my notice in today, but I don't see the point of paying rent again on the first, and I know my landlord will let me leave. I might not give a full two weeks."

Brianne paused to look at Lelah, expecting admonishment for short notice to everyone.

"Or, if you want, *you* can pay next month's rent and then stay here for a month. I don't even think I'm gonna take the furniture cause Rob's place isn't big enough, plus I'm not trying to pay for a truck. You can sell it all or keep it."

Bobbie had fallen asleep in Lelah's arms. He pulled on her shirt collar with one hand and palmed her left breast with the other, a lingering habit from his breast-feeding days.

"What makes you think I don't have a place?" Lelah asked. She whispered fiercely, so as to not wake her grandson. "Who's gonna watch Bobbie, huh?"

Brianne took a big breath. She was aware that her mother was breakable, that this right now might break her, and because of this Brianne felt both terrified and strangely energized. Years later she would look back on this early morning as the moment her adult life truly began.

"*Me*, Mommy, at least until I can find nursing work out there. Then we'll figure it out."

"You and *Rob*," Lelah said. "You and Rob will figure it out. Right. You can't just run away from your life, Brianne. You got a good job here, free childcare, and you know how this economy is. Jobs aren't just falling from the sky."

"I don't have a *life* here. I just have a job. I just work a lot, and none of my friends from college are around, and I don't have anything to talk about with the ones from high school."

Brianne swiped at a tear with the back of her hand.

"So *Rob's* gonna take care of you? After all this time of him not doing enough. You're just gonna throw away the work you've done by yourself and go lay up under some *man*? You know I did that with your father, and it didn't work. I was trapped cause I wasn't makin my own money. No, me and *you* were trapped down there, Brianne. He beat the *shit* out of me and if it wasn't for Cha-Cha comin to pick us up maybe he would've killed us, or I'd have killed him. That's what layin up under a man gets you."

Lelah realized she was yelling because Bobbie startled awake. He looked over to his mother, saw the tears in her eyes, and began crying too. Brianne reached across the table and took him out of Lelah's arms. Lelah had never told Brianne about Vernon hitting her, about the long hours of night when she sat in a corner of the living room with Brianne on her lap, with her right eye swollen shut and her lip split open, waiting for Cha-Cha to arrive. Terrified that Vernon would come back from wherever he'd gone. She always just told her that things had not worked out, and she'd forbidden her siblings from contradicting her. She had planned to tell Brianne the truth just as soon as she could tell the story and not feel the old terror and rage. That day had never come.

"You should go," Brianne said. It was nearly inaudible, but she got it out.

"Leave? What about Bobbie?"

"I'll take care of him," Brianne said.

Lelah looked around the room for something, anything that might help her salvage her case.

"Come on now, Brianne. I didn't mean to shout, but there's no reason I can't watch him today. You gotta go to work. I'm not saying Rob is like Vernon, I just—"

She watched her daughter move to the front door and hold it open for her. On the TV Donnie rode a miniature fire truck around a playground. A euphoric smile spread across his face.

"I need you to go," Brianne said. "Right now."

So Lelah went.

Brave, or at Least Brash

Cha-Cha dreamed of Alice. In that fancy bed, next to his wife and following their failed attempt at sex, he dreamed of her, and for the first time in a week he looked poised to sleep through the night. It wasn't quite a sex dream, but it produced a similar effect when he awoke. He dreamed of stop-motion glimpses of her, first behind her desk as usual, her hair gathered up in that halo style from his last visit, her arms bare. Then she was sitting on the mauve fainting couch, still clothed, a coquettish smile on her lips. Another moment saw her reclining on the couch in a lavender negligee, one of those lacy, strappy getups that Cha-Cha found enticing in catalogs but cumbersome in real life. Just as he registered his own hands extending toward the brown expanse of Alice's hips, he snapped awake. The windowsill was aglow.

He remembered Lonnie's advice, to try to talk to it.

"Hello?" he tried. "What do you want?" He felt ridiculous. He took himself too seriously to talk to a blob on the wall.

He nudged Tina. She didn't move. He shoved her, perhaps too hard, but she only mumbled, "Uh-huh, right there on the counter," and rolled over. Cha-Cha let her sleep. He lay there on his back, his eyes trained on his haint, and pondered his dream, his post-dream erection, and what it all might mean. It frustrated him that even in his dreams he could only limn the line of infidelity, could only imagine a PG-13 encounter with Alice. He always let himself down in this way. His entire life might have been different if he'd figured out a way to be braver, or at least brasher. He might have made more money, garnered more respect. In the late eighties a couple of black truckers Cha-Cha knew from the union had approached him about starting their own company, buying a few trucks and contracting out service. It had seemed very risky to Cha-Cha back then, but now he couldn't recall why. His boys were both nearly grown, and the small-business loan required was modest. It must have been that Francis was already sick, and Cha-Cha had felt his impending role as patriarch required stability. Two decades later, before gas prices went crazy and work disappeared, those black truckers sold their business for an admirable profit, and Cha-Cha was still a Chrysler peon. The same quality that read as dependable and even-keeled in his youth had crusted over and become stubborn and pitiable. Tina pitied him, and Alice likely did, too. Well, he thought, there might be time yet to change one of their opinions. He rolled over so that he no longer faced the haint. Instead he lay face-to-face with his wife. She slept with both hands tucked under her cheek, as if in prayer.

Around six-thirty Tina woke up, dressed, and looked in on Viola. Cha-Cha remained in bed, feigning sleep. At seven-fifteen he heard the doorbell ring and the booming voice of Andrew, the young Lebanese man who worked for the medical transport service Cha-Cha hired to take Viola to her physical therapy and hospital visits. He heard Andrew explaining things to Viola—"I'm going to count to THREE, then lift you UP"—in the loud voice young people who feared the elderly used. A single squeak from Viola's wheelchair, a front-door slam, and they were gone.

In the car outside of Alice's office Cha-Cha had second thoughts. It was true that this was his regularly scheduled session time, but had his episode last week canceled it? Alice might have given his time slot away. And then there was the more nerve-racking issue of what he'd say. He'd decided this morning to chance it, tell Alice how he felt about her and see what came of it. An easy enough plan, but how to execute it? He'd always valued romantic stability—knowing where his sex and his meals would come from—over the thrill of someone new and the anxiety of living a lie. In this respect he differed from his brothers. Of the seven Turner boys, four had outside children they claimed, and there were always jokes and jabs about other children out there, waiting to be brought into the ever-fattening fold. No one called these children illegitimate, and none of their fathers ever denied patronage (at least not after DNA tests), but they were living, lovable proof of the weaknesses of the Turner man. Cha-Cha had never felt so weak before.

"Charles, I wasn't expecting you," Alice said.

But was that the truth? She stood in her office doorway looking more put-together than usual. Her eyebrows, often unruly, were regulated by some sort of makeup pencil, or maybe she had plucked them. She wore a sleeveless blouse and for the first time ever a skirt, a black and white polka-dotted one that stopped just below the knee. Her legs looked freshly shaved and well greased. To Cha-Cha, everything about her appearance suggested extra, premeditated effort.

"I've unfortunately scheduled this hour for some errands I need to run," she continued. "But you're welcome to walk out with me."

The girl behind the counter looked as surprised and suspicious as Cha-Cha felt. He gathered himself up from his chair and followed Alice into the hallway.

Once out of earshot of the receptionist, Alice spoke.

"I don't have any errands to run right now, Charles, I just thought we might need to talk outside of my office. I didn't think you'd show up for your appointment, but I'm glad you did. Would you like to get coffee?"

"Coffee," he said. "Okay."

"Great," Alice said. "There's a shop right on Grand River and Farmington; I'll drive myself and meet you there."

"Okay."

This could be either the beginning of something new for them or the end of everything, Cha-Cha realized. Alice busied herself with her phone as they waited for the elevator, only looking up at him once. She pretended this was normal, what they were doing, that he wasn't a patient but a colleague, perhaps, that getting coffee wasn't a new and interesting activity within the scope of their relationship.

But I say to you, whoever looks at a woman to lust for her has already committed adultery with his heart. Trusty, pragmatic Matthew. The sin was already in motion, Cha-Cha reasoned, so he might as well see it through.

They stepped into the empty elevator, bringing their awkward silence with them. Cha-Cha wanted to start the conversation immediately, get his apology out of the way, but it seemed Alice wanted to wait until they were out of her building to say anything. She smelled like citrusy perfume—another first, Cha-Cha observed. He leaned forward with one hand extended toward Alice's face, the other supporting him on his cane.

In movies, it always seems easy enough to kiss a woman, even if she doesn't really want to be kissed. The heroine will stand there and take the leading man's advance—eyes wide open if she doesn't want it, eyes closed if she does. Reality is more complicated.

Cha-Cha leaned in to kiss Alice, and because he'd closed his eyes he couldn't see the shock and confusion in hers, nor did he feel her duck out of kissing range. His lips grazed her forehead. She tasted like salt.

"Oh God," she said.

"Shit," Cha-Cha said. If he could have pushed a button to eject himself from the elevator and into oblivion, he would have.

The door opened on the first floor and Cha-Cha followed Alice out. She walked briskly through the main lobby. Cha-Cha wondered if she was running away from him, if he was chasing her. He slowed. Alice slowed as well, waited for him by the door.

On the curb outside, Cha-Cha said he was sorry, although he didn't feel sorry. Alice shook her head quickly, like a child shaking water out of her ear.

"You were confused. It didn't happen. Nothing happened. The coffee shop is on Farmington and Grand River," she said.

There would be no affair. How had he ever thought otherwise? He now feared he'd ruined their relationship for good. What had he thought—that she'd accept his kiss right there in her office elevator, then retire with him to the back of his SUV and they'd get it on? He hadn't thought, was the problem. He'd tried to be brash and ended up looking like a creepy old man.

Inside the coffee shop Alice had her drink in hand and was prowling around for a place to sit. It was one of those tiny, over-furnished places where the unemployed and entrepreneurial set up camp for the day. Alice poached two facing armchairs near a fake fireplace. Cha-Cha wasn't supposed to drink coffee anymore, so he joined her without ordering anything.

"Look, Alice," he said. "I don't know why I did that in the elevator. I haven't been sleeping—"

Alice shook her head.

"We don't have to talk about that, Charles. I'd prefer very much that we didn't."

She spoke quickly, not waiting for him to agree.

"Obviously our conversation last week ended very badly. You don't have to apologize, because we both said the wrong things."

"I do have to apologize," Cha-Cha said. "It was out of line for me to bring up your parents. And I never should have yelled."

"But I understand your frustration," Alice said. "I undid months of trust and sharing on your part in fifteen minutes. It wasn't entirely professional, and you deserve better than that."

"Thank you," Cha-Cha said. He couldn't fully commit to the conversation; his brain was busy replaying his kiss attempt over and over.

"I've been talking to my *own* therapist, who is also my mentor," Alice said. "And we think it's best for both you and me if I stop being your therapist."

"Oh," Cha-Cha said. "I see." He had no way of knowing whether she was happy or sad to be cutting him off.

"And I've decided it would be best to explain a little bit about why I handled things between us the way I did. You do deserve an explanation, Charles, because the way I've behaved is particular to you."

"What is *particular*, Alice? The friendship we've created? Or all of the flip-flopping you did about my haint?"

Alice frowned. Her fingers fluttered with no desk full of pens to distract them.

"Both, I suppose," she said. She took a long drink of her coffee. "I wanted to know more about you, so I deliberately broke my own protocol in regards to several things, the haint just being the most glaring example."

Cha-Cha reasoned that his first suspicions about her must have been true; she'd used him for a little cultural voyeurism, some risk-free socioeconomic slumming.

"But I wasn't interested in you because my parents are white," Alice added. "This is Detroit, after all, Charles, and I'm an adult. I *know* black people. It didn't have to do with you being black, but it did have something to do with your background. Honestly, I wouldn't have been able to articulate what exactly it was had it not been for the conversations I've had with Gus."

"What was it then?" Cha-Cha asked. "I'm not that interesting."

The truth, when finally revealed, is sticky like wet dough. The majority of it stays in place as one handles it, but pieces break off and adhere, making certain facts seem larger, more portentous, than others. Alice told a story that was more than Cha-Cha imagined hearing from her, a story that made him look at their entire history differently.

Over a decade earlier, at thirty-one years of age, Alice discovered she had uterine fibroids. Despite the best efforts of doctors to minimize these growths and even an operation to remove them, they persisted, large and painful inside of her. Her doctors determined that a hysterectomy was the only viable option to ensure her health. Faced with the reality of barrenness, Alice developed a desire to learn more about her birth parents. She wanted to know whose genes she'd inherited, whether she had siblings out there in the world, and what other conditions crouched in her DNA, waiting to incapacitate her at a later date. Alice knew that her adoptive parents, the ones Cha-Cha had seen online, had been Freedom Riders in the sixties, and that after many visits and considerable bureaucratic rigmarole they'd adopted her from a small orphanage in Mississippi. Throughout her twenties that explanation sufficed, but now that Alice needed to know more, additional information proved elusive. After weeks of correspondence with county clerks, records officials in Jackson, and even a few priests, Alice learned that she'd been the youngest of seven children, and that all of them died shortly after she was born.

"No one over the phone or through the mail would tell me how they died," Alice said. "So I took a trip down there and started asking around. I questioned people at the grocery store and after church in the town where I was born. A lot of the older people remembered my family, but were cagey about what had happened to them. I eventually got the number for the retired county clerk's house and called her."

She met the elderly woman for lunch at a nearby Cracker Barrel. The woman told her that at the time of their deaths, the eldest of Alice's siblings, a boy, had been fifteen years old, and the youngest, a girl, had been two. The retired clerk also seemed hesitant to go into the details of her siblings' deaths, but Alice pressed her.

"They died in a car accident," Alice told Cha-Cha. "The car spun out of control on a bridge and ended up in a lake. Everybody but my birth father and me was inside, and for whatever reason, my birth father eventually dropped me off with a church lady and left town. It's a sad story, and I was upset about it, but it didn't explain why the whole town acted as if there was a terrible secret behind it all."

The secret wasn't based on fact at all, just a mass of rumors that over time people took for truth. The retired county clerk said the eldest son had been driving on the day of the accident because Alice's birth mother didn't know how. There were rumors that he'd tried to run away several times before the accident, but each time he'd run out of money before he got very far and come back home, or else his father would find him, give him a good whipping, and bring him back because he needed help on the farm. The rumor was that this eldest son drove the car off the bridge on purpose, and while there was no way to substantiate it, the rumor persisted, even thirty years later.

When Alice came back to Michigan she often found herself thinking about them. Bodies folded inside of an old car, overcome by silty lake water. She thought about this eldest son, and the possibility of so much responsibility so young making a person desperate. How feeling trapped within such a large family might affect one's psyche. Not until years later, when she met Charles Turner, eldest of thirteen and possibly prone to hallucinations, would she get an opportunity to talk to someone at the center of a similarly complex web.

"So," Cha-Cha said. "You humored me all this time because you wanted to know if being in charge of things for my family was making me murderous?"

Alice winced, and he knew that despite his best effort to sound empathetic, his question had come off cruel.

"There's no one-to-one correlation, Charles. What matters is that I saw something in you that interested me, so I decided to perhaps not do what was best for you in pursuit of my own interest. I shouldn't have done that."

Every time Alice apologized, the possibility of the two of them remaining friends seemed more unlikely. She was being this honest with him because she never wanted to see him again.

"But do you think that . . . that I'm hallucinating?"

Alice chewed on her bottom lip. Her hand traveled up to her hair, and she raked a stray coil back into the larger formation.

"I'm not speaking in a professional capacity—"

"I know," Cha-Cha said. "We're done with all that. I just want to know what you think; I'm not going to sue you."

Cha-Cha felt uncomfortable in his armchair. The back was too straight and the seat wasn't deep enough. He was aware of his belly hanging low and his knees spread too far apart.

"Honestly, Charles, I don't know what to tell you about the haint."

"I just want to know what you think, in your gut."

Alice took a deep breath, and her cheeks puffed out like a child's.

"In my gut I think you've always believed in this thing. And I don't know that you want to get rid of it."

Cha-Cha opened his mouth, but Alice raised a hand in the air to silence him.

"I think you have a position within your family that affords you a lot of respect but not much true friendship, or a sense of individuality. This ghost, or the memory of it, has bothered you your whole life, but it's also made you feel extraordinary, chosen."

"It doesn't make me feel special. I can't even sleep. I don't want it."

"Your wife has her church involvement, which from what it sounds like makes her feel purposeful, but what do you have, Charles? You have this haint."

"I still think it's real," he said.

"Charles, you're focusing on the wrong thing. Does it even *matter* one way or the other?"

It was a hypothetical question, Cha-Cha knew, so he saved it for some later mulling over. What he worried about now was that Alice had stood up to throw away her coffee cup, that she was digging in her purse, presumably for keys. One last opportunity to be brave. Cha-Cha stood up.

"I'm not sorry about the elevator. I mean, I'm sorry for jumping on you, but I still think there's something between us."

Alice smiled, and if she were a different sort of person, Cha-Cha imagined, she would have given his arm a conciliatory pat.

"I don't want to belittle your feelings, but I don't think you'd feel this way about me if I hadn't taken advantage of our relationship in the first place. I've just told you more about me than I've ever told a patient, Charles. That's the only intimacy I can give you."

She pulled a business card from her purse and handed it to him.

"No one would blame you for wanting to take a break from therapy, but I really don't think you should. This is my mentor Gus's information. He's smarter than me, and funnier. You two will get along."

Cha-Cha put the card in his shirt pocket. He felt lonelier already.

One Thing Was Clear

She no longer trusted herself to be on Yarrow Street alone. She had Marlene's money, and the hours in the big room would be too long. She would end up at Motor City.

If Brianne were a volatile daughter, it all would have hurt less. If slammed doors and shouting matches figured into their history, Lelah might have taken the morning's events in stride, confident that they'd get over this disagreement as they had others. She had never articulated her anger or disappointment with Lelah, save a snippy text message or two, but now Lelah saw that Brianne had it in her to cut Lelah off. Sever ties and move away. All of this time Lelah had thought that Brianne couldn't see the truth about her, that she retained an element of naïveté where everyone else in the family knew Lelah to be a failure.

David knew the truth about her, had seen her on Yarrow and not run off. So she called him. Offered to treat him to lunch at Slows, the barbecue place he'd wanted to take her to that first day they ran into each other downtown. He said he only had time for coffee, and that he needed to meet earlier than lunchtime. They met at a bakery near Wayne State with pricey pastries and nice outdoor seating.

Now that he sat across from her, she could not figure out the right way to present her ludicrous proposition: that she move in with him for a very short while as she figured things out. It had seemed a sound idea as she sped away from Brianne's, then pulled over to breathe, and think, and decide what to do. If she stayed with him, she would not go to the casino; if she stayed with any of her siblings, the temptation would still be there.

She stalled. She talked about Viola's upcoming party, about her siblings arriving from out of town. Her mouth moved without much effort from her brain. After several minutes of this she noticed that David wasn't looking at her. In fact, he was making a show of looking at everything but her. The umbrella shading them, the water bowl on the ground for dogs two tables down, a panhandling old man in a Lions jersey making his way up the block. Lelah asked him what was wrong.

David put his messenger bag on the table and pulled out an oblong, cloth-wrapped thing. He didn't unwrap it; it didn't need unwrapping. She wished she could save their relationship at this moment, keep it free from what was about to happen. Preserve it in amber like a prehistoric organism maybe, and wear it on a chain around her neck. Proof that she could be cherished by someone, if only for a while. What was about to happen and what *had* happened had nothing to do with each other. She wasn't sure how he'd procured what was wrapped in that cloth, but it did figure, given her luck, given the morning she'd had, given how secure she'd started to feel with him, and what she'd had the audacity to think possible. Before he spoke she felt herself slipping in his eyes from person to patient, lover to bad decision. She'd lost everything else, but this one thing, what her and David were starting to have, should have been hers to keep.

He did not unwrap the item, but he did explain.

With a brother like Greg and a mother so forgiving, David Gardenhire had reason to be familiar with east side pawnshops. Two summers ago he had visited every pawnshop within feasible walking distance of his mother's house with a picture of Greg taken on Christmas six years prior, and solicited manager promises not to do business with his brother because his things were surely stolen. It was a naïve, unenforceable request, but he hadn't known any other way to regain a sense of control. He returned to these pawnshops yesterday.

Gregory Sr. had been born again at Second Baptist Church in downtown Detroit as a condition of marrying David's mother, but having migrated up from that part of southeastern Texas with strong Catholic roots, he'd worn his very Catholic crucifix until the day of his death. Although David had wanted his mother to bury the necklace along with his father, Mrs. Gardenhire's penchant for memento hoarding prevailed. It was draped over the corner of the best picture of Gregory Sr. on her mantel (taken in the seventies; he has a small, hopeful afro and graying sideburns) waiting for the day when Greg finally got desperate enough to steal it.

A few pawnbrokers had claimed to remember David. Even at CHAINS-R-US, the Walmart of pawnbrokering on the east side, the elderly Vietnamese owner said he had turned Greg away.

"He said the chain was too flimsy," David explained now. He spoke to the street to the right of Lelah, but Lelah stared at his face, at that unusual elegant nose and those full lips.

David had idled at the window because he had no more shops to visit. Eventually a young woman with very thin eyebrows and a slicked-back ponytail came out of the back room. She sat in front of the desktop computer and placed an open laptop next to it. She logged on to eBay.

"I always wondered what they do with the shit no one wants to buy, you know, so I just stood there and watched her," David said now.

Thanh had opened a folder on her laptop full of photos of a knife. On the desktop computer she pulled up a listing for a similar knife on eBay.

"I *knew* I'd seen that knife before, so I banged on the glass until she turned around. I asked her where she got it, and she described you."

Lelah let out a sound, not quite a whimper, nor a sigh.

"At this point I'm pissed, like real hot," David said. "And I feel stupid. But I still ask her all these other questions, trying to make sure it was you. She ends up showing me that flute case with your name on it, and after that I had to admit it to myself."

David had tried to visualize his living room floor, the cool concrete beneath him and his breath becoming shallow. He couldn't. Instead he felt the sucking warmth of Phuket, Thailand. Remembered how he and Troy and a sailor named Tasaka from Queens had left Bangkok, tired of watching Ping Pong tournaments on TV and too afraid to seek out whores. In Phuket they found beaches, friendly Australian girls, and booze. They met a man with a boat who sold them on a nearby island with even better beaches, and a lot of Singha for the ride there and back. The rest of that evening remained hazy in David's memory, but when they traveled back to Bangkok the following day the sailor Tasaka, who was half black and half Japanese, had been upset about losing a knife he'd bought in Okinawa and had planned to give to his father. David remembered Tasaka showing the knife off early on their boat ride, using it to open beers, and he'd always figured the driver stole it when everyone got drunk. But there was the knife yesterday, stolen by Troy twenty years prior for no apparent purpose. Perhaps Troy had planned to sell it to pay off some debt and forgot. Or maybe—and this seemed very possible now—Troy Turner was simply an asshole.

"And you pawned it cause that's what you *do*, right?" David said now. "I guess you probably have to pawn shit all the time." He finally looked at her.

She didn't reply.

"I don't think we should, whatever this is," he said. "I'm not doing it anymore."

Lelah pinched the skin between her forefinger and thumb. She felt lightheaded.

"You don't wanna say nothin? Nothin at all?"

She wanted to say plenty. About mistakes, about how she had been one way so long, it was hard to turn around so quickly, but that she did feel different, even from this morning when she'd lied to her baby girl and broken something between them. She wanted to say that she just needed time, that she could dig herself out of all of this with more time.

"You want me to *beg* you to change your mind?" is what she said. She hoped she sounded strong. "I'm done lying and begging."

He should have left by now, she thought. But he still sat there.

"Look, my brother Greg's been on heroin since '97 at least," he said. He put on his Intervention Face: eyes large with compassion, mouth tight and authoritative. "My mom just keeps giving him chance after chance after chance. I can't be that person for you."

"I'm not asking you to be!"

David whipped his head around to see if anyone else had heard her.

"Don't act *crazy*, Lelah. You don't need to get loud. I'm just—"

"Nobody's acting crazy. You're trying to make me out to be something I'm not. I have problems, yeah, but I'm a grown woman. I already told you at my mom's house, I'm not asking you or anyone else to save me."

"Right. But you're staying on the east side and nobody knows."

"You know what? I should go," Lelah said. She yanked her purse off the back of her chair. She had come so close to asking him to save her.

"Look, I'm sorry. Don't leave like that," David said. He half stood. "I'm not, I'm not trying to say you ever made me feel like I had to help you, but that's how I *am*. It doesn't even matter what you need, I'd try to solve your problems, which is a problem, you know? I need to stop doing that shit. And I'm not trying to say I don't like spending time with you cause I do, I just—"

"What? You want me to call you up when I get my shit together? I'm not on *drugs*, David. Those things were junk that nobody wanted. I'm surprised I got anything for them at all. It's not like I'm running up in my mother's house and stealing her TV, or snatching cash outta her purse like your brother."

David stood up now. He put the cloth bundle into his bag. His mouth spread into a miserable, close-lipped smile. When would she see those perfect teeth, that lovely face again?

"The thing is, you're *exactly* the same as him," he said. "Maybe worse, cause you ain't even figured out how fucked up you are yet."

The words settled on her shoulders like a curse, and one thing was clear: there was no one to save her but her. No salvaged job, no daughter's forgiveness, no big-room reprieve from the world, and no beautiful, meditating man.

"Why'd you have sex with me in my mother's basement?" she asked. "If I'm just like your brother, why didn't you stop seeing me when I told you about my eviction?"

David looked past her once again, out into the street. He appeared exhausted to Lelah, his full forty-three years old. He shrugged.

"I don't know," he said. "But I shoulda never done it. I shoulda never done any of this. Biggest mistake I've made in a long time."

"Fuck *you*," Lelah said. "You don't even *know* me." She remained seated as he walked away. "Fuck *you!*" This time louder. It was either this or cry, and while she did want to weep for the loss of him, doing so would have been giving in to self-pity, and she needed to be done with that for good.

DAVID HAD INTENDED to drive to Troy's in Hamtramck, to free himself of every ounce of Turner bullshit in his life, but he turned on Belvidere instead. There was a little stretch of Edsel Ford Service Drive abutting the freeway back there that Greg used to frequent. Last February David had caught him picking through the dirty snow for scrap metal like a magpie searching for glint. Today it looked like the church on the corner had finally cleared the neighboring lots of debris. All of the grass was evenly cut, and there were no bits of houses for a person like Greg to sift through.

David turned onto Holcomb, his mother's street, at a crawl. If he saw Greg, he would jump out and punch him in the face, he decided.

Run him down with this installation van should he be in the street. Somehow blot him out. He scanned house porches for a not-so-old man in a very old pea coat and saw no one. A relief, truth be told. It was just as likely that if he had seen his brother, he wouldn't have done anything at all. He feared he might even loan Greg money if asked, that the memory of the big brother who had drawn comic book heroes and still managed to be so damn *cool* would forever keep David in its thrall, just as whatever memory his mother held on to— of a cheerful, nappy-headed little boy who used to help her in the garden, maybe—supplanted reality and made her keep on forgiving.

He parked across the street. He saw his mother walking through her empty-lot garden with Mr. McNair. They picked their way through plants David could not name. They held hands. The sun reflected off of his mother's shiny black wig, and Mr. McNair's hand moved to the small of her back. His mother and Mr. McNair. Betsy Gardenhire and Mr. McNair. David realized that he didn't know the old man's first name, that he'd never before considered the fact that McNair had a first name. He didn't know that Norman McNair had loved his mother since the day of his first wife's funeral. Arlene, who had worked for a black undertaker's family in Conant Gardens for forty years, and found both Norman and Francis Turner their truck-driving jobs at Chrysler through that undertaking family's connections. She had loved succotash. Betsy McNair was the only person to bring a dish that Arlene would've liked to the repast after the funeral.

David unbuckled his seat belt but idled, torn between getting out of his van and driving home. After a few minutes he stepped out of the car. He was halfway across the street when he noticed Greg. His brother was in the garden too, bent over red and green cabbage in their father's old overalls. Yanking up weeds with a cigarillo pinched between his lips. Greg muttered something and everyone in the garden laughed, like easy friends. Funny to feel embarrassed more than enraged, as if catching an intimate moment shared by some other family. David returned to his van and headed to Hamtramck.

Playing for Time

The casino: a different animal at 10 A.M. than at 10 P.M. The windowless, nighttime atmosphere of the casino floor does nothing to stave off the depression one feels when visiting the place so soon after breakfast. At 10 A.M. no one is at the casino for fun. They come to be redeemed, to be absolved, to forget.

Lelah's inch-thick stack of bills—mostly tens and twenties—sat in the envelope in her purse, next to her father's pipe. Marlene's money was the last company she had, and like the old gambling saying went, scared money don't make money.

Ten in the morning meant more low-minimum tables but also less camaraderie. Lelah circled the floor, waiting for someone else to sit down for roulette. Playing with just herself and the dealer was too lonely; dealers wouldn't partake in confessional conversation the way a bartender might. An older man with a close-cropped salt-and-pepper natural sat down at a table, and Lelah joined him. He nodded hello to her in that tight-lipped, formal way that gamblers focused on winning do. With $950 and $10 minimums Lelah could play nearly a hundred turns. She didn't care if she made a profit; she was gambling for time. For stillness. She was fresh out of plans except for this one.

Where Turners Had Been Known

Cha-Cha's father claimed to never drink and drive. Instead Francis Turner cradled his beer between his thighs while navigating and took furtive sips at stoplights. This was a man who had never worn a seat belt in his life, even while driving an eighteen-wheeler, so Cha-Cha knew that following his example was foolhardy. Still, he stopped at a liquor store on his way to the east side for two six-packs of beer, popped one open, and drove the rest of the way like his father.

He might have made it to work at a decent time, but he had stayed in the coffee shop after Alice left. He drank two doctor-discouraged coffees and tried to reason away the abandonment and humiliation he felt. It had been years since Cha-Cha thought another woman might be interested in him, and on this, the only time he'd worked up the nerve to act on the inclination, he had made a fool of himself. Alice had ended up being trouble, just as Tina predicted. Cha-Cha didn't fault her for dumping him as a patient, considering the messes both of them had made—the breaches of trust, the ulterior motives—but somehow he thought they'd at least be able to be friends. Instead Alice used him as a repository of very personal information, a hole in the ground to yell a disconcerting secret into, and then left him. Wired on coffee, with little desire to go to work and even less desire to go home to his wife and mother, Cha-Cha decided to go home for real.

He parked on Lambert, kitty-corner to the old, abandoned primary school and across from the basketball court. Clumps of grass the size of human heads poked through the court's crumbling blacktop. Cha-Cha turned off the ignition and opened another beer.

This was Francis Turner's drinking spot. The house under which Cha-Cha had hidden was not fifty yards away. It was now an empty lot choked with weeds. No evidence or answers about what happened there remained—not even a hint of the house's foundation. The phenomenon of disappearing landmarks used to distress Cha-Cha, mostly because new buildings never replaced them, and it felt like the old ones had never existed. But over time he realized it didn't matter; memory needed no visual cue to do its work.

He hadn't called out sick, so his job would likely call home, and Tina would discover his truancy. Cha-Cha turned off his phone. He tried to remember a time within the past few weeks when he'd felt tenderness, or any emotion at all toward Tina that wasn't tinged with resentment. He failed.

He held no illusion of safety on Yarrow Street. In the months since his mother moved away things had gotten worse. He read the news every day, and while he rarely saw this exact block mentioned, the scenes of crimes were close enough for him to understand that they happened here too. He knew his car made him stand out, likely made him look like an over-the-hill undercover cop, but the more beer he drank, the safer he began to feel. The house next to his mother's was long gone, so Cha-Cha could see the side and back of the Yarrow house clearly. The windows of the boys', girls', and parents' rooms upstairs, the late-addition garage attachment, the verdant back alley. All of it worthless now.

The thing to do was go into the big room, he knew. Confront his fears. But what if nothing happened? Part of him would rather spend every night on his couch, never sleeping more than a few hours, than muster the courage to return to that room and find it held no special truth for him. If it turned out to be just four walls and a twin bed, then Alice would be right, and he an even bigger fool. He drank more beer.

It always took a long time for Cha-Cha to get drunk. He blamed his substantial weight and Turner genes. He drank the first six-pack and remembered he hadn't eaten anything yet, so he drove to a Coney Island on Gratiot. When he returned to the neighborhood with his chili dogs and fries, he parked on Yarrow, across the street from the house.

Two men riding in a silver Dodge Charger pulled up parallel to his window and looked at him. The bass from their stereo made Cha-Cha's seat vibrate. He nodded at them without smiling. They nodded back and drove away. Cha-Cha relaxed. This was the street where the first thirteen plus two later generations of Turners had been known. A face like his must have still meant something to people around here.

Up

Hours later and Lelah wasn't destitute. Far from it, in fact. She had played at that first table for two hours, just her and the salt-and-pepper gentleman who wouldn't make small talk. She placed $10 to $20 bets initially, trying to bide her time, and her stack of chips fluctuated but never disappeared. That should have been a good thing; the plan was to spend time, after all, but stillness eluded her. The man next to her refused to smile, and the dealers rotated to the table were all business. The casino was too quiet early in the day; even the robotic pings of septuagenarian-helmed slots couldn't cut through the emptiness. By noon more people had arrived, but not enough stayers, just a bunch of bet-and-walk types who made it hard to maintain a good vibe at a table. Without the stillness, her mind ran over the things she'd done wrong, today and always. There was nowhere to put all of that self-loathing, no one place to stash the regret, but stillness, if it would just show up, could hold despair at bay. When she took a break for the lunch buffet she had $875. Only $75 lost.

After lunch Lelah stationed herself near a long, overhead-illuminated craps table, usually a logistical no-no for her, but it was the only place where the players looked jovial. Of course on the day that she didn't care to win, she won. She played only on the outside, on black and 00, and won $200. A joyless gain. She changed all of her money, the entire $1,075, for chips, mostly multicolored 50s and 20s, and marveled at how short her stack felt with higher denominations. Unsatisfying. She called the waitress over for drinks, one mai tai and then another, and sat disgusted as her pink and yellow $20 chips, the same colors as her drink, came back $50 green. A woman with a very flat chest stood next to her and whooped as Lelah's stack grew, drawing attention the way a lone wolf alerts his pack to easy prey. It was a roulette crowd—smaller, less exuberant than a craps crowd—and Lelah refused to look up at them, refused to play the role of victor. In an effort to shock and embarrass the onlookers with her recklessness she put $800 on 27, Brianne's number, and nothing anywhere else.

She won.

"Whooo!" the flat-chested woman yelled. She clapped Lelah on the back.

The pit boss came over and approved her win so that the dealer could give her the chips. Lelah's mental math failed as he slid her chips she hadn't possessed in years, $100 ones. The crowd quieted, waiting on what she'd do next, and all of their attention made Lelah nauseous. She called the waitress for a bottle of water and sat out the next round.

"If you're gonna backslide, this is the way to do it, huh?"

The voice from behind startled Lelah. She spun on her stool, breaking one of her rules by putting her back to her chips. A thirty-something white guy stood behind her. Blond hair parted to the side, out of place in an expensive-looking suit and tie.

"I don't know you," Lelah said, but her voice had the lilt of a question.

He squinted at her. Beyond the playfulness that he presented for show, something in his face was so unhappy, so desperate for commiseration, that Lelah rotated half of her body back to the table, a subconscious movement to ward off misery more frightening than her own.

"You probably don't know my real name," he said. "But you've heard me tell the same sad stories enough times to know me. I went by Zach?"

It was true. Lelah remembered a Zach and the story he told, about his obsession with watching the roulette ball spin, and his ex-wife not letting him see his baby daughter. Lelah nodded at him. She had nothing to say.

"I don't remember *you* ever talking much," he went on. "But now I see why. You're a fucking pro, huh? I wouldn't want to quit either."

He smiled at Lelah with only the corners of his mouth. His misery assaulted her senses like bad breath.

"I'm leaving," she said. She traded her smaller chips for larger ones, swept everything into her purse. Zach's eyes followed her chips as they moved, then he looked over Lelah's shoulder toward the wheel, where the ball was in motion. It was difficult for Lelah to maneuver because Zach stood so close behind her chair. He would have to take a step back for her to walk away from the table.

"Okay, good seeing you," he said. "Congrats on your win."

He extended his hand, presumably for a shake, but his palm was parallel to the ceiling. Like a priest seeking alms or a basketball coach soliciting a low-five. He wants a goodwill chip, Lelah realized. Well, he'd have to get it from someone else.

She stepped past Zach's hand and away from the table. She cashed in her winnings, picked up her car from the valet, and left Motor City behind.

When she turned onto Yarrow her car and the world outside of it, save for the inverted pyramid lit by her headlights, plunged into darkness. Both of the remaining streetlights on the block had either burned out or been smashed out. Lelah knew this was always a possibility. Dozens of blocks throughout Detroit existed in dangerous darkness as the city dragged its feet replacing the lights. She drove slowly down the block, hoping neither pedestrian nor pet jumped out into the street.

It would have been idiotic to risk fumbling with the back gate in the pitch dark, so Lelah parked out front and sprinted up to the door.

The First and the Last

Cha-Cha shocked awake from a push on his back. He sat against the big room's door, and through the crack underneath it came a faint light. The knob turned. His heart pounded and his body froze. He was still drunk, in no condition to reunite with a more aggressive incarnation of his haint. He heard footsteps retreating, and a second later a strong shove from behind knocked him forward.

Lelah switched on the big-room light and found her eldest brother in a fetal position to the right of the doorway. Two empty beer cans lay lip to lip in the middle of the floor.

"Oh my God," she said.

"Who is it? Who's there?"

Cha-Cha's lower back burned from the blow. The light was too bright for him to keep his eyes open. The footsteps moved closer to him, and he wondered if he might die before they reached him, have a cardiac event and perish at the hands of his own idiot fear.

"Cha-Cha? It's Lelah. Are you hurt?"

He groaned. His brain said sit up straight, but his body refused. Lelah dropped her purse and put a hand on his forehead. He swatted her away, rolled onto his back.

"Ughhh. I don't have a damn fever," he said. "You scared me half to death. Did Tina send you here?"

Lelah hooked Cha-Cha under the armpits and helped him sit upright on the bed. He reeked of beer. Sweat ringed his undershirt collar. She had never seen him like this before, and her fear for him made her forget that she'd just been discovered.

"You gonna throw up? You need me to help you to the toilet?"

"It's just *beer*," he said. "Of course I'm not gonna throw up."

Cha-Cha was able to keep his eyes open now. Lelah looked as bad as he felt. Her eyelids were puffy and the bottom rims red. She hunched in a way that suggested more than exhaustion; she looked spent, and skinnier.

"Let me get you some water," she said. "I'll try to find a cup downstairs."

Alone in the room, Cha-Cha took in the duffel bags pushed beneath the bed, the lone leather jacket hanging from a corner of the dresser. He hardly remembered coming inside the house, only stuffing the two remaining beers into his pants pockets and double-checking that his car door was locked. He looked around and realized that he had left his cane in the car. His knees hurt and the front of his pants were dirty. With no cane, he suspected he had crawled up the stairs to the second floor. He prayed he hadn't crawled up to the porch, too.

Lelah returned with lukewarm water in a paper cup. Cha-Cha poured some onto his hand and wiped his face with it. He gulped the rest down.

Cha-Cha knew the duffel bags shouldn't be here, and that they meant something, but he asked Lelah again if Tina had sent her.

"No," she said.

"Well, what are you doing here? Looks like . . . looks like somebody's been *living* here." He shrugged in an effort to appear less judgmental.

She started crying and nodding.

"For almost a month," she said. "I got evicted and suspended from my job cause I gambled everything away."

She sobbed like she used to when she was a little girl. So hard that her face was red and her body lurched. When Tina had babysat her, Lelah often cried like this, whether telling him how Viola wouldn't let her tag along to the flea market, or how Berniece and Sandra had pushed her out of the girls' room and slammed the door. When Cha-Cha drove her home from Missouri and she told him about the way Vernon had punched her, snatched her up by the collar and slammed her against a wall, she had cried like this. Even though he was maybe beginning to feel a little angry, Cha-Cha obeyed his impulse to comfort her by putting a hand on her back.

"And Brianne hates me because I don't know when to fucking *quit* with her and I feel like I'm ruining her with my guilt and bullshit. And I was sleeping with Troy's friend and now he hates me. I hate *myself*, Cha-Cha. I don't have *anything* and I'm tired of it. It's disgusting."

"Aw, Lelah, don't say that," he said. "Just slow down, and try to breathe."

She stopped talking. Her body heaved.

"I'm not angry at you," he said, although he wasn't sure she cared either way. "So you came back home. That's what it's for, right? It's no big deal. We'll figure all the rest of it out."

At this Lelah sobbed louder and shook her head.

"No," she said. "No, I don't wanna be saved anymore, Cha. *I'll* figure it out. I have to."

"Alright," he said. "You'll figure it out. I'm just tryna say it's not as bad as it feels."

How easy it was for him to slip into this paternal role, even when despairing in his own right. It was a gift and a burden. He thought back to the summer of '67, before fires and bricks and trains to Glory, when it was still Lelah's summer. How vastly different Lelah's experiences must have been from his own, even though they grew up in the same family, in the same house, in the same neighborhood, in the same city called Detroit.

Lelah's breath finally slowed, and she felt her heartbeat relax. This was the final confession, she promised herself. No point in telling people about her problems if nothing changed. She leaned her head against Cha-Cha's shoulder. Through the shirt his skin felt soft and clammy. Her ears rang from the sobbing, and she marveled at how the one person she especially didn't want to find her out was sitting next to her in the big room. Then, remembering the beer cans and him slumped in front of the door, she sat up.

"Wait a minute," she said. "What are you doing here?"

"I uh, I . . ." Cha-Cha started.

"Why are *you* up in here getting drunk on a weeknight?" Lelah asked. She wiped her nose with the back of her hand.

After several seconds of searching the corners of the room for an answer, Cha-Cha shrugged.

"You really don't wanna tell me," she said. She couldn't imagine any reason for him to be here, no cane in sight, passed out drunk at 10 P.M. Not Cha-Cha, leader of the family, paragon of propriety.

"Don't wanna tell you what?" he said. "I just needed to think. I've got a lot of things stressing me out."

He wouldn't tell her. That was always the way. She dumped her problems on others, they helped her solve them, but they didn't trust her. It never even occurred to them that she might be able to reciprocate.

"Will you do me a favor and turn the light off?" he asked. "My eyes sting."

Lelah flipped the switch, and the room became so dark that on the way back to the bed she used her phone as a flashlight. Cha-Cha laughed.

"What? What's funny?"

"Your phone," Cha-Cha said. "I saw your phone when you came busting in here, and I thought it was the haint. I thought a *gotdamned* cell phone was a ghost."

He laughed more and burped once. The smell of chili dogs mingled with the smell of beer.

"Marlene was trying to tell me about you and a ghost yesterday," she said.

"What *she* know about it? She calls herself being mad at me."

"Francey told her what it was about, you calling everybody."

"Oh," Cha-Cha said, then, "Oh! When you called yesterday I was in a bad mood. I shouldn't have snapped. Had I known you were here, I would have—"

"You would have been mad, Cha-Cha. It's fine. I'm not supposed to be here, and I haven't answered anybody's call for weeks."

"Nothing is decided anyhow," he said. "But you been here, Lelah. You know Mama can't come back here. It ain't safe. The stairs are steep; we'd have to put up some kind of ramp to the porch."

"Mama's dying," Lelah said, and just as soon as the words were out she wished she could take them back. Too painful a thing to just come out and say, even if true. Cha-Cha said nothing, and Lelah tried to formulate a sentence to undo her previous one.

"Tell me the story of the haint," she said.

"You know it. Everybody knows it."

"*I* don't, not really. There's all kinda stuff I don't know, Cha. All I know is Daddy didn't believe you."

"Shit, now Mama is claiming she don't either," Cha-Cha said.

He recounted that first visitation with the same animated certainty other people employed to tell the story of how their parents met, or the story of their first child's birth. It was his origin story, he realized, and if it turned out not to be true, he wasn't sure what would replace it.

"My therapist, Alice, says I hold on to this idea of a haint because it makes me feel extraordinary," he said. "But one, I don't *need* to feel extraordinary, I'm fine with feeling ordinary. And two, why would I make this up?"

"I don't know," Lelah said.

They heard a faint buzz through the window, and the streetlight popped on. Cha-Cha and Lelah sat in the orange glow of tenuous

Detroit Edison favor, and the increased visibility in the room made both of them feel vulnerable.

"I didn't know you were still seeing the therapist," she said. "I thought she was expensive."

"She is," Cha-Cha said. "And I'm not seeing her anymore. That's how I ended up here. We got into it cause she said I was hallucinating and I got mad. Then she tried to refer me to somebody else. So I got mad again, got some beers, and came here."

"After all that money she never even helped you?"

She watched Cha-Cha scoot back further on the bed and lean against the wall. She couldn't imagine what secrets he might have told a therapist. His sons, her nephews who were nearly her own age, never seemed to have any real drama, and he and Tina's relationship was more solid than any marriage she'd ever seen, including Francis and Viola's.

"No, Alice helped me," Cha-Cha said. "Like I said, I got other things stressing me out, and she was helping me with that kind of stuff."

"That's good."

"What's your game?"

"What, you mean my gambling game?"

He nodded.

"I don't wanna talk about it, Cha. It doesn't matter."

"But you been to the casino tonight," he said. "I can tell cause you smell like a chimney full of cigarettes."

She looked surprised that he would notice such a thing.

"Roulette."

"Not slots? I thought all you girls liked slots."

"No," Lelah said. She grimaced. "I don't like playing a computer, and you don't get any chips when you win, not even coins nowadays. You just get those receipts."

Cha-Cha could remember going to buffets at Motor City, Greektown, and MGM with Lelah and his other sisters, but had he ever seen her play before? Perhaps if he'd seen her in action, even once, he would have been able to tell she was hooked.

"Marlene gave me some money last night. And you know how people say they can't win for losing? Today was the only time I *wanted* to get rid of some money and I couldn't lose to save my life. I've got a few thousand now, and I don't deserve it. At least I can give Marlene her money back."

"Nobody *deserves* anything, Lelah," he said. "It's called favor. And all we can do is thank God for giving us a little bit, and do the right thing moving forward."

"You sound like your wife."

Cha-Cha shrugged.

"Have you figured out if this haint shows up at a certain time?"

"Mmm-hmm." He closed his eyes and leaned against the wall. "Between midnight and three."

Lelah checked the time on her phone.

"It's already eleven-thirty."

"I know."

"And you say it's been coming every night?"

"Yep."

"So it could show up whenever and I'll see it?"

"I doubt it. Tina didn't even feel it last night, and I figure if she couldn't feel it, then nobody but me can see it, cause it feels stranger than it looks."

"But Tina's not blood," Lelah said. When she was younger, and had felt left out, the last one still on Yarrow, she'd subscribed to this notion of blood. No matter that she didn't know the stories behind every joke, or that the Yarrow Street that Lonnie and Netti and Quincy might reminisce about had nothing to do with the one that she knew; the same blood pumped through all of their veins. When Francis held baby Brianne to his chest, she got to hear his heart, the source of his blood, the source for all of the others after him. Blood still mattered to Lelah.

"Also, you said everybody saw it that first time," she added.

"Maybe, maybe not."

"And you think Mama knows something about it but doesn't want to tell you?"

"I know she knows, Lelah."

"Maybe she thinks she's protecting you by playing dumb."

He wished Lelah would leave. Let an old man be alone with his demons, or angels, or hallucinations, whatever they turned out to be. She added another variable to his experiment, and what would it mean if she didn't see the haint? It might not be so bad, acknowledging that he'd held on to this thing like children cling to imaginary friends, but to have to admit it to himself and Lelah? Cha-Cha wasn't ready. Pride pride pride pride pride. It threatened to ruin him.

They heard a crash outside, very close to the house. It didn't sound like breaking and entering, not like a window kicked in, not even like a car rear-ended. It sounded like a heavy stack of dishes smashed on the ground. Cha-Cha saw no one on the street. From the big-room window he couldn't see the porch, just its roof, but he saw a shadow stretching from the porch onto the front walkway.

"Somebody's on the porch," he whispered. "They knocked over a planter."

"What should we do? You have a gun on you?"

"No I don't have no *gun*. Do you? You're the one who's been here alone."

"I'ma call the police." She opened her phone, and the room filled with light.

Cha-Cha snatched it and snapped it shut.

"Let's just wait a minute. Could be a drunk. I'm not tryna call the police on a drunk neighbor. They'll probably leave. They can't kick in that storm door, not with those bars."

Lelah tried to control her breathing, but was unable to be as calm as Cha-Cha looked. She remembered recent news and rumors she'd heard about the neighborhood. That a fourteen-year-old girl had been walking home when two men in a nineties-model sedan pulled up beside her, tossed her into their trunk, raped her in an abandoned house, and left her there. That a shootout with the police near Baldwin last February had ended with a six-year-old boy shot dead. She felt like a fool.

Someone paced the porch in heavy shoes, the footfalls loud enough to reach Cha-Cha and Lelah upstairs.

Someone banged on the storm door with the toe of a boot, or a strong fist. Another empty planter crashed to the porch floor.

"Maybe they know somebody's home," Lelah said.

Someone stomped around the porch again and after a few minutes began whistling a cheerful-sounding tune. A tune that Lelah vaguely recognized, she couldn't recall from where.

But Cha-Cha knew where the song was from, as well as the lyrics:

This train is bound for Glory, this train
This train is bound for Glory, this train
This train don't pull no winkers, no crap-shooters, no whiskey-drinkers
This train is bound for Glory, this train

Lelah felt her brother's body jerk. He jumped up off the bed.

"I'm not doing this no more," he said. "I'm tired."

He was out of the room and lumbering down the stairs before she could stop him.

Francis Turner had hummed the song when the two of them went fishing, when he drove them to football games, or when he worked in his tiny garden behind the house. Troy had never thought to ask Francis what the words were, but throughout his life, particularly when he was agitated, he'd caught himself whistling the tune. His eye hurt from where David Gardenhire had punched him, and he stopped kicking things over to poke at the swelling above his orbital bone. The storm door swung open, the front door after that. Cha-Cha came out, wild-eyed.

"You are not you! I know you're not you! Leave me alone!"

Troy had no time to decipher what this meant because Cha-Cha barreled toward him, low and shoulder-first like a wrestler. Troy had failed at subduing David earlier; his long, noodly limbs moved too quickly. But Cha-Cha was solid and slow. Troy bested him as he'd been trained to by the Detroit Police Department: firm downward pressure between the shoulder and neck. Cha-Cha dropped to the floor. Troy rolled him onto his stomach, put his knee into his back, bent Cha-Cha's arm behind him. The perfect position for cuffing.

"His hip! You're gonna crack his hip," Lelah said.

"Fuck his hip. He was tryna tackle me."

Cha-Cha gurgled.

"He can't breathe! What's wrong with you?"

Troy eased his knee off Cha-Cha but kept him pinned by the twisted arm. He didn't want to kill Cha-Cha, but his gut told him not to let his brother up.

Cha-Cha sucked in air as best he could. The porch was filthy, and broken terra cotta from the planters pressed into his cheek. Grit coated his tongue. He smelled the liquor sweating from Troy's pores. *I should be more surprised,* he thought; *I should be more surprised, but I'm not.* He wasn't even as angry as he deserved to be. Not yet, anyway. He'd come to Yarrow to face a supernatural being head-on, and instead it was his own kin betraying him, hurting and confusing him. And not just any kin, but the two he'd helped to raise before his own children were born.

"I came by here to take you home, cause I felt bad for you," Troy was saying to Lelah. "David told me how you two, you two been sneakin *around,* and how you been livin here just like them crackheads in that abandoned house up the street."

"You're out your fucking mind," Lelah said. "Let him go or I'ma call the police."

Cha-Cha heard Troy laugh—a fake, movie-madman cackle—and the pressure on his back slackened. He freed his hand and rolled away, up against the porch railing. He sat up, balled his fists, ready to defend himself as best he could, but Troy did not pursue him.

"Like I said. I came over here to see if what David said about you was true, but then I seen Cha-Cha's car outside. And I figured . . . I figure let me come inside and tell this nigga about himself for *once*, cause ain't nobody tellin Cha-Cha the truth, are they?"

Troy looked over to Cha-Cha with watery eyes. He'd clearly been crying, and now his black eye was swollen shut so that he seemed to be winking fiercely.

The streetlight blinked off and back on, which reminded Lelah that they were sitting on the porch past midnight, making a scene. She knew she should go to Cha-Cha, help him to stand, but she didn't move.

Troy sat with his back against the porch's stair railing. He pointed at Cha-Cha. "You had me out in the snow. Why?"

"I'm not doing this with you," Cha-Cha said. "I don't know what you want from me."

"Just leave him alone, Troy," Lelah said. David must have confronted Troy about that knife, she realized. He must have gone to Hamtramck looking for answers that Troy did not have, because Troy couldn't articulate why he'd stolen that knife any better now than he could have twenty years prior. But Lelah could imagine her brother's motives easily enough. It was rooted either in jealousy or in pride, and likely disguised as a prank. The sailor, Tasaka, might have been better with the ladies than Troy, or smarter, or perhaps just too flashy for Troy's liking. She felt sorry for Troy, for Cha-Cha, and for herself. Their attempts at getting answers, or respect, or even a modicum of stillness inside their own minds were pathetic.

A car drove by and all three of them watched it pass. None of them moved to go back inside.

"I just wanted team shoes and a fuckin jersey. That's all I wanted."

"Jesus, what *shoes?*" Cha-Cha said. He spat the dirt out of his mouth. "I bought you and Lelah whatever you asked for, whatever I could scrape up some money to get."

Troy shook his head too many times and then put his hand on his temple as if he were dizzy.

"Nah. You had me waiting out in the cold. You made me wait, and Chucky and Todd were up in that house warm."

"Oh God, Troy," Lelah said. "Let it go. You gotta—"

"No, no, no. He can go ahead," Cha-Cha said. "Everybody thinks I owe them, or did something to them. Let him get out what he thinks I did."

With permission granted, Troy wasn't sure what he wanted to say. Jillian had come home shortly after David punched him. She hadn't administered aid or provided much comfort; she instead asked what he'd done to provoke David. Even the woman who supposedly loved him did not expect him to be on the right side of a disagreement. Why would she want to be with someone like him? He'd left the house and drunk most of a fifth of Hennessy in his car, and then he'd driven here to save his little sister, to be the bigger person. But Cha-Cha's car out front thwarted even this feeble, drunken attempt to do the right thing. It seemed clear then that Cha-Cha, whether directly or indirectly, had been behind many major disappointments in Troy's life.

"You . . . you're the reason I'm back here, you know. Back in Detroit. I wanted to help with stuff."

"What stuff?" Lelah asked. Troy scrunched up his face at her. His lips trembled as if he might vomit.

"I'm talking to Cha-Cha, 'scuse me. I came back here for *you*, Cha, to help you take care of things. I even stayed here with Mama."

"Just until you could get your own place," Lelah said. "Don't lie." Troy ignored her.

"You don't listen is the problem, Cha. Like, with this house? I told you we should just short-sell it to Jillian, but no. It wasn't a good idea cause it wasn't one a *your* ideas. I was finna do it behind your back, too, you know that?"

Cha-Cha felt too many things at once. Rage: he wanted to smite Troy, to smack the taste directly out of his mouth. Disillusion: Alice had said that his role in the family earned him respect but not friendship. Now he saw that he'd never had respect, either. And finally, confusion: was he really so bullheaded, so closed off to his siblings, that they would spend real money just to do something without his consent? These feelings pinballed inside of him, and he felt like giving up, retiring early, selling his house and moving to a place where he was one of one, not one of thirteen. He no longer wanted to devote his life to these people.

"Yeah, I was handling it," Troy said. "But then Lelah had to go and fuck my friend. Know what? I don't even *care* you and David were fucking. But what you *do* to him, huh? He was damn near crying, saying we're a toxic family and some shit about the both of us . . . the both of us needing help. Like I need help! *He's* the one who can't even get his own brother clean. And you somehow got him thinkin we're worse than that."

Lelah stood up, dusted off the butt of her jeans.

"I do need help," Lelah said. "But look at you! You're a grown-ass man, coming over here crying, looking for answers from Cha-Cha like he's your daddy. Your daddy's dead, he's *been* dead! You got nobody to blame for your shitty life but yourself."

Troy stood up as well. He had to lean on the porch railing to steady himself.

"You been up in this house like a squatter. Like a fuckin bum!"

Lelah advanced on him until they were nearly nose to nose. His breath was terrible, but she did not back away.

"And you tried to do some underhanded shit to *sell* this house, or whatever you had planned. You're no better than me, Troy. Fuck you for even thinkin you were."

They were screaming. Cha-Cha knew he should separate them. Lelah was a woman, and Troy shouldn't be in a woman's face like that, but separating them reminded him too much of how he'd intervened in their squabbles as children. So he sat and watched them, a little proud of how Lelah refused to back down. These two were his protochildren, and he had failed them. He had done better with his actual sons, but that was with Tina's help. These two he'd tried to shape and mold when he was perhaps too young for such responsibility, and had failed. He was tired of failing, physically exhausted. In fact, he was just tired-tired. He could go to sleep right here on the porch. He thought about going to sleep as he looked down the length of it, to the far corner. There stood his haint. Or rather, there stood a new iteration of his haint, in the form of a skinny man in baggy slacks and an undershirt, its body backlit by a familiar shade of blue.

"Do you see it?" he whispered.

Lelah and Troy continued arguing.

"There there THERE! Right there! You see it?"

The haint reached both arms up over its head in a stretch. Opened its shadowy mouth and yawned. As if it was tired of haunting Cha-Cha, as if it had better things to do. But then it took a step toward him. It seemed to not register Lelah and Troy at all.

"Shut up shut up and look," he said, but they ignored him. The haint took three more steps. Cha-Cha felt the air leave him—the world's worst sucker punch—and then nothing.

Troy noticed Cha-Cha first. Out the corner of his eye he saw him slumped forward, mouth open. He ran to him and put his ear to his mouth. He was still breathing.

He slapped him lightly on the cheeks, and when this failed to revive him, he tried not to panic. He suddenly felt sober.

"Shit," he said. He slung Cha-Cha's arm over his shoulder. "We need to get him to the hospital."

"Should I call 911?"

Troy thought about response times and cross streets. He did not trust his fellow first responders to do right by this address tonight.

"No, we gotta just drive him. Come on."

It was slow going—Cha-Cha's body sagged like dead weight—but Troy and Lelah got him into the back of the SUV. Troy made Lelah squeeze into the back too.

"Make sure he stays breathing," he ordered.

In the rearview Troy saw Lelah shake Cha-Cha's shoulder, then pinch him on the flabby underside of his arm. Cha-cha groaned but did not wake up.

"I'm gonna just keep messing with him," Lelah said. "He's gotta wake up."

Troy sped down Gratiot with his hazard lights flashing. He was positive this was his fault. He must have used too much force when he subdued Cha-Cha, maybe leaned on his chest too hard. What the hell had he wanted? To be acknowledged? Even if Cha-Cha survived, Troy imagined he'd be excommunicated from the Turners forever. The desire to vomit returned.

"I found a water bottle," Lelah said.

She uncapped it and dumped a good amount of its contents onto Cha-Cha's face. When this didn't wake him, she let out a terrible moan.

"What are we gonna do if something's really wrong with him?" Lelah said.

Troy could not answer her. At the hospital he parked the car in front of the ER and ran in for help.

Cha-Cha opened his eyes as soon as the EMTs slid him onto the stretcher.

"Wait, he's awake!" Lelah said, but they were already wheeling him into the building.

"How do you feel?" she called out.

Cha-Cha hurt all over. But besides physical pain, he had no idea what or how he felt.

He was conscious, talking, and not showing signs of a heart attack, so the ER staff parked Cha-Cha in a wheelchair near a nurse station. They would not let Troy and Lelah back to see him, not even after Troy flashed his badge around. Not even after Troy put his badge back away, apologized for having flashed it, and tried to ask nicely. So they sat in the urgent care waiting room, next to people with more visibly urgent ailments than Cha-Cha's. A teenager with a wound to the side of his neck taped over with bloody gauze. A child with a gruesome, purple-black bruise on his bony shoulder. An older man with swollen, pus-caked feet crammed into Nike slippers. A young woman with bald spots on her short salt-and-pepper hair who moaned and sniffled. Troy begged Lelah not to call Tina, or anyone else, and she obliged because she too felt guilty.

Cha-Cha waited in the back, drinking water and trying to figure out what had happened to him, until a tall male nurse with a neat beard finally came over to talk to him.

"What happened tonight? Your son said you fainted?"

"That's not my son; that's my brother. I don't know if I fainted. I saw a . . . I had lot to drink earlier, haven't slept in a while."

The nurse repeated the procedure that Cha-Cha had already been subject to twice since arriving. He flashed a light in his eyes, checked his throat and ears. He listened to his heartbeat, stood up straight, folded his arms, frowned, and listened to his heartbeat a second time.

"You may have fainted. The fatigue and dehydration might have had something to do with it. I'm going to put you in a chair and get an IV with fluids going into you for a little while, to take care of the hydration part. And I'll take some blood to run a couple of tests, just to be safe."

He ushered Cha-Cha through the hallway into a windowless, holding cell-like room, where half a dozen patients whose ailments didn't warrant a private room but who were awaiting clearance to leave lay on beds and sat in cushioned chairs.

Cha-Cha could no longer lose sleep over this haint, he decided. He had to stop killing himself with hysteria. His brother Quincy had used that word on the phone: *hysteria*. He would take sleeping pills. At his age it was a miracle that he only took blood pressure medicine and a multivitamin; he reasoned one more pill a day for a while would not kill him. He hadn't considered sleeping pills before because he had been game to see what the haint was about, get to the bottom of it one way or the other. Now that it had reappeared in human form, moving, perhaps able to inflict harm, he was game no longer. Better it killed him when he wasn't awake.

"Did you see anything?" Lelah asked. "Like a ghost?"

"No," Troy said.

"What's the difference between a haint and a regular ghost anyway? Is a haint just a southern ghost? A black-folks ghost? Too bad Auntie Lucille and Olivia died when we were kids. They had all the stories, I bet."

She and Troy had disparate tactics for coping with guilt. Lelah tried to smother the tension with chatter, more words than Troy had heard her utter in at least a year. Troy sat very still and tried to say nothing.

Lelah pitied him. Even if it was an entitled, wrong-headed, destructive little tantrum, his outburst on the porch had been an appeal for Cha-Cha to love him. Turner men did not admit to needing love. While Cha-Cha was having his moment with his haint—Lelah very much wanted his haint to be real—she had chopped Troy down more than she'd ever chopped down anyone in her life. Called him out on selfishness dating all the way back to the hoarded boom box of their teens. Accused him of being manipulative, of emotionally abusing Jillian. Of being a cheating-ass coward (her exact words) with his ex-wife, Cara. It had felt very good to say these ugly things to him, things that were true but not really hers to say. She neither forgave him for what he'd said in return (that she was various combinations of bum-loser-liar and had ruined his friendship with David) nor needed an apology. In the game of sibling mud-slinging they had reached a draw.

The nurse returned and told them he thought Cha-Cha was fine, that after getting intravenous fluids he'd be free to leave.

Troy slumped in his chair, lightheaded with relief. For the past four hours dread had nearly choked him. Dread that something was really wrong with Cha-Cha, that he'd caused irreparable harm. The dread had not even circled back to thoughts of what it might mean for him should Cha-Cha be sick; it had stayed at Cha-Cha being hurt, and that was dread enough. It was Cha-Cha who had filled those gaps left by Francis's dodgy ways when it came to talking about love, sex, and friendship, Troy remembered. Cha-Cha who had taken him to buy condoms before junior prom (he'd already lost his virginity by then, but the gesture still mattered). Cha-Cha who had advised him not to fight for custody when Cara wanted to take Camille to Germany, that it was better for her to be with her mother, and he'd been right.

Troy had never received anything and felt satisfied with having it—not a job, not a gift, not a woman. Nothing save for his daughter, Camille, and this news that Cha-Cha was okay. Everything else he'd always turned over in his mind too many times to actually enjoy, zeroed in on the ways that a gift or an accomplishment was lacking. He felt a sudden need to be with Camille. She was his best accomplishment. He couldn't bear to face his other siblings at Viola's party, not so soon. He would go home, look online for flights, and leave for Germany as soon as he could.

At around 5:30 A.M. the nurse brought Cha-Cha out in a wheelchair; they wouldn't let him walk to the car because he had no cane.

Troy drove back to Yarrow slowly. The early-morning streets were deserted, and the first light of the day crept in from the east.

"You don't have to drive like this, Troy. I'm fine."

Troy pressed on the gas a little harder, but not much. He and Cha-Cha met eyes in the rearview.

"Cha," he said. "I'm not happy. That's it. I'm just not happy. Lelah said I blame you for stuff, and she's right. I don't even know why I came over there like that last night, knocking stuff over. I was drunk, mad from fighting with David earlier. I think me and Jillian are gonna break up."

"Mmm-hmm," Cha-Cha said.

Troy slowed to turn onto Yarrow.

"I'm tryna say, Cha. I'm tryna say . . . I shoulda never blamed you, I shoulda never acted a fool out on the porch. I definitely shoulda never pinned you to the ground like that. I was stupid. Especially for trying to sell the house from underneath you."

He parked in front of the house.

"I'm sorry, Cha. I *apologize* for all of it."

There it was, finally.

"Thank you, Troy," Cha-Cha said. "Thank you for saying that."

At the house Troy swept the porch clear of broken pottery, while Lelah brought her things down from the big room. She would stay with Cha-Cha for now.

A Real Soldier's Return

· SPRING 1945 ·

Eight months into Francis's heathen period, the war in Europe ended and lo, Odella Withers, the wide-mouthed mistress of his boardinghouse, had been married all along. Francis came up the walkway after a long day at the stamping plant on Jefferson and saw Odella sitting on the sagging porch next to a uniformed man with hollowed-out cheeks and curly coppery hair. Private Dennis Withers had returned from Italy a hero in the black community, if not the nation at large. Odella introduced her lover to her husband as casually as one might introduce any two men at a party, or even church.

"Arkansas? You came up here all alone?" Dennis's accent reminded Francis of a baseball broadcaster's — clipped, energetic, decidedly unsouthern. "Boy, you don't look a day older than sixteen."

Francis slept in his half room for the first time in weeks.

Faced with the loss of her, Francis saw that aside from Norman McNair, Odella had been his only consistent friend. Her infidelity depressed him. He hadn't imagined a woman capable of doing that, folding up the love she felt for a man, tucking it away, and never mentioning his name. A week after Dennis's homecoming, when Francis was once again just the renter of a half room retrieving his bedding from his boardinghouse mistress, he asked her when she had stopped waiting for her husband.

"Soon as you knocked on my door," Odella said. "It was almost a year and a half by then. He never wrote me. Not one time the two years he was gone, not even when he was just Down South training. I thought he was either dead or done with me. You do something like that, you can't blame a woman for getting on with her life."

"But you takin him back just the same," Francis said.

"That doesn't mean I forgive him."

He thought he understood why Dennis Withers had never written to Odella. What was there to tell a woman if the life you ended up with was harder than you thought it would be? After a few thrilling binges of liquor and nightlife, Francis had learned that Detroit, with its overcrowded tenements and crooked bosses and exclusive restaurants downtown, was a lonely, backbreaking city. It took courage to let a woman in on one's disappointment, one's fear. Francis thought about his own wife, a willful woman who may have not been as open to second chances as Odella Withers. He knew his heathen period had to end.

Quitting Time

· SPRING 1945 ·

Harold Joggets fell from his highchair one Thursday morning in May. Ethel Joggets rarely ate more than toast for breakfast, but that morning she had said, "Why not biscuits, Viola? I don't think you've made biscuits the whole time you've been here." So Viola was in the pantry, looking for flour. It had taken Viola several weeks to get into the habit of putting things back in the pantry where Ethel wanted them instead of where she thought best. She'd started keeping scraps of recipes scribbled down impatiently by her sisters in her apron pocket for all of the things she did not know how to cook. Biscuits, luckily, Viola could make without thinking. Just a little flour, shortening, baking powder, and salt. She had just found the sack of flour and wrapped her fingers around the handle of the sifter when she heard the dull thud. Ethel was at the counter, finishing the last of her coffee, her back turned to her son. In the seconds it took for Viola to trace the sound and stand up straight enough to move toward Harold, Ethel had moved faster, and reached her child first. This was all it had taken. A dull thud, then a hard slap on the face. The mother had reached her child first, and this made Viola guilty. Well, she fought the urge to slap Ethel back, but she did not help the woman in the midst of that crisis, the baby wailing at the top of his lungs, a trickle of blood sliding down from his temple. She collected her hand-me-down coat and pocketbook and walked out.

The first bus that came stopped for her. Midday drivers apparently had seats to spare for colored maids. Viola sat up very straight in the back, searching for the relief she had imagined feeling when she finally quit Ethel Joggets. Instead her thoughts skipped between hurt babies and raw fear. She had to leave, go to Omaha or Cleveland, where one of her brothers would have to help her make a way. Arkansas was over. Yes. She would call Clyde or James or Josiah, and one of them could come get her, or she would use the little she'd saved on train fare to go. She'd never had a wedding ring. Seemed a pity now. There would be no proof of her good intentions, no proof that she'd been a wife before a mother, and that she'd tried to be obedient and wait for her husband's word. She looked through the bus windows at this place, not the Virginia where her grandparents were buried but closer to it than wherever she imagined she would end up. The rich earth, the boisterous trees. The ditches already flooded with wild-flowers.

Viola waited at the side of the road for the second bus. She'd never left the Joggetses' house early before and had no idea if the second bus even ran all day, or only during those hours necessary to cart Negroes back and forth to work. She needed to pee but feared the bus would drive by as soon as she sought out a suitable tree. After twenty minutes no bus had come, so she hustled behind a big hickory about thirty yards off the road and tried to prevent her stockings from getting wet.

Back at the road a Packard waited where she had been standing. Viola hesitated to approach it, thinking Ethel Joggets had sent her husband—a man Viola had never seen—to fetch their housekeeper and prosecute her. If the baby was hurt badly or dead, something could be pinned on her. Neglect, or a more malicious charge. Who would believe that a young colored woman just wasn't any good at being a maid? That her only crime was not knowing how to locate things in a crowded pantry quickly enough?

She couldn't run; it was seven miles to her parents' shotgun house, and there was no other road to take her there. Viola trudged through the dewy buffalo grass back to the road. A black man sat behind the wheel of the Packard. He had no passengers. It was Reverend Charles William Tufts, her missing husband's former benefactor and her only son's namesake. He rolled down the passenger window. He wore a black hat with a narrow brim and a gray wool coat over his suit.

"Ah, the young Mrs. Turner," he said. "It would appear that you are in fervent need of conveyance."

Viola nodded. She would gladly put up with the reverend's speechifying as long as he took her home.

The reverend drove as if they had nowhere in particular to go, both gloved hands planted on the wheel and never over twenty miles an hour. Viola thought he might be trying to protect his fancy vehicle from dips in the road.

"I assume you've been discharged by your employer," he said. "I'm sorry. That is always unfortunate."

"Discharged," she said. "What gives you that idea?"

"The welts on your face. The same number as fingers on a hand, Mrs. Turner." He brought his own gloved palm briefly to his stubbly face. Viola was surprised that he hadn't shaved this morning. "Red marks may not show on complexions like ours, but the raised skin can still tell quite a story."

Viola said nothing. The sooner she could forget Ethel Joggets, the better. She made a promise to herself right there to keep that vignette of humiliation to herself. And she would, for her entire life. They passed the filling station that marked the halfway point to the shotgun house.

"You don't have to explain for my sake," Tufts said, and then after a moment of thought: "Anyhow, you should be going north soon, shouldn't you? I imagine Francis has devised a timeline for you and the little one's departure."

"I ain't heard from Francis, Reverend. He mailed once, but I ain't heard since."

Was he making fun of her? No way Tufts hadn't heard the town gossip. He'd clearly heard enough to know that she had a job to get *discharged* from in the first place.

"And with all respect due to you, Reverend, Francis would still be here with me and the baby if you hadn't put it in his mind to leave."

Tufts smiled his patient, I'm-going-to-teach-you-something smile, eyes deliberately bright. The smile he used right before he drove his message home at church.

"Fair and true," he said. "But I never advised him to go and cease contacting his wife. You must remember I wrote a letter of introduction for him. Had he utilized it, I have no doubt your young family would be together now."

A good point. Viola's mind wandered back to her three older brothers, to which one might facilitate her escape. It infuriated her to have to put her fate in the hands of men once more. She wanted out of this life. More immediately, she wanted out of this car.

She turned to the reverend again.

"But why'd he have to leave, huh? His mama sent you what little money she had, and you took it for half his life—"

"Now, Viola, I don't think fiduciary matters should be your concern."

"My *concern* is that I married a man who had a call to be a preacher, and then outta nowhere he talkin bout goin up north to be a ... I don't even know what! You had him up under you, tendin to your church, runnin your services, for what? You oughta be ashamed."

Other than a quick nostril twitch, the reverend's face was still. He considered a large part of his own calling to be to help his people conquer their emotions, to channel their volatile feelings into structured Missionary Baptist works. To make spiritual pillars of the race out of them, if not intellectual ones. He had been one of the first black preachers in that part of Arkansas to add the word *missionary* to his church's name. He prided himself on conducting his congregation just as well as any of the white Missionary Baptist churches in the region. He waited until his heartbeat felt familiar to him once again, until he could trust his voice to come out even, and not as angry as he felt. Then he asked Viola Turner whether she believed in ghosts.

· WEEK FIVE ·

Spring 2008

When the End Is Near

A young fool was much more forgivable than an old one. Tina feared she had been a fool for too long. Pastor Mike would have prescribed forgiveness, would have reminded her that no man on this earth was without fault, that marriage was built on understanding. Tina wasn't sure if she believed all of that anymore. Infidelity was heartbreaking, but the unprecedented changes in Cha-Cha's day-to-day behavior were worse. It was too late for him to require so many adjustments from her. Had he done this when she was thirty, forty-seven, even five years ago at fifty-five, she might have been able to forgive and adjust, do her best to forget. But at sixty Tina found it all too disruptive; an unwanted hiccup in her otherwise satisfactory life.

The news at Viola's doctor visit the morning before had been alarming, downright distressing, so Tina called Cha-Cha's job to relay it to him immediately. He wasn't there. He hadn't even called out sick. Hours passed and he didn't come home, sent her phone calls straight to voicemail. At dusk she snatched the piece of paper with Alice Rothman's office number from out the kitchen junk drawer. Tina dialed with no real plan of what she'd say. Maybe recite the lyrics from that Shirley Brown song? *Woman to woman, if you've ever been in love . . .* She had counseled plenty of friends over the years in this position: on the trail for proof of what they already knew in their guts to be true. She'd always advised them against confronting the other woman. She'd said ridiculous, pious, turn-the-other-cheek things like "God will deal with her in His own time." How idiotic. The other women deserved to get cursed out, at the very least. Alice's phone rang and rang and rang until Tina finally put the receiver down. She checked the time on the clock over the kitchen sink. If she and Cha-Cha were together, then Alice clearly wouldn't be at work at 7 P.M.

Early the following morning, she sat down on Cha-Cha's little desk chair and sifted through his printouts. She'd stacked them up after his first episode but hadn't bothered to look through them. Ugly websites with typos in their headers. How crazy had Cha-Cha become? Halfway through the pile hid an image of Alice Rothman, flanked by two older white people who looked like liberal types. The elderly woman had a salt-and-pepper wiry bob and thick-rimmed glasses. The man, whose hairline was receding, wore a blue button-down shirt and a chocolate cardigan, although judging from Alice's off-the-shoulder black dress, the occasion called for more formal attire. Alice wasn't even very pretty, Tina thought. Her hair looked healthy enough, but her edges were sparse and her greasy forehead reflected the camera's flash. She was neither as different nor as similar to Tina as Tina had expected her to be. She was clearly taller than Tina, with a smaller bust, but her skin was almost the same shade, and she didn't look like she was in better physical shape. A decade ago Tina had put on weight steadily, but she'd started a walking group at church and had stayed within the same ten-pound range since. Of course, Alice's face was younger; she didn't have bags under her eyes or the beginnings of smile lines on either side of her mouth. And her clothes looked more fashionable. Tina put the picture close to her face, trying to determine if it was really a dress or a shirt-skirt combo Alice wore. Let her start getting hot flashes, Tina thought; then we'll see whether she won't want clothes with a little more drape and flow to them. She folded the paper in half, then folded it again and put it on the arm of the loveseat next to her. Who printed out a picture of their therapist? Tina imagined Cha-Cha on one of his compulsive Google binges, printing out the picture and hiding it in the pile of haint "research." One would think he'd have the decency to put more thought into covering his tracks.

He could have cheated on her hundreds, if not thousands of times in these thirty-some-odd years, on trucking runs at least twice a month. And if he ever had, Tina would have liked to believe it was a single indiscretion, never an affair. Something not worth telling anyone at all. She would never tell her girlfriends, but Tina was an avid believer that one transgression, one night of succumbing to the weaknesses of the flesh, need not be confessed, dredged up, and displayed to ruin what two people had built through child rearing and sacrifice. She'd told this to Lonnie right before he went and confessed to that smart girl he'd somehow convinced to marry him out in California. Had he listened, they might have not divorced. It was selfish to confess to such a trifling thing. But what Cha-Cha had done wasn't a one-time slip. It was a full-blown emotional and maybe even intellectual affair. How could this be forgiven?

The front door opened and Cha-Cha walked into the living room with what looked like a spring in his step. A self-satisfied smirk on his face. Then he noticed Tina at the desk in the corner and his face collapsed. He looked like a large child, she thought. A big, fat, philandering baby. She opened her mouth to say the most hurtful thing she could think of—she didn't even know what, maybe just a loud groan—but Lelah walked into the room. The two of them looked like they had been jumped, drugged, and tossed out the back of a van. He *would* come home with her, Tina thought, or anyone who could delay the confrontation he knew was coming. Cha-Cha thought decorum would always overrule anger for Tina, and he was usually right, but today there were sufficiently hurtful things she could say in mixed company.

"Your mother has cancer," she said.

"*What?*" Lelah said. Tina watched Cha-Cha's face for a response. She'd broken a cardinal rule of their relationship: never talk about any big family development without running it by him first, so that he might determine the best way to disseminate the information.

"What?" Lelah said again. She dropped her duffel bag on the living room floor.

Tina ignored Cha-Cha's death glare and explained.

"Last time we went to the doctor she was complaining about pain in and around her armpits, and after the doctor felt some swelling there they did a scan. Well, today they said it looks like something is there in her lymph nodes, which means it's gonna spread fast."

"Something?" Lelah asked. "They don't know for sure? Can't they do a biopsy?"

Cha-Cha rubbed his temple but didn't speak.

"She's probably awake in her room right now, Lelah," Tina said. "Go on in and ask her what they said and what *she* said too."

"Okay," Lelah said, as if finally registering the tension in the room. "Good idea."

Can a human being ever truly know another person's heart? Tina had thought it possible. How could she have been wrong? Cha-Cha sat on the arm of the love seat closest to her and knocked the folded-up printout of Alice onto the floor. Tina ignored the proximity of the knees of his dirty pants to her face and focused on the paper. He smelled like beer and dirt and mildew. She refused to speak first. Back when she had been closer to her sisters-in-law, Francey and Netti in particular would tease Tina for her inability to hold Cha-Cha accountable for his mistakes. "You give in too easily," Netti used to say. "I love Cha-Cha, but he's the type of man that'll only change if you put him in the doghouse for a while." Tina never did. Some women put men in the doghouse, she thought, and others just up and quit when they've had enough.

Cha-Cha touched her forearm.

"Why didn't you tell me about Mama sooner? I woulda gone with y'all yesterday. I had no idea—"

"Are you out of your *mind?*" Tina swatted his hand away. "I'm not about to sit up here and explain *anything* to you."

"I'm just trying," he started, and stopped. "Cancer is *serious*, Tina—"

"And what, I don't know that? You must think I'm *so stupid*, and weak. But I'm not."

Cha-Cha stood up, put his hands in his pockets, and sighed. As if he somehow thought he'd get around this.

"Nothing happened, alright? I should've called to check in, but *nothing* happened yesterday, or any other day. I swear to God."

"Don't you swear for my sake. You and me must have very different definitions of the word *nothing*."

"I slept on the east side at Mama's house," Cha-Cha said. He turned around and pointed toward Viola's closed door. "Ask Lelah. She was there. I found her there and brought her back with me. She's messed up, Tina. She just needs a place to stay—"

Tina jumped up from her chair so that she was eye level to Cha-Cha's chest.

"I don't care I don't care I don't care I don't care! When have I *ever* cared about somebody staying here, huh? You didn't go to work, Cha; I called. And you didn't pick up the phone all day long." She took a deep breath before asking: "Did you go see Alice?"

Cha-Cha's jaw hung open, which was answer enough.

"That doesn't mean I slept with her! It just means . . . I needed to work some stuff out. Truth be told, I needed alone time more than anything."

Tina laughed.

"*Alone* time? *You* needed alone time? That's all you do, Cha. You've got to sleep alone to figure out your haint situation. You've got to weasel out of helping me with your mother on account of an argument y'all had. You've got to keep your Alice conversations to yourself, and you walk around here like somebody's teenager, resentful of me like *I'm* your mother. Well, I'm not, alright? I'm sixty years old, and I'm not about to be anybody's fool anymore."

Tina jabbed a finger at her own chest.

"You got no right to humiliate *me* just cause *you're* having a crisis. Especially after I offered to listen, to help, to do *whatever,* and you pushed me away."

"Alright," Cha-Cha said. "I think we both need to calm down some. At least come outside before Mama gets upset."

He walked over to the sliding glass door leading out to the deck, gestured for Tina to follow him. Tina picked up the folded printout on her way and pushed it against his chest.

"Matthew five twenty-eight," she said. "I know you know what it says."

Cha-Cha unfolded the paper. The Rothmans looked up at him. For a moment he considered capitulating; he had indeed been unfaithful under Matthew's parameters, and by proxy Jesus', but then he saw an opportunity for leverage.

"See, that right there is what all of this boils down to, Tina. You don't even see me as a person anymore. I'm just a body to toss scripture at and guilt-trip all the damn time."

"Oh, that's *real* clever—"

"You act like I'm not saved enough for you, but that's not how belief *works*. Just cause you wanna spend all day churching with your friends doesn't mean I'm not worthy. It doesn't make me the devil."

"All day churching? You *never* come to church anymore, Cha. Not ever. And I know it's not cause you don't believe, it's cause you think you're better than everybody there. Smarter than everybody there. But you can't even figure out why you're seeing ghosts! I'm not gonna let you blame me and what *I* do at church for this. Try something else." She turned her back on him and walked to the far end of the deck. Cha-Cha followed.

"It's not about blame," he said. "It's about giving each other what we need."

Tina spun around, incredulous.

"What we *need?* Sounds like some stuff you got from that shrink. For the majority of my life I've given you everything you've asked for, and a whole lot more you didn't, and I don't think you ever really thought what it took for me to give all that. The other night you acted all miserable because your body wouldn't cooperate when you were ready to make love. Well, guess what, Cha? That's been the story of my life since menopause! But do I blame you and ruin things? No, I blamed myself. I got hormone pills and crazy bottles of lube and stuff from the ladies at church—oh, I know you think they're too stuck up to have that kinda stuff, but they *do*—and I made it work. I did it for you, not to *keep* you, but because I love you. But I bet you thought it was all magic, huh?"

"Tina, I . . . this isn't . . ." Cha-Cha tried. "Nobody ever said—"

"And the thing that's really embarrassing is that I still *want* you, old as we both are. Last night and too many nights. I'm embarrassed by it, Cha-Cha. Really."

She covered her mouth with her hand and stifled a sob. Cha-Cha knew better than to say anything else. He could elicit pity by telling her about his trip to the hospital, simply lift up his sleeve so she could see where the IV had been. But that did not negate the feelings he had for Alice—feelings that had not quite disappeared—and he was not interested in Tina filling the role of caregiver anymore. She walked back to the sliding glass door.

"Your mother is *dying*, Cha-Cha. Ain't no more quick fixes left for her. And you two don't even talk. More than everything else, that's a problem. I'd like to be here for her until she's gone, but after all of this—"

Tina did not finish the thought. She slid the door open and left Cha-Cha outside.

LELAH AND VIOLA sat on the edge of Viola's bed, perfectly still, trying to eavesdrop. After Cha-Cha and Tina moved to the back deck and out of earshot, Lelah convinced her mother to lie back down.

Viola's weight loss was evident: her thick blue diabetic's socks, usually tight, pooled around her knobby ankles. The springs in the bed, which Lelah recalled being loud, made no noise under Viola's weight. When Lelah first walked in she had found Viola sitting on the edge of the bed trying with all of her body to listen to the argument unfolding on the other side of the door. She was trembling from the effort, her torso sloping to one side.

"Were you even supposed to be sitting up, Mama?" Lelah said. "I thought you had to rest your neck."

"It don't hurt. I'm all doped up now," Viola said. "I been telling them doctors I need stronger medicine. They didn't never wanna give it, but now cause I'm dying for real they went on and gave me everything."

They heard stomping through the living room, then the hollow clang of the garage door slamming.

"What exactly did the doctors say?"

"Cancer in my lymph nodes, and some in my lungs, too."

Lelah sat down in the little armchair wedged between the bed and the window. She picked up bottles of lotions and nail polish and pretended to read their labels.

"And what did you say to that?"

Viola blinked several times and yawned.

"Oh, I don't know. It was cold in there. You remember how that chemo did Marlene? All that weight gone, then back, then gone. Ain't enough of me for that."

Lelah nodded. She had often detected an undercurrent of melodramatic dread in her mother's words. Growing up it was if Viola had expected to lose a child, or that she'd never expected her own life to go on for as long as it had. How to act when the end was truly near?

"So you got more drugs for now," she said. "Then what?"

"Nothing. Cancer takes too long. That's why I'm not foolin with no treatments. It's just gone drag it out more. Naw, baby, not for me."

Viola closed her eyes and wiggled her feet under the blanket. She was high off of pain meds. Not enough to be incoherent, but enough to make her sassier than Lelah had seen her in a long time. Lelah climbed into the bed next to her mother. The corners of Viola's mouth turned up in a smile.

When Cha-Cha rescued Lelah and Brianne from Missouri, he had brought them to this house. Lelah had slept in this room for an entire day, and Tina had looked after Brianne. Lelah had heard Brianne's cries through these walls, or thought she did, but she could not muster the strength to go to her daughter. It was like she'd been drugged. The weight of her own body, thinner than she would ever be again, was too much to maneuver. Lelah had not cried; she just stared at the ceiling and tried to figure out why she'd married Vernon in the first place, why she hadn't thought of any other plan for herself. At the twenty-four-hour mark she sat up, a new question in her mind: what would she do now? She was twenty-two years old, and the only answer that came was *work and raise your daughter*. Now, back at this place, Lelah saw it had cost too much to aim for so little.

"You're not even afraid to die?" she asked.

Viola scrunched up her nose and shifted her torso as if trying to get away from Lelah. Without the upper-body strength required for a full scoot, she ended up rocking from side to side for a moment and resettling. She opened one reproachful eye.

"You smell like smoke. Like a pool hall or someplace. When you start *that?*"

"You know I don't smoke, Mama. I was around some smokers yesterday. I need to take a shower."

"I don't know what's worse, smokin or drinkin. Your daddy used to drink, you know."

"Everybody knows that."

"Your daddy was always *worried*, worried himself drunk. So worried about what *didn't* happen at his job, with the house, on the street. Worried about heaven and hell. Waste of time."

"Let's talk about something else," Lelah said. "When's the last time you seen Marlene?"

"Marlene came by and gave me some lace gloves. Lace! They was pretty, but where I'm goin with lace on? I threw them under the bed. Troy been by too. He get your fingerprints yet? He came by for mine, but I *know* he was lyin about something, I don't know what. He can't lie to save his life."

Lelah looked. No gloves under the bed. A good thing. It would have been cruel of her sister. Viola's hands were too knotted and her nails too thick for lace. She had no idea what she meant about Troy, but she hoped Viola was mistaken about him too.

"Now, your daddy," Viola said. "Maybe if he didn't buy so much liquor, he'd of had less to be worryin about in the first place."

"Yeah, well, he stopped drinking eventually, didn't he?" Lelah said. "Plenty of people never stop, Mama. It's hard."

"Shit," Viola said. She looked to the left and right of her, and whispered, "Your daddy ain't stop nothin. That doctor told your daddy his liver was about to up and quit on him. And you think he wanted to stop? *No.*"

Viola made a clucking noise in an attempt to scratch the back of her throat.

"I made Cha-Cha follow your daddy around, and sure enough he was drinkin still. Got to the point I told him if he had another drink, I would kill him dead myself. I'da done it, too."

Lelah propped herself up on an elbow.

"What are you saying, Mama? You know that's not true. Daddy quit cause he wanted to. I remember he used to carry his flask around for show, but he never—"

"He didn't quit nothin!" She shot Lelah an impatient look. "He just chose to stay alive is all. And lucky for him his liver held on. Mmm-hmm. That's why you need to quit that smokin now, girl. Fore you mess around and get sick."

And just like that, Lelah's last illusion died.

Viola muttered to herself about tobacco pipes and beer money and something Lelah couldn't decipher about ham hocks. Other Turner children would have forced Viola to remain alert, ply her with questions aimed at sharpening her focus and fighting the morphine-induced confusion, but Lelah saw no point in making her mother work hard at anything anymore. Soon Viola fell asleep, heralded by a soft whirring from her nose. Lelah turned over in the bed and grabbed her phone out of her purse on the floor. No missed calls. She wanted to call someone up and tell them the truth about Francis Turner and his drinking, but really, who cared but her? Better to let the myth of the man who beat his demons live on. She called Brianne instead. The phone went straight to voicemail, and Lelah wasn't sure what message to leave. She hung up.

In the living room Cha-Cha sat with his head in his hands. Lelah came and sat on the arm of the couch next to him.

"Tina's gonna be fine," she said.

Cha-Cha shrugged. "I don't wanna talk about it."

"Okay," Lelah said. She stood up to leave, but Cha-Cha grabbed her arm. Even with his red-rimmed eyes as proof, Lelah couldn't imagine him crying.

"You can't tell anyone about Mama. I'm not ready," he said.

"Huh? You mean don't tell her other eleven children that she's dying? That's not fair, Cha."

"Now hold on a minute. Nobody said she was dying. Just give her some time. We can get her to do the chemo, I know we can. She just likes to be dramatic."

Lelah sat back down. She pictured her mother, wide awake once more, straining to sit back up and eavesdrop on them. She lowered her voice.

"She's *dying*, Cha. Sooner than you realize, I bet. Go ask her and she'll tell you herself. It's not even about the cancer as much as it's about her being ready to go. You know once somebody her age decides to stop fighting, it's pretty much over."

Cha-Cha slapped his leg and Lelah flinched.

"Gotdamnit, regardless of that, I'm asking *you* not to tell anybody, alright? Not until we have some sort of plan. Can I trust you to keep this between us?"

Seeing as how she was staying under his roof, Lelah did not consider herself in a position to disagree.

A Multiple-Man Operation

He wanted to tell her that every second she stayed away he felt bereft. But Chucky, his own son, was playing bouncer. His shorter, stout body was planted on the threshold, his arms crossed. His face—more Tina than Cha-Cha, with small eyes and narrow nose—was veiled in artificial indifference. Cha-Cha would have punched him if he didn't love him.

"I know you think you're doing the right thing," Cha-Cha said. "But you need to go on and let me in so me and your mom can work this out."

"Just let her have a couple days to herself, Pop," Chucky said. "She just needs a couple days."

"It's already been a day and half! She just ran off and didn't tell me or your grandma or anybody where she was going."

"You knew she'd be here."

"Doesn't matter! She knows I don't know nothin about the pills Mama's got to take, or what appointments she has or—"

"She obviously called Auntie Lelah and told her everything, or Grandma would already be in trouble."

Was he talking smart? Cha-Cha thought so. He really could have punched him.

"So what, if I try to come in, you're gonna *hit* me? Is that it? You shouldn't be choosing sides, Chucky. Especially since you haven't even heard my side."

Chucky uncrossed his arms and put a hand on Cha-Cha's shoulder. Cha-Cha stifled the impulse to flinch.

"She's not trying to see you right now, Pop. That's huge. In all the years y'all been married, she ever stay mad at you longer than a day?"

"I know it's huge! I don't need you to tell me about my own wife. Why do you think I'm here? We *made* you, remember that. If she wants to stay here for a while longer, fine. But we at least gotta talk."

Inside the house, Chucky's son, Isaiah, yelled, and someone immediately appeased him. Having been publicly cuckolded by his ex-wife made Chucky think he had a right to moral superiority when it came to relationships. If Todd were here, he would have cooperated, Cha-Cha thought. Todd, his spitting image, would remind Tina that she'd invited folks to a party that was supposed to be happening in two days, and that the person who really suffered by her staying away was Viola. Too bad Todd was stationed in a faraway desert, getting ready for a second tour in an even more dangerous desert.

"You're worried about her forgiving you," Chucky said. "But you need to be worrying about why you're acting up in the first place, Pop." He stepped back into the entryway and gently closed the door on his father. He might as well have slammed it.

A smashed silver Lexus sat in the middle of Cha-Cha's driveway. Oil leaked from underneath and trickled toward the gutter. A diagonal gash across the passenger side revealed a mangle of folded metal and plastic. California plates, all four cheaply tinted windows rolled down to different levels. Cha-Cha parked on the street and stuck his head through the driver's window on the way to his front door. A film of grease-dappled burger wrappers obscured the backseat and floor, some from fast food joints not found on this side of the Mississippi.

The front passenger seat held a heap of tape cassettes. The chemical-sweet stink of Luster's Pink lotion crowded Cha-Cha's nostrils. The sum of this detritus was Lonnie.

In the kitchen Lelah beamed as she made breakfast for dinner. She put down her spatula, hugged Cha-Cha round the neck.

"He's been here an hour and Mama's already *so* happy," she whispered. "I think he's a little drunk, though, which is why I'm making breakfast."

"You didn't tell him nothing about Mama's, uh, *new* news, did you?"

"God, Cha-Cha, no. Just go in there and say hi."

"I dreammmed of a city called Glor-rry, / So bright and so fair. / As I entered the gates I crieeed ho-ly, / And the angels met me there."

Someone had used every pillow in the room to prop Viola up. Her dressy black sequin turban perched on her head. She squinted in rapture, and tears shimmied down her mole-flecked cheeks. Her right hand rested lightly in her sixth child's upturned palm.

Lonnie's bony limbs folded into the armchair. His black leather baseball cap sloped low over his brow. Mustache: a scraggly broom; eyebrows: two inverted checks. Legs possessed by their trademark jitter inside navy blue track pants. Baby-sized teeth chipped here and there. But his voice? His voice did much to make up for all that mess.

"They carr-rried me from mansion to man-sion, /And oh, the sights that I saw. / Then I said I want to see Je-sus, / The man who diiieed for us all."

They froze in time, Cha-Cha silent at the door, his mother closed-eyed, and his brother looking out the window, stalling before he started the chorus. Lonnie and Viola communing in a way Cha-Cha could hardly imagine. Lelah walked in, breaking the spell.

"I've got eggs, Mama. Just a little bit, and some bacon. Lonnie, yours is on the stove. What're you lurking in the doorway for, Cha?"

"Big brother Charles!" Lonnie stood up and flung his right hand to his forehead in sloppy salute. "You're lookin desk-job sharp in your business-casual slacks."

"Oh, Cha-Cha's home!" Viola said. She tried to straighten up on her pillows and wiped her face with her hand. "Where you been, Cha? You ain't came to sit with me in a long time."

She held out her hand to him, so Cha-Cha had no choice but to take it, lean in, and give her a peck on the forehead. He wondered whether his mother even remembered forsaking him in his time of need.

In four swift steps Lonnie crossed the room and clapped Cha-Cha on the back. Lelah shooed them into the hallway.

"Your car looks terrible, and it's leaking," Cha-Cha said.

"Hit somethin in Ohio. Fell asleep. Don't worry about that. How are *you* doing?"

Lonnie walked into the kitchen. He shoveled eggs into his mouth with a wooden serving spoon.

"I'm fine. You drove here?"

"Yahp," Lonnie said. He broke a piece of bacon in half and put that into his mouth too. "After we talked, Tina called and said Mama wasn't doing so great. That combined with your own predicament made me hop in the car. I borrowed some money from Lily, the girl from Hawthorne I was tellin you about? We back together, I think."

Cha-Cha remembered that he'd promised Lonnie a hundred dollars on the phone. Those desperate calls seemed so long ago.

"Miles and the girls flyin in Friday," Lonnie said. "My girls is flyin with em, too. Didn't wanna drive cross-country with me, I guess. Duke's flyin out from Oakland, but it's just gonna be him I think."

A Turner invasion and Cha-Cha had nowhere to hide. Soon they would be hitting him with judgment and unsolicited advice from all sides. A room full of funhouse reflections of himself, distorting what he knew to be true.

Lonnie washed down his bacon with a cup of coffee from Tina's favorite mug. He wiped his hands on the front of his track pants.

"So, what you got goin on right now? It's still light out. You know what *I* always wanna do first thing I get in town."

Cha-Cha knew: head to Yarrow Street and see what was going on.

"You remember Courtney the man? He used to wear that lime-green jumpsuit, runnin around the east side lookin like a bolt of lightning?"

"I don't remember any men named Courtney."

"Sure you do. He started the Yarrow Gang, but he didn't run it for too long cause he tried to hold up that liquor store with a hammer. Remember? He was high out his mind. A gotdamn *hammer*. Clerk shot him in the face."

"Oh."

"Remember Terry Randolph? Had a twin named Tyrone? Tyrone owed some people some money, but they killed Terry instead. Slit his throat, I think, right on the basketball courts. This was around '73."

"No, I had Chucky by then. Working too much."

"I *know* you remember how Lydia Osage got shot by the police. They were chasing down somebody who robbed somebody on Fischer and shot her when she came around the corner with her groceries?"

"Can we just ride, Lonnie? Can we just ride and not talk about who's dead and who all got shot?"

"Sure. I'm sorry. You know I like to reminisce."

Lonnie drummed his fingers on his knees and stared out the window. The streets were alive to him, Cha-Cha did know. Lonnie—the hallway pisser, the brick scavenger, the lead singer—had been more social, mischievous, and curious than Cha-Cha, and as such spent his teenage years making friends and enemies on blocks, dance floors, and basketball courts throughout the city. To him listing the too-soon-dead was paying homage; to Cha-Cha it was depressing.

"So you worked out the haint situation, huh?"

"What makes you think that?" Cha-Cha asked.

"Lelah said y'all had some sort of 'experience.' And that you're snoring up a storm in the house."

"I don't know what happened, but I got too much going on to worry right now. I'm sleeping again, that's true."

He had been taking sleeping pills since that night on Yarrow Street. He didn't know if the haint was still coming to him, but since he was still alive and well, he liked to believe that it was not. He was also now determined to disprove Alice's main hypothesis; he wasn't so pathetic that he needed a ghost to give his life purpose.

"I can't keep thinking about something I can't control."

"Sounds good to me," Lonnie said. "You been by that shrink's house again?"

"What makes you think I been to her house? I've *never* been to her house. Lelah's been runnin her mouth to you, and she don't know what she's talkin about."

Lonnie tugged at his crotch and shrugged.

"I would've gone to her house. I'da gone to her house and no one but us two would've ever known anything, I'll tell you that much. Specially if I'd have been as good as you been your whole life. You got a picture of her?"

"Yes. No. Not anymore." Cha-Cha turned on the radio to discourage further conversation.

Someone had stolen the garage. The aluminum-sided late addition to the house was gone, and if it weren't for the fact that the brick on the back of the house there looked fifteen years cleaner than the rest, it would be as if it had never existed.

"Mother*fuckers*," Cha-Cha said. He pulled the car into the back alley.

Lonnie whistled.

Some sort of ingenious, stealth operation must have taken place because the back gate lock was intact. Save for the heap of geriatric sundries on the ground, one would have been hard-pressed to find a fingerprint or scrap of evidence.

"I was just here two days ago," Cha-Cha said. He jiggled the handle of the kitchen door. Still locked.

"Somebody missed their calling in life," Lonnie said. "This right here's some MacGyver shit. A multiple-man operation. For scrap metal! They musta dragged it over the fence in sections. Why not just cut the fence? They already had the tools."

"Where the hell were the police? Where the hell was *McNair*, huh? The hell I'm payin him for if he can't even tell me somebody up and stole a piece of my house?" Cha-Cha circled the pile of junk on the floor like a carrion eater. He kicked a box of Depends as hard as he could. Its side crumpled too easily. He hit the walker with his cane, lacquered wood to cheap aluminum.

"Mother*fuckers!*"

"Calm down, Cha, before you throw that hip out," Lonnie said. He smacked at something between his teeth. "Thought you was lettin the bank have the house anyway."

"I never said that! Nobody ever said that! I was *just here* with Lelah. And Troy. I never said that. I'm paying almost seven hundred dollars a month for this place, gotdamnit."

"We got insurance?" Lonnie asked. "They might cover somethin like this, maybe."

"Mother*fuckers!*"

Lonnie stood and witnessed Cha-Cha's tantrum. His round, ungainly brother cursed and swatted at the air and cursed again. For a moment Lonnie worried whether Cha-Cha could rile himself up into a heart attack, but since he had never been one to stand between a man and an outpouring of emotion, he let it continue. Lonnie looked at the house, then to the corner, where a car stopped longer than the sign required before driving on. He muttered a quick thank-you to God—a more open-minded and ethereal god than the one Cha-Cha envisioned—that he had never developed a taste for the truly hard stuff, the kind of stuff that made a person snatch a rickety garage under cover of night.

Leverage

Lelah saw the moving van parked in Brianne's reserved spot but refused to believe it belonged to her daughter. It had only been two days. It was too extreme for her to have rented a van already, too final. She parked in a guest spot and walked over. From what she could see through the rear windows, the van appeared to be empty. That was a small relief. But then she saw Rob standing at the top of the apartment stairs with Bobbie in his arms. Bobbie spotted her and called out.

"Gigi! Gigi, come here *now*." His squeaky voice mimicked the bossy tone of an adult's.

She climbed the stairs with her hands outstretched for her grandson, offering Rob the smallest amount of eye contact one could dole out without appearing rude.

"Hi, Rob, hi."

"Hi, Ms. Turner," Rob said.

He actually seemed to be mulling over whether he was going to hand Bobbie to her, weighing his options, as if he had options. After about five seconds he passed Lelah her grandson. Lelah kissed Bobbie, squeezed him so tight he squirmed, and then handed him back.

"Brianne's inside," Rob said.

Rob was an inch or so taller than Lelah, with a smooth, medium-brown complexion and the sort of swirly, light brown eyes that made boys look more innocent than they were. He was likely not used to people staying upset with him for long—those sparkling eyes underneath his thick eyebrows compelled you to forgive him. But Lelah had not forgiven him for his early absence in Bobbie's life, nor had she forgotten the hypocritical, self-congratulatory behavior of his parents. Once Rob had changed his tune and decided that he did in fact want to be a father, his parents had thrown a belated baby shower at their house in Grosse Pointe. Lelah, Marlene, Francey, Netti, and Tina had gone together. The unapologetic bourgieness of his parents—with their not one but two Romare Beardens on the front-room walls that they just *had* to point out—the way they lavished attention and affection on Rob, the baby boy of his family, as if he were doing a valiant service by deigning to be a father to his son, never mind his short-term negligence—it had all been too much bullshit for the Turner women to stomach. Francey had made a very Francey-like comment—not out of malice but for the sake of small talk—about how times had surely changed, because she could remember when a black family couldn't even buy a house in Grosse Pointe thanks to their now infamous point system. Rob's parents had looked at her blankly and changed the subject. Every Turner woman but Lelah and Brianne had left within the hour. She pushed those memories down now and gave him a shoulder squeeze.

"Thank you, honey," she said. "It's good seeing you."

Inside the apartment, the scene reminded Lelah of her own recent eviction, the sort of chaos that resulted when there was no time to see one packing project through from start to finish. Heaps of clothes in every corner, dishes stacked on the couch, a wastebasket overflowing with ripped-up documents. A foreboding sense that many items would be permanently lost or trashed in a mad rush to get everything out the door. Brianne, in pink sweatpants and a white sports bra, dragged a duffel bag through the hallway to the kitchen. She plopped it down with a grunt.

"So you're moving out today?"

"Yep," Brianne said. "Gotta give the landlord keys by three o' clock."

Lelah's phone said that it was already 11 A.M. No way this place would be packed in four hours, not with Rob futzing around with Bobbie. Brianne left the room and came back with a plastic bin of toys. She set the bin outside the front door and yelled downstairs for Rob to come pick it up.

"Can I help?" Lelah asked. "I'm pretty good at moving out in a hurry."

Bad joke, she realized too late.

Brianne shrugged. "No, we got it. Thank you."

"So Rob's driving the van, and you're gonna follow in your car? Tonight?"

"Yep, as soon as we drop off the keys."

"Oh." The lack of eye contact rattled Lelah. "Well, are you gonna come back Saturday for Grandma's party?"

"Don't think so. We need to get settled, and Bobbie's been on too many long car rides lately."

"You know, Grandma's sick."

"I do know that."

"Like for-real sick. Really sick. Worse than whenever you saw her last."

Brianne knelt in front of the couch and wrapped dinner plates with bath towels from a hamper. She carefully placed the wrapped plates in a box.

"Do you think you guys can wait? It's just two days until the party, and then y'all can leave early Sunday morning."

Brianne's hands stopped moving.

"I am turning the keys in at three, and we are getting on the road to Chicago before it gets dark." She said this like a chant, as if saying it repeatedly might make it come to pass.

"Alright, well. I want you to have this."

Lelah reach into her purse and pulled out the thousand dollars she'd set aside for Brianne at Cha-Cha's that morning. She held the money out to her, but Brianne did not budge. Lelah set it on the arm of the couch.

Brianne went back to wrapping plates. Rob walked in with Bobbie, saw Brianne sitting on the floor, the helpless look on Lelah's face, the money on the couch, and turned on his heels.

"Please take it, Brianne."

"You want me to take that?" Brianne pointed her chin at the stack of cash.

"Yeah. Why not? I don't want you moving to Chicago with nothing. If you're determined to go, then I support you, fine. But you shouldn't go empty-handed. It's just some just-in-case money."

Lelah wanted to add something about not moving in with anyone, especially a man, with nothing to offer, but she thought better of this.

"Where's that money from, Mommy? That's the money Auntie Marlene gave you?"

"Yeah. Well, kinda, yeah. It's some of her money in there."

"Oh my *god*," Brianne said under her breath, but Lelah heard her. Brianne pursed her lips and went back to wrapping plates.

Rob returned, holding Bobbie.

"I'm sorry," Rob said. "I just, I'm gonna pack up more stuff in the room so we can make time. Sorry." He shuffled through the living room and shut the bedroom door.

Brianne stood up, picked up the cash, and held it out to Lelah.

"You want me to be codependent with you. That's what you want. *Co*dependence. But I won't, Mommy. I can't. I can't take this money. I know where you got it from."

These practiced lines — perhaps Googled, perhaps fed to her by that Tawny person she kept mentioning the other day, or Rob himself — didn't sound right coming out of Brianne's mouth. Lelah split the money in half, put one stack of bills in her purse and held the other stack back out.

"Just take a few hundred. Gas alone for that van, plus your car is gonna be a couple hundred. I don't want nothing for it. I swear."

Brianne dumped the papers from the overflowing wastebasket into a big black trash bag. She stopped a few times to fish out certain slips of paper and tear them into smaller pieces.

"I am sorry, Brianne, genuinely *sorry* for the other morning. I came at you all wrong, cause I was embarrassed to have lost everything. But I'm okay now, money-wise, for a little while. And I didn't mean what I said about . . . about anything I said."

It was very hard to say. Evidently Troy wasn't the only one who was out of practice with apologies.

"How about this?" Brianne said. "I'll take the money if you promise to go to GA."

Lelah could picture her searching online for such a solution. Brianne had always been solution-oriented; a list maker, a task manager. Lelah tried to focus on the obvious love behind an action like that, but it was humiliating. How did Brianne have all of the bargaining chips? She was *giving* the child money, damn near throwing it at her, and still she had no leverage. No leverage at all.

"GA stands for Gamblers Anonymous, Mommy."

"I know what it stands for. I been there before. I don't know. I gotta keep looking, maybe something else besides GA is for me. I'm not gonna sit here and promise to go do something, and then maybe not go. I'm done lying to folks."

Brianne shook her head and laughed, incredulous.

"Okay," she said. "Well. Here's what you can do for me. This is about the *only* thing you can do for me at this point, so if you say no, then I guess it just is what it is. You tell me everything, from beginning to end, about Vernon Greene, and you and me, and Missouri. Everything you can remember, and I'll take that money."

A not unreasonable request. It troubled her that her daughter might consider this the hardest thing she could ever ask her for. What sort of person denied her child such basic information? And how had Lelah convinced herself that Brianne would be fine without having it? Flawed as it had been, it wasn't a fling that conceived Brianne but an actual marriage to a person whose last name Brianne still carried.

The things we do in the name of protecting others are so often attempts to spare some part of ourselves.

It took nearly three hours for Lelah to re-create Vernon for her daughter, starting from the very first time she'd seen him jumping hurdles at a track meet at Cass, to that final afternoon she'd seen him nodding off in the freezing rain. Lelah filled the stories with details she hadn't thought about in decades, like his first car, a 1980 Cutlass Supreme, and what she'd worn to their courthouse marriage (a baby-pink knee-length dress with aggressive shoulder pads). She took her time, because she never wanted to repeat these stories again. The two of them folded clothes into bags, packed boxes, and sorted through piles and piles of junk. By three o'clock they'd gotten Brianne in good shape to leave her mother and Detroit behind.

To Let Go or to Hang On

Humans haunt more houses than ghosts do. Men and women assign value to brick and mortar, link their identities to mortgages paid on time. On frigid winter nights, young mothers walk their fussy babies from room to room, learning where the rooms catch drafts and where the floorboards creak. In the warm damp of summer, fathers sit on porches, sometimes worried and often tired but comforted by the fact that a roof is up there providing shelter. Children smudge up walls with dirty handprints, find nooks to hide their particular treasure, or hide themselves if need be. We live and die in houses, dream of getting back to houses, take great care in considering who will inherit the houses when we're gone. Cha-Cha knew his family was no different. The house on Yarrow Street was their sedentary mascot, its crumbling façade the Turner coat of arms. But it disintegrated by the hour. Mold in the basement, asbestos hiding in the walls, a garage stolen. He understood these things pointed to abandonment. He knew he should walk away from the place, let it become one more blasted-out house in a city plagued by them. But what to do with the house and what to do about his mother's sickness were problems to which Cha-Cha possessed no simple solution. In both cases his impulse leaned toward preservation, but at what cost?

If Viola wanted to die, who was he to stop her? If the house was destined for atrophy, why fight it? What he'd felt in that backyard with Lonnie was helplessness; it had only looked like rage. What happened to control? Control used to come effortlessly to Cha-Cha, and not because he was power-hungry or ego-starved. A pack of wolves. A murder of crows. All groups needed order. He felt the loss of control like a loss of basic reason. A dark splotch on his frontal lobe. Why not give in to every impulse, break free and go insane, if he lived in a world where people made structures disappear overnight?

On Thursday morning Russell arrived, as did Sandra and Berniece. The former claimed the second guest room. His sisters went to Francey's. That evening Miles, Duke, Quincy, a passel of nieces who were improbably womanly, and nephews newly graduated from knuckleheads to respectable young men descended. A full house if Tina wasn't missing.

The visiting Turners filed into his mother's room one by one or in pairs. They sat and watched TV with her, brought her food, and filled her in on what the beings that had sprung from her being were doing out in the wide world. Everyone wanted to go to Yarrow and inspect the scene of the garage heist. Cha-Cha let them take his car. He didn't join them. On Friday night, the eve of the party, the out-of-towners met up at Cha-Cha's and piled into cars for a casino buffet. Cha-Cha begged off, as did Lelah, for obvious reasons. She claimed to be exhausted and went to bed early, without checking on Viola or saying good night. Cha-Cha inflated all of the air mattresses and left a heap of comforters on the couches for pallets on the floor. It was 8 P.M.

OLD FOLKS WERE supposed to be accustomed to suffering. Viola knew this. No one wanted to hear an old lady complain about aches in her chest, or throbs under her armpits, or stinging, scalding sensations in her disobedient legs. The young couldn't keep an old lady from hurting, so they'd rather think that there existed a threshold one crossed where it ceased to matter. Selfishness. Viola counted getting

the doctors to prescribe her stronger medication as her last significant victory on this earth. She was proud of speaking up for herself
and claiming what little say-so she could about what happened to her
body. For saying no more of *this*, but I do need more of *that*. The only
drawback was the fog. When she felt the least amount of pain her
thoughts became the most jumbled. Following a single thought to its
logical end was like trying to catch a fish with bare hands. But when
the drugs subsided, and the hurt hammered down, her mind was as
clear as ever. Right now she could feel every part of herself. The pain
had yanked her awake, if she had indeed been asleep. She had stopped
keeping strict track of time when she moved off of Yarrow and into
this room, but she estimated that if no one brought her any pills, she
had half an hour before the truly crushing, vision-blurring pain began. She couldn't remember when her fear of pain had first started
trumping her fear of death.

To her relief, someone was in the room. A son sat in her armchair.
Dozing with his chin on his chest. Looking as old as his daddy when
he died. Viola remembered something.

"You got three years, Cha."

"What's that?" He wiped his mouth with his hand.

"Your daddy died at sixty-six. Three years and you got him beat.
Your granddaddy, too. Both granddaddies."

She kept track of no child's age except Cha-Cha's. Her age minus
eighteen. She could never forget that she had been eighteen, she and
Cha-Cha sleeping in one bed in the living room of the shotgun house
while Olivia and Lucille slept in another bed. She had been eighteen
during those long months when she thought her husband was gone
for good.

Cha-Cha shook out her pills, already sorted, into her hand. He
picked up a glass of water from the nightstand and positioned the
straw close to her lips. She looked him in the eyes, grateful, but he
looked away. Viola remembered something else. A question he'd
asked that she had not felt brave enough to answer. Sending him away
with doubt in his heart. She kept the pills in her hand.

"Tina's asleep?"

"Gone," Cha-Cha said. "At Chucky's. Not talking to me."

"Oh." She was afraid to ask anything else. She should just take her pills and banish her aches and let her mind float off, she knew, but guilt wouldn't let her.

"She's gonna be back," she said after some time.

"Mama, maybe she shouldn't come back. I don't know."

It was difficult, talking like this. They were not built for these roles.

"You remember that little farm your auntie Lucille and Olivia had back home? How we used to go down there in the summer sometimes?"

"Uh-huh," Cha-Cha said. "I always tried to milk the male cows. Lucky I never got kicked in the head."

Viola smiled. She would have liked to sit up high in the bed, but she couldn't manage it. Keeping a tight grip on the pills in her hand took all of her strength.

"I want you to know that I never seen no haints, Cha," she said. "Never in my whole life, but I do know folks see them."

Her son looked doubtful, crestfallen.

"It was your daddy that seen them," she added. "Not me."

She considered telling him how she knew this. About her ride with Reverend Tufts the day she'd walked out of Ethel Joggets's house and decided to be done with Arkansas. But she couldn't tell him that story.

"If Daddy saw haints, why'd he say he didn't?" Cha-Cha asked. "Why'd he look me in the face and lie?"

"Cause he wanted you to be satisfied. Your daddy tried to be satisfied his whole life. Oh, he was happy. He had all you children and him an only child. But somethin bout that haint messed up his spirit, Cha."

Viola's mouth felt dry. The pills in her damp palm stuck to one another. If she didn't take them soon, Cha-Cha would have to throw them away. A waste she couldn't bear.

"Your daddy loved everybody but himself. Never was content with his own self."

She watched Cha-Cha's face as he turned what she'd said over in his mind. If anyone besides her knew of Francis Turner's melancholy ways, it would be her eldest son.

"You know I had an uncle named Friend?" she said. "That was his real name. You never met him. I never even met him. Folks say he had a haint follow him from Virginia before I was born. He was supposed to be riding his horse to Arkansas cause my daddy had a job lined up for him layin bricks someplace. Well, Friend must've owed the haint somethin when it was alive, like some work, or maybe he done somebody wrong back in Virginia and tried to run from it. They found him in a hole somewhere between Memphis and Pine Bluff. Deep as a grave. Looked like a horse had kicked his skull in, but his own horse was tied up a ways away.

"*That's* the kinda haint to be worried about, Cha. I think you and your daddy, whatever kind y'all got can't hurt you unless you let it."

Cha-Cha tapped the side of the glass of water and looked down at his lap. Viola knew he was deciding whether to let go, to let his haint continue to be a mystery but no longer a preoccupation, or to hang on. After about a minute of this he positioned the straw close to Viola's mouth once more, and she swallowed her pills. There was always a period of anticipation before the medication hit Viola's bloodstream, when the pain felt more akin to pleasure, because she knew it would soon be gone.

An Old Man in Faded Slacks

Cha-Cha left Viola's room determined to hold one final vigil for his haint. He would not be its unwitting victim, as his great-uncle Friend had been, nor would he spend the rest of his life taking sleeping pills, or denying its existence as he believed his father had done. He would stay awake and demand to know what it wanted. Both Lonnie and Alice had suggested confronting it; Cha-Cha finally felt ready to do just that, without any beer muddling his perception. He adjusted the pillows on his side of the bed until he sat upright, turned off the lights, and waited, nodding in and out of sleep, for the blue light to appear around its usual time.

Two A.M. The man did not glow blue this time. It was very close to Cha-Cha, less than four feet away. Up close, Cha-Cha could see its features better. Its mustache extended past the corners of its mouth. It looked at Cha-Cha and showed teeth, but was it a smile? There was a gap between the front two. A confirmation.

"You're not real, Daddy," Cha-Cha said. "You're not alive." It was a statement for a third party. Surely the haint knew what it was and wasn't.

The haint did not wear what Francis was buried in—an old blue pinstripe suit from Hudson's with a garnet necktie and pocket square.

He wore clothes that Cha-Cha did not associate with his father at all. A white T-shirt, an undershirt, really, which was tucked into his hitched-up, faded brown slacks. His chest sagged as an old man's is wont to do, concave and thin, the shadows of his nipples visible through the cotton.

"Get out from under there," the haint said. "You think you hidin, but I know you down there. I don't *never* hide."

Its voice was quiet but stern, more country than Cha-Cha remembered it. Its eyes focused below Cha-Cha, under the bed. Cha-Cha wondered what might be under there, but he once again had trouble moving.

"I need to know what you want," Cha-Cha managed to get out. He thought the question silly now that he faced this man, a haint who looked as flesh-and-blood as he did, but he had no other plan for what to say.

The haint did not answer him. Cha-Cha noticed that it wore no shoes or socks.

"Come on out, now," the haint said. "Don't you have no pride? Look at you, down there like a possum. That's what you doing, huh? Playin possum? I bet you is."

The haint laughed and laughed, and for a moment Cha-Cha felt angry. Was it laughing at him? The face resembled his father's, but Cha-Cha didn't recognize the laugh at all. High-pitched and nasal. The haint leaned against the wall to steady itself and laughed some more.

"See now, I know you're not real," Cha-Cha said. "You're saying what I wished you'd have said when I was up under that house." He didn't realize this was what he thought until the words were out.

"You knew I was down there, didn't you?" Cha-Cha said. "You knew I was down up under that house, and you made a fool of me. Why?"

The haint reached down and scratched the bottom of its left foot. Its toenails were filthy. Its chest still heaved from laughing. Its eyes still focused under the bed.

"Boy, ain't nobody thinkin bout you," the haint said, almost tenderly. It shook its head. "Folks got their own business to tend to. So you just come on outta there like I say. It's late."

Cha-Cha watched the haint watch whatever it saw under the bed. He realized he was holding his breath and tried to take a deep one to make up for it. He was suddenly worried about his health. Perhaps the haint was here to collect him, take him to heaven or hell. He had no intention of dying so young, not even outliving his father. He thought maybe he should tell the haint that it wasn't welcome here, that it should go toward the light, or some other variant of things people in movies say. But Cha-Cha didn't feel he had a right to say such a thing, not even if the haint was just something he'd made up.

"Well, do what you want then," the haint said. It spat, but no liquid reached Cha-Cha's carpet. "I never knowed you to be no coward."

The door opened, and Cha-Cha turned to look at it. It was Lonnie, come so late to look for extra pillows, and when Cha-Cha turned back to the windowsill, the haint was gone. For the first time ever, he wished it would return.

How Three Went North

· SUMMER 1945 ·

On the ride back to her parents' shotgun house that morning, Reverend Tufts told Viola there was something heathen and hysterical in Francis. That her husband had claimed to see haints, and worse, that he claimed they were from God. It was not surprising Francis had gone north and turned feckless, he said; he likely succumbed to depravity shortly after stepping off the train. Tufts tried to console Viola. "You shouldn't be overly upset," he said. "A practical, good-looking girl like yourself will find an honest man to take care of you." Viola hoped more than she'd ever hoped for anything that Tufts was right. She didn't care much about haints; she just knew she couldn't wait anymore. It wasn't fair. And just as she refused to ever recount the story of her short stint as a white woman's help, she told no one what happened in that car next. She watched the reverend remove his glove from his right hand and reach for her thigh. On the surface it might have looked innocent, a comforting pat, but Viola felt the warmth of his palm and the need in his fingers. Push that hand away, she thought, but she did nothing. She let his fingers settle there, and with a slight shift of her thighs she gave him permission to connect with what he wanted. With only one hand on the wheel the reverend pulled the car onto a gravel road flanked by oaks. Then he took off his other glove and put his hat on the dashboard. She did not wait for him to move toward her. She went to him, slid over to his side of the wide Packard. Viola did not know what she expected to happen afterward; she was not naïve enough to think the reverend would be the "honest man" to take care of her. The best he could possibly do was give her money to get to one of her brothers Up North, but Viola knew she would never ask him for it. She simply felt alone, and trapped in a life that should not have been hers. Francis had betrayed and abandoned her; she would betray him as well. She was eighteen years old. She thought it would be the lowest day of her life.

It wasn't. Just as he'd known to wait on the side of the road for her that first time, Reverend Tufts appeared again in his Packard on the perfect patch of isolated road as Viola walked back from an errand a few days later. He again opened the door. She once again climbed in. Soon enough she started walking the long way home whenever possible, passing in front of the reverend's porch where he might happen to be sitting outside for a smoke. They never talked much, a relief to Viola because as much as the love-starved part of her needed him to touch her, she hated when he spoke. He had certain turns of phrase that reminded her of Francis, and the shame quadrupled when she heard them. After each time, she returned to the shotgun house and swore to never walk the long way again, but she could hold out only a few days. He aroused her, and he repulsed her. *A woman without no options is waitin for a man to come by and ruin her.* It was a lesson that Viola would pass on to her daughters years later.

A month after she quit the Joggetses, Francis stood at the door of the shotgun house. Pounds thinner, dirty. Dressed even poorer than when he left. It was the middle of the day. Viola was home alone with Cha-Cha.

"I've done wrong," he said. "But I got a good job lined up and I'm here for my family. I'm gonna be here for now on."

I've done wrong, too! Viola had wanted to shout, but she did not.

Nothing good could have come of telling her husband this. She let Francis into the house, handed him his child. He had ridden buses and hitched rides back south so that the three of them—husband, wife, and son—could afford train rides north. She pumped and heated water for her road-weary husband, bathed him, and set their baby down for a nap. Then Viola and Francis made slow, quiet love in the front room of the shotgun house.

They forgave each other without sharing the details of their betrayals. They would spend the rest of their lives atoning for those months when they had not only forsaken their marriage but given up hope. Each child became a consecration, further commitment to stay put and be happy. And they often were.

Losing the Call

A boy like Francis had reason to see ghosts. A father in the ground so young from a poor man's ailment. A mother away. Shortly after he lost them both, a haint visited him. A man with pale skin, hitched-up trousers, and bare feet. Francis had no picture of his own father, so he could not say for sure if this was him, but he had no reason to think it was anyone else. His yearning for his father had been so deep that he did not dare question how the man had found a way back to him. If haints could be conjured, called forth from the hereafter, then young Francis had accomplished it. The haint returned every subsequent Arkansas night, not always as a man, sometimes just as a light in the darkness of a room. For years he told no one because he did not want intercession. One man's haunting is another man's hallowed guest.

At twenty, married and father to one, Francis wanted a place in church leadership. Reverend Tufts, the man who considered himself a scholar, pushing his church toward pragmatism, fashioning a model, modern congregation, and above the need of even three old deacons, doubted his ward's worthiness. Francis had received little formal education, after all.

"How do I know that you've truly received the call as opposed to doing what you think I expect of you?"

A simple enough question, and Francis could have answered with a verbose citation of scripture or a simple, fervent oath, but he spoke about the haint that had visited him for ten years right under the reverend's roof. He likened it to the angel Gabriel, counsel to Daniel and comforter of Mary. He said he knew his place was in the church, helping to shepherd their humble congregation however he could.

It was the wrong answer. Reverend Tufts did not take kindly to superstition or root work, and claims of otherwordly visitations fell under that umbrella for him. Never mind the ghosts in the Bible. The reverend detested the tendency of Negro churches to prize the sensational at the expense of more complex concepts. He said he would consider what Francis wanted, but he did not. The next week he gave Francis a letter of introduction to a Detroit pastor and advised him to shoot for a better life up north.

Starting his first evening in Detroit, and every night for the rest of his life, Francis saw nothing. Not hide nor hair of the haint that had helped give his life purpose. He spent no small amount of time pondering why. Could have been that his father's spirit, if the haint was indeed his father's spirit, was unable to travel so far away from where its earthly body lay. Or maybe Francis, finally grown and gone for good from the sort of poor, sharecropping life that had killed Francis Sr., no longer needed protection. Either way, his conclusion was the same: there ain't no haints in Detroit. When his firstborn son claimed to have seen a ghost, to have fought with it, Francis refused to believe. His haint had been a blessing, nothing to fear.

Francis never returned to Arkansas after collecting his family. And the call to something greater—to preach, to lead, to be anything other than a man who worked too much and made too little—either had stayed in Arkansas with his haint or had never really been within him. For funerals and summer trips he would drive Viola and the children as far as her brothers in Cleveland, and as they made the journey south, Francis would turn back to Detroit. He would continue to take things that happened in the city personally—white flight, the government-sponsored demolition of Black Bottom and Paradise Valley, plants closing, drugs arriving—but he would love the city just the same, even if he did not love who he had become within it.

Every Turner Dances

There truly ain't no party like a Turner house party. Like a single-celled organism, it can change shape and reproduce itself with little fuel. The food runs out by 9 P.M., no matter how much they make, but the booze never ends. The children, in a pop- and candy-fueled ecstasy, will do doughnuts on their Big Wheels in the basement. Or, minus miniature vehicles, they'll play video games on the old big screen down there, standing up, jostling one another, fighting the big screen's static, and only stopping for Faygo and pee breaks. In the absence of any toys at all — which is unlikely because Cha-Cha's basement doubles as a toy graveyard — Turners under the age of twelve may resort to old school play, linking arms and running as fast as they can in a circle until someone vomits, playing tag in the dark until someone gets a minor concussion, or simply screaming at the top of their prepubescent lungs until an adult comes down and threatens them into silence. The adults will play dominoes, bid whist, and Po-Ke-No. They tell the same embarrassing stories about one another and guffaw as if they're new. They make liquor runs; they make new boyfriends uncomfortable; they make neighbors consider calling the police. They will eventually kick the children out of the basement, tuck them away upstairs, and dance in the belly of Cha-Cha's house to classics from the disparate decades of their youths.

But first: preparation. Quincy gathered his brothers and their adult children in Cha-Cha's living room, put his sisters on speakerphone, and devised a game plan. Tina's absence necessitated this pre-party huddle. Cha-Cha went along with the plans as if it wasn't his house and he wasn't supposed to be hosting. He couldn't face the day, with its marathon drinking and joking and inevitable arguments, without Tina. What he needed was solitude to think about the mess he'd willingly made of his marriage. A Turner house party had no room for solitude.

Quincy, Russell, Miles, and Duke left the house and came back with enough farm-animal limbs to start their own butcher shop. Then Miles and Duke, the Californians, marinated beef for carne asada and brined their chicken in lime juice and beer. Quincy and Russell, the southerners, changed into short sets and Panama hats, puffed on cigars, and began the complicated process of concocting rubs for their ribs. Lonnie foraged through the house for music. The nieces and nephews staked their claim on adulthood by going out to buy the first haul of booze.

Cha-Cha hosed out old moldy coolers in the driveway and wondered how long he could get away with going back to bed before someone noticed. Lonnie opened the garage door, presumably for more light to help him as he sifted through the boxes of cassette tapes and records stacked behind a tangle of rusty bikes. He didn't speak to Cha-Cha, and Cha-Cha was grateful to him. He felt like a hostage in his own house. He saw now that these parties were larger than him and Tina, and even Viola. That his family could go on party prepping in Cha-Cha's house when his home life was an obvious wreck indicated of a lack of respect. This was what happened when an open-door policy—something Cha and Tina had prided themselves on—ran amok. When *mi casa es su casa* was taken literally. His house had become an extension of the Brotherly Banquet Hall of their youths, except his siblings slept here too, and paid no security deposit for damage. In exchange, Turners thought their presence was expression of love enough; that they'd booked flights and crossed state lines to invade Cha-Cha's space was supposed to be some sort of gift to him. It felt more like an ambush.

Miles came around the side of the house with two hot links on a skewer and a Corona in each shirt pocket.

"Early spoils of the war," he said, and pulled off a link for Cha-Cha. Cha-Cha found no joy in the taught, salty skin of the link, nor in the spicy, juicy meat inside, but he ate it anyway, because historically he loved hot links. He put the Corona in his own shirt pocket for later use.

"So," Miles said. "I looked into tearing down the house. Not to sell it, but I figure we could tear it down and keep the grass mown till we wanna rebuild or whatever. Less hassle. Plus it wouldn't be uglying up the block."

"Let's just focus on getting ready for the party," Cha-Cha said. "So everybody can have a good time."

"Shit, I'm already having a good time. I got a link and brew, don't I? I'm just sayin I *get* it, is all. Turns out it'll cost at least eight thousand to tear that sucker down and haul the junk away. And then we'd still have to renegotiate the loan. It ain't an easy decision."

"Who's tearing what sucker down?" Duke said. He sauntered over from the side of the house, beer gut first. "The house?"

Miles and Duke had always been a package deal, so inseparable that folks on Yarrow thought they were twins instead of a year apart. Cha-Cha vacillated between envying their built-in friendship and being suspicious of it. He now saw it as a way for neither brother to truly grow up, an annoying Frick and Frack routine they'd never stopped performing.

Duke stared at Cha-Cha, waiting for an answer.

"Nobody's tearing anything down," he said.

"Good," Duke said. "Cause I been doin some math." He mimed punching numbers into his calculator palm.

"Me too," said Miles. "That's what I was just sayin. It costs at least eight thousand—"

"Three thousand seventy-six a piece!" Duke yelled over him. "That's all it is per child to get the loan paid up. Don't try to tell me that all a these *grown-ass people* can't come up with three thousand. Three Gs, as the young folks say."

"That's a lot of money for me," Lonnie said. "I'm on a fixed income." He did not look up from his boxes of music.

Miles and Duke exchanged quizzical looks and snickered.

"Well, according to Russell, that's money down the toilet," Miles said. "He won't pay it cause a what already happened to the garage."

"We might as well hash all this out before the party starts," Duke said. "Before folks get that liquor in them, and the girls come over and get emotional."

"Marlene gonna kick your behind if y'all do this without her," Lonnie said, walking toward them.

"Ain't nobody scared of Marlene," Duke and Miles said in unison. This was a lie.

"I'ma go get Russ and Quince," Duke said.

Cha-Cha could not stay for this. He didn't care that this was his house, and that he was the one who would have to sign for any final decision. He saw why Troy, wrong-headed as he'd been, thought it was easier to just do what he wanted and fill in his siblings later. Nothing would be decided in this driveway roundtable, with his sisters excluded and meat still grilling in the backyard. He walked past his brothers to the front door, set down his Corona on the entryway table, and picked up his keys. He turned up the radio as he sped away, and only faintly heard his brothers calling after him.

WORD SPREAD THAT Cha-Cha had taken off, and while Miles, Duke, and Russell wanted to call him, drag him back against his will, Lelah and Lonnie convinced everyone that the show had to go on. It was for Viola that they had come, after all. Shortly after Cha-Cha left,

Marlene came over to help get Viola ready. She and Lelah bathed their mother, dressed her in her favorite color. Yellow muumuu, yellow slippers, yellow pillbox hat to crown a shiny brown bob wig. "Y'all don't have to do all this," Viola repeated as Marlene painted her nails pink, as Lelah lotioned her feet. "We just goin to the living room." When she saw the finished product in the mirror she smiled, showing off strong teeth that were mostly still hers.

Marlene stopped Lelah in the hallway, held her by the elbow.

"How much medication she take today, Lelah? She can't even keep eye contact. You think you gave her the wrong amount? We can call Tina and check."

"She's got cancer, Marla. And it's at the point where she gets whatever she wants whenever she wants."

"Oh. Well. Oh."

"Cha-Cha isn't ready to tell people, and I guess Mama isn't either or she would've told you."

Marlene pulled her into a hug.

"If she doesn't wanna tell anybody, that's her choice," she said.

"But don't you think the outta-town folks should be able to say goodbye?"

"Maybe she don't want goodbyes. Trust me, you start to feel a lot more dead when other people find out you're dying. That's how I felt when I got sick."

"But you didn't die."

"Nope. But I wasn't eighty-two years old."

Lelah slipped the $950 Marlene had loaned her into her purse when she wasn't looking.

The other sisters arrived with foil trays and ceramic boats of food. Without Tina, the menu lacked the cohesion of a usual Turner party spread. Francey brought vegetarian lasagna with an unappetizing white cream sauce and bread crumbs sprinkled on top. Sandra and Berniece brought potato salad, macaroni salad, and deviled eggs. Netti brought chicken biryani that she'd just learned how to make in India. The rice looked too dry. Henna still decorated her hands. "It was like a honeymoon, but it was so hot! I had a flash about every five minutes, and had to buy water on the street. Rahul was scared but I *never* got sick." Marlene's son, Antoine, arrived with his wife, their new baby girl, and banana pudding. A chorus of coos filled the foyer for several more doorbell rings. Lelah stood in the entryway, feeling pressure to greet these arrivals in the absence of the homeowners. She kept hoping that the next people through the door would be Brianne and Bobbie, or even Rob. She'd told Brianne everything she could remember about Vernon, and that had been enough to get her to take $300. She knew it had not been enough to get Brianne to trust her again, to get her to stop thinking of her as a problem that she should either fix or avoid. Only time would change that.

"WE'RE ON THE way to your house," Chucky said at the door. He carried a huge pot of something with both hands.

"Who? You and your mama?"

"Me and Isaiah. I just strapped him into the car. Mommy doesn't wanna—"

"Oh, well then, excuse me." Cha-Cha sucked in his stomach to squeeze past Chucky and into the house.

"Pop, Pop! You can't just . . . Oh, whatever," Chucky said. He shut the door.

Tina sat in Chucky's living room, flipping through the DVR queue for something to watch. She seemed neither surprised nor relieved to see him.

"You wanna know what the funny thing is, Cha-Cha?"

He said nothing. He was afraid of what the funny thing might be.

"Everybody thinks we gotta make up. That old as we both are, we *have* to. But that's exactly why we *don't* have to. It's been thirty-seven years, Cha. Mostly good years. That's already beating the odds."

"Tina, I was confused with Alice, not happy with my own life and confused. I'm sorry."

Tina shook her head.

"It's bigger than Alice. What do we even have in common anymore, besides other people, besides our family? Just me and you, what do *we* have? You don't even like the things I like. You think they're silly, which is fine."

"It's not fine. It's not fine for me to make fun of things that make you happy."

"But we also can't . . ." Tina went on. "We hardly *touch*. Like, not even walking by each other in the hallway. Nothing. Maybe we've finally grown apart."

She looked at him straight on.

"You and me probably have twenty years or so left, if it all goes right, and that's it. We'll be gone. If I'm not what you want for the next twenty years, then you should go find it. I'll do the same."

Cha-Cha sat down. He had an inkling of what he wanted. To be satisfied. He recalled what his mother had told him the night before about Francis's haint. About his father's private unhappiness. He did not want that inheritance. He could accept a haint visiting him at night but not a life defined by regret. He thought about Troy, twenty years younger than himself and already wrecked by bitterness. This morning he'd been reminded of how smart Tina was, socially adept in a way that Turners were not. The party hadn't officially started when he'd left, and it was already missing a certain Tina-ness, an inclusionary spirit that he'd heretofore taken for granted.

He put his hand on top of hers, and she did not pull away. He kissed her the way he used to when they'd lived in that drafty apartment off Van Dyke and he had a six-pack and two real hips, that long ago. She kissed him back, and they made love on their son's sectional. Not quite the same as they had during their Van Dyke days, but very well nonetheless.

PARTY TIME, OFFICIALLY. Tradition obligated everyone to come out of their hidey-holes and make a show of familial togetherness in the living room. There were too many people to sit down at the formal dining table and eat, so knees and palms cradled plates as people leaned against walls and sat cross-legged on the floor. Small groups absconded when they could.

Out on the deck, four Turner men and Rahul smoked cigars and drank Hennessy and Heineken.

"It's a lose-lose situation: white men won't vote for a woman, and *nobody's* gonna vote for a black man. Not even enough black folks."

"Yeah, well, all *kinds* of folks been donating to Barack's campaign, so that's gotta mean something."

"Shit, all kinds of folks donate to Feed the Children, but that don't mean they want your black ass over for dinner."

"Say, Antoine, what's that you got tattooed on your neck?"

"What's it look like?"

"Rahul, you still got that convenience store off of Ford Road?"

"You don't wanna know what I think it looks like, it looks like a—"

"No, I sold it last year. Too much hassle."

"See, I don't understand why you young guys wanna go and get neck tattoos. What's it gonna look like when your stuff starts hangin down like this, huh?"

"Can't get a job with a neck tattoo. No real job."

"It's a *fist*, Uncle Duke. It's Joe Louis's arm and fist. Like the statue downtown?"

"I hear it, I hear it. You still have those apartments around there though, I assume?"

"I do. I thought about selling them two years ago, but lucky for me I didn't. Everyone who's been foreclosed on needs a place to rent right now. It's sad, but—"

"Ohhhh. Yeah I see it. You gotta kinda turn your head to the side, but I see it."

"Nothing sad about it. I'll tell you, I remember when Hubbard, the old mayor of Dearborn, said he wouldn't ever have any niggers living in his city. He said it right on TV! They kept voting his *fool* self back into office, too. Now look. You and your A-rab brothers *own* that town. It's a beautiful thing."

"That's not what I was gonna say it looks like. It looks like you got a big old dick tattooed on your neck, you ask me."

"Well, I just own those apartments."

"That's real funny, Uncle Duke. Real funny."

"And, I'm not Arab, you know. Indian, Quincy. But it *is* something, you're right."

Lelah walked out onto the deck, hands on her hips. The party was going okay without Cha-Cha and Tina, even without Brianne. She wasn't happy, but she wasn't miserable, either.

"Enough man talk already," she said. "DJ Lonnie's got the basement set up, and if y'all don't come downstairs and dance, he might cry."

Every Turner dances, two left feet or no. Even Russell, oafish by nature, floated and swung to the right combination of seventies soul and egging on. They hustled. Lelah and her sisters spent three songs breaking down the moves for their nieces, and finally on the fourth it came together, a miracle of steps and taps and pauses and turns. "Finished" it might have been, but Cha-Cha's basement never lost its earthy, cave-like essence. The warmth of bodies made the loamy smell rise, and it felt like dancing in a bunker made of earth.

Around nine o'clock Marlene brought Viola from her room, where she'd been napping. She had a fresh batch of pain pills in her bloodstream and looked like a high-noon sun in all of that yellow. Those who had been dancing came upstairs to give birthday tribute speeches and cut the cake. On a nephew's insistence, and after a little back-and-forth about young people's hypersensitivity, and aggressive Turner communication styles, they used a kitchen towel to regulate who spoke when. Marlene encouraged Lelah to go first.

Lelah stood in front of the huge flat screen, thinking of what to say, still sweating from dancing, and wringing the kitchen towel with both hands. Just then Cha-Cha and Tina walked into the living room. Someone whistled, and a few people clapped.

"It's Tina Turner, ladies and gentlemen! Tina Turner!" Duke yelled. An old, unfunny joke.

"Oh, you should go first, Cha," Lelah said.

Cha-Cha sat on the arm of the couch nearest Chucky and shook his head. He suddenly remembered Lelah at fourteen at a party similar to this one, for Viola's birthday, playing the flute he and Tina had bought her. She'd worn a serious expression when she played, and her body became rigid, but the music itself had sounded effortless.

"The last can go first tonight," he said. "Go on."

"Well, I guess. Hmm. I just wanna say that as the thirteenth, I looked up to you all so much. I wanted to be each and every one of you at some point. But now I just wanna be myself. I don't know. The point is, I love you all. I'm happy to be a Turner. And I love you, Mama. Happy birthday."

Viola nodded and smiled.

Lonnie went next. He pinched the towel with two fingers. His eyes darted around the room, challenging anyone to butt in. "Now, I don't wanna bring us all down with talk of death."

"But you're about to, huh?"

"Excuse me. I said I don't wanna bring us down. But by now you all been to the east side, and you seen what they did to the house. I know people feel frustrated about it, but think about this: I'm alive. Me!"

"Lord knows *that's* a miracle."

"It *is* a miracle. I'm not gonna go into too much detail, but if the only thing we have to complain about all these years later is that some fools ripped off a piece of our house, then we are very fortunate. Thank you for that, Mama."

Francey jumped up and grabbed the towel.

"To piggyback off of that. Ahem, I said to piggyback off of *that*, can we talk about the love my daddy had for this woman? So much love. You know, I remember when I was little, one time, when we stayed in that rented house on Lemay and Mack . . ."

And so began the overly specific anecdotes. They had their moment, as did shy grandkids and even brand-new significant others, mortified to be put on the spot. The jokes inevitably took a turn to the crude, and some speeches slurred more than others. The love pivoted between hard and unwieldy and tender and sincere.

People began to feel antsy, ready to keep the party going in their own ways. But no one moved. Viola had yet to address her children. She waited for the room to quiet down, for everyone to have a turn. For her there was no rush. Her thoughts cleared up with each minute; the words solidified in her head. She thought of the longing she felt to get out of that shotgun house so many years before, how as the three of them went north, she had no inkling what this city might be like, no idea that she was capable of loving so many. She had not cared for her children equally, and never had time to worry about the good or bad of that fact. They were individual parts of herself. She knew it didn't matter what she said right now because her children were the proof, as were their children, and their children's children, whom she could not name. They had crowded her thoughts, burdened her heart, and wanted too much from her over the past sixty-four years, and it had been worth it to try to give. Much better than being a regular old preacher's wife.

She would be gracious. She would talk about strength and pride. She would tell a little joke. They would all feel loved.

For Better Things

Francis had returned to the salt mines, to breathing in dry ocean air deep beneath the city. He'd pushed down what needed pushing down inside of him in order to make it through each shift. He did this for Viola and Cha-Cha, and soon enough for Francey too. They first lived in a tenement on Elmwood Street in Black Bottom—more crowded than Odella Withers's boardinghouse, and in worse condition. While Francis worked at the mine, Viola looked after their children, and the children of neighbors for extra money. She did not complain about the rats, the shoddy plumbing, the poor heating, the rude policemen on the street, or the smell of the rotting gutter behind their building. As long as they were there together, these were temporary inconveniences. They lived there for four years. The job at Chrysler meant daylight again for Francis, and feeling as if he could stand upright. They moved to a house on Lemay and Mack, a rental with a coal stove, on the edge of a neighborhood whites were quickly fleeing.

The summer afternoon they moved into 6257 Yarrow was humid. Rainwater dampened the front lawn. The Turners stood on the sidewalk and regarded their home; it promised more space than anyplace they'd lived in yet. Francis unlocked the front door, and Cha-Cha, seven years old by then, ran up the stairs and straight to the middle room, thereby claiming it for boys for the next forty years. Viola, five months pregnant with Russell, held Quincy's hand as she inspected the kitchen, the basement, and the bathroom. She did a short, celebratory dance in the hallway upstairs. Francis lingered on the porch with little Francey in his arms. He smiled down at his daughter. He allowed himself to hope.

Acknowledgments

For showing me that families are their own universes worthy of exploration: my aunties Valerie Moore, Sharon Dunbar, and Leisha Williams. Thank you to my stepfather, Bob Harper, and his children, Jasmine and Joshua. A very partial list of cousins: Style Bell, Terrence, Angie, and Thomas Dunbar, Damon Hawkins, Jason Moore, Tadia James, and Latonia Curtis. Thank you to all of the Hempsteads, especially Aunt Rose.

I am indebted to the work of Thomas Sugrue, author of *Origins of the Urban Crisis: Race and Inequality in Postwar Detroit,* for showing me that you can't talk about the history of Detroit without talking about housing discrimination. The stories collected by Elaine Laztman Moon in *Untold Tales, Unsung Heroes: An Oral History of Detroit's African American Community, 1918–1967* shed light on how it felt to be there as the city changed.

Thank you to my agent, Ellen Levine, for your patience, your sense of humor, and your willingness to step in and advocate for me. To Jenna Johnson at Houghton Mifflin Harcourt, for working tirelessly for this book, and for buying those nachos. Margaret Wimberger helped me wrangle my dates and character ages, which was no easy task.

I've had so many wonderful teachers. I'm grateful to Michelle Huneven and Alexander Chee for being insightful advisors and excellent friends. Thank you to those who have read some incarnation of this book, and to those whose lessons made my writing stronger: Lan Samantha Chang, Marilynne Robinson, Elizabeth McCracken, ZZ Packer, the gracious and generous Allan Gurganus, T. C. Boyle, Daniel Alarcón, and Michael Martone. Thank you to Connie Brothers for being kindhearted and no-nonsense, a winning combination.

For reading my work, laughing along, pushing me, and believing: Emma Borges-Scott, Evan James, and Jihan Thompson. A million hugs and a grand jeté for the brilliant, understanding Robert Valadéz.

Thank you to Justin Torres and Ayana Mathis for taking me seriously even when I did not take myself very seriously, and for showing me how the work can be its own reward.

A mi hermana Yuly Restrepo: abrazos a vos por todo.

Thank you to my girlfriends Zoé Zeigler, Vallery Lomas, Sophia Williams, Jasmine Alexander, and all of my Somerville family. Let's keep shining. To Gene Demby, PostBourgie mastermind, for nudging me to see issues differently and inspiring me to hustle harder.

To Stephanie Parker, Kiana Butler, and Martinique Williams: happy ten years to us! Thank you to my Sorors from the Upsilon Chapter of Delta Sigma Theta Sorority, Incorporated, for your constant cheerleading, and for letting me crash on couches near and far.

Thank you to John Roussel for our decade.

To my younger siblings, Jordan Harmon and Joy Flournoy, thank you for being constant sources of happiness. To my older sister, Candice Marie Flournoy, you showed me how to love hard and laugh harder. We made it.